the older brother

by USA TODAY bestselling author
GINGER SCOTT

THE OLDER BROTHER

A Rival Brothers, Age-Gap Romance

GINGER SCOTT

Chapter 1

THE VALETS HAVE ALREADY STARTED PARKING cars by the time my best friend Cami and I pull up to the Anderson estate. Technically, the open land behind my ex-boyfriend Caleb's family home is State Trust land. Still, it's only a matter of time before their family bids on it—*owns it*—so nobody is going to blink at the fact they're lining the open desert with G-wagons and Range Rovers. That desert will be theirs soon enough.

"We don't have to pay for this, do we?"

Cami offered to drive and I gladly let her, because I plan on drinking every expensive thing offered to me tonight. Nobody checks IDs at an Anderson party. Besides, it's my graduation party too, damn it. Who cares if I'm sharing it with the guy who dumped me less than a week ago because he wanted to start college "fresh," and to "find himself." Truth is, the fucker wants to sleep around without consequences. Just like his dad.

I should have known better than to fall for him our senior year. Caleb and I were better off as friends. We were thrust together by proximity in fifth grade—my mom works for his father—and we attended the same school. Cami says I never really loved him; I simply got used to him being around. She doesn't think he and I should have even been pals, but Caleb's the person I've been closest to for most of my life. There are things he knows about me that I haven't even told Cami. He was my person. And then he turned eighteen and became an Anderson through and through.

"We don't pay for anything at the Anderson house. Besides, they're hiding your rat-ass Chevy Malibu way in the back. They don't want people seeing us commoners here." We both burst into laughter over the harsh truth of my statement, but go silent when the bright beam from one of the parking attendants' flashlights hits the windshield.

Cami rolls her window down just as the attendant shifts his light toward the ground, and I barely have a second to swallow the instant lump that forms in my throat from seeing Caleb's older brother for the first time in a year.

"Fuck, he just gets hotter and hotter," Cami mutters before turning her attention to the tall, tatted man suddenly leaning against her open window.

"Hi, ladies. I'll take it from here if you'd like."

Rowan Anderson's voice enters my system like an Old Fashioned, the timbre deep yet soft, like he's constantly telling someone a secret. His lips have the power of hypnosis, his smile slightly sinister—*always*—and the dimple faint yet accented by his constant stubble. He was my first crush at age ten, dreamier than any of the teen heartthrobs I tore out of magazines and taped to my walls.

And the older he gets, forever older than me, the more that swirl of green and blue in his eyes bewitches me. He's a safe crush. A fantasy. A cute boy to dream about who'll never break my heart because I am invisible to him in that way. Nothing like Caleb.

I feel compelled to lean over Cami's console to make sure

our eyes meet. I think I will always get a rush from his attention, even if he thinks of me as a little sister.

"So, are you on the payroll for tonight? Or is this a favor
to Caleb?" I tease.

Rowan is very much the black sheep of this family. He did
a stint in juvie when he was seventeen for setting fire to his
family's beach house, and he's been treated like a problem
ever since. Even now, at twenty-four with a successful business
of his own, Rowan is the unwanted guest. He's out here
parking cars while his dad's partners and clients sip cocktails.

He lowers his head to peer through the window, and his
eyes flicker a hint when our gazes connect. It feels nice, and
the panicked drumming in my chest slows a little thanks to the
quick dose of confidence. I had hoped my black bikini top and
cut-off shorts would turn some heads tonight—and make
Caleb choke on regret.

His tongue peeks out between his teeth as his smile slowly
spreads. He shifts his body, resting his forearms on the roof of
the car as he leans further in the window. I snicker to myself
when I catch Cami breathe in his cologne. She doesn't even
bother masking the drunken smile that paints her face as her
eyes flutter. Her brother Miguel has been friends with Rowan
since they were kids, so Cami's crush on him is probably the
only one that rivals the duration of mine.

"I should ask you if you're crashing this thing to embarrass your ex?"

His lip ticks up on one side. I guess Caleb filled him in. I
don't know why the fact that other people are aware embar-
rasses me, but knowing our break-up is now public knowledge,
at least to some extent, makes me feel small.

I sink back in the passenger seat, suddenly less sure of
myself.

"I had to come. My name's on the damn cake. But I
wouldn't hate it if you push your brother in the pool when he

isn't looking." My eyes shift to the side to meet his just as his lips form around his signature laugh—faint, raspy.

"I'll see what I can do. Now, come on, let me park this thing somewhere safe," he says, pulling the door open for Cami. He trades places with her as I step out of the passenger side.

"Are you really going to hide my car in the back?" Cami asks as I step in beside her and link our arms together.

Rowan shifts gears, then revs her engine while pressing on the brake before blinking his focus to us.

"Your brother's my best friend, so I'm gonna park this baby right up front. And to answer you . . ." His gaze shifts to me, his right brow arching higher. "No, I'm not getting paid. And fuck Caleb for breaking up with you."

The comforting warmth creeps back inside my chest, and I utter a quiet "Thanks" as he pulls away and parks Cami's eleven-year-old sedan with a dented bumper right inside the gates, where every new guest is sure to see it.

Cami and I follow the flagstone pathway that winds from the circular drive around the east side of the house, and I steel myself when we reach the set of sliding windows of Caleb's bedroom. The shade is drawn, the room blacked out, which is probably for the best. I don't know how I'd feel seeing his rumpled sheets and the giant TV mounted on the wall with his streaming service that's probably still paused on the show I was bingeing with him the day before we broke up.

"You okay?" Cami's hand slides down my arm until our fingers thread, and she gives me a squeeze.

I nod and pull my focus away from the windows to my best friend.

"I'm not even sure why I'm sad about it, to be honest with you."

"You're sad because he did it first, before you got to be the one to end things. Because you know they were going to end eventually." Cami shrugs and twists her mouth into a guilty smile.

I draw in a slow breath and let her truth sit in my head for a beat before nodding. She's right in many ways. It's not as though Caleb and I are headed in the same direction. In three months, he's going to follow in his father's footsteps at Mount Fortus Business School in New York so he can become a finance bro. I'm going to Northern State, three hours away, on a swimming scholarship. I've decided I hate swimming, so we'll see how long that lasts.

"Let's go see this stupid cake," my friend insists, tilting her head toward the open-air kitchen as we step onto the covered patio.

I nod and follow her lead, but sneak a quick glimpse of the massive infinity-edge pool that's currently filled with everyone Caleb and I graduated with. I don't even like most of these people. I'm staring at the couple making out on the lounger for a full second before I realize I'm glaring at Caleb and Neveah, our student body president. Thankfully, Cami tugs my arm to force my attention away before anyone notices.

"I guess he's finding himself in her pants," Cami jokes.

I roll my eyes and breathe out, "I guess."

My pulse speeds up again, my body tingling with the familiar anxiety that numbed my skin before we got here. Everything inside of me is resisting. I didn't want to come tonight, but my mom will be here, and I couldn't bear the thought of disappointing her. She put the catering together and ordered the cake, party-planning one of the many hats she wears as David Anderson's assistant.

If I didn't show up, all everyone would talk about is how awkward she must feel that her daughter didn't come to her own party. We're cut from the same cloth, she and I. Case in point, I'm not necessarily jealous seeing Caleb throat wrestle Neveah by the pool. However, I am dreading the way everyone here is going to look at me because of it.

"Well. There it is," I say, the two-tiered cake accented by golden and black folds of frosting centered on the massive granite countertop that divides the professional-grade kitchen from the vast great room that overlooks the Valley's lights.

"What flavor is it?" Cami glances to both sides, then swipes a small rivulet of frosting from the base of the bottom layer.

"Vanilla, I think." I shrug, not sure what Caleb picked. I told him I didn't care.

"That tracks," Cami jokes.

I smirk, but it fades as I take in the crowded space around us. I don't know most of the people in this room. I've never been interested in Brogan-Tackerly Hedge Fund clients. When David hired my mom when I was a kid, the firm and the wealthy clientele were all my mother talked about for months. I used to think the snobbery of it was what drove my dad away, but as I matured and understood the nuances of relationships, I realized that a gig musician with a wandering soul was not suited to my mother's type-A lifestyle.

Cami and I make small plates of olives, cheese, and prosciutto, then head outside, where at least the median age is eighteen, like us. We pick a dry area on the deck and dip our feet into the cool water of the pool while we pick at our plates from the charcuterie spread my mom probably spent days perfecting.

"The cheese is weird," Cami says, spitting her bite into a cocktail napkin, then discarding her plate on the deck beside her, the rejected and wrapped bite tucked under it.

"Good to know," I say, nudging the cheese to the edge of my plate with the toothpick I'm using to eat.

A rush of testosterone-fueled former football players from our school barrels into the pool a moment later, casting tidal waves of chlorinated water into our laps. We scream from the surprise. Cami lifts her gauzy cover-up dress over her head and tosses it behind us before pushing off the edge and rushing toward two of the footballers who doused us. She splashes them with two hands, and Warren, her on-again, off-again ex, quickly wraps her up in his arms. The two of them are giggling and play-splashing one another within seconds, which means I'm going to be solo for the rest of the night.

I spot one of the party servers headed in my direction with a tray of champagne, so I stand and wave him down, swapping our plastic-crystal plates for a flute of golden bubbles. I tip my head back and swallow down half of it in one gulp.

"Don't embarrass me tonight, Saylor." My mom's hushed voice at my side tempts me to guzzle down the rest, but I'm not here to pick a fight. I'm here to keep up the façade, to make sure she can continue to work for these people and hold her head high.

"Wouldn't dream of it," I say as my gaze drops to hers.

Our matching resting bitch face expressions duel for a second, and she's the first to break, slipping on her famous "everything is fine" mask.

"You look cute. Has Caleb seen you yet?"

She leans in and kisses my cheek, and I breathe in her citrus-floral scent that somehow matches the eyelet sundress and hemp mules she's wearing. Her long brown hair rests on her shoulder, woven into a messy braid that I'm sure took her an hour to perfect. My mom's effortless beauty requires a lot of effort, and the fact I don't put in the same work, given that our appearance is nearly identical except for the obvious age difference of seventeen years, drives her nuts.

"He may have caught a glimpse when he came up for air," I say, nodding toward my ex-boyfriend, who is now hovering over a bikini clad Neveah, his teeth tugging at the string between her breasts that's barely holding the triangles of her top together.

"Ah, I see." My mom's mouth falls back to its natural flat line, and my stomach twists.

"I'm going to get some cake," I announce, extricating

myself from her. She has this way of making me feel guilty for the most ridiculous things that are not my fault. I'll be damned if I'm going to stand here and let her make me feel bad about Caleb breaking up with me.

"Saylor, you have to wait for us to make speeches. We won't have cake for another hour."

I groan quietly, then force a faint smile on my face when I turn back to face her. *I have to be here for an hour?*

"Fine. I'll swim," I say, my lips forming a tight, pursed smile.

I down the rest of my champagne, then hand my mom the empty glass before marching back to the now-soaking deck where Cami and I were sitting. I slip my sandals from my feet, then unzip my cut-offs, making a point to work them over my hips with a little sway before wriggling them down my legs. I kick them to the side, near my shoes, then run my palms over my hips to make sure the strings are snugly tied on my bottoms.

I scan the pool, hoping for a few sets of eyes on me. It's a new suit, and it barely covers things. I bought it four hours ago, and so far it's not pulling its weight. The eighty-dollar-price-tag garment has only gotten a glimpse from Cami's ex, who is the *last* person I need noticing.

Defeated, I head toward the steps to slip slowly into the water. I'm not in the mood for a splash battle. I pause at the second step to scoop water onto my tummy and arms, and when I lift my gaze, someone is finally staring at me. Rowan pulls the cap from his beer, his lip tugging up on one side as he raises it to me in a toast shared by only the two of us.

I laugh silently and shake my head as he tilts the beer back to drink, then slowly pulls the rim of the bottle from his lips, his smirk still exactly the same. His eyes fixed on me. The attention is enough to make me forget for a moment about Caleb's make-out session a few feet away, and I'm grateful.

Sinking into the water, I push off from the steps and glide

toward Rowan. He's changed out of the dark slacks and white shirt he wore to park cars, and he's now shirtless and wearing dark blue board shorts that ride low on his hips.

The physical differences between him and his brother are almost laughable. Caleb is fit, with muscular arms and a ripped chest and back, thanks to diligent workouts and years of competitive basketball, which he's only giving up in college because his fancy New York school doesn't have a team. Everything about Caleb's appearance is color-by-numbers. The perfect hair. The preppy wardrobe. The daily grooming to ensure he's never unshaven, unkempt, or sloppy.

Rowan's body, on the other hand, is chiseled from life. The ink that crawls up his neck and down his arm tells a story about an older son who nevertheless grew up in second place and never figured out how to win. His round biceps were forged by self-taught manual labor, from hours spent sanding classic cars and hoisting tires. And his smile, well, that must have come from a deal with the devil.

My fingertips slide up the stone edge of the pool and I lay my arms over one another, then rest my chin on them and blink away water droplets from my eyes.

"What are you looking at?"

He knows I like his attention. I think he's always known about my little crush. My teenage adoration made him feel good about himself. I'm sure of it.

Rowan lifts his beer to his lips, pausing.

"Nothing," he says through the devil's smirk.

I blush. I feel the heat on my cheeks. Laughing softly, I turn my head to my right and catch Caleb's stare. He's still glued to his current fascination, but he's finally spotted me doing something he doesn't like. And I like that.

Rowan and Caleb love one another, but they hate each other, too. Their love stems from obligation and familial contracts. Some of it is from good memories, probably, like when Caleb was young and Rowan got to play the part of the big brother he looked up to. But years of living in this house have worn most of that away, and now, the resentment that exists between the two of them is thick enough to taste. It's bitter, almost rancid.

"My mom says I can't have cake until they give their speeches," I say, moving my eyes back to Rowan.

His face tics with a short, silent laugh.

"I'll get you cake," he says, leaving his beer on the deck beside the lounge chair and marching across the manicured lawn.

I rest my cheek on my forearm as I watch him walk as if he's the boss inside a house that hasn't been hospitable to him for years. When I spot him pull a knife from one of the drawers, I chuckle and lift myself out of the pool. I grab the large white towel draped on the back of Rowan's lounge chair and wrap my body in it before sitting on the end and folding my legs up.

Rowan snags my shoes and shorts on his way back to the chair, then drops them to the side before handing me a plate with a heavily frosted triangle of cake. I was right about the vanilla, but there's a vein of raspberry running through the fluffy white that I hope is intentional. I love raspberries, and I'd like to think my mom made that special request just for me.

"Thank you," I say, sliding the fork through the tip and taking a bite. The frosting is rich, but melts on my tongue as the soft pillow of cake dissipates in my mouth. It's sweet, but the tartness of the raspberry cuts it perfectly. I chew with my mouth closed in a grin and look up at Rowan's expectant expression.

"Well?"

"*Mmm*," I moan, digging in for a second bite as he chuckles.

"Good. It's your party, too, damn it, and if you want cake, you should get cake." He flops back into the chair, crossing his legs behind me as he leans against the reclined back.

I do my best to savor the flavors, but it's hard not to glance Caleb's way, especially as he's now dancing in front of a swooning Neveah. He doesn't look like a fool, though I wish he did. He's confident, and the way he knows all the words to the song he just turned up makes him rather magnetic. Even my wing-woman Cami is smiling and clapping along as she sits perched on her ex's shoulders in the pool.

"He's doing this to get at you, you know," Rowan says. I swivel my head, but not all the way.

"I doubt that. All Caleb thinks about is what makes Caleb happy." I feel a twinge of guilt for calling him out, especially since I spent most of my life defending his narcissism.

"That's true. But it makes him happy to see you unhappy. He gets that from our dad."

I turn the rest of the way to meet Rowan's eyes, and he shrugs, then lifts his beer from the deck. His eyes stay on me as he takes a drink, and for the first time tonight, the attention feels like too much.

I blink away, glancing back at Caleb. He catches me looking just as he lifts his head from kissing the top of Neveah's head. He kissed me like that two weeks ago, and damn it, I swooned. I feel so stupid.

"Hey, we should start the movie!" Caleb announces, moving his gaze from me, then scanning the crowd clustered in and around the pool.

A few people whistle and cheer, so Caleb straightens the blow-up screen that's been parked near the deep end of the pool since I got here. He nods to someone behind me, and I crane my neck to catch a glimpse of his father as he switches on a projector and turns up the sound on the tower speakers they've set up on both sides of the pool. He heads back inside seconds later, where my mom and two of his clients are waiting for him.

The roar of cars racing drowns out most of the chatter, and soon, my now former classmates are all piled into lounge chairs or rafts in the pool as the latest *Fast and Furious* movie lights up the dark desert yard. Caleb moves back to the chair with Neveah, sliding his body behind hers and wrapping his arms around her. I can't see much in the dark, but every few seconds the screen lights up enough to show off the way he's nibbling at her neck. I'm in the back, where nobody can see me, yet I feel as though everyone is looking.

"I'm full," I say, turning to hand my plate to Rowan.

He takes it in his hand but holds it still between us as his eyes lock on mine. His gaze drifts over my shoulder and lingers for a full breath, maybe two, on the scene his brother is making before he sets the plate on the ground, then shifts his legs to make space for me to sit between them.

"Come here."

He pats the tan cushion between his knees, and I blink a few times. I'm overcome with hesitation, but the pre-teen who dreamt this very moment so many times is screaming at me from deep inside to get over myself.

"It's more comfortable, Saylor." Rowan's head falls to the side, his eyes dimming and seeming to express the annoyance I'm more accustomed to from him over the years.

"I'm still wet."

His lip twitches, stretching his smirk, the second those words leave my lips, and I gasp and bury my face in the corners of the towel.

"From the pool!" I whisper-shout.

A tugging sensation on the towel accompanies his soft chuckle as he pulls it away from my face.

"I know. Just sit with me and forget about my jackass baby brother. He's not worth it."

I glance to my lap, the skin on my thighs beading with goose bumps from the cool night air. My gaze flits toward the screen, toward Caleb, who is quite comfortable with Neveah on his lap. Without giving myself a chance to think my way out of it again, I unravel my towel from my body and scoot into the space between Rowan's legs, lying back against his chest before pulling the towel over myself like a blanket.

"There. That better?" His breath is warm against my ear, and my mind instantly wishes for a graze from his lips, his nose, teeth, tongue. Anything.

"Yeah," I say, the shiver from my chill causing my voice to quaver.

Rowan breathes out a soft laugh that warms the crook of my neck, moving his palms up and down my biceps over the towel, I think to warm me up.

"Thanks," I say as I scan the pool and deck, curious whether anyone sees us. We're behind everyone, though, and I'm the last thing people are curious about. I feel silly worrying so much about how everyone would react tonight. They've all basically erased the fact that Caleb and I were once an item. Like . . . days ago.

Rowan's hands continue to slide up and down my arms, slowing as the minutes pass, and I finally exhale a deep breath and turn my attention to the movie. I saw this two weeks ago in Caleb's room. It's still good, though. He hasn't ruined that, at least.

My body warms and dries after a while, and Rowan's hands move to the armrests on either side of us. His chest is hot against my bare back, and when I concentrate, I swear I can feel his heartbeat against my spine. The scent that put my best friend into a trance when he parked her car has fully invaded my senses, too. He may have refused his father's money, but he smells of wealth and privilege—embers of mesquite, linen, and the sweet lingering tail of a half-smoked cigar. He smells like every Christmas afternoon I spent at this house when his father held private parties for his clients and staff.

I'm locked into the feel of his chest as he breathes when he moves his right hand back to my bicep, this time under the towel. My eyes widen as his fingertips brush my bare shoulder, but I force my face to remain still—a true poker face with zero hint at what I feel inside.

When his fingers travel over my right shoulder, across my bikini strap and along my collarbone, I swallow hard, and Rowan's touch stalls. I turn my head slightly, just enough for him to notice, my gaze dropping to where his hand rests inches from my now ice-hard nipple. My lips part with a quiet but audible gasp, and his hand slides toward the center of my chest. When his fingertips reach the edge of the small triangle of fabric covering my left breast, I steady my breath and inhale deeply, hoping he'll sense my invitation.

He does, his fingers inching over the material until they gently run over the hard tip aching underneath.

My lips part with another gasp, one I swear others can hear, but a quick scan in front of me says otherwise. Everyone is either making out with their significant other, or their *current* other, or watching the movie.

Rowan's fingers circle my nipple, and more than once, I hope the tease of his thumb will finally work in concert to pinch the hard bud. When his hand moves, my shoulders drop as I exhale in disappointment. A short breath warms my ear, and I turn my head again, enough to catch the faint smile on his lips before his chin stubble brushes against my cheek. Just then, his hand slips underneath my bikini top, and he gives me what I'm desperate for, squeezing my nipple between his finger and thumb, then rolling it as I shift my hips, needing relief somewhere else.

"Say yes."

His words are a whisper, but I don't imagine them.

"Yes."

He rolls my nipple in his vice again, and I arch my back against him, suddenly wanting to push myself harder into his hand. I'm no longer wet from the pool; I'm wet from him. My bikini bottoms soaking with need. My mind buzzing with caution and thrill. My heart racing. Stomach tightening.

Rowan's left hand tugs on the slip knot fashioned at my hip, pulling the strings free and loosening my bikini bottom. My legs part under the towel, my knees falling open and resting against his as I sit between his legs and feel his growing erection. His hand glides under the fabric that covers my lower abdomen, his fingertips moving softly over the small strip of hair before his finger slips between the juncture of my thighs and dips inside of me.

"Oh," I breathe out, still quiet, but maybe not enough. I focus on the people closest to us, but I'm starting not to care.

"Say yes again," Rowan says, this time his tongue flicking my earlobe. My core tightens, an orgasm begging to be set free.

"Yes," I croak in a breath.

Rowan tugs my nipple and sinks his finger into me while pressing his thumb against my clit, and I writhe beneath the towel.

"Shit," I mutter, unable to stop the small swivels of my hips that match the circles Rowan is now making against my pussy with his thumb.

"Come."

His word is a command, and my body listens as I fall apart on his hand, every nerve ending in my body firing away, practically rejoicing. It took him seconds to undo me. And he drags every rush of pleasure from my body before pulling his hand away.

"I've gotta go. But happy graduation, Saylor. And fuck Caleb," he whispers, then places a kiss just below my ear.

Rowan slips out from the space behind me, and I look up at him, practically—no *definitely*—helpless as I look up at him with what must be awe on my face. His devil's smile graces me one more time just before he puts his finger in his mouth, sucking the taste of me before he leaves.

Under this towel, my raw nipple pulses, exposed and wishing for that warm hand to come back. My bottoms are untied and open, my pussy wet and still flickering from the welcome onslaught to my swollen skin.

What the fuck just happened? And how the hell do I get that to happen again?

Chapter 2

SO MUCH FOR Cami being my responsible and sober driver. She's still asleep on the leather sectional in front of the Andersons' massive stone fireplace. She's also wearing Warren's—her ex's—football jersey, which he will never wear again since we all left high school behind a week ago. Whatever went down with them last night is likely going to mess with my friend's head when she finally wakes up. I should probably put that off as long as I can. She's not a fan of my honesty when it comes to her relationship decisions. Just like I'm not real interested in hearing all the ways she was right about me and Caleb.

I tiptoe my way into the kitchen, quietly sifting through the rack of coffee capsules until I find an almond one. I push the cup into the machine and snag a mug from the cupboard, sliding it into place, and staring at its empty center while I wait.

One of the nice things about growing up with the Andersons is that I have first dibs on my favorite spare bedroom when I need it. I haven't slept in that room since I was a preteen, though. When I was with Caleb, I was always in his room, in his bed, whenever I stayed here. Maybe it's the years between, but the spare room felt a lot colder than I remember it. I slept hard with the help of alcohol, but it took me an hour to fully crack my eyelids open this morning, and that time was spent taking in all the things that have been abandoned in that room. Old photo albums and boxes of mementos. A painting that Caleb and Rowan's mom, Cora, did of their beach house in Malibu, the same one Rowan burned down eight years ago. And me—the discarded girlfriend. Rowan's plaything. The spare girl screaming to be seen as a woman.

I had a few more champagne flutes after Rowan left me bewildered last night. And I tossed in a couple of tequila shots when I discovered Cami was doing them and had zero plans to drive us home. I needed the buzz to get through the speeches. To hear my mom gloat to a roomful of my peers and forty-year-old business partners I don't know—all my accomplishments, my swimming dedication, my scholarship, my plans for grad school—*news to me, by the way*—all on my way to becoming a powerful CEO.

I squeeze my eyes shut and pinch the bridge of my nose to force out the puffiness and rid my head of replaying her speech again. The missing slice of cake never came up, but she also never offered me a piece, which was probably because she knew I already had one.

The last few droplets of coffee fall into the mug, and as I grasp the handle, the space gets tighter behind me. Caleb smells the same as his brother did last night, yet somehow my physical reaction is vastly different. My neck still pebbles with goose bumps from the nearness of his chin to the curve of my neck, and when his fingertips brush against my shoulder, I visibly shiver.

"Your top is coming undone," he says at my ear. A place he doesn't have a right to be anymore.

I clear my throat and step to the side, setting my coffee on the counter, then covering the loose knot with my own hand to remedy.

"Hazard of sleeping in a bikini top." My eyes lift to meet his briefly before I tuck my chin to my shoulder and retie the long swimsuit strings.

"Maybe you should have worn a one-piece," he says in a flat tone, grabbing the bitter, plain coffee-flavor pod, swapping out my empty cartridge for his. I'm about to comment on his lack of taste when he spins to face me while sporting a truly pompous smirk.

"But you knew a bikini would get my attention. Didn't you?" His gaze lingers on mine, his eyes bloodshot from the heavy drinking and pot he smoked last night.

The breathy laugh that leaves me is a surprise. I didn't expect to be this strong in his presence. And I definitely don't think Caleb expected it. I've only ever been two ways with him: a loyal friend or a smitten teenager.

"I didn't wear it for you." Sure, it's a lie . . . sort of. I mean, I hoped he would notice. I hoped *lots* of people would notice. And I hoped all that attention would eat at him. Clearly it has, given it's the first thing he brings up this morning.

"Am I supposed to think you wore that for Rowan?" He leans back against the counter, gripping the sides and arching his back to show off his bare stomach and chest, the untied waist of his sweats that hang low enough to expose the ridges along his abdomen, and his apparent lack of boxers.

I roll my eyes as I leave him alone in the kitchen, taking my coffee into the dining room, where I pull out the head chair and sit with my legs folded up. I cradle the mug in my palms and wait for it to cool, blowing along the surface enough to make tiny ripples in the liquid.

Caleb joins me after a minute or two, taking the seat closest to me. My lips pop open to protest his company, but as I'm about to speak, he drops a pile of envelopes on the table in front of me.

My brow draws in as I set my mug to the side and spin the

top envelope so the cursive *Saylor* written across the middle in golden ink is facing the right way.

"Your portion of the graduation gifts. Remember? The whole point of the party?"

Caleb lifts his brows for a half second before blowing on his own cup of coffee, and I give in to the gravity pulling me into the velvety padded chair. I'm sure people gave Caleb cash and gifts, but he doesn't need them the way I do. Yet one more reminder from him of our differences. "We come from different worlds," he said when he broke it off with me. One of his many reasons why we should split before college.

I tap my finger against the ribbed envelope that I'm sure contains a seriously overpriced card. I wish whoever gave me this simply added what they spent to the check I'm sure is inside. They could have folded the check in a sheet of legal pad paper for all I care.

"Thanks," I croak, suddenly feeling like an Anderson family charity case.

I slide the cards into a stack and grip them in one hand while clutching my mug in the other. Suddenly, waking up my friend and enduring a day of her relationship drama seems like the winning choice.

I push my chair back under the table with my hip, my cut-off shorts still a bit damp from being splashed and left on the ground most of the night. I can't wait to get home and shower.

"Hey, Saylor? One thing."

I'm nearly out of the dining room before Caleb stops me. I glance over my shoulder to meet his blue-eyed stare, and the way he twists his lips and furrows his brow sends my pulse racing.

"Be careful." His gaze lingers, his mouth a thin line that evokes a sense of judgement, yet also a hint of caution.

I blink after a few silent seconds and nod once before leaving him behind.

He saw me with Rowan. I'm now sure of it. He noticed everything, too. Not just my suit. And while it feels good that it made an impression, his warning also makes me a bit uneasy.

What's more is that I suddenly feel the urge to be defiant. I don't want to be careful at all. Careful with Rowan, with my summer, with my future. I want to be off script for once in my fucking life.

After a few gulps of my coffee, I discard the mug on the marble sofa table before getting on my knees and brushing my best friend's tangled brown hair away from her face. Cami scrunches her nose and groans as the hairs tickle her cheeks.

"It's time, Cam. We gotta get out of here," I whisper.

"One more hour. Please," she whines. Her eyeliner and mascara are smeared so much she looks like a linebacker wearing eye black in the rain.

"No, babe. We've gotta go now," I urge. In another life, I'd let her be and crawl under Caleb's covers for another hour of sleep of my own. But I'm not welcome here like I once was. I felt it in the guest room. I felt it in the kitchen. And though nobody's watching me or my friend, I feel it now. This place isn't for me anymore.

We come from different worlds.

"Fine, but you're driving." My friend rolls into the corner of the sofa and pats her thigh, probably searching for a pocket with keys. She's still drunk. She's not wearing pants.

"Cami, you're naked, and . . ." I clear my throat and tug on the hem of the familiar Seton Prep football jersey.

Cami manages to peel one eye open enough to glance down at her body, and promptly covers her face with her palm.

"Shit. I fucked up." She pushes herself into a sitting position as I scan the floor around the sofa, then glance out the open glass panels to the pile of clothing near the hot tub.

"Just a little," I say to appease her while I skip out to the patio and grab her bikini and cover-up.

I guide her feet into her bikini bottoms, then dial her number to track down her phone and keys.

"I feel it," she says, wobbling into a stand and pulling up one of the cushions.

She grabs her phone, then hands her keys to me as Caleb steps into the room. He's carrying a bowl of cereal, and pauses his spoonful of fruit-flavored loops a few inches from his mouth when our eyes meet.

"You get her pants on?" He gestures toward my friend with his spoon.

"Fuck you, Caleb," Cami bites out. My ex fails at holding in his cocky laughter, so I swoop my shoulder under my friend's arm and guide her toward the door before he has a chance to pick a fight.

Cami throws up in the middle of the circular driveway, so I pop the trunk on her car and dump out the workout clothes from her sports pack, handing the pack to her in case she gets sick during our drive home. We're nearly there when her phone buzzes in the cupholder of her center console.

"Shit," she mutters when she flips the screen over to face her. "It's my brother. I forgot I have the spare key for his truck that he's selling today. Can we swing by the garage?"

"Uh," I stammer as she answers her brother Miguel's call and promises him we'll be there soon.

"Sorry about this," she says to me after ending the call.

"It's fine," I say, though the way my insides are bubbling says otherwise.

Miguel and Rowan are partners in a vehicle restoration business. It's been Rowan's dream for as long as I can remember. His grandfather on his mom's side was an Army mechanic with a passion for older cars, and Rowan would tinker with engines alongside him any time they visited his grandparents in California. Miguel has the same eye for detail, but where Rowan's expertise is the precision under the hood, Miguel's is all about the body. In two years, they've flipped enough junkers to buy prime garage space right off the highway.

This little pitstop would have been fine yesterday. But today? I'm trying to make sense of what happened by the pool last night. I'd fill Cami in, but she's still drunk enough to lose her shit in front of Rowan and her brother. I'm certainly not in the mood to take that on.

It takes us twenty minutes to get to the garage, and after not seeing Rowan in person for a year, I ready myself to come face-to-face with him for the second time in a dozen hours. My eyes instantly go to the historic license plate on the back of his seventy-four Camaro. The RJ007 brings a smirk to my face. His middle name is James, and for a few weeks of high school, he tried to get everyone on board with calling him James. Because boys are, well, boys . . . he became James Bond instead.

The doors are both rolled up when we park, and Cami waits for a few seconds in the passenger seat as I get out and round the vehicle to open her door.

"Ah, shit, is my sister hungover?" Miguel's familiar laugh brings a smile to my face, and I turn toward him as Cami pushes her door open with her foot. I wrap my arms around his neck in a hug, looking into the garage over his shoulder. Rowan's jean-covered legs shift along the ground as he scoots his body underneath a rusty Bronco.

"Yes, she is. Do you have anything to drink in that place?" Cami whines. She fans her still-clean backpack toward the garage.

"We got beer," Miguel answers, reaching out a hand to his sister. She grasps it, but he quickly shakes her off.

"My keys, you pain in the ass." His lips purse as his sister glowers at him, but she eventually pulls the spare key from her console and places it in his palm.

"Now, help me to your couch," she says, waving her hand at her brother until he gives in and helps his sister to her feet.

"Don't you dare puke on me," he warns, bracing her until she seems to find her balance.

I hang back as the two of them wade toward the garage, a few extra seconds to myself so I can suck in some air and brace myself for whatever's to come.

Cami flops on the dusty black leather sofa near their business office within seconds. Miguel pulls a cold one from their fridge, and the crack from a beer cap pings across the garage. The sound must pique Rowan's interest as he slides out from under the Bronco a second later. His gaze finds me right away, but his expression is blank, as if he's looking at a stranger.

"Kinda early to start, no?" His head swivels as he looks at Miguel. Away from me.

Miquel holds up the beer, then tilts it toward his nearly passed-out sister on the couch.

"Hair of the dog," Miguel says.

Rowan chuckles, then scoots himself back out of sight. My legs suddenly feel weak, but unlike my friend, my tremors have nothing to do with the alcohol I drank last night. I'm simply perplexed to the point that it's making me dizzy. It's not that I expect Rowan to rush me at first sight and sweep me into his arms, but I didn't exactly anticipate a cold shoulder.

I move from the arm of the sofa to the space right next to my friend, nudging her so she sits up and stays awake.

"Rude," she gripes.

"I kind of want to go home and take a shower," I remind her.

She lets out a heavy sigh before grumbling, "Fine."

"We've got a shower in the back," Miguel suggests.

My eyes go to Rowan, his legs unchanged, hands working at the underside of the vehicle he's buried beneath. I doubt he even heard his friend.

"I don't exactly have a change of clothes," I say through an awkward smile. I'm still wearing cutoffs and a bikini top, and I'm tired of smelling like chlorine.

Showering here isn't ideal, but also, there's a part of me that wonders what Rowan would do. Before Miguel can take the offer back, I get to my feet and huff out, "Okay, whatever. But can I at least borrow a shirt?"

Rowan's movement isn't fast. He wheels out from under the Bronco in an almost lackadaisical fashion, wiping his hands on a grease-stained rag before hopping to his feet and opening the Bronco's driver's side door. He pulls out a long-sleeved gray T-shirt and walks it over to me, not an inkling of emotion anywhere on his face. He hands the shirt to me, but doesn't let go immediately when I grab it.

Our eyes lock, and for a moment, my body flashes white hot. My lips part as I sneak in a tiny breath. Rowan licks his lips, but the dimple never comes. No flicker in his eyes, either. But I feel it. Despite the lack of physical clues, there's a thread between us. A pull. It's brief, and it dies a second later when he's back on the floor, wheeling himself back under the Bronco.

"Thanks," I say, lifting the shirt in acknowledgement before returning my attention to my friend, only to find her face buried in her phone. Her brother is doing the same as he sits on a stool by the tool counter.

Nobody saw that. Not that there was anything to see.

I laugh silently at myself and carry Rowan's shirt toward the back hallway that leads to their work shower. It's not a very sexy room, more like a gas station restroom than anything. The space is tight, but it feels good to strip away a day-old swimsuit and stand under a hot stream of water. I spend ten minutes lathering my body with the masculine-scented body wash I find on the shelf, turning the shower off when the hot water feels as though it's running out. I swipe my hand over the glass door to clear away the condensation before popping it open just enough to reach for the sky-blue towel neatly folded by the sink. I don't realize the towel is resting on top of my borrowed shirt—

and a suddenly appeared pair of gray sweats—until I wrap my hair in it.

I didn't come in here with a towel or those pants.

My heart kicks and my tummy twists. Not from fear, but from thrill. It was probably Cami. In fact, I'm sure it was. *But what if?*

My hand slides from my neck to my breast, then down the center of my body to my stomach as I look back toward the still frosted glass of the shower. I'm not sure how much of me there was to be seen anyhow.

Rather than spiraling any deeper with this stupid fantasy, I finish getting dressed, ignoring the overwhelming scent of Rowan's cologne on the shirt as I pull it over my head. I hang the towel to dry, then make my way back to the garage, where Miguel and Cami are exactly where I left them.

"Feel better?" my friend asks, not bothering to peel her eyes from her constant scrolling on her phone.

"Yeah," I hum, my gaze drifting to the now-lowered Bronco. Rowan's back is to me as he moves a mop around the glossy floor near the rolling doors, but I keep my eyes on him, waiting to see if he glances at me over his shoulder. I study every twist of his arms, the way his body sways as he moves the mop back and forth. I search for a tell. But there isn't one.

Shaking my head, I move to the other corner of the couch and flop down to sit next to my friend, pulling my phone into my palms and joining the doom scroll party. The clatter of the mop handle falling against the corner of the brick wall snaps me from my sudden trance in time to catch Rowan's back as he heads toward his Camaro.

"Make sure you pick up more invoice slips. We're running low," Miguel shouts to his friend.

Rowan raises a hand in response, then gets into his car and revs the engine.

"Fucking show off," Miguel says through a chuckle.

My phone buzzes in my hand, so I drop my gaze to my

screen and slide up on the message notification. The number isn't familiar. But it doesn't matter. I know exactly who it is.

> UNKNOWN: You look good in my things.

My eyes dart to my right to make sure Cami is still lost in her own world. Then to my left, where Miguel has moved on to a laptop where he seems to be researching car parts. When my phone buzzes again, I jolt, cupping my phone to hide the screen as I read Rowan's follow-up.

> UNKNOWN: And don't worry about getting anything . . . wet.

I bite my bottom lip, unable to hold back the smile or stop the heat that rushes to my cheeks. *Fuck. Me.* In fact, I almost type that in response. Thankfully, I have enough sense to think before texting. I wait until Rowan pulls away before I finally hit send.

> ME: I'm keeping the shirt.

I hold my breath while I wait for him to respond. And when a few minutes pass, I remind myself that he's driving. After thirty minutes, however, I give up and tuck my phone in the pocket of his sweatpants, and resolve to quit indulging in something that's clearly played out as far as it's going to go.

Chapter 3

THE LAST THING I want to do is have a meal with my father and his protégé, Caleb. Yeah, yeah, he's my brother. Blood is thicker than water. All that shit. I might have believed in that cliché before my brother stabbed me in the back. Not now, though. He chose sides. He chose our father.

He chose wrong.

Naturally, Caleb's sitting at the table alone as I walk into the posh lakeside restaurant. I'm sure our dad is running late. He's never on time, especially for his family. We come last.

"Good afternoon, Mr. Ander——"

I lift my hand before Rob, the maître d', can finish my last name. It makes me feel like that guy in the *Matrix* movies when he greets me that way.

"I see my brother. Thanks." I pat Rob's shoulder twice as I pass the hostess stand, and his shoulders drop the invisible bags of cement that are likely resting on them. That's how people are around my father knotted, messy, stressed-out wrecks. Even when he's not directly their boss. My dad's been coming to Patrick's by Lakeside for years, and Rob may as well be on the Anderson payroll. The amount of shady shit I bet that guy has overheard and had to bury deep down and try to forget must be epic. One of these days, I'm going to offer him a job far away from this place and pay for his therapy.

Caleb swivels his chair and leans back as I approach, stretching his legs out to force me to walk around them on my way to my seat. He's wearing gray dress slacks and a fitted white button-down, the standard summer corporate attire for my dad's company. I threw this denim button-down over my T-shirt and swapped my jeans for a clean pair of Dickie's out of respect for Rob. He shouldn't have to track down a coat for me to fit in with the clientele in this joint.

"Rowan." Caleb nods, still chewing the roll he stuffed in his face as I walked in.

"Hey, baby brother. Happy graduation, blah blah blah."

I snag a roll from the silver bowl in the center of the table and slink down to match his disrespectful posture. I don't really love seafood, so I'll fill up on carbs while I can. And Caleb doesn't like it when I call him *baby*, so I figure we both may as well not like something about this lunch date.

"Hey, thanks for parking cars for my party. Real classy of you." He snaps off another bite from a roll and smirks at me as he chews.

"Yeah, well . . . you know me. I never turn down an opportunity to case a lot full of high-end cars." I mimic him with my own bite, and we spend the next several seconds in a death stare while chewing.

It's been more than a year since I called on my brother to be a character witness after a con man dropped off a stolen Bentley at our shop, as if it were his own. I was too eager to make our shop succeed, too naïve, and I leapt at the chance to work on something rare. When the guy dipped from the country, though, we were left holding the bag—or wheels, in this case. An unsealed juvenile arson record meant I took the hit. I wouldn't let it touch Miguel, so I pled my way out of things and wore an ankle bracelet until last week, since my brother refused to put his name on the line. My dad paid for the shitty lawyer, so now, I'm working off that debt by giving him my time, something I swore I wouldn't let him have when I walked out of the house six years ago.

Caleb breaks our standoff first with a laugh, dropping the half-eaten roll on the small plate in front of him, then leaning into the table, resting his elbows on either side of it while he rubs his palms together.

"You're the one running a chop shop, Rowan. Don't act so high and mighty." His mouth falls into a straight, emotionless line while I fight to keep my pulse in check. I'd like to deck him across this table, but that won't accomplish anything.

"Believe me, Caleb. I don't set foot near you high and mighty folks if I can help it," I say, not even bothering to correct his smear. My business is legit. Always has been. I know it. Miguel knows it. And the real collectors and gearheads who come to us know it. That's all that matters.

I'm not sure what I prefer, sitting here alone with my brother or making it a three-top with our dad. The choice is out of my hands, though, as my dad walks into the restaurant, his phone pressed against his right ear while he nods at us and points with his right finger to a table he would apparently prefer.

Caleb scrambles on command. I sigh as I pick up the bowl of bread and move three tables to our left, closer to the water and farther away from the staff. I wonder what kinds of things dear old Dad doesn't want others to hear.

"Listen, Jack. I've gotta go. I just got to my appointment, but this all sounds great. Let's talk it through over drinks tonight." My dad ends the call after that, and I hope Jack, *whoever that was,* is used to his typical abruptness.

"Sorry for making you wait. Did you guys order?" My dad flips open one of the menus Caleb carried over from our first table, as if he needs to study it. I'm sure he has it memorized, and besides, the chef will make him anything he wants.

"We waited for you," Caleb says, sitting up straight and dropping his cloth napkin in his lap to protect his stupid fucking slacks.

"We waited for you," I mutter in a hushed, mocking tone as I snag a menu to scan.

"Fuck off," Caleb fires back, his voice low but not exactly quiet.

"Knock it off," our father grunts without looking up from his menu.

"Sorry," Caleb is quick to apologize. I roll my eyes, owning the childish way I baited him just now. It's so easy to get under his skin. It was playful when we were kids, but now I do it purely out of spite.

I honestly don't know why Caleb tries so hard to impress our dad. I'm clearly the outcast in the family. I'm the black sheep. Everyone knows it. All he needs to do is breathe and stay out of jail, and he'll forever remain the golden child. If it's an inheritance thing, I've made it abundantly clear that I don't want a single penny of my father's money. That's why Miguel and I took out a business loan on our own. I'd rather climb out of debt for a few years than feel obligated to that man—or worse, let him feel entitled to our shop. He already lives to take jabs at me and what I do.

When our server comes, my father orders three lobster tail salads, so I close my menu and toss it on top of Caleb's. My brother never even bothered to open his. I stare at his face until his eyes shift to meet mine for a beat, and I blink slowly and shake my head. Caleb quickly glances the other way.

There was a time when my brother was as annoyed by my father's controlling ways as I am, but I guess the promise of power and money is too alluring for him. Hell, the kid gave up college hoops to make our dad happy. We both wanted to play, but I lost my right the second I confessed to dropping a match in the Malibu beach house. Caleb traded a possible run in March Madness for creased dress pants and a pathway to securities management exams. I'm not sure when he cashed in his dreams for my father's, but I'd guess it happened around the time he told the detectives working my case that he couldn't vouch for me on account of my criminal past. That was enough to get a judge to approve unsealing my arson conviction.

Feeling antsy, I flatten my palms on the linen-covered table and lean in.

"So, what's the occasion?" I have a million other places to be. Well, places I'd *rather* be.

"We can talk business after we eat. I want to hear about my boys." My father must have a doozy for us. He's laying it on thick.

He stands to take off his jacket, but Rob flies in before my dad's pulled his second arm free. My father pulls a thick envelope from the inside pocket and sets it on the table, along with a gold pen, before Rob rushes his coat away to the closet.

"That guy deserves a raise." He chuckles.

I smile faintly, wishing he would actually do something to make that happen. He won't, though, because helping Rob in no way serves him.

"Caleb, did you like your party? Your guests seemed to have a good time. I think the last one finally crawled out of the house an hour ago, according to the security cameras."

My brother breathes out a short laugh and nods. My attention, however, is divided between their conversation and the envelope that is clearly the reason why we've been summoned.

"It was perfect." Caleb's response is confident and clipped.

My dad's gaze lingers on my brother for a beat, and the longer it lasts, the more my brother squirms in his seat. Caleb and I have both endured that look enough times to know it's masking something. Caleb's feet shift under the table, and he straightens his spine in preparation.

"Good. I hope Saylor enjoyed herself, too. It must have

been awkward for her. You certainly didn't help make her comfortable."

And there it is. It's not that my dad has some special regard for Saylor. It's more that he has a complicated relationship with her mom, Allison. Nobody holds more dirty secrets about my dad close to their chest than her. He wouldn't want her to be unhappy, and making her daughter unhappy is a bit of a threat to the peace he's miraculously been able to keep with her. But these are nuances my brother hasn't been old enough to notice. While he was busy with club basketball practices and running for homecoming king, I was growing up fast and taking notes.

My father doesn't like people causing a scene that might reflect poorly on him. The irony of that isn't lost on me, given the choices he's made. I suppose when you're the king, you're privy to all the resources required to bury ugly little secrets. My dad clears his throat as he shifts his gaze to his empty wine glass and the bottle of red being presented by our server at his other side.

My dad swirls a sample of the wine in his glass, then swallows it.

"That's fine, yes." He nods while reading the label. Our server pours a glass for the three of us, and I push mine toward the center of the table when he leaves. My father wrinkles his nose.

"You have a problem with wine?"

I shake my head.

"Just trying to keep a clear head."

"She didn't have to come," Caleb says, finally responding to my father's jab about Saylor being cast aside at her own party. I grab the water glass to my right and take a sip to keep myself from snickering.

My father's palm slams down on the linen-covered table, the silverware and water glasses clattering with the sudden tremor. Caleb jumps in his seat, and I sink back, getting more comfortable for the show.

"Allison has been loyal to this family. To me."

I cough out a short laugh that earns me a sharp glare, my father's nostrils flaring. Maybe even smoking.

"Sorry, loyal. Continue." I lift my hand and swallow down all the bullshit I know about how far Saylor's mom's loyalty goes. Besides, I know better than to deflect for Caleb. My days of taking the heat so he can skate by are long gone. He's a big boy.

"Allison pulled your little party together. Every little whim you had, she made happen. You'd be wise to remember that," our father continues, his ire back where I'd like it to stay. Directed at my brother. "And maybe have a little respect for her daughter, who I believe was shacking up in your room only a week ago?"

My brother's eyes haven't left the center of the table since my father's hand came down on it, but he manages to squeak out, "Yes, sir."

The cloud of tension settling over us bursts with the delivery of our salads, and my father shifts his personality again, pretending to give a shit about Caleb's fraternity bid when he gets to college. My gaze drifts back to the envelope, which has been pushed aside to make room for our meals. But its presence is everything. I know it in my gut. I nudge the leafy greens around my plate and pick out some nuts and tomatoes until I can't handle the small talk that doesn't involve me any longer.

"I've got a busy day, Dad. Can we get to the point of this?" I wipe the corners of my mouth with my napkin, then toss it on top of my barely eaten lobster salad. My father's gaze remains fixed on my slight of the meal for a breath before he sets his knife and fork down and dabs the corners of his mouth with his own napkin. He sets the linen to the side and brings his elbows to the table, rubbing his hands together as his head falls to the side and his eyes zero in on me.

"I'm sorry, Rowan. I didn't mean to interrupt your booming oil change business—"

"Okay, you know what?" I get up from my chair, not really in the mood for my father's insults about the direction I decided to take my life.

"Relax, relax," he says, gesturing his splayed hand toward my abandoned seat. I take a deep breath and sit down, my hands spread out on my thighs, giving me something to squeeze and release my frustration.

My father's gaze sticks to mine as his right palm covers the ominous envelope. He lifts it, balancing it on its edge and tapping it on the table almost as if to show off its weight. When he finally unfolds the top and pulls out two sets of folded documents, both my brother and I lean in with our forearms on the table, like good students.

I have a feeling, though, that our motivations are vastly different. Where Caleb is likely curious, maybe even excited, I'm soaked in caution. If the years I have on my brother of watching and studying my father's every move have taught me one thing, it's that anything David Anderson puts on paper is probably written in poison and blood.

"As you both may or may not know, my marriage last year to Lindsey prompted a review of my estate, and I've been putting off updates to my will because, well, I don't have a good taste in my mouth when it comes to dying."

Caleb chuckles along with my father, but I remain stone cold silent. My father's gaze squares on me.

"Maybe you're warmer to the idea of me no longer being here."

He couches his dig as a continuation of his morbid joke, but I note the subtle shift in the tone of his laugh. It's loaded with passive aggression.

"I just don't like thinking about you and death, is all. There's so much finality to it."

My response is honest, but I don't voice my motivation. I don't like thinking about it because it's going to come with more emotional stress for my mom, renewed disappointment in my brother, who will no doubt salivate at the wealth he'll inherit, and I will be forced to take my share of money I never wanted in the first place. Unless, of course, this lunch is about taking me out of the will completely. I perk up.

"How benevolent." The way my father's tongue curls around that word reminds me of a snake.

"*Hmm.* Indeed," I say, glancing to the papers my father continues to cradle between his hands.

"Right." He splits the documents and passes one set to me, the other to Caleb, and we each spend a few seconds silently reading the cover page.

"It's all there, very standard. I'm not cutting Lindsey into the will. She will have her own earnings from being my wife, and that should serve her fine."

"Romantic," I joke under my breath.

My father clears his throat, but I remain unfazed. I don't like Lindsey. She's only four years older than me, and my father married her after meeting her on a whirlwind ski trip last year. She's a viper. But I guess, who isn't. Everyone linked to my dad seems to be one, or at least in training to gain their fangs.

"Everything will be divided equally between you two, into trusts. This will codify that," my father explains.

"Equal?" My brother's objection makes me smirk, but I don't divert my attention from the words I'm trying to decipher on page two.

"He is your family, Caleb. Just because he doesn't believe in working a proper job—"

He's baiting me, but I know better than to engage. I

merely glance up from the pages while my brother does the work.

"I'm the one coming to work for you. This will be my hard work, too." My brother whines a lot for a guy about to head off to college.

Our father flattens his hand on Caleb's contract and forces my brother to look him in the eyes.

"And I have no doubt you will one day soar far beyond me and be an incredible success." My brother blinks at my father's syrupy praise. It makes me want to vomit, but my dad seems to have uttered the perfect phrase to cast Caleb back under his spell.

With the timid nod of a spoiled child who was just handed a consolation prize and told to be grateful, Caleb takes the pen my father holds out for him and scribbles his name on a line next to today's date. It's a tiny clue that stabs at my gut, and when I flip to the final page of my document, I find the freshly typed date there, too.

"You pull this right from the printer or something?" I quirk a brow and tap on the date with my finger.

My father shrugs, taking the pen from Caleb's hand and holding it out for me.

"I don't know when Allison printed them. She handled the details."

My father has incredible discipline. It makes him a shark in business. It's let him pull apart companies under the guise of helping the little guy. I can't help but feel I'm sitting opposite him at a high-stakes poker table in a basement somewhere.

"I'd like to take it home and read it first, if you don't mind," I say, pushing his hand down and refusing the pen.

His mouth pulls tight, the slight flex where it puckers at the edges the only physical sign that I've made him mad. But he is angry. I smell the shift in the air. It's acrid, like dawn after a gunfight.

"Sure," he says, moving the pen away. Giving in. I don't buy it, though. "I probably should have held off when you needed that lawyer, too. You know, to make sure I fully vetted the situation you found yourself in before coming to the rescue."

He slowly slides the pen back toward me. I chew at the inside of my cheek as our eyes duel briefly, my heart paused, probably considering how much it's worth to keep beating if I'm stuck in a situation like this.

I take the pen. He knew I would. My brother's knife saws against his plate as he digs in to finish his salad. He's the only one left eating. I lost my appetite the moment my father called for us to meet.

My gaze drops back to the signature page, the date now hitting me like a vital timestamp that I will forever remember. Adjusting my elbow on the table, I glance up to meet my father's glare. He blinks slowly.

"One day you can donate everything you inherit. Does that make you feel better?"

"Only mildly better than burning it," I respond, scratching my name across the line before dropping the pen to the paper and pushing them away.

"You do seem to like playing with fire," my father incites.

Unlike Caleb, I only feel beholden to this man to a point. I signed his fucking trust papers. I am not, however, sticking around for dessert. Or more insults.

"Caleb, it's been nice. Sort of. Dad, it's been . . ." I draw in a deep breath as I stand from the table and remind myself that I'm building a legacy of my own far away from this toxic one being thrust at me.

I nod to Rob as I leave the restaurant, his shoulders once again ratcheted up to his ears with stress. Pausing just before the exit, I fish out my wallet and pull out the two hundred dollar bills I won at pick-up basketball last weekend, and turn back to hand them to Rob.

"Thank you for your hospitality, or something," I mutter, not sure how to couch this tip.

"Wow, uh . . . thanks," he says, tucking the cash in his suit jacket as I wave off his gratitude. I don't want him feeling like that's a payoff. If anything, it's restitution for years of empty promises from his most difficult clientele.

I pull my phone out of my pocket when my feet reach the parking lot, and when I read the message from Miguel asking if I'm down for a trip up north this week to pick up an investment car he found online and wants to flip, I jokingly ask if I can leave right now.

> MIGUEL: It's not ready until Thursday, but you do you, man.

A four-day road trip with spotty phone service is tempting after that lunch, but I guess I can drown myself in engine work until then. I open my other notification.

> SAYLOR: I'm keeping the shirt.

Or other distractions.

Chapter 4

WHEN I FIRST JOINED A SWIM TEAM, I did it because being underwater for hours at a time gave me peace. It still does, to an extent. Pulling my cap over my head and gliding through the water twenty-five yards at a time is the one place where I can quiet the constant critiques from my mother, coaches, and Caleb. Honestly, it's the only reason I'm still swimming.

I hit the swim club early this morning to put in my laps. It was an excuse to get out of breakfast time with my mom, and for a moment, I worried she might try to accompany me. She has thoughts on my undeclared status for my freshman year. She says I'm ignoring my natural business savvy and my penchant for number crunching.

I'm good at math; it doesn't mean I love it. And I absolutely don't want to do it for the rest of my life.

The echoes of my mom's lecture during dinner last night resurface in my head the moment I leave the water. The reprieve is always so short-lived, but I can't stay in the pool forever. Damn, to be a mermaid.

"Saylor, I'd love to chat with you before you leave, if you've got a minute?" My old team coach, Christen Tellez, has been trying to get me on board to coach this summer.

How do I tell her I'm probably not the motivating factor she thinks I am for her group of young swimmers? I'm liable to slip at some point and tell them how much I hate competing, how the only reason I'm here is for the audible drowning it provides.

"I can't today. I have an appointment. Next time," I say, holding my hand up as I pick up my steps toward the locker room and rush by her at the pool's edge.

"It won't take long. I'll follow you out," she insists.

I sigh as I walk, and I know she sees it. I don't care.

"We're scrambling to get a coach for the fifth and sixth graders. And you've always been so good with the youth here. It would really mean a lot . . . to the kids."

We round the corner and enter the locker room, then stop at my stall. I flatten my hand on my locker and stare at the leftover sticky outline from where I pulled my nameplate away a few weeks ago. Fucking hitting me with her famous "the kids" speech. I drop my chin and nod.

"Okay, I can fill in until you find someone permanent. Make sure the parents know I'm temporary." And disgruntled. And only good at swimming because I'm excellent at running away from my problems.

"Of course. Thank you so much, Saylor. You're saving our asses, truly."

I glance over my shoulder, and force a smile to match my former coach's relieved one. It feels nice to help her, at least. And I do like working with kids. Maybe I can find a way to use this to get my mom off my back about my future. She's always admired teachers. Maybe that's what I'll become. Of course, teachers are poor. Like musicians. And since that's always been a sharp criticism of my dad, I'm not sure how much grace the teaching route will buy me.

"I'll have Megan set you up with paperwork tomorrow. Drop by whenever you can," she says, tugging on the lanyard that holds her whistle around her neck before spinning on her heels. She practically sprints out of the locker room, probably afraid I'll change my mind.

Smart move.

I already am.

After a quick shower and change into my blue cotton romper and sports bra, I head out to my car without running into any more unwelcome conversations. The AC for my car has been tricky lately, as in working every third attempt or so, but my car is twenty years old, so at this point repairs are weighed against the price of a new ride. I'm sure my mom would help pay for a car, but that would be one more piece of leverage she would have in dictating my decisions. If I can just make it to school in the fall, I'll walk everywhere I need to go and figure out what to do for transportation next summer.

It's still early in the morning. There's no way Cami is awake, but it's also too early to guarantee my mom has headed to the office. I drift out of the swim club lot and weave around the wealthy neighborhood that surrounds it to kill time. I roll my window down to take advantage of the morning air, which is only a brisk ninety rather than triple digits. It helps that my hair is still wet from my swim, but I'm going to start sweating soon.

I dip into the drive-thru for Swig soda shop and order an extra-tall lemon soda with ice while sending up a quick prayer to the AC gods before attempting the refrigeration again. I'm next in line and idling with my palms held out to test the vents as I mutter, "Come on, baby," to myself until one of the middle vents flickers to life with a slight burst of coolish air.

"I know a guy who can fix that."

I jump in my seat and clutch my seat belt against my chest before twisting to find Rowan leaning in my open window.

"Fucking hell, man!" My heart is pounding so hard I think my vision is pulsing.

Also, Rowan is shirtless. And gleaming with sweat.

"You holding a car wash or something?" I glance over my

shoulder, checking to see if he's left his car parked behind me. He chuckles as he stretches into a stand. His taut stomach is within reach, and it's the first thing my eyes find as I turn back to my open window.

"You sound like my father with that joke. Poor Rowan, charity case," he mocks, and I instantly recoil.

"Oh, yuck. Don't say that." I lean my head against the window frame and flit my eyes up at him. It takes him a second or two to drop his gaze to mine, and when his green-blue eyes connect with mine, my insides jolt as if he startled me again.

"I come out here to shoot around a little, at the park," he says, gesturing toward the tree-lined street across the main thoroughfare.

I glance out my windshield in response to his direction, toward the neighborhood that is much more like mine. Caleb always plays pick-up games at the club. I didn't realize Rowan still plays.

"Maybe I'll come watch a bit—" I say, but Rowan cuts in before the words completely leave my mouth.

"Hey, about the other night . . ."

I blink my gaze back up to him. My heart is pounding again, remembering how Rowan made me feel, his touch, the things he did with only a few fingers.

He breathes out a soft laugh and bites his lower lip, and my lungs inflate with the airy joy of hope. It takes him half a second to collapse them.

"I'm sorry. I was out of line. I should have respected the boundaries—"

"Boundaries?"

His eyes shift to mine, and his head tilts a hint, his brow furrowed with confusion.

"Saylor."

He says my name with authority. Like a parent. Or an older brother.

"Rowan." I dish it right back.

He blinks a few times before chuckling, his hands grasping the edge of my window as he leans back.

"Look, I know you and Caleb just broke things off, and it was wrong of me to take advantage of . . . the situation."

Of me. Take advantage of me. I want you to take advantage of me.

"Right," I croak, squinting as sunlight reflects off the car in front of me as they pull away from the drive-thru window.

"You're next. I was just coming to grab a water. I should —" He points a thumb over his shoulder, to the pointless park game he finds more important than this conversation.

"Yeah," I say, my stomach tight and my mind ping-ponging from frustrated to hurt.

Rowan pats the window edge a few times and utters, "Okay," before stepping away. He makes it a few steps, then turns around and grasps the corner of my window again.

"You're like my little sister, is all. I mean, I watched you grow up. Hell, I babysat your ass more than a few times. And I shouldn't . . ." He stammers, and for a tiny moment, I swear his cheeks flush.

"Shouldn't what?" I challenge him.

His eyes meet mine, and he bites the tip of his tongue while holding back a full smile.

"I *shouldn't* a lot of things," he finally says. The way his gaze lingers makes me crazy, and I can't help but wonder what that list of things he's ruminating on entails.

"Miss?" A blonde girl with her hair twisted into space buns is leaning out the drive-thru window ahead.

"I'll see ya," Rowan says, patting the window's edge again and this time leaving me behind without pause.

I let my foot off the brake and roll forward slowly, my mind barely able to handle the wake of WTF Rowan left behind, let alone manage payment instructions from the peppy Swig worker waiting for me to scan my phone or card on her payment device.

"Five sixty-four?" she prompts again. I shake my head and snag my phone from my passenger seat and tap it to her screen. I give her a five-dollar tip for putting up with me, then take my soda and move to the open spots along the driveway.

Little sister. That's what he said. Is that really what he sees when he looks at me? Because the hard-on pressed against my ass the other night by the pool says otherwise. And he didn't have to stop to talk to me just now. He could have waited for me to drive off without seeing him.

No. I'm not buying it. Rowan Anderson didn't mean that apology just now, nor do I want one from him. And fuck whatever guilt he seems to be wrestling with over the things he did to me—*that I let him do.* Full consent between two adults. Not a baby and her sitter.

I work myself up so much that by the time I pull out of the parking lot for Swig, my back wheels peel out from my swift punch of the gas. I race across the main road, only slowing when I spot Rowan's form a few blocks ahead. There's a public pool at this park. I remember it well from my youth swim meets, and I doubt it's changed much over the years. I pull to the side of the road to let Rowan make his way back to the park before I blatantly follow him.

The game is in full swing when I pull into the familiar lot. I glance at the pool to my right, fond memories of my first leaps off the high dive pulling up the corners of my mouth. I roll my car window up and shut off my engine, snagging a hair tie from my glove box before grabbing my drink and exiting the vehicle.

Rowan's back is to me as I walk up, but a few of the guys playing with him glance my way, a couple bumping elbows and snickering to one another. I climb up the small set of bleachers and pull my sunglasses from the front of my romper, slipping them on so I can stare without it being quite so obvious. It takes Rowan a few minutes to spot me, and he pauses his run across the court for a beat when he does.

I slip my flip-flops off and rest them on the bottom bench, making a cushion for my heel as I cross my feet and hike the hem of my jumper up to sun my legs. I twist my hair up with my tie, then lean back on my elbows before glancing to the two boys whispering not so quietly to each other to my right.

"Hi, boys," I say, smiling. They both laugh nervously, their braces gleaming in the morning sun.

My guess is twelve, maybe thirteen. Their skateboards are propped against the side of the bleachers. They're probably waiting for Rowan and his friends to finish up so they can practice whatever tricks they think will impress the girls in their grade. I remember the boys like them. I was impressed back then. It takes more than a few tricks to get my attention now, though. Apparently, it takes a twisted form of playing hard to get, along with a full sleeve of tats and a trove of family drama.

"Hey."

I swivel my head to the other side to meet the unfamiliar voice. The guy standing at the end of the bleachers flips open the top of his water bottle and immediately gulps down what I assume is water as his eyes linger on me.

"Hey," I repeat.

He's a good-looking guy, probably about Rowan's age. Maybe younger. It's hard to tell anymore, and Rowan wears his years a bit heavier than most. He's lived what feels like more than the twenty-four years that he is.

"You watching your boyfriend or something?" The guy lifts a brow with his question, and I glance beyond his shoulder as a few other guys from the game wander toward us for their break. Rowan remains on the court, shooting jump shots that rattle the chains as they repeatedly sink through the hoop.

I shake my head as my gaze works its way back to my new friend.

"Nope. No boyfriend for me."

His grin moves in swiftly, as does his quick laughter.

"Well, that's good to know. You, uh . . . You like anything you see?" He quirks a brow again, taking another long drink when I don't answer right away.

Is this guy for real? Is this what pick-up lines are now? The level of ick crawling over my skin is smothering, but I do like the way Rowan keeps glancing at us. There's a protectiveness in his expression, one emphasized by the regular flex in his jaw.

"Oh, there's a lot of things I like seeing out here . . ." I tip my chin, awaiting his name.

"Brady," he says, as a curled lock of hair slips over his forehead.

"Nice to meet you, Brady. I'm Saylor." I pull my glasses from my eyes and reach forward with my other hand to shake his.

His grip is firm, though a bit damp. His gray athletic shirt is drenched with sweat, but it's clear he's got a decent build underneath. Maybe I should be open to a guy like him. Perhaps an entire summer of Bradys. Flings I can use to forget about the rules my mom is trying to enforce around my decisions about my future. Summer fun to wash away memories of the boy I thought of as a best friend, who ditched me to find himself and have a summer of his own hook-ups. A date night, perhaps, with Brady . . . to forget about the way my body teems with electricity at the mere thought of Rowan watching me from afar.

"I'd love to buy you dinner, maybe some drinks."

I smirk, glancing back to Rowan for a second, just long enough to catch his eyes on me. He quit shooting, and is standing in the center of the court with the ball tucked to his side as he watches me turn up the flirt with his friend.

"Well, I'd love dinner. But I'm not quite twenty-one, so drinks might be a little hard to manage." I bat my lashes and brace myself for the inevitable question.

"How not quite twenty-one are you?" There's an edge to Brady's tone, and he may actually be worried I'm younger than I am.

"I'm eighteen. I leave for college in August," I say, and his relief seems instant as his shoulders drop with a swift exhale.

"Dinner it is, then. Can I get your number?" He moves toward a small gym bag resting on the ground near the bleachers, but before he can pull out his phone or a pen, I slip my shoes back on my feet and stand.

"Rowan has my number. He's practically my brother, so just tell him I said you can have it." My lips pull into a puckered smile, and I let my fingertips graze along Brady's shoulder as I walk around him.

"Sounds good, Saylor," he says to my back. I glance over my shoulder with a smirk, but my gaze never reaches Brady at all. It stops at Rowan.

Playing games is not like me. None of the way I've acted or felt for the last week is like me. But I'm tired of being whatever I have been for most of my life. Complacent. Quiet. Willing to push my wishes to the side for whoever needs center stage at the time. The good daughter who appreciates her single mom's hard work and never mentions that she misses her dad. The third wheel to the Anderson boys; the one who needs a babysitter.

Fuck that.

I might not be ready to break all of my good girl promises, but this one? Where I pretend that I don't want Rowan Anderson? I'm done faking that.

I make it back to the house before my phone buzzes in my center console with Rowan's call. I sink back in the driver's seat while idling in the driveway and enjoying the nice chill from the AC I finally got working.

"Hello, this is Saylor. Are you calling about the babysitting job I posted?" It's hard to keep the innocent tone up, and I fight not to break into a laugh.

"Ha ha, very funny. No, I am not looking to babysit anyone." Rowan doesn't sound amused, which somehow pleases me more.

The sound of an engine revving in the background fills the line. Probably one of his friends' trucks or cars. Rowan seems to have lost his.

"Okay. Then, why are you calling?"

It's quiet between us for a few seconds, so I clear my throat to prod him to respond.

"Hang on. I'm getting in the car," he grunts.

"I'll wait." And I do. I take in the various sounds of his car's ignition engaging, his phone connection switching to his car's speakers as his engine rumbles to life. Even the way his car sounds is sexy.

"Brady fucking Campbell?" he finally spits out.

"Is that his last name?" I bite my knuckle, loving how irritated he is by this.

I don't know that Caleb was ever truly jealous. Even when it came to me flirting with his brother, which I'm still not entirely sure he noticed. Caleb's warning to me to be careful was more about his dislike for Rowan than any emotional connection to me. It's territorial. And maybe Rowan is being territorial too. The difference is I'm not aiming for anything more than that, than to be wanted in a way that makes me feel alive. Beautiful. Sexy.

"Yeah, that's his name. And no, he can't have your phone number!"

I laugh out loud.

"I'm glad you find this funny," he grumbles.

I hold my fist to my mouth, covering my smile.

"It's a little funny. I mean, why can't your little sister get to know your friends a little better? Maybe Brady and I will hit it off."

"Like hell are you dating a guy like Brady fucking Campbell. All that dude is good for is a few hundred bucks every time I beat his ass on the court." Rowan's engine roars again, and I picture where he's likely at, probably getting on the highway to head to his garage, which gives me an idea.

"Hey, did you mean what you said about my car? Do you really think you can get my AC working?"

What's the worst that can happen here . . . my air gets fixed?

"Yeah, I can. Do you have time today to swing by the shop?"

I suck in my lower lip, giddy at the thought of pushing his buttons in person. I shift my car into reverse and slowly back out of my driveway.

"On my way," I say.

When he doesn't respond immediately, I add, "Maybe Brady will stop by, too?"

"No, he won't," he gripes. "Just get your ass here."

Rowan ends the call, but not before letting a groan slip over the line, the kind that comes from deep inside, from living on the edge of something you want. I intend to push him there.

Chapter 5

WHAT THE FUCK *am I doing?*

Did I know Miguel was gone for the rest of the day meeting with our tire supplier? Yeah. I did. Just like I knew Jersey was still out of town with his girlfriend. I'm always here. Vacations feel frivolous. Plus, I love my job. I'm not good with negotiations and shit like that. I'm good at details, at making things work. I like working alone and focusing on a problem I can fix. That's why engines have always excited me. They're logical, even when they're complicated. And they're quiet, at least when they're broken.

Alone time equals relief. But when Saylor pulls her Toyota into the garage and proceeds to grab herself a beer from our fridge before sliding up on the workbench along the back wall, I keep my mouth shut. I don't breathe a word about how long this will take, or how I don't work well under observation. All I think about is the way those flimsy shorts on her jumper hike up her smooth thighs.

"You need a new compressor," I mumble around the small flashlight clutched between my teeth, fighting to keep my eyes on the problem. Away from the opportunity.

"That sounds expensive." Her voice is raspy, a trait I've

noticed but never fully appreciated before. Fuck, I love a raspy voice.

I pull the flashlight from my mouth and rest my hands along the front of the engine bay, willing myself to keep my gaze fixed on the debris-encrusted parts under this hood. I make it three seconds before conceding failure, leaning to my left to stare straight down the front of Saylor's bra as she leans over her thighs, her elbows propped on her knees. She's . . . flexible. Raspy and flexible. Fucking hell. I wedge my tongue between my molars, but I can feel the smirk tugging my cheeks up.

"I mean, usually? Yeah. It's about a fifteen-hundred-dollar job. But I know a guy . . ."

Don't do it, Rowan.

Saylor sits up, her fingers wrapping around the edges of the workbench on either side of her legs.

"You know a guy?" She quirks a brow.

I'm doing it.

I chuckle as I wipe my hands clean from her engine, then toss the rag to the side as I saunter toward her. My head tilts, matching my crooked smirk.

"Yeah, I know a guy," I say, my gaze dipping to her feet, her flip flops dangling from her toes, ready to drop to the ground. I take my time dragging my attention up her long legs. Somehow, I also maintain my slow steps as she relaxes her thighs and lets her knees part slightly. This would be a whole lot easier if she weren't sending me silent invitations.

"Do I know this guy?" She pops her tongue against her teeth, then smiles.

My eyes meet hers as she lifts her chin. Her dark, wavy hair slips from her shoulders and falls behind her. I rest my palms on the outside of hers, caging her in front of me as I stand close enough for her kneecaps to brush against my thighs and her breath to mix with mine.

"Yeah, his name is Brady Campbell." I hold her gaze

hostage while her eyes flinch, her mouth fighting against laughter as she deciphers whether I'm fucking with her. God, I wish I was. Brady's a good friend. His family also owns an online parts distributor. They have access to a lot of used parts —like the one I need.

"Shut up," she finally laughs out.

I drop my head and rap my fingers along the benchtop next to her. Those fucking perfect thighs. I could lower myself between her legs right now and take a bite out of one, trail my tongue along the inside, press my lips to the edge of her panties, tug the fabric to the side with my teeth.

Stop.

This is Saylor Kelly. Innocent, sweet Saylor, who I promised I would always take care of when her mom left me in charge when we were kids. The girl who refused to let anyone put a Band-Aid on her cuts and scrapes but me, because I always blew on the cut first to make it hurt less. I was just doing what my mom did for me. Caring for her. Like a sister. Being the adult, though I was barely a teenager.

I lift my head to meet her stare, my mouth pulled into a tight smile to hide the ebbing willpower silently telling me to do the right thing.

"Let me give him a call, see if I can get the part today. It'll be reconditioned, but it will be better than what you've got in there and should buy you some time before you have to really spend some money."

I stand up straight, dropping my hand in my right pocket for my phone, but Saylor halts me when her fingers wrap around my forearm. Mentally, I flash to the version where I grab the back of her head and pull her mouth to mine.

Focus, Rowan.

"I've got maybe a grand left in my checking account. Will that—"

I cover her hand with mine and fight the temptation to weave my fingers through hers and lift her arm above her head, along with the other one. Her fingers flex lightly under my palm, so I pat her knuckles twice and take a full step back from danger.

"I'll get you the part for free. Don't worry. And I'll do the work for free, of course." I turn my attention to how I'm going to keep Brady's ass away from this place when he finds out who the part is for. I'm sure he'd give it to her for nothing, but the last thing I need is to give him some sort of connection to exploit.

Brady's a good guy, but he's not the kind of guy Saylor needs to hook up with. He'll smother her. While he's not a player simply looking to hook up with a hot girl once, he does love a beautiful toy he can show off. And he likes to choose Brady before anyone else. Saylor isn't anyone's trophy. She sure as shit wasn't Caleb's.

I press Brady's contact info, and he answers on the second ring. He's probably hoping I've changed my mind about giving him Saylor's number. I have not.

"Hey, man. I need you to do me a solid," I say, pinching the bridge of my nose as I meander out the open garage bay doors toward the roadway. I don't need Saylor overhearing this part.

"You mean like the way you cock-blocked me this morning?"

Yeah, he doesn't need to know this is for Saylor.

"I told you, she's like family. It's a hard no, dude. You'll live. I'm calling about a part, and it's kind of rare." I try to shift him to business, and thankfully he follows my lead.

"Let me guess . . . it's for a rush job?" There's a slight waver of laughter threaded through his words. I guess I do hit him up with a lot of rush requests. But we always pay, or, at least, our clients do.

"Ideally, I'd love to grab it today." My request is met with an earful of laughter.

"I'll do my best. It's gonna cost, though."

I open my mouth, pausing for a short breath as I weigh the cost-benefit of dropping Saylor's name as the client or forking out the cash myself. It's been a good month at the shop. We can afford it, and I know Miguel would agree. Jersey can barely balance his own checkbook so he'll never notice. I'll pay it back in two weeks.

"I can cover it. I'll send you the serial number. Let me know what you can do." I end our call and head back into the garage, grinding to a halt when I spot Skyler bent over the hood in front of me. She's making this—*me*—hard.

"Thinking of changing it yourself?" I tease as I pass.

She flips her hair over her shoulder to glance at me, still bent over the fucking engine bay. She's literally mimicking the poses from my favorite hot rod posters of my teen years. Hell, there's one up in the business office right now. I grab the back of my neck and dig my fingers into my skin, forcing my head straight as I move to the laptop on the work desk.

"I'm just impressed with this stuff. With you, I mean."

I blink up from the computer screen, and thankfully she's now facing me. She's still leaning against her car, however, and somehow, making leaning sexy.

"I'm not that impressive, believe me," I laugh out, suddenly hearing my father's voice telling me how I'm wasting my talents on trivial things.

Dropping my gaze back to the computer, I push those negative thoughts back to the fringes. Seems Saylor has different plans, though. I sense her approaching about a half second before she pushes the screen down. I was literally on her part listing.

"Say—"

"Why do you do that?" she breaks in.

Her gaze dives deep, like she's probing me from the inside out, somehow knowing I'm about to feed her a line of bullshit. Her brown irises are cut into golden slices that grow smaller with the expansion of her pupils. It's as if she's a witch casting a spell, and I have to shake my head to break her hold before nudging the computer screen upward again.

"I know this is a blue-collar life, is all. I don't pretend it's anything more than it is. I'm not saving the world." I chuckle.

"You're saving me." Her soft voice tugs that place in my chest that's weak for her, and I give in and flit my eyes upward until our gazes meet.

"I'm not saving you. I'm making your air conditioner blow cold." I click the mouse without looking, and blink twice before returning my focus to my screen.

"In Arizona, cold air is a precious thing. Believe me, Rowan. You're a hero."

I breathe out a soft laugh at her continued praise. It's sweet of her to say, but I come from a family that works in commas and zeros, in crypto and cool cash. I'm secure in my place in the pecking order because I have my soul. That's enough for me. It's more than my brother can say.

I type the number that comes up into my phone, then set it on the counter before giving in to this sudden, constant pull to look Saylor directly in the eyes.

"I should know in a few minutes whether I can get this done today. If so, I can give you a ride home if you want. Or if you want, call Miguel's sister. Or—"

"I'd rather stay here. Maybe watch you work? If that's okay?" She tucks the corner of her lower lip in her teeth, and I'm losing this battle. I never stood a chance.

"I mean, I'm pretty boring." I sink my hands into my front pockets and ball them into fists. "But if you want—"

"I do want. To watch, I mean."

Our eyes are locked, and the quiet seconds drag on in slow motion, tension wrapping around my throat, slipping down my chest and into my veins. This is a slippery slope, and Saylor is playing with fire.

I take a step back and laugh softly, flitting my gaze to the open bay doors behind her, willing someone—anyone—to walk through and save me from the pending terrible but tempting decisions.

"Saylor, what are we doing?" I level her with my gaze, my mouth pulled into a disciplined line, my head slightly askew, my fingers fisting even tighter.

Her eyes shift from mine as she blinks her focus to the center of my chest while she draws in a deep breath. She flattens her palms on the desk across from me and raps her fingers a few times before pulling her mouth in tight and falling back on her heels.

She makes her way back to the workbench where she was before, when she was sitting and scrolling through her phone quietly and at a safe distance. I assume she'll go back to that, so I slide a pile of invoices next to my computer and begin looking them up on our system to see if checks have cleared yet. I'm not normally the accounting guy, but I know what I'm doing in the software. And frankly, I could use the distraction.

"You shouldn't diminish your dreams, Rowan."

I flinch at her words, but something about the genuine care in her tone forces my eyes up from the screen. I shrug.

"I don't diminish them. I'm doing exactly what I want to do, and I know how lucky it is that I can say that. Believe me . . . you don't have a two-hundred-pound parole officer unlock a monitoring anklet and not feel grateful about the good shit in life."

She smirks, and her gaze drops to the open space beneath the desk where my legs are on display. My skin warms, and though the anklet is gone, the place where it encircled my leg throbs from the memory of its weight.

"I'm sorry you went through that."

Her tone is quiet but not the ashamed kind my brother and father sometimes use with me. Her gaze has shifted up a bit, too, though it's not fully on my eyes.

Rather than dismiss her apology with the typical write-off I typically use, saying, "It's no big deal."

I decide Saylor deserves my honesty. I wasn't lying when I told Brady she was like family. She's more family than my brother and father at this point. Besides, I'm sure Caleb filled her head with his perspective. It's only right I get the chance to counter it.

"It stung more than anything. I thought Caleb had a higher opinion of me, is all," I say, biting my tongue when Saylor's brow pulls in.

Maybe she doesn't know.

"Caleb was my character witness. I assumed he told you." My eyes dim as her gaze drops with the shake of her head.

A short, breathy laugh causes my nostrils to flex, and I flip over the gold-plated pen weighing down the stack of invoices. I'm tempted to throw my brother under this massive bus right now, but despite our mutual disdain, I can't lie about him completely.

"He didn't say anything that wasn't true. He just shared a little too much." I lift a shoulder and pull my mouth into a crooked smirk.

Saylor sinks back, resting her shoulder blades against the brick wall.

"He told them about the fire?" She exhales the words in one breath.

I nod.

"Yep. They unsealed that sucker faster than the final lap at Daytona. I learned closing a case is sometimes more important than getting it right, so I took a deal." I grimace from the memory of that moment, when I knew I was going to have to fall on another sword. At least, in my past I was the one making the choice. This sword left me with few options, if any. And it was sharp.

"Is your sentence done now, or do you have a parole officer or community service hours?"

I nod.

"Parole Officer Steve and I have a standing date every

Thursday. At least for the next eighteen months. Unless there's overwhelming evidence of good behavior."

My eyes flash to hers, and there's a snap in the air that I don't think anyone can hear but me. Saylor's head falls to the side as a wry grin etches into her cheeks.

"We both know your behavior is questionable at best," she jests.

I chuckle, then flip the pen over again to rid my hand of nervous energy that builds during the brief silence.

"What about you? Collegiate swimming is a big deal. I still remember the lanky girl flapping around the swim club pool, trying to pull off the butterfly stroke."

We both laugh at the memory, and Saylor stretches her arms out wide to mimic the stroke, at least the way she did it back then.

"I was better at drowning." She laughs.

I shake my head, though, because even with her unpolished technique, she was always the fastest in the water.

"I distinctly remembering you smoking my brother in a race after your first practice. You were a natural."

Her lips settle into a faint smile as her gaze drifts to the side for a beat.

"Caleb doesn't tell it that way," she finally says, her gaze hesitating but coming back to me.

My brow draws in.

"He's told that story a few times, like to people at school or to your dad. In his version, he wins."

My chest burns with this tiny piece of intel, and I know it's not important, but I can't seem to shut off the defensive flood that suddenly eats at me inside.

"Why didn't you correct him?"

I know why. The same reason I let other people's versions of my story go unchecked.

It's easier that way.

Her shoulder rises as her mouth bunches.

"It seemed way more important to him, I guess," she says in a soft voice.

I nod and match her tight-lipped, resolved expression.

"I understand."

A brief silence settles into the garage, but my phone buzzes on the tabletop before it becomes unbearable. I flip to the screen in my palm and am instantly filled with a mix of excitement and trepidation at reading Brady's response. He has the part, and it's mine if I want to pick it up today at their warehouse. It's a mere six hundred bucks, which I would laugh at out loud if I were alone. Since I'm not, I keep the sticker shock to myself. It's still the best price I'll get for it.

"Is that Brady?"

Saylor slides off her perch as I hold up a finger, pretending to still be reading his response. I'm not sure I can make it through this day without touching her, and I've already crossed the line plenty.

I type Brady back.

> ME: Awesome. I'll swing by on my way home
> for the day and leave cash with Bev.

Bev is Brady's mom. She runs the books, and she loves when I operate in cash because, well, she also cooks them.

As soon as Brady sends me a thumbs up, my shoulders relax. Before Saylor can invade my space again, I tuck my phone into my back pocket and move across the room to snag my keys and wallet from the locker in the corner of the garage.

"The good news is he has the part. The bad news is it won't be ready for pick up until the end of the day, so I'll have to do the work tomorrow."

Her lips curve down with disappointment, and my own mouth twitches from guilt. It's too late, though. I've spun the tale, and I know in my gut that I need to get the two of us out of this space. This way, tomorrow, I can work at my own pace and without the smell of her citrus shampoo and chlorine invading my senses.

"I can give you a lift, though," I offer.

Her eyes light up, but before I can fully catalogue the new world of trouble getting her alone in my car could cause, our private conversation is interrupted by the high-pitched hum of my brother's electric BMW.

Caleb pulls into the bay between Saylor and me, and I can't help but chuckle at his obvious play. I'm not sure what the hell he's doing here, but I one-hundred-percent recognize his jealous behavior. He cuts his engine, and the quiet whir ceases.

"Having car trouble, Saylor?" His back is to me as he gets out of his car and glares at Saylor from across the roof of his vehicle as if he owns her.

"She is. What do you want, Caleb?"

My brother turns to face me, and I silently connect with Saylor before I give him my attention. I can't tell whether her wide eyes are twitching because she's freaked out that Caleb is here or because I just took over answering for her. I shouldn't have, but my brother pushes me into auto-defense.

"Dad needs to get a scan of your license for the trust paperwork. I offered to come by." He keeps glancing back at Saylor, obviously rattled by her presence . . . here. He finally nods at her.

"You know, we've got a service through the company. I could have given them a call to get you a rental, had them pick up your car and diagnose—"

"It's not your company, Caleb," I say. It's annoying when my brother speaks as if he and my father are on the same level, like they're partners. He's barely out of high school. And he bailed on his AP math courses. I honestly think it will be a miracle if he passes the security exams.

My brother's glare narrows on me, but after a moment, his brow ticks up on one side.

"Unless this is a charity thing. It's nice of you, Saylor. Keeping my brother in business. Family supports family and all that. I get it." Caleb's cocky expression shifts between the two of us as he sits on his hood.

"I was about to take her home. So, if we could just hurry up with your little errand," I say, pulling my license out and handing it to my brother.

He snatches it from my hand but keeps his challenging glare on me, his mouth frozen in that half smirk he wears when he feels superior.

"I can take you home, Say. I'm heading that way. I'm sure my brother has a lot of work to do." Caleb doesn't look over his shoulder to meet her eyes. If he did, he'd see the crease deepening between them as she scowls.

I spin my keys around my finger, partly to draw Saylor's gaze back to me, but she's locked in on the back of Caleb's head.

My brother fishes his phone from his pocket, palming my license as he snaps a photo while his mouth lingers in that arrogant grin that never seems to leave his face. He hands my ID back, and I take it while splitting my focus between him and Saylor as she cradles her phone and rapidly types out a message. I secretly hope to feel my phone buzz in my pocket, but after a few seconds pass between the time she puts her phone away and then marches toward the garage drive, I concede that whoever she was texting wasn't me. It wasn't Caleb either, though, and I'm a bit smug at that thought.

"You know it's bullshit, right?" Caleb says, his voice low. He has yet to realize that Saylor's walked away.

"You driving over here to do something I could have done myself with a text? Yeah, Caleb. I know it's bullshit."

He came here to gripe about me getting a share of the family fortune, I'm sure. He didn't get to say to me everything on his chest during our lunch with Dad, so he made up an excuse to see me and take up round two.

"You don't have a right to any of it. You gave that up the second you torched our home." His whisper-shout would have easily been heard if Saylor were still there, and as much as I like the idea of her seeing more of Caleb's ugly underbelly, I don't want her hearing more of the same old story about the disturbed Anderson boy who liked to play with matches. I'm sick of that tale myself, and I'm the one who fucking wrote it.

Caleb glances over his shoulder as he seethes, his spine straightening as soon as he realizes Saylor's gone. Spinning on his feet, he turns toward the roadway where his ex is holding out a hand and waving to someone not quite in view.

"Saylor! What the hell?" Caleb throws up both hands, perhaps incensed that she does not need him, or maybe irked that she dares to leave without a word. She left me, too, but unlike my brother, I'm willing to respect her choice and own that this time, I probably didn't deserve her goodbye.

Cami's car pulls into view within seconds, and Saylor holds up a middle finger before getting into the passenger seat and slamming the door shut.

"I was taking you home now! Why you gotta be that way?"

I chuckle silently as my brother shouts at Cami's taillights. And when he turns back to finish his lecture to me, I decide to take a page out of Saylor's book, turning my back to him and flipping him the bird on my way to the back room where I live and can lock the door.

The click feels good, as does the way my brother futilely calls me a dick from the other side of the door before leaving. But then I'm all alone again, with nothing but a fleeting mental snapshot of Saylor's smile and her broken air conditioning.

Chapter 6

THE LAST PLACE I want to go is to my mom's office. Caleb will be there, and after his little performance yesterday, I can't guarantee I won't wrap my hands around his neck upon first sight. I have no problem acting on that urge, but I don't need to cause a scene at my mom's work, or make issues for her with Caleb's dad.

As irritating as my mother's constant critiques of my life are, I can't ignore how hard she works to give me opportunities. She managed to transform a two-year associate's degree in office management into a steady career with a solid retirement forecast. We might not be up in the hills, living behind the gate, but we have a nice home, and I got to attend the same private school that the Anderson boys did. I owe that to her.

I'd forgotten that I promised to meet her for lunch today to set up new beneficiary paperwork. I'm not sure that would have stopped me from marching out of Rowan's garage to leave him to bicker with his brother, but it would have made me rethink leaving my car behind. Now, I'm without wheels for the day, and Cami is not remotely reliable before ten in the morning. I could put this off for a day, I guess, but then I'll have to explain to my mom that my car is at Rowan's garage, which will lead to me enduring a new round of lectures about staying away from the older Anderson brother. I'm not interested in hearing any opinions on that, which is probably why I haven't mentioned anything to Cami about him . . . er, *us.*

The thought of *us* makes me snort laugh. I shake off my fantasy and search my Uber options. The rides showing are all around a hundred bucks to head downtown at this time of day. I could charge it to my mom, but she'd get an alert, which would, again, lead to questions.

"Fuck it," I mutter to myself, stuffing my phone in the back pocket of my shorts before snagging my crossbody and phone from my dresser and shoving my feet into my sneakers without socks. I don't have time to dress for a formal office visit, which I'm sure I'll hear about from my mom. But if I'm going to catch the bus and get there on time, I have to head out *now,* in shoes that can accommodate a brief sprint from the blue line to the express stop by the freeway. I snag a water bottle from the fridge and lock the door behind me.

I twist my hair up in a clip, letting the sun hit the back of my neck while I rush to the corner of our street. There's a woman waiting with a walker under the bus stop shelter, and she looks to be struggling with several grocery bags.

Two men are waiting on the other side of her, both perhaps in their early thirties, though it's hard to tell given the weathered scruff on their faces. Their shoes are in rough shape, one pair peppered with holes. Thankfully, the man has a new pair of socks underneath to shield his feet from blisters. The skin on their noses is peeling to the point of forming wounds, and their shoulders and arms are a deep, painful red, which leads me to believe they're either homeless or outdoor labor workers. Maybe both.

As the bus approaches, I move closer to the woman and eventually scoop up two of her plastic grocery bags to help her get on the bus. Her long hair is twisted in a bun at the base of her neck, but several strands have fallen out, leaving the long hairs to stick to her sweat-soaked neck and back.

"It's pretty hot out here to be making a grocery run," I say.

She laughs softly, her eyes squinting against the sun as she looks up at me with a smile.

"It's hot out here for months at a time. A woman's gotta eat, though, so it's not like I can put it off." She coughs through her laugh, covering her mouth with a tissue wadded in her palm. She shoves it in a loose pocket on the hip of her long sun dress before adjusting the bags looped over her right arm.

The bus squeals to a stop in front of us, and I hold my arm out to help the woman balance in the entrance while one of the men waiting with us lifts up her walker.

"Thanks, Chad. I'll get it," the driver says to the man, taking the device in two hands and unhooking a clasp that allows it to fold easily. He slides the walker into a nook behind the driver's seat while I help the woman get settled in a seat near the front. She pulls out a cell phone to scan the payment code, and I do the same, taking a seat directly across from her. The men move to the middle, the one who didn't assist curling up on his side along two seats. The other man, Chad, pulls a set of earbuds from his pocket and unwinds the cord before plugging them into his phone.

"Do you know Chad?" the woman asks, pulling my attention back across the aisle to her.

I shake my head and offer a soft smile.

"Oh, I figured maybe you did. Most of us regulars do." She settles into her seat, but I keep my gaze fixed on her, suddenly curious about Chad, the bus regular, and wishing she'd share more.

"I take it you know Chad?" I prompt.

She shakes with a silent laugh and leans toward me while waving her hand.

"I would hope so. He comes to the apartment for dinner every Sunday."

We're both laughing, though I'm not entirely sure why, as I'm not certain how I'm supposed to have known that. There's something about the woman that sets me at ease.

"How long have you known Chad?" I ask, bracing myself as the bus jerks to life and the driver closes the door and shifts into drive.

"Let's see . . ." She looks up at the bus ceiling, her lips moving with silent counting before she drops her gaze back to me and declares, "Seven years."

"How did you meet?" I'm really having to work at piecing together this Chad mystery.

"I live at the Beatitudes. Chad works in building maintenance, and the day I moved in, my sink decided to explode all over my cabinets and flooring. Chad fixed it right up, though." She leans toward me and waves me to do the same, like she's about to reveal a secret. I do as she asks, and she cups her mouth.

"He replaced the flooring for me, too, even though he wasn't supposed to. He wouldn't say so, but I know he went and bought the tiles himself. I've been feeding him Sunday dinner ever since." She sits upright and crinkles her eyes as she smiles. I find myself matching her expression, and I turn back to glance at Chad again with a sudden warmth in my chest.

We get to the retirement home's stop about ten minutes later, and Chad pulls out his earbuds and winds up his cord before stuffing them in the pocket of his well-worn jeans. I help the woman make her way down the bus steps while Chad carries her walker. He sets it up for her, then takes over holding the grocery bags as the two of them walk toward the entrance. My gaze lingers on the pair for a few seconds, my mouth stretching up on the corners as Chad makes her giggle, and she responds by squeezing his arm.

There's a definite sense of envy in my chest, but it's not

like the feeling I had when I saw Caleb kiss another girl. It's more like the way my insides feel when my dad sends me photos from one of the cities he's in, or from some stage in the middle of Ohio in a bar with hundreds of people there to hear him play. I long for those texts from him. I know I can't exactly tag along for the ride, but I hate not being a part of his routine. There's a part of me that wishes the woman had dropped me an invite to Sunday dinner.

It takes another twenty minutes to reach the express line and, as I predicted, I need to sprint to catch the next bus. The only seat left is smack in the middle, and I have to climb over a burly man to sit by the window. I tried waiting for him to shift or get up, but he was clearly more interested in making me feel small and intimidated. The feel of his meaty, khaki-covered legs rubbing against my thighs while I stepped over him lingers until we reach the downtown hub. Thankfully, he's quick to exit his seat, and he heads in the opposite direction from me when we get off the bus.

I've worked up a good sweat by the time I reach the lobby of my mom's building, so I pace in the cool entryway as I send her a text alerting her that I'm here. A full minute passes without a response, which means she's either in a meeting or on her office phone, so I let my head fall back and blow up at the few strands of hair stuck to my forehead, then shuffle my way toward the bank of elevators.

Karma kicks me right in the teeth the second the doors open, as standing there wearing dark gray suits are the brothers who have monopolized my thoughts for the last twenty-four hours.

"I didn't know you were coming in," Caleb says, his mouth forming a surprised grin as he moves to one side to make space for me.

I hover in the doorway.

"Weren't you getting out here?" I jerk my thumb over my shoulder and bounce my gaze between the two men.

"Yeah, but that can wait. I'll take you up," he says, moving his attention to his brother, who also seems hesitant to leave the elevator. "You go on, Rowan. I'll meet you at the car."

Rowan's deep chuckle is swift.

"Yeah, not a chance," he says, reaching across my body to the buttons and pressing the nineteenth floor to promptly close the doors again.

I stare straight ahead as the lobby disappears, squeezed between two metal doors that seal me off from an escape. The silence makes the space feel tighter, plus it's easier to hear the squeal of the gears and belt working to take us up nineteen stories. I swear to God, if this elevator breaks right now, I'm going to have to do some serious reflecting on my sins.

I can feel Caleb's eyes on me at my left, so I shift my gaze to the right, where Rowan is typing something on his phone, probably to avoid having to speak.

"Are you learning the ropes, too?" I ask, pulling his attention from his screen. His eyes blink a few times as his mouth contorts between the hard line that comes naturally and the irritable smile I provoked.

"No."

I hold my eyes on his for a beat, waiting for him to elaborate, but when his mouth shifts into a triumphant grin, I accept that's all I'm going to get for now.

"Huh. Okay, then," I say, turning my attention back to the metal doors about a half second before they open.

I step out and to the right, toward my mother's office, thankful Rowan heads straight ahead to the leather sofa by the windows. Caleb tails me into my mother's office. Sadly, she isn't in it, leaving me with no choice but to speak to him alone.

"What's the deal with you and my brother?" He's trying to sound curious and light, but I can hear the edge of jealousy in his tone.

I move to my mother's desk and flip through the paper calendar to make sure I didn't mess up our date. When I see my name highlighted at noon today, I sigh. I almost wish I had it wrong, because then I could leave and not entertain Caleb's encroachment on my space.

"Say? Did you hear me?" He leans a hip on the edge of my mom's desk as I flop into her chair and let it spin halfway around before shuffling my way back to facing him.

"I heard you. I just don't have anything to say. There's nothing. No deal. Is that what you want?" I mean, I wouldn't *mind* a deal, or at least another tryst. Maybe something more for the summer.

Caleb's head drops forward as he nods, a slow laugh airing out through his breath.

"Makes sense now. He's trying to get to me," he says.

I roll my eyes but take in his assessment. Is that all the flirting is about? Getting under Caleb's skin? It's not like Rowan knew Caleb would show up at the shop. He doesn't have to fix my car for me. That doesn't feel like a show for Caleb's benefit.

"Didn't we break up?" I blurt out.

Caleb straightens his posture, dropping his hands into the pockets of his slacks as he rolls his shoulders and meets my eyes.

"We're going to different colleges, Say. It just makes more sense, and we're young. I don't know who I'm going to be in four years, and neither do you." He's delivering the same bullet points he gave me when he broke things off, which is not what I need to hear right now.

I nod.

"I was there for it the first time. You don't need to repeat yourself. But for a guy who ended things, you seem awfully interested in being jealous."

He flinches at the J word, and my mouth pulls into a tight, smug smirk because of it.

Caleb's head falls to the side a tick, his lips parting as he seems to be pondering the appropriate words.

"I'm not jealous, Say. I just don't want you getting mixed up in any of my brother's chaos. He can't help it. Trouble just seems to follow him everywhere he goes."

He shrugs as if what he just said is some simple, obvious fact. And to an extent, there's truth to it. Rowan has had a lot of struggles, for sure. But the more I get to know him as an adult, the more I wonder if those struggles are of his own making or, at the very least, a result of being an Anderson boy.

"So, no jealousy . . . at all." I rest my arms on my mother's desk, folding my hands together as I stare Caleb directly in the eyes.

His head falls back in laughter, then shakes as he rights it.

"None at all. Only worry for you. I swear."

He crosses his chest with his finger as my inner voice screams, *"Liar!"*

Our silent agreement is broken up as my mom pushes the door open wide behind Caleb. Her cell phone is pressed to her ear, and her other arm is weighed down with a pile of white binders. She plops them on her desktop, then shifts the phone against her face as she looks at me.

"I'm so sorry, Saylor, but I'm slammed. Can we try again tomorrow?" she whispers, returning right back to the phone conversation with a full volume, "Of course. We can pull that together for tomorrow. Uh huh. Uh huh."

I draw in a long breath before snagging the pen from her desk and using it to draw a line through my name with an arrow pointing to the same time tomorrow. I tap on it to get my mom's attention, and she twists her neck to read the appointment that seems to be in the way.

"Shoot," she mouths, taking the pen from me and sliding it along the week until it's into the middle of next. There's a pretty big gap around noon ten days from now, so she circles it and writes my name down, never bothering to confirm that it's okay with me. Of course it is. What else could I possibly have going?

Chewing at the inside of my cheek, I nod and stand. I type the new date and time into my phone as I head around one end of my mother's desk while she circles the other. Places now swapped, I leave my mother at her desk and find my way back to the lobby, where Rowan has propped his feet up on the slick granite coffee table as he scrolls through his phone.

"Hey, since your mom bailed on lunch—" Caleb says over my shoulder. Rowan's eyes shift up to mine.

"I don't want to have lunch with you, Caleb." I breathe out an exaggerated sigh, then spin on my heels to face him with a shrug. "We're just in different places, and I . . . well, I just don't know the person I'm going to be after lunch. I want to dine on my own, you know . . . to figure that out."

"Say, that's not . . ."

I turn my back to him, ignoring his hurt feelings. I embarrassed him in front of his brother, who smirks back at me like he wants to offer me a fist bump for dropping the mic.

"At least, let me drive you home," Caleb says as the elevator dings and I step inside.

I turn around fast and flash an open palm. I'm taking this ride alone. I'd take the stairs nineteen flights before riding with the two of them again.

"I'm good. I've got my car," I say, flashing my gaze to Rowan's and hoping he catches the hint just before the elevator doors close. The flash of green and blue, along with the twitch of his upper lip, tells me he did.

Chapter 7

THESE FAVORS for my father are piling up. At some point, I'm going to have to refuse to indulge him, but I haven't hit the breaking point yet. He's still too influential over my life and the business I'm fighting like hell to get off the ground. One grudge from him could sink us, and I know it. I've seen him do it to others for petty reasons. It doesn't matter that I'm his son. When David Anderson's ego is bruised, he fights dirty, with every financial tool in his pocket.

When my father requested my attendance for photos this morning for the big profile piece *The Financial Times* is running on him, I begrudgingly agreed. I even accepted the suit he had ready for me when I stepped foot in his office. I'll admit, it did help ease my discomfort that Caleb was annoyed to have me there. My brother is loving being the anointed heir, and it's apparent my presence makes him feel threatened. But as terri-torial as he is over our father's attention, it's nothing compared to the way his hairs seem to stand on end when I come near Saylor.

My hunch is confirmed the moment I exit the elevator in the parking garage and spot her leaning on the back end of the Camaro. I drop my hands in the pockets of the expensive slacks my father bought me and pause just outside the elevator doors, indulging in a few moments of staring at her.

The sweet girl who has always been my favorite family member, despite having zero relation to me, has become my siren. The thoughts that run through my mind are bad; I own how wrong it is to think about stripping her naked and sinking into her while she clutches my skin and screams my name. But I've never wanted a woman more. And the fact that me wanting her makes my brother sick to his stomach is simply the cherry on top.

"I got your invitation," I say, pulling my key fob from my pocket and pressing the unlock button. My car beeps, and the taillights flash on either side of Saylor.

Her smirk dents her cheek with a fresh dimple as I approach, and I let my gaze travel down her body. She's wearing a white tank top, and the dark green strap of her purse crosses between her breasts. It would be so easy to run my thumbs over her perfect nipples. It's tempting.

"For a guy who claims to be the black sheep, you sure do seem to be in the center of the Anderson family functions a lot." She crosses her arms over her chest and tilts her head.

"Yeah, well, money gives people power." I loosen my tie, then slip off my jacket before moving to the passenger door.

"You want a ride to your car?" I tilt my head as I pull the door open.

Saylor's lips pull into a suspicious smile.

"Courtesy driver on top of mechanic. I'm impressed," she says, sliding past me.

I hand her my jacket when she settles in the seat, and she lays it across her thighs. I glance across the roof of my car before walking to the driver's side. The garage is quiet, which surprises me. I was sure Caleb would follow me down here when I backed out of grabbing lunch with him, but his BMW is still tucked in the corner, away from any possible door dings.

Saylor has slipped her arms into my jacket by the time I

climb into the driver's seat, and the visual is unmistakably sexy. The coat covers her shorts, so it's nothing but her sun-bronzed legs and my imagination, which naturally pictures her wearing nothing under my coat.

"So, it's fixed?" She arches a brow.

I crank the engine and let the rumble vibrate up my spine in that familiar way that puts me at ease. There's something about this car. Maybe it's because the engine sounds the way it does because of my own two hands. This car is priceless to me. I will never be able to put a price tag on the hundreds of hours I've spent under the hood.

"Yeah, I told you it would be an easy fix once I got the part. I had it done—" I stop myself, suddenly remembering I told Saylor I wouldn't be able to get the part until late yesterday.

"Let me guess," she says, sucking in her lips as her gaze drifts up in faux thought. "You were up until the wee hours getting it done for me."

Her eyes drop down to meet mine, and I can tell by her smirk that I'm caught.

"Something like that, yeah," I say, my voice laced with a wry smile.

I roll out of my spot and take my time winding down the levels of the garage. When we reach the exit, I idle for a few extra seconds before pulling onto the roadway. My motivations aren't pure, and my body rushes with dopamine when I spot my brother walking along the front of our father's building toward the brunch spot we had planned to go to together. It's the short pause in his step that I catch in my rearview mirror that really ups the endorphins, though, because I'm almost certain he saw two people in this car. The sudden vibration in my pocket from my phone seals the deal. I don't even have to look to know it's a text from him.

"What's that smirk for?" Saylor asks.

I roll my head to the side after pulling to a stop, smirk stamped in place.

"You know what's satisfying?" I counter.

Her brow pulls in.

"What?"

I chew at the corner of my mouth as a silent laugh pulls it higher.

"When people get exactly what they deserve. Karma, I guess." I hold her stare for a beat, her eyes hazing as she seems to be working through my cryptic words.

"Tell me, then, Rowan. What do you think *I* deserve?"

The directness of her question hits me surprisingly hard, jolting my pulse for a few beats as I blink and refocus on the stoplight and the roadway ahead. My insides twist with her question, torn between wanting to tell her every dirty thought running through my head and the desire to protect her from men like me. From *all* the Andersons, really.

"Better," I finally say, punching the gas at the green light and peeling through the intersection the way only a man craving attention can. "You deserve better."

I leave my air conditioning on high as I race from interchange to interchange on our way to the shop. It's plenty cool in the car, but I love the way Saylor looks in my jacket, so I want to make sure it remains a little *too* cold for the duration.

We pull into the shop's driveway just as Miguel is pulling out. I stop right next to his truck, roll the window down, and take note of the way his eyes dart to Saylor, then back to me. There's a warning in them. You haven't been friends for as long as we have been without a good understanding of what certain expressions mean.

"She's just getting her car," I say, which does little to quell the guarded haze of his eyes.

"Ah, okay. Nice to see you again, Saylor," Miguel says, leaning against his steering wheel to look past me and at his little sister's best friend.

Fuck, this is all kinds of wrong.

"Hi, Mig." She waves and my jacket slips down her body, and when my gaze returns to my friend, I sense just how guilty the situation makes me look.

"You need me to help zero that out?" Miguel glances to his side as he tilts his head back. I already told him I wasn't charging Saylor for my labor. It's an easy invoice to reconcile. Even I can add a bunch of fucking zeros. He's offering me an exit before I drive full speed into trouble.

"I got it," I say.

My friend chuckles and shakes his head, squeezing the top of his steering wheel as he looks straight ahead for a beat, then returns his gaze to me.

"All right then. I'll see you later. I'm going to pick up Jersey and his girl from the airport. Don't forget . . . it's poker night."

"I won't," I say, nodding.

I'm relieved when my friend rolls up his window and heads out to the road. My conscience is bad enough; I don't need Miguel's sticking around to judge me.

I force myself to head directly to the back office instead of opening the passenger door for Saylor. The trick to good behavior, I think, is limiting opportunity. But a quick glance at the text from my brother after I pull Saylor's key out of the lock box has me rethinking.

CALEB: *Why is Saylor in your car?*

I snicker quietly under my breath, hovering on the response for a few seconds. I decide it's better to leave him lingering with his own paranoia, justified or not. What did he think was going to happen when he ended things with her? That she would forgo ever spending time with another man? That she'd hole up in her house until college and cry fat tears on her pillow? Is my brother really that arrogant to think he's the peak of the gender and it's all downhill after dating him?

"Are you sure I don't owe you anything?" Her voice is distant, so I exit the office to find her running her fingers under the front of her car's closed hood, her tongue pushing inside her cheek.

"You checking my work?"

She flips around, seemingly startled by me, and lets out a nervous laugh as her fingers hook under the slim gap beneath the hood.

"I wouldn't know what I was looking at. I can't even open the hood." She lifts a shoulder as her hands fall to her sides.

"Let me show you."

I step toward her, and she doesn't move as the distance between us grows tighter. Our eyes meet as my shoe taps against hers, and I lean to her left and feel under the hood for the release latch. The heavy metal pops with the release, and Saylor sucks in a tiny breath.

I turn into her, and our faces are only a few inches apart. My gaze dips to her mouth just as she licks her lips. This is dangerous territory, which is probably the reason I like it so much. Temptation always finds me, and I'm not always great at saying no.

My eyes move back to hers, and her lashes seem heavy. Her breath is noticeably slow.

"You just need to know the right spot." Her eyes widen a hint at my words, and her lip ticks up on one side.

I lean into her more, my chest brushing against hers as I pull the hood up behind her.

"Do you want to see what I did?" I nod behind her toward the open engine bay, but she bites her lip and shakes her head.

"Not really."

"Are you sure?"

We both know I'm no longer talking about looking at her car. She lifts her chin and nods.

"Positive."

I let the hood slam shut only a few inches behind her, and she jumps at the harsh clank of metal on metal, her hands flattening on my chest to steady her balance.

"I've got you," I say, my lips grazing against her earlobe.

Her hands drag to the center of my chest, and her fingers wrap around the gray silk tie hanging loose around my neck. My palms slide up her bare thighs to her hips, and I lift her onto her hood. She undoes my tie, then drags it from my collar, gathering it into a ball that she clutches against her chest. I would love to see those wrists tied up with it sometime.

"Lie back," I say, walking my fingertips up her stomach to the center of her chest. I coax her body flat atop the hood, her head resting against the windshield. Her hands fidget with my tie as she bites her lower lip, her faint smirk practically daring me to take things further.

I lean over her body and run my thumb along her cheek. She turns into my touch, her lips parting with a slight breath that tickles my wrist as her eyes flutter shut. I pull the clip from her hair and let the waves fall along the glass and onto her shoulders before setting it to the side.

"I like it when your hair is wild and messy," I say as she blinks her eyes open on mine. Her lips curve into a bashful smile that pushes into her cheeks. They rush with color, a soft pink that mimics the sun-kissed color on her nose. I like it when she's embarrassed, too, but I'll save telling her that for next time.

There will be a next time.

My hands trail along the front of her body as I move to stand in front of her, and she arches her back when my fingertips graze along the hard peaks under her tight cotton tank top. Fuck, I can't wait to feel those again. Her nipples are so hard, so round and perfect, like candy. I want to bite them.

Her knees part as my palms run down her thighs, and I lift them so her feet are flat on the edge of the hood.

"I'm afraid I got your shorts a little dirty," I say, running my finger along the hem of the white linen cuff on her inner thigh.

"I don't like them much anyway." Her voice is barely above a whisper.

My hand breaks the barrier of her shorts, and I glide a fingertip along the wet strip of cotton between her legs. Her hips shift with the faint touch, so I press the swollen skin underneath and smirk at her.

"Are you wet for me, Saylor?"

Her cheeks grow redder, but she nods as her lips part with a tiny gasp.

"Oh, you're *very* wet," I say, slipping my finger under her panties and along her wet pussy. Her knees move wider, and the thought of her opening herself to me makes my dick ache.

I'm not fucking her out here. I want to, but there's a chance anyone could pull in at a moment's notice. I have to hear her come for me again, though, and while we may get interrupted, at least we're alone until then. I want to know what she sounds like when she's not holding back so much.

I sink a finger inside of her and she moans, moving her hands to either side of her head and stretching my tie across her own eyes as a blindfold. My cock flexes at the sight. She's so fucking hot, and so innocent. I want to ruin every piece of her, steal that innocence, and know that I do things to her that nobody else ever can. There's no way Caleb made her feel this good. He's too selfish.

Since I can't simply unzip these stupid pants, I adjust my cock in my slacks with my free hand while I work her panties to the side so I can see the aching pussy beneath. It's so fucking beautiful, the tiny strip of hair like an arrow pointing to pleasure and fortune and the loss of my soul. I lean over her body and wrap my arms around her legs, hooking a finger in her panties to hold them to the side as I cover her swollen pussy with my mouth.

"Oh, fuck!" Her hips buck in response, but her hands stay where they are, holding the tie in place over her eyes.

I suck on her clit before punishing it with my tongue, her sweet taste making me drunk.

"Your pussy is so fucking soft, Saylor. So perfect," I say, my lips moving against her swollen skin. She writhes under me with every teasing touch.

"Uh huh." Her voice is raspy, her breath ragged, and it's making me so hard.

I want to fuck her like this, on the hood of *my* car. And I will. Many, many times. Because this isn't merely something you sample. It's not just a taste. Saylor Kelly is an addiction. And I'm an addict.

I flick my tongue against her, then switch to long, torturous strokes when her hips begin to circle. She hums with every touch, a soft moan as I push her to the brink, then refuse to let her fall over the edge.

Saylor drops one hand into my hair, threading her fingers through it and holding me to her as her breathing grows more urgent. When she pulses under my tongue, I glide one hand up her body, slipping under her shirt and bra to the hard nipple begging for release. I roll it between my finger and thumb, pinching harder as she lets out a gasp that echoes in the garage bay. While one hand holds her to my face so my tongue can work her pussy, the other rubs her hard nipple raw to the rhythm of her bucking hips. Finally, a high-pitched shriek leaves her lips, and both hands grasp my hair, pressing my head into her as she fucks my tongue.

I drink every drop of her soaking wet pussy, my tongue wide against the shattered nerves still pulsing between her legs. I hum as I get slower with every pass, and her fingers unfurl from their tight grip on my hair. When her hands finally fall limp at her sides, I stand and wipe my chin as she gazes at me with sleepy eyes and a wide, dreamy smile.

"We have company," I say as the buzzing of my brother's

engine clicks off. He stays in his car at the end of the driveway for a few seconds, probably trying to decide whether he saw what he thinks he saw.

He did. I knew the minute he pulled in. It was the exact moment I made his ex-girlfriend come in my mouth.

Chapter 8

I ROLL to the right of my car and slide my legs to the ground so I'm shielded from Caleb's view while I adjust my shorts and panties. My thighs are wet from pleasure, and my heart is pounding from the jolt of adrenaline that rushed through my body the second Rowan announced we have company.

Caleb saunters into the garage as I move to stand by the passenger door, maintaining a full ton of metal between us. It's bad enough having to endure his glare.

"You had to bring your car back already, huh? Hope this guy gave you a warranty on his work." Caleb's tone is obvious, but if he wants to go at this with lies, fine. I'll play along.

"Actually, his work was so good I thought I'd have him do some more," I say, letting the double meaning float in the air between the three of us. Rowan coughs out a hard laugh, but Caleb's reproachful glare only narrows on me. "You know what, though? Another time, maybe. It looks like you two need some alone time, so I'm gonna . . ." I turn my back to them and march to the workbench where I left my crossbody, then snag the keys out of Rowan's hand as he dangles them for me to take.

I open the driver's side door and slip inside, holding my

breath the entire time. The stale air burns my lungs until I crank the engine and allow myself to exhale. My gaze flits to Rowan, whose lips are raw from pleasing me. My neck warms and I can feel a blush creeping up, so I back away from the shop—and the Anderson brothers—before I tear up from embarrassment.

It's not so much that I care about being caught—or *potentially* caught—in an intimate moment. It's the layers of the situation—that it's Caleb, and that it's with Rowan. I shouldn't care, because it's not as if Caleb gave two shits about my feelings at our graduation party. Or, fuck, maybe ever.

I need a voice of reason, but since the person I used to go to for emotional advice is now my ex and part of the problem, I decide it's time I get Cami up to speed. She's going to lose her mind.

The call rings through the speakers of my car when I push her contact info, and I redial her twice before she finally picks up. It's close to one in the afternoon.

"What, Mom? I'm up. Gosh!" She whines like a teenager. I have serious doubts about my friend making it through college without me. She has zero discipline. Her brother has his shit together, at least, and thankfully, she's staying local so he can keep an eye on her habits.

"I don't know how you expect to become a nurse from bed," I say, glancing over my shoulder as I merge onto the highway.

"I'll work nights. It will be fine. Besides, I have like a million years of school, so I'll be ready when the time comes."

I roll my eyes at my friend's rationalization.

"If you ever get up for school. You know I worry about leaving you alone in two months."

"So, stay. Go to school with me. We can join a sorority, hit all the parties, date some football players—live the dream!"

I laugh silently.

"I think you're missing the point." I follow my words with

an audible sigh. My friend mumbles something about me not being any fun.

"Are you on the highway? Your car is super loud," she groans. I picture her finally stretching her body awake and rolling out of her bed. The only reason she can get away with the lazy life is because her parents both work in healthcare and leave the house at four in the morning.

"I'm heading back from your brother's shop, actually." I snap my mouth shut and wait for my friend to pick apart my story while I barrel toward her house.

"Something wrong with your car?" She yawns through her words.

"My AC, you know. It's cold now." Cami's always complaining about riding in my car. The vinyl seats and zero air make for a sweaty ride.

"That's good. Miggy hook you up? He didn't say anything."

I don't respond, and it takes only a few seconds of my silence for my friend to make the connection.

"Shit! Rowan fixed your car? Did you stay the whole time while he worked on it? Did he take his shirt off? Why didn't you call me and take me with you? Bitch! I need photos of that man working on a car. It's creepy for me to take them myself when my brother's hanging around."

I chuckle at my friend's spiral, then suck in a long breath and brace myself for the storm I'm about to brew.

"I didn't exactly watch him work on the car."

My body hums with a rush of tingles from my mere insinuation. The way Rowan makes my body feel, even from memory—*my God.*

"Saylor, don't fuck with me. What are you saying? I need you to give it to me straight. Did you? Are you hooking up with Rowan Anderson?"

I nod vehemently because I know Cami can't see me, but I manage to temper my voice when I respond.

"We've done . . . things. Let's just say my air is working and so is Rowan Anderson's tongue."

"Bitch!" She squeals into the phone, and I laugh at her tirade. I know she's not truly jealous, and she's going to want embarrassing details—specifics that are going to require a few drinks before I share.

"Get your suit on and grab your club pass. I think we're overdue for a pool day, and my mom's membership still covers me until I leave for school in August."

My friend orders me to put the pedal to the metal and get my ass to her before we end our call. I'm going to have to endure some probing questions for the next hour for sure, but once I get Cami up to speed, maybe she can help me figure out how to navigate what the fuck all of this means, and put the whole brothers aspect into perspective. I don't want to feel ashamed for having a fling with a hot older guy, but I also can't help but feel like a chess piece on an unfair gameboard. I need someone to help me see the play for what it is, so I don't end up losing more than I bargain for.

"And Caleb was just . . . there?"

It takes about an hour to download all the details to my friend. Thankfully, the Arcadia Club's pool isn't very crowded this time of day, because Cami insists on revisiting each aspect about a dozen times, and her questions are not remotely close to modest. At one point, I have to flat-out hold her hands and meet her eyes as I say, "No, I have *not* seen Rowan's dick."

But I want to. I keep that bit to myself.

"My two cents? Caleb is not the same goofy junior high boy you hung out with at the mall. Maybe you two made sense in high school, you were that couple people wanted to see together. He was the popular jock, and you've always been—"

I roll my head against the back of the lounge chair and pull my sunglasses down to give my friend a hard glare.

"Always been what?" I know she's not going to say popular, because I never really hung out with any crowds, *in* or otherwise. I swam. I hung out with Cami and Caleb. I got good grades and was kind to everyone, but beyond those two, I never really let people in.

"Sexy and mysterious, I guess?" My friend scrunches her nose, and it pushes her glasses up.

I chuckle and shake my head as I turn my focus back to the ripples in the pool. A few guests have shown up with kids, and I hear one of them shout the word *cannonball*. I pull my legs up and run my palms over my knees, and the memory of Rowan pushing them apart warms my tummy.

"Is it weird that I'm doing things with Rowan? Not just because he's Caleb's brother, but because—" I turn back to my friend and lift a shoulder.

"Because when he was eighteen, we were playing with Barbies?"

I cup my palm over the instant O my mouth forms and shake with a silent laugh.

"Fuck, we really were," I admit.

That warm feeling hasn't left me, though. If anything, Rowan's maturity draws me to him even more. His physical traits are appealing, the way his body is fully formed, the life lived on his skin with intricate tattoos and hard-earned muscles. There's a scar across one of his hands, probably from working with them, and a deep texture to his voice that's a far cry from the boyish tone of his brother's.

It's easy to see why any girl would desire Rowan Anderson's attention. But there's something else that has him stuck in my thoughts. Sure, there's the way he makes me feel—sexually. And maybe that's all this is, part of my grand awakening, a moment in time to send me off to college to fully become the woman I'm meant to be. I just can't seem to shake this premonition, though. Rowan is peeling back my layers, and it feels like they've been waiting to bud for him and him alone.

"Look, babe." Cami sits up and shifts her legs to the space between our loungers, then pulls her sunglasses down her nose. I take mine off to meet her eyes.

"Caleb was the one who called it quits. And as much as I think he's an arrogant tool, he was right about this being the time to learn who you really are. And if the person you are is someone who feels confident and beautiful when she's around Rowan, then that's where you should be. So, he's Caleb's brother." Cami shrugs, and I try like hell to feel as casual about the idea as she is.

Besides, maybe I'm twisting myself into knots for nothing. It's not like Rowan and I are a couple. We're messing around. I'm still going off to college and living the life my mom wants me to. And I'll probably meet some pre-law student who checks all the boxes. What harm is there in indulging my teenage fantasy for a little while? If it bothers Caleb so much, then maybe he's not as ready to be single as he thinks he is.

The cascade of water from a rotund, pink-skinned pre-teen soaks my friend and me from the waist down, and we both rush from our chairs with screams.

"I guess pool time is done," Cami huffs, running her hands down her hair, then wringing out the ends. She's wet, but it's not like she took a trip in the dunk tank.

I laugh it off, mostly because I saw it coming well before the execution. I glance at the pool, where the red-headed boy is floating and holding on to one of the lane markers. He grins and raises his eyebrows a few times, and my friend flips him off.

"Cami!" I swat her hand down and instead offer the kid my quiet applause. Then he blows me a kiss and dips completely under the water.

"Great, now another age gap is in love with you," she teases.

I push her shoulder lightly and tell her to shush as the pool attendant comes over to take our empty glasses away and settle the bill. I look a lot like my mom, and she never comes here, so I use one of her old IDs and sign her name when Cami and I want to enjoy a few margaritas without a lot of questions. We've been doing it since the summer of our junior year, and while we got a few questioning looks the first two times from the cantina bartender, most of the servers working the pool are college guys who don't give a shit if we're breaking the law. In fact, the one taking the bill from me seems pretty interested in my friend, even going so far as to crane his neck to stare at her as he walks away.

"Looks like someone else is sexy and mysterious, too," I say.

"Bitch, damn straight I am," my friend says, fogging her sunglasses with her breath and cleaning them with the linen cover-up slung over her arm.

We indulge in forty-minute massages since there are open timeslots at the spa, and we need to sober up. I'm sure Cami falls asleep during hers, but I spend the entire time replaying the first half of my day. Caleb's contemptuous glare has stuck with me, and I hate that I'm letting him dictate how I feel about everything else that happened. It's getting in the way of the fun part. I lived a literal fantasy this morning, and I will never be able to wear those shorts again without picturing Rowan tugging them to the side and burying his face between my legs.

I'm probably the only person to ever leave a spa treatment room feeling more tense, and I catch my fingers shaking when I hand over my mom's membership card at the counter. I sign her name again on the invoice, using two of the dozens of massages that come with her membership. I don't think she's ever booked a single visit.

Cami and I are halfway to my car in the parking lot when my phone buzzes in my tote bag. I fish it out, then hand my keys to my friend when I see it's my mom on the line.

"This might take a minute." I flash the screen toward her and she nods.

"Hi," I answer, bracing myself for the myriad ways the impending lecture could go.

Cami heads to my car and turns on the amazing new air system before moving to the passenger seat to wait for me.

"I see you've been out spending my money today," my mom says. She only pulls the "my money" phrase out when I'm not doing things the way she wants. If I were out loading up on women's pant suits, she would be thrilled.

"It was just an afternoon at the pool with Cami. We both had time off today, and—"

"Time off would mean that the two of you had jobs to take time off from. I don't seem to recall there being jobs in either of your summer plans."

I'm going to enjoy correcting her on this.

"Actually, I *have* a job. I'm going to be coaching the younger kids at the club. I start at the end of the week." So what if it's something I'm dreading. It's a job, with my own paycheck attached. And I like it a lot more now than I did five minutes ago, mostly because it lets me be smug.

"Well, how nice for you. That pays, what, fifteen bucks an hour? Maybe? I'm sure you'll be loaded by the time summer is done."

She's in a mood. I have a feeling she had to discipline someone for David. My mom handles a lot of the HR-type stuff at the office, and she gets emotional when things like firing people or corrective action land in her lap. Maybe that's why I'm getting the hyper-critical reaction right now.

"It's a job. And I'm giving back to the club that helped me get a scholarship, so it's also a nice thing to do." That's how they sold it to me when they wrangled me into the gig.

My mom sighs. That's her signal that she feels guilty for laying into me. I hear her sigh a lot.

"I just don't want you settling on yourself. You've got more potential. And sure, there's a time in life when jobs like that, or retail or food service, for example, are okay."

"And here comes the *but*," I say, wiping the sweat from my forehead and staring at my car, which I'm sure is cold inside. I'm roasting on the pavement to spare my friend from hearing these lessons that are tailored specifically for me.

"No *but*, Saylor. However—"

"However is kind of like a but," I point out. It's a snarky thing to say, but I'll take the sigh it earns.

"I made an appointment with Dr. Addleton at North State for Thursday. He's the dean of the business school, and he's a friend of David's."

My eyelids flutter, and I spin slowly where I stand.

"Great," I groan, moving my hand to my nape. I push my hair up off my neck and wish for a breeze. It's still as death outside, though, and pushing one-fifteen.

"You'll have a good spot in the program. And the connections you'll make will set you up for success. Just hear him out. That's all I'm asking."

I blink a few times and bite the end of my tongue. She's not asking. She's telling. And I'm not going to be surprised if my mother hasn't already persuaded the college to switch out my fall schedule from the exploratory liberal arts path I chose to nothing but accounting and finance.

"What time?" If I don't agree, she's simply going to find a way to kidnap me and drive me up there herself. I may as well do it on my own without her as my chaperone—aka puppet master.

"Eleven. And your coach said to stop by after and check out the new uniforms. I'm glad it works out."

"*Hmm*, yeah," I passively agree. It's as if I planned it. What a convenient turn of events.

My mom is interrupted by someone at her office door, and she muffles the phone half-heartedly, telling whoever it is that she'll be in the conference room in thirty seconds. Our call is done after some half-hearted "I love yous."

I yank open the driver's side door and flop into the cool interior, letting my forehead rest on the steering wheel as the vents blast air at my cheeks.

"And what did Allison Kelly want today?" Cami mutters from the passenger seat she has fully reclined.

"To dictate the rest of my life," I mumble, rolling my head along the wheel until I meet my friend's gaze.

She grimaces.

"Maybe you should have asked her about your little problem with the brothers."

I puff out a hard laugh, then move in my seat so I can pull the safety belt over my chest. I pat my friend's thigh, my way of telling her to sit up and get her damn seat belt on. She does, and we're on our way to her house seconds later. I think I'll stay there tonight. As amusing as it would be to run my dating quandaries by my mother, I don't really want her opinions to bleed any deeper into my life than they already are. And as it stands, I'm not certain Caleb won't surprise me with a visit just to let her in.

Chapter 9

AS MUCH AS I hate hauling cars on our rickety-ass trailer with Miguel's lifted truck, I need this alone time to get my head straight. The drive up north on the Seventeen has always had a way of resetting my soul. It's quieter up here. The peace comes at that point when dirt and cactus finally dissolve into Ponderosa pines. When I was a kid, I used to pretend I was passing through a magic wormhole into another world. The temperature suddenly dips twenty degrees, and the sky gets smaller thanks to tree-peppered mountains.

Getting under my brother's skin seemed like a good idea until the fucker started showing up more often, and inviting me to shit just so he could passive aggressively interrogate me over his ex-girlfriend. I stuck to our story when he showed up in the garage two days ago, but I know he saw more than he let on. Fuck, Saylor's leg was still wrapped around my head when I heard his pussy-ass motor idle into the driveway. I refuse to confirm anything for him, though I can tell his thoughts are torturing him. And I'm not stupid. I know the real reason he invited me for a round of golf yesterday morning with some of our father's clients. He wanted to pair up and get me alone so he could probe more, see if Saylor and

I are a thing. The joke was on him, though, because I charmed one of the clients so well that he insisted we share a cart so we could talk more about classic cars and the upcoming auction in Scottsdale.

I roll my window down and breathe in the air, still a warm eighty-four outside but a far cry from the triple digits I left behind. The Welcome to Flagstaff sign greets me just as my phone buzzes in my console. I prop my phone up and swipe the message open so I can glance at it while I'm in a traffic lull on the final stretch into town.

It's from the seller, a guy named Mike.

MIKE: *I'm at Dante's Diner right off Main. I grabbed a booth. You'll see the car parked out front.*

I give the message a thumbs up, then groan over the fact this guy seems to want to chat over lunch. I was hoping to hook the car up and head back to town before rush hour hit the city. Miguel didn't give me a lot of details on the deal, other than the magic words—classic Corvette. I guess it's in rough shape body-wise but the engine is solid, so it's mostly going to be a body job on Mig's end, maybe a few upgrades under the hood by me and Jersey when he gets back into town this weekend. The price is set, at least it better be, because I'm carrying a cashier's check for fourteen thousand and nothing else.

The exit for Main comes up in minutes, and I'm parked next to what looks like a '67 Vette seconds later. Miguel was right about pouncing. I exit the truck and round the car, eyeing it for opportunities and money pits as best I can before heading into the diner. She needs a new hood, but the doors can be buffed out, and once Mig hits the body with a paint job, we're looking at doubling our investment, at the least.

I flip the truck keys around my thumb, glancing over my shoulder one last time as I head into the diner. The hard stop I make the moment I'm inside, though, trips my feet a little. Parole Officer Steve slips out of a booth in the far corner of the diner and nods at me as if he's expecting me. A quick glance around the restaurant fills in the gaps as he's the only single dude in here, and he's dressed in a casual gray T-shirt with jeans. His peppered gray hair is a little messy, like he just pulled a ball cap from his head. No court badge or white button down with a pocket protector. This version of the man standing before me is more weekend warrior, fresh from his kid's club soccer game.

"Rowan, nice to meet you. I'm Mike." There's a directness to his tone, so I reach out and take his hand before sliding into the seat across from him.

"Nice to meet you . . . Mike." My molars grind together as I search the table for context clues about what the fuck is going on. There's a folder flipped open with what looks very much like a car title. I twist the folder to face me so I can read the name, and sure enough—Mike Gillespie.

"What can I get you all?" The waitress breaks my confusion spiral.

I pop my gaze up to Mike-slash-Steve about a half second before uttering, "Just coffee for me."

He leans forward, pulling a pair of black-rimmed glasses from his pocket and sliding them on the bridge of his nose while dropping his gaze down the menu.

"I think I'll do the pastrami. And coffee here, too. Thank you." He tucks the menu back into the slot behind the canister of sugars and creamers, grinning at our waitress, an older woman with a tightly wrapped bun atop her head.

"Thanks, sugar." She winks at him, pushing her pen into the bun before tearing the ticket from her booklet and marching toward the kitchen window behind the counter.

"So, Mike . . ." I roll my head back to face my parole officer head on.

He chuckles and pulls the glasses from his face before pinching the bridge of his nose.

"For this meeting, right now, it's Mike. You understand?"

The grin on his face feels forced, and I'm not sure whether I'm supposed to be smiling back.

I laugh softly and lean back into the booth, keeping up the performance because I understood that much from his vague clues.

"Can't say I do, Mike. Why don't you fill me in?"

He pushes the folder toward me and slides the title sheet to the right, uncovering what looks like a copy of an email sent from my father's office to a man named Lionel Petersen.

"Mind?" I glance up at him for permission to bring the documents closer.

"Of course. You need to know exactly what you're buying." Fuck if that's not a loaded statement.

The first email reads fairly boring to me at first, the usual exchange of talking points I've heard buzzed through a million times—profit and loss numbers, company business models, legal agreements, including those pending.

I shrug and glance up to meet *Mike's* waiting gaze.

"Seems like things are in order here," I say, about to push the folder back his way. He nods at it, though, hazing his eyes, which I think means I should flip through a few more pages.

That's when I see it.

The red herring.

The same numbers the company's CEO sent my father look to have been recalculated a day later, and while they are closely aligned, they aren't exact matches. And a few of them, specifically cash-flow statements, are wildly different.

"So, whose numbers are right here?" I lift my head and pull my brow in.

"That's where you come in," he says. My stomach tightens, but I drop my head and read on.

I see Saylor's mom's name on a lot of the emails, which is normal since she's my father's executive assistant. What troubles me is that her account seems to be the one repeating the changed data, and my father's email isn't linked. At least, that's what I glean from these printouts.

"He's inflating the value," I mutter. I've suspected my father of this very thing before, but I never had any actual proof. That evidence went up in flames along with the beach house.

"That's what I'm hoping you can help with," my parole officer says.

I flip through a few more pages, taking a deep breath as they all seem to be more examples of the same behavior.

"That looks like three different investments, am I right?"

"It's four," Mike-Steve responds, adding, "That we know of."

We. As in an agency, likely the attorney general's office.

"You want me to get you the hard proof." I sigh and push the closed folder back across the table. My head is throbbing. So much for drives up north offering me a respite from stress.

The waitress drops off a plate piled with pastrami and layers of bread, along with a mountain of fries, then quickly returns to fill our coffee mugs. I peel open about a half dozen packets of cream, diluting the harsh black coffee with creamer as well as a few ice cubes from my water glass so I can down it quickly. I'm not awake enough to handle this shit.

"Is the car even a real thing?" I lift a brow and give him a hard stare. It's going to be hard to explain not coming back with a Vette to my partner.

"The car's real. I think you guys will find it's a pretty good deal for you. And for you personally?" Mike-Steve leans back in the booth, slinging an arm along the seat-back as his eyes meet mine searching for silent understanding.

"What kind of a deal are we talking?" I feel like throwing up, but at the same time, there's renewed energy rushing through my arms and legs at the thought of giving my father some kind of justice, the kind I always suspected he deserves.

"Your record will be clean. Like it never happened. None of it."

I lock on his stare while I hold my breath for a few seconds, waiting for the *but* or *if* to come. I know there's one there.

"The arson *and* the bullshit theft?"

He gives me a wry half-smile, still not buying the bullshit part of the theft, I'm guessing.

"Exactly."

I lift my coffee mug and gulp down the remnants. I'm gonna need another one of these.

"What's my end?" I don't meet his eyes when I ask, instead staring at the closed folder thick with incriminating documents in need of a final push.

"You'll take that title, give me the check, which will be held in an account for you should there be any expenses incurred for your work."

"Expenses." I pull out that one word.

He waggles his head side to side, pulling his mouth in on one side.

"You might find you need to walk the walk with a few of these guys, and they can hobnob at some pricey places. You may need to buy dinner a few times, maybe get yourself a few suits."

I hold up my hand.

"Wait, wait. You want me to work for him?" I lean in with this question and lower my voice. I get we're supposed to be discreet here, but I feel pretty good that grandma and grandpa enjoying the daily soup four booths away aren't secret spies. Then again, I thought Parole Officer Mike-Steve was just a disgruntled federal worker.

"Rowan, this has been in play for months. Your arrest for the vehicle gave us an opportunity to put a few things in play. What did you say the last time we met? Owing your father means you must spend a lot more time with him than you'd like. Well, all we're asking is that you take advantage of that time and get as close as you can to his business deals."

I chuckle softly, but it grows louder the more I think about what he's asking.

"Why are you so amused?"

I rest my palms flat on either side of my empty mug, smiling up at our waitress as she stops by to top me off.

"Mike," I use his new name. "I think you're overestimating my father's opinion of me. He likes showing off the idea of being a family man, but I'm not the guy he's going to invite to the table to really learn the business. If anything, the only reason he updated the trust I signed a few days ago was for tax purposes. I'm sure it's a write-off, or—"

"Or a way to make you and your brother take the fall?" He quirks a brow. The twist he offers lands in my chest with a thud.

Before I can open my mouth with more questions, he pulls a second folder from the leather satchel next to him and drops it in front of me. Now, the buzzing in my limbs is less from excitement. This burn is from dread, and my fears are confirmed as I flip the cover open and see the stamped copy of the document I signed a few days ago.

"It's not a trust agreement, Rowan. Your dad is setting you and your brother up to take the rap if his house of cards comes tumbling down. And if you want to keep your ass and your brother's out of federal prison, you'll find a way to make your dad's opinion of you rise. You could say your future depends on it."

Fuck. I could. Because it fucking does!

I flip through a few pages, catching my signature in the key spot, along with words that read a whole lot more like a partnership agreement than an inheritance document. I knew something was off about these. The date alone, now so obviously a hire date.

"My guess, which comes from a lot of years working cases

like these, is that you'll see your dad's firm putting out press releases in the coming months with a lot of that false information. And I am guessing you or your brother will be sourced on those press releases. And then when securities blow up and inevitably come crashing down while your father conveniently shorts them—"

"Anyone who looks too hard will think Caleb or I rigged the system," I finish his case for him.

"Exactly."

I close the second folder and push it across the table, just as I did the first one.

"Are you even a parole officer?" I lift my gaze, which now feels heavy with the weight of the world.

"To everyone who matters, yes, I am a parole officer. And our weekly meetings will continue. I'll be your point. As Steve."

I draw in a deep breath that burns my now-quivering lungs. I'm not one to be afraid of things. I've almost flipped my car drag racing out in the desert. I've taken cash from dudes I hustled at pick-up basketball who could easily have kicked my ass or stabbed me. I took my share of beatings and gave them right back when I was in juvie. But this shit now? It has me off my game. There's a lot riding on it. Caleb might be a shitty family member, but he's still my little brother. I can't let him go down for my father's criminal behavior. He tried this same shit with our mom, right before he cheated on her. I protected Caleb from those things back then, which, upon reflection, I shouldn't have guarded him against so closely. Now he idolizes a man who is capable of horrible things. And he hates me.

And then there's Saylor's mom. I wonder if she knows just how deeply her poor decisions have dug her. Allison has her faults, but I don't think federal financial crimes are on her resume. Trusting the wrong men? Definitely. But fraud? From what I know about her, she seems to play by the book.

"Want to take a look at the car?" He flashes a wide grin. He's barely taken a bite from his sandwich, so my guess is he'll stick around here after I leave, playing up the role-playing he's taking very seriously.

"Guess I should see what I'm buying," I groan.

He snags the satchel and folders from the booth, and I slide from my seat to follow him toward the exit. In any other scenario, I would be doing back flips on my way out to the parking lot. He wasn't lying—the price is a good deal. This is going to make us a nice profit. And apparently, I'll be using the money we're giving him on partying with the assholes I hate.

"You all need a check?" The waitress catches us on our way out, and Mike-Steve flashes a toothy grin.

"No, no. I'm not leaving that sandwich alone for long. I'm just going to get my buyer his keys and settle up. I'll be right back."

He winks at her, and I swear she blushes when she says, "All right, darlin'."

I don't open my mouth until we get to the back end of the car.

"Witnesses, huh?" I assume this keeps his cover—and mine—intact. The need for a cover has me wondering just how bad my father's associates truly are—or how dangerous *he* is.

"Nothing unusual about two people making a private car sale, should anyone mention it to your dad. And you'll have the car, and I'll have the money for it."

"Yeah, yeah. I get it. I'm not meeting with the feds," I mumble.

The curt way he clears his throat and proceeds to pop open the trunk indicates I should keep my mouth shut about what's really happening and follow his lead. I realize exactly how serious this all is when I spot the recording gear and wired vest in the trunk. I'm getting him on tape or digital, or whatever the fuck they do for audio now, in his own words.

I swallow hard while Mike-Steve proceeds to talk about the spare tire and jumper cables, as well as the jack and a few extra parts from the engine rebuild. Meanwhile, he shows me exactly how the recording system works with his hands hidden deep within the well of the trunk. It's a lot like the movies, and I'm a technical guy, so when I tell him, "I got it," I mean it.

Handing me the keys and a copy of the registration and a pre-signed bill of sale, he offers his other hand for a shake on the real deal we're making. We grasp hands and lock eyes for a beat, and in that moment, the earth's gravity feels like it's pulling me down twice as hard.

"Pleasure doing business with you . . . Rowan. It is Rowan, right?" A few people are walking by in the parking lot, so I play along.

"Yep," I confirm. "Thanks again, Mike. If we have any questions, I'll be in touch. I'm sure she'll run just fine, though."

He smiles and nods, with nothing in his expression indicating that anything more than a normal private car sale occurred. He's inside before I even get the driver's side open. I crank the engine and feel the roar turn into a violent purr around me. This car is a work of art, and I wish it weren't a Trojan horse. But it is. And that makes me hate it just a little.

It takes me a solid thirty minutes to get it locked down on the trailer, and I've worked up a decent sweat by the time I climb back into the truck cab. I've also built up a pretty good appetite, and the lukewarm coffee left me feeling awfully thirsty. There's no way I'm going back into that diner, though, so I pull away from the scene where my life experienced a major shift and make my way deeper into town, to the gas station where we used to load up on snacks before we went to the lake when I was a kid.

At first, the silver Toyota with the hood propped up right

outside the station's front doors doesn't strike me as strange at all. There's a lube shop on the north side of the service station, and a lot of people end up with battery emergencies when they climb to this elevation. I've seen this scene dozens of times. But I've never been quite this lost in my thoughts, and I'm practically standing next to Saylor when I recognize her.

"Are you following me?" I'm only half joking, because what are the odds that she's here right now? Plus, it's been a strange morning, so I'm half expecting her to flash me her FBI badge.

She jumps at my question, though, and I feel bad when her hand flattens on her chest.

"You scared the shit out of me, but man am I glad to see you."

I nod toward the open engine bay as she twists her hair up into a tie, her neck moist with sweat. Fuck, did her AC fail? It's not as hot up here, but it's not exactly cool.

"I can't get it to start," she sighs.

"Let me take a look." I lean over the engine and feel around for a few obvious solutions, but nothing seems disconnected, and everything feels dry. The compressor I installed looks fine, too.

"Give it a crank for me," I direct her. She skips to the driver's side and gets in. A few seconds later, there's a lot of clicking, but nothing more.

It's her alternator, which is not something I can pick up here and snap in to send her on her way.

"Well? What's the diagnosis?" She rests her palms on the fender and blows up at the few loose hairs sticking to her forehead. She's wearing a university T-shirt and tight little shorts that hug her ass. My guess is she was up here for a visit since she'll be coming here in the fall.

"Looks like you're riding home with me. Good thing I brought the big trailer." I hold out my hand for her keys, and she hands them over with a groan before folding her hands along her forehead.

"Geeze, my company that bad?" I tease. I know for a fact it's not. And I'm not that disappointed to be riding home with her next to me for the next two hours. I'm not looking forward to my brother's reaction, but given the shit day I've had, this seems like the universe making good on a few things.

"Can we make a stop first? And, like, soon?"

I stop before getting into her car, and meet her gaze across the roof.

"I have a meeting with a dean, and I need to see my coach. It shouldn't be more than an hour or two, tops. And you'd be saving me."

Two tops means three. I am aware of how those estimates work, and I've known Saylor long enough to know that she's not quick about anything. Not wanting to make her feel bad by blatantly pulling my phone out to check the time, I mentally run through the math and figure it's about one in the afternoon. With any luck, we'll be hitting the road by three, but more likely four, which lands us coming into town in the thick of rush hour.

"I'll make you a deal," I say, deciding to take a little more from the universe than I deserve. Fuck it, though—I deserve a whole hell of a lot after today.

"What kind of deal?" Her eyes narrow with suspicion, so I let my smirk grow.

"We hit the road in the morning," I say, tilting my head to the right, toward the Timber Lodge Resort, which, if memory serves me correctly, is a lot more lodge than resort in room amenities.

She sucks in a long breath and holds her gaze on the lodge's sign as she hums, "*Uhm.*"

"I could really use a shower, so I'll check in after I drop you off. Plus, it's fish fry Thursday, and I mean . . ." I hold up my palms, and her mouth inches slowly into a grin. Soon, she's laughing and nodding.

"Fine, we can stay. I mean, who can turn down a fish fry in the middle of the desert, right?" We both laugh at what is sure to be the worst fish fry ever fried.

I send Saylor into the store with my debit card to grab me a few snacks and drinks while I load her car on the trailer. She skips out, and I take the drinks from her before she pulls herself into the truck. The coconut scent of her lotion or shampoo mixes with the engine oil coming from my arms and hands. I can't help but feel like I'm sullying her simply by sitting this close to her, but then my mind drifts to taking a shower with her and ruining her in a whole different way. By the time I pull into the main campus lot, my cock is so hard it's threatening to bust the zipper on my jeans. I'm going to need a cold shower when I check in, if I can make it that far. Thankfully, a text from my brother interrupts my imagination by the time I return to the lodge parking lot.

CALEB: Dad wants to know if you'll be joining us for drinks at the Guild House tomorrow.

I smirk to myself and cradle my phone in my lap as I type.

ME: If I get back in time. In Flagstaff for the night.

I have a hunch he knows Saylor is up here for school. He still keeps tabs on her, and he talks to Allison throughout the day at the office. My suspicion is confirmed in seconds.

CALEB: Is Saylor with you?

I chuckle as I push my phone into my back pocket without responding, then lock up the truck before heading into the lobby to reserve a king room with an extra-large shower.

Chapter 10

I SEE why my mom wants me to meet with Dr. Addleton. He's slick, rather good-looking, and it's hard to ignore his personal wealth. Especially since he lowkey brags about it in so many not-so-subtle ways. The rotating slideshow on his computer screen behind him shows him with celebrities on red carpets, in exotic places for vacations, on his yacht—it's all part of his hard sell, I'm sure. And if I were more like my mom, I'd probably be walking out of this meeting dreaming of building a life just like his by taking that first step with the North State business school program

But I'm not like my mom. At least, not when it comes to ambition. I don't want to accumulate *things*. I want experiences, but I don't need them to come with caviar and servants. I want to be useful, to help people, and to avoid a life of titles and name plaques, and a closet filled with pant suits.

I'm carrying the weight of sitting through that hour-long meeting with Dr. Addleton into this one with my swimming coach, Becca Cruz, and my cheeks ache from all the fake smiling. At least, her office is attached to the indoor swimming facility and comes with a cleansing waft of fresh chlorine. Maybe the fumes will clean out my mind.

"A lot of our athletes come up a week early. It's an option for you, but not mandatory." The way the last word tumbles from my coach's tongue gives me a sense that while I'm not obligated to show up early, I am expected to.

"Thank you, Coach. I'll give that some serious thought." I shake her hand at the exit from the swimming venue, the rumble of Miguel's truck apparent about fifty feet behind me. My coach's gaze drifts over my shoulder as our hands part.

"That your ride?"

I glance behind me, my eyes going right to the tatted arm stretched out the driver's side window. Rowan's other hand is draped over the steering wheel, and his ballcap is pulled low over his brow. He appears to be napping.

"Which one?" I chuckle when I turn back to face her.

"I'm assuming the one being driven by that sexy guy with tattoos." Coach lifts a brow when our eyes meet, and we share a silent but mutual acknowledgement that Rowan is incredibly good looking. "It looks like the other two aren't really road-ready."

"Yeah, he's my ride. The ugly Toyota on the trailer is mine, and I lucked out running into him."

"As in, you just met and he's already hauling your car around for you and driving you back to the Valley?" She laughs through her words, and I realize how I made it sound.

"No, not like that. Rowan and I are . . . old friends." I chew at my lip for a second, and my coach lets out an audible, "Ha!"

"I have an old friend like that. He became my husband," she jokes, but the insinuation lands heavy in the center of my chest.

"Really, we're just friends." It's a lie, and even I don't believe it the way it sounds coming from my mouth. But I don't exactly have terms that define whatever the hell it is Rowan and I are doing. And I'm not telling my coach that he's my ex's brother and we're potential fuck buddies.

"Keep me posted on your plans, if you plan to come up for the early week and off-the-books training. Oh, and let me know how the coaching works out. Maybe I can catch a meet when I head down there for recruiting this summer. You can tell me which fifth and sixth graders to keep an eye on."

We exchange a pleasant laugh as I nod, then turn to head toward Rowan. My jaw pops as I stretch my mouth open wide, erasing the smile from existence. I'm exhausted from pretending to be excited about any of this, and I feel guilty that Coach Cruz likes me so much. I like her! In fact, I wouldn't mind getting a few coaching pointers from her. I'm simply not jazzed about competing anymore. But who knows, maybe I'll find that spark before the first week of August rolls around.

"Excuse me, sir. There's no loitering here," I say in a deep voice that still sounds exactly like me.

Rowan's mouth quirks up on my side, and he stretches both arms out over the steering wheel before pulling his hat from his head and running a palm through his incredible hair. He tosses the hat on the dash.

"You texted me to be here at five. I can't help it if you ladies got chatty." He taps the watch on his left wrist.

I wince and utter, "Sorry."

He leans his head toward the passenger side.

"Come on. Get in."

Four simple words, but somehow, uttered in his deep voice, they make me feel all tingly.

I skip around the front of the truck and climb into my seat, dumping my stack of business school brochures and application onto the center console. Rowan slides his hand over it while I buckle up.

"You thinking of following in your mom's footsteps?" He squints as he glances up to meet my eyes. I sense his disappointment, and I want to quash it fast.

"Oh, God, no! I did her a favor and met with the dean.

That's as far as that goes. I can't imagine a life of spreadsheets and boardrooms."

He nods, then sweeps my stack of papers into a neat pile and deposits it into the groove between my seat and the console.

"Good. I don't see that life for you either. You're meant for something . . . more." He nods with that final word, and hearing him say it with such confidence fills me with a little bit of my own.

"Thanks," I croak.

He winks, then turns his attention to the front of the truck, shifting gears and slowly pulling us around the athletics parking lot and onto the road.

The lodge isn't far, and the air smells of fried fish the second we exit the truck.

"Would you be against ordering a pizza instead?" I plead.

"Good idea," he laughs out, pulling his phone from his pocket as we head toward the lodge's lobby doors.

"Supreme? Cheese? You pick," he offers, passing the phone to me with an order app ready and waiting.

"How do you feel about mushrooms?" I quirk a brow.

"Fucking disgusting."

I smirk, then select the Supreme. I'm tempted to get double mushrooms just to be a brat. It's something I would have done when we were kids. But I don't feel like teasing Rowan that way as an adult, so I ask for them to only be on half, then hit submit and hand him back his phone.

"I would have eaten them, by the way," he utters as we pass through the lobby. "But only for you."

He chuckles, and I know he's simply being flirty and cute, but the sentiment makes me swoon like a schoolgirl. I could smell his fresh-showered scent in the truck, but somehow in the closeness and quiet of an elevator—the two of us alone— the fragrance is even more intoxicating.

"Is that the hotel's shampoo I smell?" I ask.

He laughs silently and pivots so he's facing my left side, then drops his mouth to the curve of my neck. His lips are soft and send an instant rush of chills down my body.

"I think it's called Amber Rain. You like it?" His mouth moves up my jawline, then nips at my ear.

"I think I might, yeah," I say, my eyes fluttering shut as the beeps counting the floors sound their way to eight.

The doors open, and Rowan backs out slowly, holding a hand out to me. Our fingers tether, the connection so easy and natural.

"The top floor, huh? Did you reserve the penthouse for us?" I know this place doesn't have those, but still, I like that he put us on the top, and as we make our way down the hall, it seems he also put us at the end. Away from everyone else. Private. Alone.

"It might not have a hot tub inside, but it does come with complimentary water and the best mattresses, according to reviews on Yelp and hotel booking sites."

"Ooooh," I tease.

Rowan keeps our hands locked as he reaches into his pocket with his other hand and fishes out a key card that he presses against the door sensor. It unlocks and pushes the door open, dragging me behind him and tossing the card into the room before spinning me around so my back is against the door the moment we're inside.

With my wrists locked in his hands and held above my head, Rowan has me caged between the door and his body. My breathing stutters, and my eyes lose focus as the lids grow heavy. Through everything, we haven't kissed. The way Rowan's mouth is hovering over mine—his lips so close but not quite, his tongue tempting to taste but not giving in—has me feeling drunk.

"We have thirty minutes until the pizza gets here. But I'm hungry now," he says as his eyes sear into mine. The green is showing off tonight. His hair is still damp from his earlier shower, and the longer strands have curled over his forehead. I've never felt the rush of desire so quickly. One look from him has me soaking wet. His touch, both rough and gentle, has my breasts aching. My mouth wants to bite into his, to tug on his soft bottom lip, then sink into the hard muscles along his shoulders.

"So, eat," I finally say, my voice raspy with want.

"Fuuuuuuck, Saylor. The way you have me," he growls into the crook of my neck.

He keeps my hands locked under one of his while his other hand drops to the bottom of my T-shirt, gliding up my stomach to the cotton bra underneath. He pulls the cups down and rolls my hard nipple between his finger and thumb, and my body buzzes with both relief and need.

He pushes my shirt up my body to expose my breasts, sinking his mouth over my nipple and holding it hostage between his teeth, sawing the tender peak with sweet, gentle pressure.

"Oh, fuck," I moan.

At the sound of my voice, Rowan leaves my hands and tugs my shirt over my head, then strips me of my bra, tossing it behind him. His mouth moves from one breast to the other, his tongue flicking my nipples before his soft lips suck them until I cry out.

My hands sink into his hair, and I'm tempted to hold his mouth against my breasts until the pink skin is so raw I'm unable to take the assault from his tongue any longer. But I want to kiss him too much. I move my palms to his cheeks and coax his mouth upward until his hands slide up my breasts and move along my throat, stopping at my jaw. He holds me still against the door, his thumbs stroking my cheeks as our gazes lock.

Our breaths tangle, both of us panting, but we don't dare break our stare. I think he knows I want to kiss him, and he's making me wait on purpose, somehow making the connection of our mouths feel sacred and worth more than everything else.

With his eyes on me, he drops his right hand to the button of my jeans, unfastening it with ease, then drawing the zipper down. The loose-fitting denim hangs on my hips, and I'm grateful that I chose the white lace panties today instead of the less sexy boy shorts that I almost wore.

Rowan's hand sinks into my pants, his fingers gliding over the silky strip a few times before dipping underneath. His touch against my wet skin makes me quiver, and my lips part with a gasp. Rowan leans into me until his forehead rests on mine, and my eyes fall shut as I swim in the nearness of his lips to mine.

"I want to fuck you, Saylor. Do you want to feel how bad I want to fuck you?"

"Uh huh," I whimper.

Rowan guides my palm to his hard cock under his jeans while he continues to stroke my pussy with his other hand.

"Do you want that inside of you, Saylor?" His dirty words make my pussy swell and my knees grow weak.

"Yes," I cry.

"Show me," he says, his mouth softly passing over my plump bottom lip. I chase after his kiss, lifting my chin to reach for more, but Rowan stops me with a soft chuckle.

"Patience, Baby Girl. We've got all night," he says, sinking a finger inside of me and drawing a loud moan from my chest.

I work the zipper of his jeans down after unbuttoning the top, and his pants slide down his hips enough to let his cock stretch out between us. He's not wearing boxers or anything under his jeans, and the thought that he's been planning for this since his shower emboldens me. I wrap my hand around his thick shaft and stroke him, running my thumb softly over his tip. He moans against my neck, so I tuck my chin as a silent request for him to kiss me.

When he finally gives in, turning his head just enough so

our lips touch, everything intensifies with a fire so hot I may have fallen into hell. If this is purgatory, though, I'll live with my sins. I accept them. More than that, I want them.

Rowan stands taller, his mouth hungry for mine, his lips caressing my bottom lip with a gentle pass of his tongue. He takes my lip between his teeth, tugging me as he growls and walks us toward the king-sized bed.

I pull the black T-shirt over his head, and our mouths find each other again quickly at the foot of the bed. Rowan breaks our kiss abruptly, then pushes me onto my back as he kicks off his sneakers and steps out of his jeans. Standing before me completely naked, he looks like a god. The ripples on his stomach and chest are painted with vines and stories I can't wait to hear. His muscular arms flex with every fine movement as he pulls my shoes from my feet, then tugs my jeans from my legs. I'm left in nothing but scant white lace panties, but rather than feeling self-conscious, I feel powerful. The way Rowan's gaze rakes over me makes me feel sexier than I ever did with his brother. I feel like the woman I've been dying to be—I feel seen.

Rowan lifts my right leg to trail kisses along the inside of my ankle, leg, and knee, until finally resting his elbows on the bed between my legs so he can press his lips to the inside of my thigh. His mouth covers the strip of silk over my pussy, and his teeth grip the fabric, giving it a gentle tug before his hands move up my thighs and strip my underwear down my hips and legs. Bare and wanting to feel all of him, I lift my knees and part my legs, welcoming him inside.

"Yes," he says, nodding as he grips his cock in his hand and strokes himself a few times to make his dick even harder.

He moves toward his jeans, I presume to get a condom, but I stop him before he reaches for them.

"I'm on the pill. I want to feel you. Every inch of you." I bite my lip and roll my hips to quench the desire that's making me tingle.

Rowan tilts his head as his mouth snakes up on one side.

"You're going to fucking ruin me, Saylor Kelly."

His hand grips my right leg as he rests on his knees before me.

"I hope so," I respond, provoking his grin to grow more sinister.

He lifts my hips and guides his cock to my center, running the tip along my wet folds before sinking in only an inch or two. I gasp at the penetration, then whine as he pulls out too quickly. His devious chuckle makes me growl, and I lay one arm over my eyes, then bite my knuckles on my other hand.

Rowan paints me with his cock, sliding his tip along my pussy and pausing at my entrance several times before finally pushing inside. He sinks in slowly, as if he's seeing how deep he can go. My legs widen with the desire to take all of him.

"Fucking goddess," he groans when he fills me completely.

I uncover my eyes, wanting to see him as he pushes into me. His arms flex with his weight as his hips rock back, and his cock leaves me empty. I whimper until he sinks back inside, this time his thrust faster. Harder. And I yelp when his cock presses to my deepest nerves inside.

My hands roam his stomach and chest, but as he thrusts into me faster, I find I need to hold on to his biceps to steady my body before he pushes me through the wall. Every new rock of his hips sends his cock into me harder, and my body hums with his rhythm. The sensation building deep in my core lingers on the edge, my hips lifting to meet his as I chase the climax that seems to run away the closer I get. Maybe I simply don't want this to end.

My cries grow louder when my pussy begins to spasm around his cock, and Rowan lifts my right leg higher, giving him access to drive deeper into me. He pumps into me hard and fast, our skin slapping as we pant and fill the room with hungry, primal sounds. My orgasm teases me until the very end, and when I finally fall over the edge, the sensation leaves me breathless. Rowan's cock swells inside of me, and he fills me with his warmth, pulling out as his cock spills cum over my pussy and onto my stomach with the few final strokes of his hand.

Rowan runs his thumb through the slick, pearl white cum, then paints my lips with it like some sort of ritual that deems me his. I lick my lips, tasting the salty evidence as my body aches to feel him between my legs again. The cool air beads my skin, and Rowan tugs the billowy white comforter up from the right side of the bed to cover me before crawling over me and pressing his lips to my forehead.

"I'm going to draw you a bath. I'll let you know when the pizza comes. And then I'll make you come again."

He drops his mouth to mine and leaves me with a chaste kiss. He also leaves me bewildered and breathless.

Rowan

Chapter 11

I like the way Saylor's upper lip curls when she sleeps. She reminds me of those tiny porcelain dolls my mom kept in a curio cabinet when I was a kid. Some of those dolls were angels. That's what Saylor is—an angel.

What am I doing? I'm going to ruin her life if I keep this up. How am I supposed to infiltrate my father's criminal behavior, spare my brother, report it all to my mystery handler —who is very much *not* simply a parole officer—*and* be present for Saylor? I can't do it all. And I haven't even factored in how any of this affects my mom, or Saylor's mom. My father's web is sticky. It's hooked on so many lives, and even those who have broken away retain the remnants of once being a part of his world.

Saylor is going to feel the blowback regardless. Her mother is my dad's right hand, and they have so much history. There are things Saylor doesn't know, doesn't *need* to know. I should give her up now while things are still new, before I get used to waking up with her in my bed.

But when she sleeps, she looks like an angel. And I like that.

Her phone buzzes on the nightstand on the opposite side

of the bed, stirring her awake. I should shut my eyes, pretend to still be sleeping, but instead, I take in the way she stretches her arms above her head until her fingertips brush against the padded headboard. She rolls her head to the side as her eyes open, blinking slowly, her mouth curving into a faint but coy smile that I want to kiss raw.

"Good morning." Her voice is gravelly and soft.

"You're getting a text message, I think," I say, nodding across her body to her phone. I brought Miguel's cord in from the truck last night so she could charge her phone. I was concerned that her mom was worried about her, but she never used it to call anyone. And until now, it doesn't seem as if anyone has been looking for her.

The crisp white sheet slips from her chest as she rolls to her side to pick up her phone, exposing her fucking perfect breasts. Her nipples are puckered into hard pebbles from the cold air of the room.

Fuck it.

I curve into her body, pressing my cock against her bare hip while my mouth covers her tit and suckles on the cherry bud tip.

"Rowan, how am I . . ." She swallows her words with a gasp as my tongue flicks against the tip of her nipple.

"Go ahead, take care of whoever . . . *that* is. I'll just be over here, you know," I smile against her breast and nip at her nipple one last time before urging her to roll on her side so my cock has somewhere to go.

"It's Caleb. He wants to know when you're coming home."

A low chuckle tickles my throat.

"I'll call him later," I say, snaking a hand under her arm so I can palm her breast.

"Did you tell him we were here together?" Her tone has a hint of panic. I'm a little surprised she cares.

"Are you worried about him finding out about us all of a

sudden?" I question, distracting her by rolling her nipple between my finger and thumb, then sliding my other hand around her waist to slip between her legs.

"Rowan, don't . . . Wait a second."

My hands freeze in position, and Saylor shifts to face me. The puzzled expression denting her forehead makes my lungs suddenly feel heavy, so I scoot back a few inches to give her space.

"I'm sorry. I would never . . . I don't mean to presume that you want . . ." Fuck, I suddenly don't know how to speak. I squeeze my eyes shut and bring my hand up to pinch the bridge of my nose. "I'm not a creep. That's what I'm trying to say. And we don't have to do anything else, if you don't like . . ."

Nope. Not coming out any better.

Saylor's hand moves to my face, resting on my cheek, and I'm relieved to see a tiny smile tug at the corners of her mouth.

"Last night was . . . everything. You aren't a creep. And what you were doing now, I want that, too. I'm pretty sure you could feel that." Her cheeks blush, and it's fucking cute as hell. I did feel it. She's wet for me.

"Just, there are some words I need to get out first. Okay?" Her thumb brushes along my jawline, and somehow, that small gesture settles the pounding in my chest. Lying with her is calming.

"Anything you need. I'll keep my hands in check. My eyes, however—" I suck in my bottom lip as my gaze drops to her breasts. Her smooth skin is begging for my touch. It's too perfect. It needs the roughness of my hands, my whiskers scraping against it, my fingers digging in, teeth biting.

"Eyes up here, buddy," she jokes, nudging my chin upward.

"Sorry," I whisper, and the soft laugh it draws from her

releases my breath, but only temporarily. Within seconds, her worry lines are back.

"The other day, in your garage . . . did you know Caleb was going to show up?" Her eyes scan mine, tiny shifts in her pupils as she studies me, like she's dissecting my tells and uncovering clues. I won't lie to her, not about this. There are too many other things that I must keep buried.

"I had a feeling about it, yeah. He saw you in the passenger seat when we left the garage."

Her mouth bunches to one side.

"Oh," she says, her eyes dipping to my throat.

It's my turn to lift her gaze to mine, so I run my knuckles along her jawline and coax her chin upward.

"Hey, that's not why I let things progress the way they did. My desire for you has nothing to do with my hate for my brother."

Her brow furrows.

"You hate him, huh?" Her eyes seem heavy, her gaze struggling to remain fixed on my eyes. I run my fingertips along her cheek.

"Only sometimes. Caleb and I . . . we're complicated. He's blood, and I'll always honor that, even if he won't. But there are things between us, ugly shit, that's festered for too long. And I won't lie to you about that, about Caleb. He's walking in my father's footsteps, and I've spent my life trying to side-step them. Our paths are going in opposing directions. Doesn't mean that there's not love deep down, under a lot of scars. I just don't feel it very often."

I haven't felt it in months. Maybe years.

"So, this . . . being here . . ." Her gaze circles the room behind me, then finds its way back to my face. "Is this just part of a revenge plan? Is that why you suggested we stay for the night?"

Shit. I said I wouldn't lie about this. About Caleb.

"No, but also . . . maybe. Not consciously, because believe

me, Saylor, my body wanted you in this bed. I wanted you all to myself. But I can't say the thought of it somehow torturing Caleb a little didn't sway me into putting it out there."

She draws in a deep breath through her nose, then nods.

"I want to be here with you. That's the root of it all. That's the truth, Saylor. I want to be here with you, right now, like this." My hand trails slowly along the curve of her neck, and she drops her chin, following the path as her eyes flutter shut.

"I believe you," she whispers, slowly rolling on her side so her back is to me again.

"I didn't plan for this," I say, tracing along the muscles on her shoulders and back with my fingers, tickling her gently until her skin is peppered with goose bumps.

"Neither did I," she murmurs.

I kiss the center of her spine, closing my eyes as my nose grazes along the curve.

"What are we going to do?" I breathe out.

She's quiet for several seconds, and I spend the time taking small tastes of her skin, running my fingertips down her side, and pulling the sheet down with my hand. I flatten my palm against her hip, then inch it around her body until she shifts her leg just enough to give my hand access to the wetness building between her legs. My fingers glide against her, and she moans.

"Tell me, Saylor. What are we going to do?" My words are a rough whisper against her back.

"Fuck," she says, pushing her ass back just enough to press my hard cock between my stomach and her body.

My tip is wet with precum, and I paint her with it, gripping my shaft and guiding down her ass until it slides into her wet center, gliding against her swollen pussy. I coat myself with her arousal. She arches her back slightly, just enough to give me access, and I guide my dick inside her pussy, sliding in slowly while she groans with the stretch to accommodate me.

Two sides of my brain are warring with one another. Part of me is really growing attached, caring in more ways than the obvious ones, at least for me. Saylor and I have history, *complicated* history. She's Caleb's ex. I'm pretty sure they were both each other's first. And for much of her life, I've been a protector. I've always cared about her, thought of her as a sister more than anything. Until now.

Now, there's an animal inside of me that doesn't know how to stop. The considerate half of my brain is screaming about the mistakes, warning me to be careful and to tread lightly. But the animal wants to feast. And I've never had a meal as delicious, as decadent, and special as Saylor Kelly.

I push into her with a hard thrust, holding her hips in place so she can take it. And she does.

"Yes!" Her scream is more than permission. It's a pass for the monster, a loud approval that what we're doing is more than just allowed, it's wanted both ways. It's mutual. She wants to be ruined. She wants *me* to ruin her.

And we're both a little happy that Caleb doesn't like the thoughts invading his jealous fucking mind.

My hands glide up her front, clutching her breasts as I pound into her from behind. Her ass pushes into me, meeting me for every thrust. My mouth falls onto her shoulder, and I suck in her skin, leaving a faint purple bruise behind, proof that I was there.

"I'm going to come soon, Saylor. You're too fucking hot. I can't hold out this time," I say, driving my hips faster. She reaches forward, bracing her body on the edge of the nightstand, keeping her from falling onto the floor from the impact.

"Fuck, I need to have you," I say, rolling her body with mine so she's lying flat on top of me, her back to my chest, my dick deep inside.

I lift her back, guiding her to a sitting position while my cock impales her. She works her legs underneath so her weight is on her feet and calves, and she bounces on me and moans wildly while my hands hold her hips steady to keep her from falling.

Rowan is no longer here. This is all the beast. And he is happy. And hungry. So . . . fucking . . . hungry.

"Your ass is so goddamn perfect. I'm going to fuck that next time, Saylor. I'm going to fuck every single inch of you. I'm going to ruin you."

"Yes," she whimpers, her hips quivering in my grip.

"Come for me. Come with me," I command, driving my hips up as she slams down on me. She sways her hips in fast circles when her orgasm hits, and her pussy clenches around me as my cock swells and then spills inside of her until I'm empty.

Our bodies are covered in a sheen of sweat. I should get both of us into the shower. We need to hit the road soon. I must convince my father of a lot of things, most importantly that I *want* to spend time with him, to learn. But the beast is still present. My dick is still inside of her, and it feels too good to leave. I roll our bodies to the side and hold her to me, finally pulling my cock out but keeping her in my arms.

"Rowan?" Her voice is a faint whisper, and I'm not sure if it's because she's satiated or having doubts.

"Yes, baby." I kiss her shoulder blade.

"I think I want to be ruined."

The beast smiles. And so do I.

Chapter 12

I DON'T WANT to go back. I want to stay here, two hours away from our reality, and pretend it's always been Rowan and me. But I can't run away. Neither can he. We have obligations, people attached to us, expecting things. Though, I think we'd both be fine disappointing those people. I know I would.

My mom texted me early this morning, sometime before Caleb did, probably while Rowan and I were both asleep. She pieced together that we're both here. Probably cluing Caleb in. Her text was fairly to the point.

MOM: *Just don't be stupid, Saylor. I hope you met with the dean. We can work on your enrollment when you get home.*

I haven't responded. I won't, not in text. This conversation needs to happen in person, not that my mother will actually pause to listen to me. I don't want to be a business major. I don't want to work with money, to sell things, to climb a corporate ladder, or have my own office. I want to be outside somewhere, working with humans and putting something good into the world.

Rowan's hand brushes along my thigh from across the console of the truck, pulling my eyes from my mom's message. I glance up at him with a faint smile.

"Something wrong?" He nods toward my lap where my phone rests.

My mouth puckers on one side as I lift a shoulder.

"Something's always wrong. Just my mom, wanting to make sure I don't throw my life away."

"Ah," Rowan says, turning his gaze back to the road. He sucks in his upper lip as he glances at the rearview mirror, then checks the side ones.

There's very little traffic, which is making our trip home pass quickly. It feels as though I'm waking from a dream. The faint music filling the cab isn't enough to distract me from my thoughts, and there's a new tightness clutching at my chest from the inside. I'm anxious, and I can feel the energy tingling in my arms and legs. I kick my shoes from feet and shift in my seat, tucking one leg under the other as I lean into the door for a better view of Rowan as he drives. He smirks at first, then lets out a breathy laugh as he glances my way.

"You know, it's hard to focus on the road with you looking at me like that." He grabs the back of his neck and squeezes it as he laughs a little more.

"I like watching you drive. I get to see the little things, like the way your forearm muscles shift underneath your skin when you move your arms. And the length of your eyelashes. You have very long lashes, by the way." I cross my arms over my chest as if I'm jealous of his lashes. I may be, actually.

"You like them, huh?" He blinks rapidly and glances my way again.

I shift my body again so my feet are now resting on the console, and my back is flush against the door. I stretch my left leg out until my toe reaches Rowan's side, and do my best to tickle him. He stops me, though, snagging my foot in his hand and moving it to the center of his lap, then pressing his thumb into the pad of my food while squeezing my arch.

"Oh, God, that's incredible," I say, my entire left leg relaxing with his touch.

"You're tense," he says, massaging my foot while his other hand remains on the wheel.

"I think I am. I've been a little stressed."

Rowan's hand moves up to my ankle, and as he rolls it with his hand, it feels like a decade of rust crackles away from the joints. I shut my eyes and exhale slowly through my nose to aid in my muscles' relaxation. I've fought tendonitis since my junior year of high school. Years of using my feet the way a dolphin uses a fin have taken a toll. I can't imagine how I'm going to feel by the time I complete four years of swimming at the college level.

"I hope I'm not adding to your stress," Rowan says. I peel my eyes open and find him looking back at me before quickly moving back to the road.

My brow pinches as I unclick the seat belt, which I've already contorted into a useless position. I pull my foot from Rowan's lap and fold my legs up against my body so I can wrap my hands around his arm.

"*Hey*," I hum. He glances at me with a wry smile, his expression suddenly guilty. "Where's this coming from?"

My fingers curl against his skin, and he slips his arm from my grasp, exchanging it with his hand. He threads our fingers together, then pulls my hand to his mouth, kissing the back.

"Your mom isn't totally wrong, is all. You shouldn't throw your life away. And maybe what we're doing—"

"Uh uh." I cut him off, moving my hand to his chin and pulling it to me for a second, just long enough for him to see the sincerity in my eyes. "Nothing about last night, or this morning, or last week. Nothing about you and me is a mistake. If anything, Rowan, for the first time in my life, I feel brave enough to confront the hard choices down the road. To stand up for myself and say what I want. And what I don't."

My heart is beating so hard, and I'm not sure whether it's from this growing pull I feel toward this man or the new muscles building alongside my resolve. Maybe it's both.

"I don't want to study business. I don't want to be anything like my mother." These thoughts I've said internally feel so good out loud. Sure, I've said this to Rowan before, but this time . . . I hear myself. And I know I'm going to do something about it.

"Then, what do you want?" Rowan puts the idea out there and I find a smile pulling at the corners of my mouth as I sit back in my seat.

"I helped this sweet older woman with her groceries the other day. Remember when I took the bus to your dad's office?"

Rowan's mouth curves into a sinister half smile, and I swat at him playfully. He remembers going down on me later that day.

"I'm talking about a life-altering experience, Rowan!"

"So am I," he laughs out.

I blush, shaking my head and fighting off the bashful smile that wants to take over my face.

"I'm sorry. Continue. I want to hear about this life-changing grocery trip." He smirks, but I can tell he's not teasing or belittling.

"It was such a small thing, really. She was managing a lot of grocery bags along with her walker and public transit, and I helped a little. Then there was this guy named Chad, and he was on the bus—"

"You can skip the part about Chad," he jokes. Sort of. There's a little honest jealousy flexing his jaw, I think.

"Okay, okay. What's important is what the woman told me while we were on the bus. Chad works at the retirement complex, and he helps her get on and off the bus or carry her groceries all the time. It's the helping part that stuck with me. I want to be a Chad, I think. I mean, not a maintenance guy with a heart of gold. I'd rather just do work that has heart. Help people navigate life. Make things easier for someone. I don't know . . . maybe I'm just being stupid."

I put my safety belt back on and shift my gaze out my window, but after a few seconds, Rowan's hand finds its way to my thigh again. I look down to find his hand turned up waiting for mine, so I fold our palms together. He gives me a gentle squeeze, and I gaze up to find a softness in his eyes, along with the small dimple on the right side of his mouth.

"You're not being stupid, Saylor. If anything, you're maybe the most grounded person I know. You've learned something about yourself that others never find."

I tip my chin up and tilt my head slightly.

"What's that?"

"Purpose," he says. "You want to be the helper. There's a reason that Mr. Rogers guy always touted the helpers. They're the good ones. The real ones. And I gotta tell you, Saylor. I'm not surprised at all that you want to give more of yourself to others. The world is lucky to have you."

I've never really felt my heart explode from a compliment before, but it does now. It's as if one of those ultra-wide, bright-burning fireworks from the Fourth of July just went off in my chest and sent embers coursing through my veins. My mom always talks about my potential, but she's not really talking about me or my dreams—she's talking about her own. But Rowan? He sees a better me.

"Thanks," I croak, covering his hand with my other one and hugging it close to my chest. I want to keep it for a while.

My phone chirps from somewhere under my seat, so I let go of Rowan's hand and feel along the space between the seat and the door. I pull it from the crevice and brace myself for yet another passive aggressive message from my mom. I'm pleasantly surprised, though, when it's from my other parent. The one I miss and rarely see. The one my mom doesn't like me visiting or having a relationship with at all, it seems.

"It's my dad," I say, flashing my screen to Rowan. His eyebrows lift.

"I didn't know you talked to him."

I waggle my head.

"Not often, but when he's between gigs or, well, sober, he'll text me. Sometimes it's a phone call. He's in a new city every time. It's kind of exciting to piece together his route through our phone calls and messages."

Rowan's brow pulls in, and I realize how sad I made my relationship with my father sound. I squeeze his arm once, then cradle my phone to take in the selfie my dad just sent.

"It's not a sad thing, so don't feel bad. I know how different he and my mom are, and I truly believe they both wanted to do right by me. I'm not harboring any strange resentments. Though, I do wish I could see him play sometime. It's been years. I remember him playing songs in our living room, but those memories are getting fuzzy. I need new ones."

I zoom in on the photo to find context clues about where my father's at. He always waits for me to guess. There's a New Mexico plate on a car behind him, so I take a stab.

> ME: Santa Fe?

My father loves that town. It's full of artists. Creativity is vital to his fabric. I wish I had more of that part of him.

> DAD: Close! Taos. I'll be in Cave Creek this weekend, though.

"Oh!" I sit up tall and cover my mouth.

"Is that a good *oh* or did you get stung by something?" Rowan chuckles.

I turtle my head into my shoulders sheepishly and peel my hand from my mouth.

"Sorry. It was a good one. My dad is going to be in Arizona! Next weekend."

I dive right into typing.

> ME: Where? What time? Is there an age limit?
> I want to come!

I watch the dots on my phone come and go a few times, and my heart leaps every time they appear. Eventually, though, they stop showing up. I'm sure he's on the road or simply got busy. He'll let me know where he's playing for sure. Why wouldn't he?

"Did he invite you to the show?" Rowan asks after a few quiet seconds.

"I asked if I could come. I haven't seen him since I was sixteen, and he had to pick me up, so, you know . . . he had to see Mom. They were cordial, but it was weird. I'd rather just visit him on my terms, without having to share it with her. It's *my* relationship, you know?"

Rowan nods and pulls his mouth tight on one side.

"Yeah, I get it. I'm sure you're invited."

He glances over his shoulder as he switches lanes, and when his eyes pass over me again, I sense something lingering behind them. I'm not sure about much lately, especially when it comes to Rowan and me. But I have to try.

"Hey, would you want to—"

My phone buzzes, cutting me off, and I drop my gaze to read the name of the venue, along with an address and a guarantee that my name will be at the door.

"He sent it! It's next Saturday! I'm going to see him in one week!" I'm practically bouncing in my seat as I type back that I'll be there.

"That's great, Saylor. I hope you get a chance to spend extra time with him, too. I'll think of you while Mig, Jersey and I roam the Tucson auction for more investment cars to flip."

"Oh," I say, my tone a little too obvious with disappointment. "Yeah, that's next weekend too, I mean. I forgot."

"Yeah, it's the biggest one for us because the price points

are usually pretty low. Who knows, maybe I'll find another gem like that Vette back there." He leans his head back, and I twist in my seat to take in the murky headlamps on the car strapped to the trailer behind us.

"Yeah." The word slips out in a haze, and as excited as I am to see my dad, my chest aches because Rowan won't be there for it.

"I'm really glad for you, though."

"*Hmm?*" I turn my attention to his profile. He reaches over and taps a finger to the tip of my nose. I follow it in and out, letting my eyes cross and uncross.

"I'm happy you're figuring out the things you want, I mean. I'm happy you're getting some of them. Like seeing your dad. It's good. You deserve to get those things."

His gaze lingers on me for the briefest moment, and I start to lean in just as he turns away. I sit back instead and return my attention to the black and white highway markers counting every tenth of a mile as we whip past them. I clamp my teeth down on my thumbnail after propping my elbow along my window and draw in a deep breath.

I want you, too.

The thought slips in and out of my head as we roar down the mountain highway and into the Valley. I open my mouth a dozen times and push those words out, to vocalize them, but something stops me every time. I don't want to sound like I'm trying to be seductive. It's not some simple flirtatious line meant to get his hand in my pants. I mean it. As in, I want to explore this *us* thing we've started and see where it goes. I want to do more with him beyond having sex. I want to show up places together, hold hands, and kiss in public. But those things might be too much to ask for, given who we are and how we became . . . whatever it is we are.

Maybe Rowan and I are a spark in time, a fleeting event that creates change. It doesn't make it any less special. It simply makes it brief. And that . . . that makes me sad.

Chapter 13

I COULD GET USED to ignoring my brother's phone calls. I did it so well for months, all the way until my father asked that I show up for him more often. "Be involved," he said. It all came with the side order of owing my father a favor for keeping my ass out of jail.

I'm not sure how that equates to owing Caleb for anything, however. Maybe because it's easier to sink his teeth into my brother if we're both competing for attention. Granted, I don't want the attention. I want the bear off my back. But that bear got a whole lot bigger when Mike-slash-Steve fed him.

The bear is the entire reason I'm responding to Caleb's text now as I sit outside our mother's Tucson salon. Apparently, my presence is required for more documents and a press conference.

> CALEB: Don't worry. You won't have to speak. You're just there to stand in the back and keep your mouth shut.

The low chuckle that slips through my lips every time I read my brother's last comment is a symptom of our growing mutual resentment. I wonder whether Caleb really thinks I'm stupid or if he is simply taking stabs at me to make himself feel better. My gut says it's the latter.

I've been working on the right words to respond with for about ten minutes. I'm sure our mom is wondering what the fuck I'm doing sitting out here in my car, keeping it idling like some getaway driver. She keeps glancing at me through the massive storefront window while she blows out her client's long platinum hair.

> ME: Tell our father I'll be there. BTW, it's cool he made you his personal assistant. Good for you.

I finally hit send and watch our text string just long enough to see my brother's response dots come and go a good five times before he finally sends his best retort.

> CALEB: Fuck off.

I kill the engine and pocket my phone and keys as I leave my car and head into my mother's salon. It's a simple space in the heart of downtown Tucson, steps away from the college campus. Most of her clients are sorority girls willing to drop major bucks for extensions and highlights. The woman in the chair today doesn't quite fit that bill—she looks to be in her late sixties, and her hair is a silky white blonde. She's admiring my mom's work with a hand mirror as I walk in.

"I love it, Cora. You work miracles, I swear," the woman praises. I step to the side and lean against the bookcase filled with fancy shampoos and hair oils while my mom runs this woman's credit card through a reader.

"It's my pleasure, Vivian. You know you're my favorite," my mom says, giving the woman a copy of her receipt and a hug. "See you in six weeks."

The woman pauses when she's a few feet from me and

scans me from head to toe. It would feel invasive and objectifying if it weren't so blatant. I think that's her goal.

"Well, this one got his mother's looks, didn't he?" She reaches for my shoulder with her hand and softly taps it, the weight of the three gold rings on her fingers giving it a little extra *plunk*.

"Thank you, ma'am. I owe my mom for a lot more than looks, though. She put a good head on my shoulders," I say, tapping my temple.

Her deep red lips spread into a crescent smile as she taps my shoulder a few more times.

"You're a good son, for sure. And cute to boot!"

I chuckle, a little embarrassed by her compliment perhaps, but I wish her a good day as she slips through the door and leaves me alone with my favorite person.

"You didn't have to make the drive. I would have gotten time off to drive up to Scottsdale eventually," she says, reaching toward me until we're embracing. Nobody hugs like Cora Anderson. When I was a kid and the world felt chaotic, probably thanks to having a father who liked to take his bad days at the office out on his family by disparaging us with swear words, my mom would make the noise go mute with one simple hug. I feel a bit like she's doing that now, and I think she can feel me relax in her arms.

"Take a seat. What's up?" She pats the back of her chair when we part.

I didn't come here for a haircut, but if she's offering, I'll never turn it down. Owning this place was my mom's dream. It was one of many things my father thought of as embarrassing. How could the wife of a hedge fund investment officer, who works with millions of dollars, want to spend her days cutting hair? My dad never understood the creative pull my mom felt, much like he doesn't get why I find joy listening to motors hum. We're built differently—us and him.

I can't really unload everything on my mind to my mother, though I wish I could. The recording equipment and wire I now have hidden under the front seat of my Camaro isn't something I can tell anyone about. Just like I can't breathe a word about the arson I went to juvie for. Or the dominoes that led to my parents' eventual divorce. It doesn't leave me with much other than Saylor Kelly. But my mom is probably the only person I can talk to about her, so maybe this was kismet.

She swoops the black cape around my chest and fastens it behind my neck, tugging the cloth straight around my body before running her hands through my hair and pressing her fingertips into my scalp. I close my eyes and breathe in slowly through my nose.

"You remember Saylor, right?"

Of course she does. My mom and brother haven't been total strangers. He shared his relationship with our mom, or at least mentioned it.

"How could I forget her. The girl who tried to sneak my maltipoo home in her Care Bears backpack when she was eight."

My mouth forms an instant smile as my mom laughs at the memory.

"I forgot about that," I say. "When her backpack started barking, she acted like she had no clue where the noise was coming from."

We both laugh at the absurdity. My mom nudges my head to one side as she bends down behind me to look at my reflection straight on.

"Maybe just a little touch up on the sides, and a tiny trim?"

I nod.

"Sounds great." I think she's bummed my hair isn't in worse shape. I feel guilty that I've gotten it cut by someone else. It's tough to make it down here often enough, though, and I was starting to get a bit shaggy. I wanted to look good for Caleb's graduation party, mostly so my father had one less thing to pick at. It's bad enough I work in a garage, I don't have to look like I do . . . at least, according to him.

"I know it's been a few years since I've seen her in person, but she grew into a lovely woman, didn't she? At least, from what I see on your brother's social media. I'm assuming they're still together?"

The scissors snip above my head as I wince, squinting one eye more than the other.

"Well?"

My mom stops cutting and shifts her body weight, jutting out a hip as her hand with the scissors moves to the side.

"Rowan."

Her tone is the scolding kind.

"Don't make assumptions. It's not like that," I start.

She punches out a short laugh, then goes back to trimming the top of my head.

"So, it's not like you decided to hook up with your brother's girlfriend, who you've babysat, might I add?"

Ouch. She had to add that part?

"In fact, no. It's not," I insist, though her summary is fairly accurate. "Just so you know, Caleb broke up with Saylor. There wasn't some sordid overlap of her hooking up with both of us."

"My God, I hope not, for her sake. You're both *a lot* in your own ways. I can't imagine the baggage she'd have to deal with if she were stuck between both of you."

I purse my lips, and my mom softly laughs, stopping the trim to squeeze my shoulders briefly.

"You know I'm saying this with love, and, well . . . I take ownership of most of that baggage. But lord help that girl if she's found herself at the point of an Anderson brother love triangle."

"Ohhhhh, no. No, no, no, no—" I wave a hand in front of

my body as if I'm cleaning a window. "This isn't a love story. No L word. It's not like that. It's just—"

"Rowan, I know we have a close relationship, but if you're about to tell me this is just about sex, and it's with a girl I helped raise in many ways, well—"

I squeeze my eyes shut tight. I should have kept Saylor off the discussion table, too. I pinch the bridge of my nose and exhale.

"I'm not. Of course, I respect Saylor more than that. I'm just saying it's not like I was waiting around for her to break up with Caleb. I wasn't pining after her for years. Hell, until this summer, I still saw her as the bratty little sister who wanted to sneak into my room and snoop through shit."

I flash back to the time Saylor found my weed under my bed and took it to my mom. I think my mom is remembering that too, based on the faint smirk on her face.

"All right. I'll let you off the hook. Let me just say this . . ." My mom pauses with the scissors above my head again, sucking in her top lip as she appears to think. "However long you've seen Saylor with new eyes, you can't forget that she also carries a history with you. So, navigate this situation with care, for you . . . and for her."

My gaze meets my mom's in the mirror.

"Did you give Caleb that same warning when he started dating her?" My chest tightens at my word choice, *dating.* Thankfully, my mom seems to acknowledge it with only the slight tilt of her head.

"Caleb and Saylor have a different history than you and she do, and you know that." We hold our stare for a few long, painful seconds. My mom is part of that history too, even though she doesn't verbalize it. She doesn't have to. It's a scar that she and I share, a wound we both try to heal for each other. And I get where she's coming from. Saylor doesn't have that wound, and I have the power to keep her safe from it.

"I understand," I finally utter.

My mom nods, then flits her gaze down to the top of my head before finally beginning to trim my hair again. I keep my mouth shut for the next several minutes while she works, and I almost feel my shoulders begin to lower by the time she runs the hot towel along the base of my neck.

She pulls the apron from my body and shakes away the tiny golden-brown hairs, and they fall to the floor like dust. I grab the broom from the corner while she carries the cape to the back. I'm sweeping the clippings into the central vac along the back wall when she exits the back room with the velvet box I drove down here to retrieve.

"Thank you again for picking this up and giving it to your brother. I would have been at the ceremony, but I couldn't close the shop for a whole day, and . . . well . . ."

I nod, excusing her from saying the painful part. She wasn't really invited. Not to the graduation, and not to the party at my father's house afterward. Besides, showing up would have reopened a lot of ugly chapters we've all worked hard to put behind us. Me, her, Saylor's family, and my dad.

"It's fine. I like seeing you anyhow. I just wish Caleb could have come himself."

I search my mom's eyes for evidence, but she's gotten good at masking, and quickly pulls her mouth into a well-practiced smile as she waves her hand.

"Oh, he's busy. I remember that time in life, the last summer before college. He has more important things to do than seeing his mom for lunch or whatever. I just wanted him to know I'm thinking about him, and that I'm proud. What do you think?" She nods at the box, which is now in my hands. I crack it open to reveal a pair of modern-styled platinum cuff-links, perfect circles with a thin line scratched along the edges.

"I think they're perfect. He'll be the most fashionable freshman in business school," I laugh out, snapping the box shut and pushing it into my pocket.

"Good," my mom nods, running her palms along her hips.

I'm not sure if she's dusting away the hair from my cut or clearing sweaty palms from feeling anxious. I would understand if that's the case. I have the same habit and affliction.

"I'll tell him to give you a call too," I say, the big brother role coming so natural to me.

"No, no. He doesn't have to—"

"Yeah, he does," I say, almost scolding her this time. She puts up with too much sometimes. My brother has no idea what a saint our mother is. It kills me that she craves a better relationship with him, yet he spends his energy sucking up to our dad.

"All right, be nice. Just tell him I'm proud."

I nod and pull her in for a tight hug. This time, I'm the one doing the soothing.

"I will," I say in her ear, my eyes falling shut for a moment.

"I'm proud of *both* of my sons. So incredibly proud," she says as we part.

"I know," I say through a forced smile. It's not that I don't believe her, either. I know she's proud. I just wish that our family weren't so fucking broken. It's hard to put on a positive face sometimes.

"I'll call you this weekend. And tell that Viv lady to keep her hands to herself," I tease, skipping toward the door as if I'm trying to run away from Viv's hands. My mom's head rears back with the kind of laugh I hear so rarely from her. It's the perfect final note before I leave her behind.

Lost in my thoughts for most of my drive home, I keep my radio turned down low until I reach the city limits again. I put on my new playlist when the traffic starts to frustrate me, and when I'm idling on the freeway at a complete standstill, I pick up my phone and shoot my brother a text.

ME: Where are you now? I have something for you from Mom.

He doesn't answer, which, of course, is no surprise. When

it's me needing something, it's not a priority. Also, I said it's something from Mom, which he knows will come with a lecture from me. My brother can say all he wants to about me running away from family drama, but he's just as much the king of avoidance as I am.

After thirty minutes of bumper-to-bumper traffic and no response from Caleb, I call my father's office. The traffic is just starting to flow again when Saylor's mom answers.

"Brogan-Tackerly. This is David Anderson's office. How may I assist you?" So formal. I wonder if Allison was always so polished or if that came later in her career with my father.

"Hi, Allison. It's Rowan. I'm looking for Caleb. Is he in the office by chance?" If he won't answer me, then I'm simply going to have to show up.

"Oh, hi, Rowan. No, he's on a late lunch, but I think he mentioned he was going to the sports club. Hope that helps." I can tell she's busy, and I'm glad she's not giving my brother's and my relationship too much of her mental space. She knows he and I don't get along. Thankfully, she gives me enough grace not to try to fix it. I think deep down, she knows she's the last person I want to take family advice from.

Allison ends the call first, which . . . fine. I exit the freeway and trek back two miles to the sports club on the way to my father's neighborhood. Most of the people who work for my dad have memberships. My brother and I don't even need to flash our cards anymore. The owners of the club basically watched us grow up on their indoor courts and in their weight room. I haven't stepped foot in here in years, though. Not since quitting basketball and turning down the D1 offers and choosing to apprentice with a mechanic instead. I'm a little hesitant when I reach the desk, but thankfully, Penny, one of the owners, flashes with recognition seeing me step up.

"Call the press, both Anderson brothers have been found," she jokes, rounding the front counter to give me a hug. She's barely over five feet tall, so I have to hunch over to embrace her.

"It's been a while, I guess," I admit.

"Uh, years," she says, falling away from me but grasping my bicep in her palm and giving it a squeeze. "I see you're working out somewhere."

I chuckle.

"More like working. It's amazing how heavy engine blocks are."

"Okay, Mr. Hotshot. Good for you! I heard you got a shop going. I think your brother mentioned it, or maybe your dad."

I smile politely. I'm sure my dad mentioned it with disgust, but Penny's always been above all that status bullshit. She's in this neighborhood because she runs a business. She admires hard work.

"Caleb on the courts?" I nod toward the gym doors beyond the counter.

She leans her head in that direction.

"Sure is. Seems like he's working through something. He's been going for an hour and a half straight. You thinking of giving him a little competition?"

I glance down at my legs and bunch my mouth. I am wearing joggers and decent enough sneakers.

"Maybe," I consider.

"Well, go on in," she says.

My pulse kicks with the excitement of competition. I don't miss the organized game of basketball. I was never going to play professionally. Sure, I might have been a decent college player; better than Caleb, for sure. But for me, it was never about the carefully structured plays, the defensive strategy, the passing and setting of picks. I was a selfish player because I loved the one-on-one. I liked the duel. So many things in my life were about accommodating others. It's in my nature. But on the court? I liked to be king. And there's only room for one of those.

I push through the double doors and am greeted with a *yawl* from a player being knocked to the floor. The guy plays up the flop, immediately getting to his feet and rushing at my brother, who merely stands in place while slowly dribbling the ball at his side.

"Fuck you, you know that was a foul!" The guy pushes his chest into Caleb's, and I lean against the wall to watch from a distance. I'm curious how my brother handles confrontation with others. I know how he deals with me. He puts up a good front, but underneath, I know I'm the one walking away on top. Caleb fears me as much as he wants my respect. That's where his insecurities are rooted, and I'm enough of a dick to exploit them.

"Yeah? You think that was a foul? How about this?" Caleb shoves the ball into the man's chest. His opponent is maybe a decade older, but he's in good shape, his leg covered in tattoos that appear to honor military service. My brother is bold to think he can handle this guy. He might be taller than him, but I have a feeling this dude's seen some shit. Caleb hasn't even seen the bottom of a clothes hamper.

"Watch yourself," the guy barks, dribbling a little too hard as he marches to the line.

I know before he even releases the ball that the guy's going to toss up a brick. The ball ricochets hard off the rim, but rather than feeling embarrassed by his bad shot, dude rushes in for the rebound, body-checking my brother to the ground on his way to a lay-up.

"What the fuck, man! *That* was a foul!" Caleb hops to his feet and immediately shoves the guy in the chest.

I push away from my quiet spot against the wall and saunter onto the court, reaching the duo, now surrounded by their teammates, just as their sweat-soaked T-shirts are wadded in each other's fists.

"You two about to kiss?" I tease.

I get instant scowls from them in return.

"What the fuck are you doing here?" Caleb grunts, letting go of the guy's shirt and pushing him away with a flat palm to the ribs.

I step between them before the guy has a chance to retaliate, and I do my best to meet the stranger's stare with my own.

"He's my brother. But don't think I'm sticking up for him. He's a fucking dick. I'd just like to be the one to deal with him." I shrug a shoulder and squint my right eye as the guy glances over my shoulder but backs away.

"Yeah, all right. I'm done here anyway. I better not see you starting shit again," he says, pointing at my brother.

Caleb opens his mouth because he can't help it, but I manage to face my brother before he can form an actual word. I slap my hand over his mouth.

"*Shhh,*" I hiss.

He backs away with a jerk, his face red with rage and his eyes fixed on me now. Good. That's where his focus should be, because I have shit to say.

"I brought your graduation gift from Mom. You know, the one you should have gone to get yourself?" I pull the box from my pocket and flatten it against his chest. He fumbles to take it before I walk away and let it drop to the floor.

"I would have gotten around to it," he huffs, turning his back to me and walking to the bench where his workout bag is sitting. He tosses the box in without even opening it.

"She put a lot of thought into that. You're not even going to look?" I should have let that guy throw a punch before I broke them up.

"I'm sure it's nice. I'll look later." His head tilts back as he guzzles water from a bottle. He snaps the cap back in place, then turns to me after tossing the bottle in his bag along with our mother's gift.

I shake my head at him.

"Sorry, fine. I'll look," he whines, reaching into his bag. He pops the box open for two seconds.

"Cufflinks. Nice. Tell her thanks," he says, dropping the box back on top of his change of clothes.

"Tell her yourself, asshole." I start to walk away, knowing that if I stick around much longer, I'm not going to be able to restrain myself.

When the ball hits me in the back of the head, though, I turn around and stare him with dead eyes. Seems Caleb wants to be challenged. He must be craving the same kind of pain I am. He wants a fight.

"You're just jealous that Dad sees something in me. He sees potential that you don't have. You're nothing more than a familial obligation." The cocky grin on my brother's face almost makes me proud. He's getting better at shit talking.

I smirk and chew at the inside of my cheek, barely holding in the low laugh as I toe the basketball to a bounce, then dribble it up into my hands.

"Jealous, huh? Interesting word." I slap the ball with my opposite hand, then launch it into my brother's chest. He catches it just as fast. His brow arches.

"You wanna go?"

I sniff and nod, dropping my keys and phone on the other end of the bench.

"Yeah, let's go. Twenty-one. You're up top first."

I pivot while my brother dribbles to the top of the three-point line, the other half-court game slowing as the players notice what's happening over here. My brother and I were both high school stars. We've both been written about for our basketball talent, hype and all that shit. I bet a lot of people simply assume I played college somewhere, and I'm sure they think that's what Caleb's going to do. People like to brag about having famous athletes in their community, as if somehow that makes them winners.

"Check it," Caleb says, bouncing the ball to me.

I bounce it right back and move to the balls of my feet, ready for his move. It's always the same, and this time is no different. Caleb spins to the right, then rushes left, trying to pass me for a quick layup. I block it easily and take the ball up top while wearing the same cocky grin he tried to pull on me.

"We're just getting started. That was lucky." he defends.

I chuckle, then pull up for a jump shot at the top of the three-point line. I sink it without a sound, except for the claps behind me from our fans.

"Whatever. Lucky shot," he says.

I do it again.

"More like skills," I say.

Our battle continues, Caleb sinking a few of the breaks he takes inside, even dunking on me once, which I swear he only does for attention. I don't take him inside a single time, and that's because I see his weaknesses. I always have. Caleb counts on the physicality of the game over the finesse. I'm taller. He's thicker. He figures he'll bump me out anytime I get close, but that means he's leaving me all sorts of room and time to take good shots. And I drill them shot after shot, until it's twenty-one to ten.

I predict his eventual meltdown, too, so when he drops the ball to kick it with his foot, I bump him with my body so he misses and ends up rolling the ball through the center of the court rather than at some innocent dude's face.

"It's time for you to grow up, Caleb."

I snag my keys and phone while he limps his way to his gym bag, feigning some injury that he'll no doubt use as an excuse to the guys in this room when I leave.

"I know you think Dad can buy you the life you want, but all money can buy you is distractions. At some point, you're going to have to deal with the shit messing with your head. Call Mom."

I let my gaze linger on him for a second, not bothering to hide my disgust before turning and striding toward the double doors.

"Leave Saylor out of this, then. Don't bring her into your

bullshit. She deserves better," he says, and I pause my steps but only for a second.

"You're right about that. She deserves better than both of us. But . . ." I give myself exactly a half second to consider shutting my mouth. Nope. I'm saying it. "I'm the one she's with now, and I like her way too much to quit."

Chapter 14

I'D RATHER RIDE my old banana-seat cruiser with flat tires than bother my mom for a ride while my car gets fixed. She didn't seem to notice it wasn't in the driveway. And she also seems oblivious to the fact I haven't been around in twenty-four hours. The only thing she made sure to check off her list when she called me during her lunch today was that I, in fact, met with the dean and am filling out the application. Rather than open the debate with her over the phone, I simply said, "Yes."

I lied.

I should feel bad about that, but I don't.

Cami has been a good sport. While I would ride my old bike, I don't have to because my best friend offered to chauffeur me to my new job, then to the lake tonight for beer and unsafe fireworks with a few of our friends. She's been sweating her ass off on the bleachers while I teach an unruly group of twelve-year-olds how to flip turn for the last hour.

"You should have brought a suit," I holler to her from across the pool as she dips her feet in the water while sitting on one of the free towels they give away at the counter.

"Next time. How long did Rowan say it would take to get your wheels fixed?" She squints against the sun as I shrug.

"He didn't. He said Jersey would have to help him with part of it."

I don't know Jersey well. His real name is Tyler Gris, but he transferred to our high school from New Jersey when Miguel and Rowan were freshmen, and some nicknames have a way of sticking for life.

"Ugh, that's not good," Cami says, stretching her arms over her head with a yawn. She knows Jersey better than I do.

"Yeah?"

I squint one eye, the weight of having to piece together transportation for the next several days making my belly twist.

"He's just not very punctual, is all. He's a genius, like, legitimately. He can simply look at things and mentally take them apart and put them back together before he even touches a tool to anything. But he's lazy." Cami kicks her feet in the water, splashing.

"Why do the guys put up with him?" I ask. Cami shrugs.

He's rich. I think he floats a lot of things when they can't pay the bills.

I nod as I drop my gaze to the ripples in the water. Rowan is from money too, but he refuses to tap those resources. I admire him for it. His principles.

The last few swimmers in my class are climbing out of the pool, so I hold up a hand to high-five them as they pass. Even the simplest positive reinforcement goes a long way. I remember being that age. I felt slow in the water until one day, when one of my coaches called me lightning. That's all it took.

"Give me five minutes to clean up and change," I say as my friend pulls her feet from the water.

"Finally!" She drags her feet along the deck, accentuating her pouting. I know she's just being funny, but I feel guilty taking up her time—even if she has nothing better to do.

I swap out my one-piece black suit for the floral bikini I

brought for the lake. I run my hair through the shower to get the stench of chlorine out, then twist it on top of my head with a clip. I slip my white gauzy cover-up over my body and stuff everything else in my drawstring backpack, then skip out to Cami's waiting car.

When we hit the highway that cuts north through the mountains, I lean forward and turn the music up, ready to clear my mind of the constant unanswered questions that have been plaguing me since Rowan dropped me off. At the top of the rotation is finding a way to see my father next weekend if my car isn't fixed yet. And then there's the man repairing it for me. For free. Again. The debt feels heavy, but the gesture also sets off a strange ache in my chest.

I sit back in my seat and shut my eyes for a deep breath, but before my lungs have a chance to fill, Cami turns the music down to nearly zero. My eyes pop open a hair before her inquisition begins.

"Okay, girl. We've got an hour drive ahead of us. Spill it!"

"Ugh, I don't know. There's nothing to spill," I groan. I needed to unpack this Rowan thing with someone, and it had to be Cami. But she's making me regret not simply stewing over things on my own more and more.

"Saylor, you spent the night in a hotel room with the finest man to ever come out of this damn state. There's plenty to spill, so . . . go on." She sweeps her hand at me, prodding me to open up, and my cheeks blush as the first memory to rush through my mind is of Rowan's mouth on my breast.

"Oh, there's more than I thought," Cami laughs out, punching my shoulder in jest.

The coy smile pulls the corners of my mouth into my cheeks, a reaction beyond my control, and my body warms from both embarrassment and the memory of Rowan's hands . . . everywhere.

"Okay, fine. Yes, things happened."

"*Things*. Bitch, elaborate."

A hard laugh flies from my chest and I choke on it, coughing while my cheeks burn. Cami has no shame when it comes to sharing about stuff like that. She made a video with her ex, Warren, that she keeps on her phone. I've seen it. Well . . . parts of it. Begrudgingly.

"Cam, I love that you're free and open, with absolutely zero hang-ups about your sexuality. I think it's beautiful. That's your feminism, and I applaud it. But I'm a bit more modest. Can you respect that?" I bunch my mouth up on one side and hold my stare on her, waiting until she glances my way and gives in with a roll of her eyes.

"Fine. I'll back off. But tell me one thing." She pushes up the sleeve of her thin, cropped sweatshirt and holds her fist up with her elbow bent.

"What am I supposed to do with that?" I think I know what she's getting at, so I mentally prepare myself with an answer.

"You start at my fist, then draw that line down my forearm until it's in the ballpark. I want a visual representation of what my girl is dealing with."

"Cam," I protest.

She shimmies her arm, though, urging me to play along, so I do. My finger draws a slow line down her wrist, inching toward her elbow as flashes of exactly how big Rowan is creep into my mind. I stop around the ten-inch mark and tap my friend's skin.

"Fucking hell, Saylor. How's your vagina holding up?"

I slap my palms over my face instantly and giggle.

"Oh. My. God!" I can feel my hot skin against my hands. Cami is torturing me, but also, what an incredible thing to be teased about. This is the fantasy. I'm sure we giggled over this very subject when we were freshmen. And now here I am, possessing hard facts, so to speak, of exactly how big Rowan Anderson's cock is.

"It was . . . a lot," I finally admit, peeling away a few

fingers and glancing at my friend. Our eyes meet as she laughs.

"I'll bet!" She slaps the steering wheel, then wraps her hand around it to mimic me gripping Rowan, I suppose.

"It got easier, though. I mean . . . *a lot* easier." I can't believe I'm sharing this much.

"Oh, I see. Okay, okay. This thing is good for you, whatever is going on between you two. My girl is having an awakening."

Awakening. *Hmm.* I suppose I am. I sink back with that thought, letting it settle over me while my skin tingles, replaying our night together. I like the woman I am with Rowan. I like her a lot. She's bold, and a little wild. But there's more to it than the sex, at least I *think* there is. I don't know if I would have had the guts to admit my desires for my future out loud if it weren't for Rowan's gentle support. He makes it feel safe to step out of line. To dream.

"Caleb texted me looking for him when we were together," I share.

"Oh, that's interesting. Kind of a nice bonus, I suppose . . . making that joke jealous." Cami's dislike for Caleb doubled when we broke up.

I waggle my head.

"Kind of. I mean, my spiteful side likes watching Caleb suffer. But I think Rowan likes it, too. They're not exactly close, and I wonder how much of what we're doing is about him shoving it in his brother's face, and how much of it is real."

My friend doesn't have an immediate response for this question, offering me nothing more than a crooked, wry smile and a heavy sigh. I haven't shared the details Rowan gave me with her, about how Caleb sold him out. That's Rowan's story to tell, when and if he wants. I won't betray his trust. But it's that bond, the one beyond the physical appeal and the sweet revenge byproduct, that has me feeling so conflicted.

The party atmosphere is in full swing by the time Cami pulls into the lakeside dirt parking lot. Within minutes of arriving and rubbing our bodies down with sunscreen, I have a cold beer in my hand and an offer to take over a beach chair from some guy I barely knew in high school.

"I'm good. I think I'm going to take a dip first," I say, fluttering my eyes at him for practice. I'm not exceptional at flirting; at least, I don't think I am. There's no harm in practicing, especially if this thing with Rowan is temporary, which I'm starting to think it is.

I pull my coverup over my head and toss it on one of the towels Cami stole from the swim club. I take my friend's hand as we tiptoe our way through the rough desert sand until our feet hit the cool water.

"How can it be so damn hot in this state yet this shit is still freezing-ass cold?" My friend inches her way deeper, stopping when her foot is covered to her ankle.

"You're never going to get in at that rate. You've gotta just go for it," I say, pulling the clip from my hair and tossing it toward my towel on the shore. I rush into the water with my next breath, skimming across the water in a manic breast-stroke as my breath is taken away from the instant chill.

"Woooh!" My lips pucker as I pant and fight to get a full breath. It gets easier the harder my legs work to tread water, though, and within a minute I'm able to dunk my head under and float on my back.

I'm almost relaxed for the first time since graduation, my muscles giving way to the slap of the current, when a wave of water instantly crushes my peace. I know it can't be Cami. She always takes a full twenty minutes to get to waist level, so I dip my head back for a dunk, then twist to face the cannonball intruders.

"Hey, gorgeous," Caleb says, his hair slicked back and his smile all toothy and proud.

"Great," I mutter. There goes any hope for fun today.

I glance to Cami, wishing she would suck it up and swim to me just this once. Knowing she won't, though, I start to paddle my way back to the shore, so at least I'm not outnumbered by Caleb, Cami's ex, Warren, and two of their other friends.

"Come on. Don't be like that. Just cuz we're not together doesn't mean we can't be friends." Caleb splashes me, and I don't know in which world he thinks I would enjoy it, but it's not this one.

I look toward the shore and notice Neveah, his new fling, stretching out on towels with a few of her friends. She's quick to undo the back of her bikini to avoid tan lines. I'm sure she's planning ways to accidentally forget and stand up to flash everyone a nice view of her expensive tits.

"*Hmm*, you have enough friends here," I say over my shoulder. His gaze moves from me to Neveah as he laughs.

"Come on. You can't be jealous. You have no right, Saylor. I mean, you're fucking my brother."

His crass call-out halts me in the water, and thankfully, I've made it to a shallow-enough place where my feet touch the ground. I turn, careful to steady my feet on solid rocks rather than slick or jagged ones. I manage to keep my mouth shut, but glare at him with a silent warning. I would never want to betray Rowan, but Caleb is pushing me to let him know exactly what his brother has told me about him. He's not such a golden child. In fact, I've come to believe he's rather rotten.

"Are you saying you're not?" Caleb's long arms sweep along the surface of the water as he treads in place, his eyes dimmed with resentment. A low laugh rumbles from his throat. "You're not denying it."

I fight the itch to engage with him, but I can't let him off the hook so easily. Rather than answering him outright, I simply let my expression morph into a devious smirk. I feel the ache in my guilty face, the way my cheeks are pushing up. I won't blush in front of him, though. I'm not ashamed, and he's not worth bringing blood to the surface of my skin.

"Fuck!" Caleb splashes water toward the calm water behind him.

The fact I was able to anger him with nothing more than the curve of my lips is enough to give me the confidence to march my ass back up the shore and pull my top off, not giving two shits who sees my tits before I lie on my stomach. The whistles and whispers don't faze me. And when my bestie crawls onto her towel beside me and holds out a fist for me to pound, I do it with pride.

"That's my girl," she says.

The hour-long nap that follows is pure bliss. I haven't been sleeping well, other than the night I spent with Rowan, and my eyelids are so heavy when I'm awake. I probably could have lain under the sun for hours, burning my skin to a crisp, if it weren't for the low rumble of a familiar Camaro stirring me awake.

"This should be interesting," Cami says. I roll my head to the side, where she's sitting up, doomscrolling on her phone and tanning her legs.

I push up on my elbows, stopping when I become aware of my undone top.

"Give me a hand, would ya?" I nod over my shoulder, and my friend helps to tie my strings so I can sit up as Rowan and Miguel stroll toward us.

"I may have invited them," Cami says, not even masking her sly grin.

"You just love to start shit, don't you?" I scan the water and spot Caleb in seconds. He's floating on a tube along with a few of his friends, but his plaything, Neveah, seems to have moved on to better things. She's nowhere to be found. Good for her.

"This seat taken?" Rowan pulls his shirt over his head and drops it on the ground next to me before sitting on it.

"It is now," I say, testing out some flirty behavior. I always feel like I sound trite with him, young and naïve, and I squeeze my eyes shut hard when I hear how I sound now.

"Damn right, it is," he says, tipping my chin up and dusting my lips with his. It's the first time he's done that in public, and the display of intimacy swallows me whole. It's suddenly hard to breathe, and my eyes can't focus as they roam the familiar faces still around us.

There's no way people didn't see that. They're talking. They're whispering. I'm sure of it.

Rowan pulls his Vans from his feet, along with his socks, rolling them up and tucking them in his shoes. He's wearing gray board shorts that sit low on his hips, the golden trail of hair from his navel to the waistband an in-my-face reminder of what's underneath. I swallow the sudden ball of anxiety lodged in my throat before looking up at his beautiful face through my lashes.

"Your brother's here," I utter in a low voice.

Rowan's gaze skims the water, and he squints as the sun reflects into his eyes.

"Yeah, I see that." He takes a long, deep breath, almost like he's readying himself for battle. About ten seconds later, I realize that's exactly what he was doing.

"Shouldn't you be under some hood?" Caleb flicks water droplets at both of us as he shakes out his hair. I run my palms down my arms to brush them away, but Rowan doesn't move a lick. He doesn't even flinch.

"That's the thing about working for yourself. You get to call the shots. I wanted a day off, so here I am . . . enjoying some fine company." Rowan's palm moves to my thigh, and my eyes dart down to take it in.

Caleb chuckles, but it's obvious by the way his posture shifts and he drops his hands in his pockets that he's bothered by it. That's why Rowan is doing it. I both like it and hate it, and I'm not sure what that means about my own feelings.

"Brace yourself for the breakup, sweetheart. Rowan doesn't stick around long. He's a love 'em and leave 'em kind of guy. He'll be done with you soon. *She's a prude,*" Caleb tacks on with a loud whisper.

"Maybe you were just a shitty lover," Rowan fires back.

My lips twitch with a proud smile, but I keep it tempered. Rowan standing up for me feels . . . well, it *feels*. It's sexy, sure. It's also more than I've ever gotten from anyone.

"He was definitely a shitty lay," I say, something strong crawling to my surface. My eyes flicker with shock, and Cami chuckles at my side. Rowan's fingers squeeze my thigh.

"You thinking about fucking my dad next, Saylor?" Caleb's words cut through any tough skin I thought I'd grown, and my only reaction is a silent gasp that leaves my eyes feeling the hot sting of angry tears. Before I can find my breath to push out the words, though, Rowan is on his feet, and he's shoving Caleb back several feet.

"You apologize for that shit right now!" Rowan growls.

"Relax, brother. I'm just giving you shit. What did you expect?" Caleb's nervous laughter is a tell. His bravado is thin, a fake coat of armor.

Caleb holds his hands up to his sides, almost as if he's baiting Rowan to throw the first punch, to look like the abuser, the villain. But Rowan's too disciplined to fall for it. Instead, he saunters backward a few steps until he's at my side again, and he drops his hand down with his fingers flexed.

"Come on, Saylor. Let's go for a swim."

His gaze remains fixed on his brother while I take his hand and let him pull me to my feet. His fingers intertwine with mine with a familiar ease, despite having held it so few times and only in private. I let Rowan lead, and he doesn't bother to veer around Caleb as we walk toward the water, instead checking his brother shoulder to shoulder as he leads me toward the water's edge.

The chill is more biting this time, the cool stinging against my pink skin. I shouldn't have slept without reapplying sunscreen. I breathe through the suffocating cold, though, siphoning away the heat from Rowan's body as we dip lower into the water. Finally, when the surface covers our shoulders, Rowan swivels my body into his and wraps his arms around me. I reciprocate with my legs, feeling him hard against me.

"Was that show for him, or me?" I ask as he spins us in a slow circle in the water, every pair of eyes at the lake on us, for certain.

He leans his head to the side a tick and glances up as if in thought before meeting my gaze.

"A bit of both." His expression remains still, devoid of clues, as his eyes search mine. I wish I knew what thoughts are racing behind those eyes of his. I'm not sure what came first, the blue-green water or the shade of his eyes.

"He can't talk to you like that. I don't care what's happening between us. He has no right. Never did. Never will. Nobody will. Not if I can hear it."

His gaze bores into me, and I lick my dry lips, suddenly nervous and excited. My heart pounds in my chest, inches away from his. I'm sure he feels it.

"Thank you," I croak. They're the only words I can think to utter. I know my worth. I've just struggled my whole life to announce it to others. But Rowan is showing me that there's power to my voice. There's power in telling people what I don't like, in voicing what hurts me, and what makes me feel whole. I need to say what I want.

"I want to stay with you tonight. In your bed." I hold my breath, ready for him to stop our slow dance in the water, but his body continues the slow spin, and his eyes never leave mine. He doesn't even blink.

"Okay."

Chapter 15

I SHOULD STOP ASKING myself what I'm doing. It's a stupid question. I know *exactly* what I'm doing. I'm getting involved with my brother's ex, a girl I always thought of as my little sister. And it's not simply about hooking up. I'm starting to feel things. Possessive things. Protective, but less like a brother, and more like . . . fuck, I don't know. Hell, I brought her here. To my place.

It's strange having Saylor in my personal space. She's not a girl I picked up at the car show, or one of the women who hang around the courts to watch me shoot. I have always been upfront with any girl I brought home with me for the night. It's always *for the night*. There's an agreement between us. No expectations or false hopes beyond two people making each other feel good for a while.

No matter how hard I try to force that conversation with Saylor, though, I can't seem to get the words out. I don't want this to be the only time she's here.

And that's a problem.

For a lot of reasons.

"You must really love your work," she says, dropping her small backpack by the door, then running her palm along the small kitchenette counter in my studio apartment attached to the shop.

"Saves on security costs," I joke, tossing my wallet, phone, and keys on the small card table that doubles as my dining room.

Saylor glances at me with a short breath and a smile.

"So, that shower I used the other day . . ." She tilts her head toward the open door that leads to the garage and the short hallway to the shower.

"It's more of a shared shower, but yeah. That's mine," I say, my mind drifting to the memory of her naked, wet body through that barely opaque glass. Her gaze lingers on mine for a moment, her lip curled up on one side in this half-guilty, half-seductress way.

I pull out one of two wooden chairs at the table while she continues to explore the room, pausing at the set of framed photos propped up on my dresser. She picks up one of Caleb and me when we were kids at the go-kart races.

"How old are you in this?" She flips the frame around and clutches it to her chest. I don't need the visual, though. I remember that day as if it were yesterday. It was one of those few perfect family moments, before . . . well . . . *before*.

"Ten, I think. Caleb was five. It was his birthday, but he wasn't tall enough to drive on his own, so he rode with me." I chuckle through a growing crooked smile. "His helmet was too big, too, so our mom took the pads out of her bra and stuffed them in the helmet to keep it from slipping over his eyes."

Saylor's laugh is soft, and her gaze shifts back to the photo as she puts it back in its place.

"It's probably dusty up there. Sorry," I say, my head falling to the side as I study her.

She shrugs before blowing the dust from another photo.

"You keep a tidy place. You can't be perfect," she says, her eyes crinkling at the sides to match her wide grin.

"I don't get a lot of guests."

Her eyes dim as her lips purse.

"*Hmm,* I doubt that. I bet there's been a few *guests* in this place. Maybe sleepover guests?" Her brow arches, and her curious expression makes my chest tighten. I don't want to talk about the women who have been here for some reason. I would rather she thinks of this place as a tightly guarded secret that I'm only sharing with her. Because in many ways, it is.

"Okay, there have been a few, but no one who . . ." I leave it there, perhaps a little afraid of my own next words.

No one who matters. Nobody like you.

Rather than nudging me into a confession, Saylor simply keeps her eyes on me as she strolls across the room. She kicks her shoes off and nudges them to the side with her toes, then pulls the white coverup over her head and tosses it behind her to the foot of my bed.

"I'm guessing this isn't the kind of swimsuit you compete in?" I reach forward and tug one of the strings tied in a bow at her hip. It unravels, and the small triangle of floral fabric covering her pussy slips just low enough that I can see the thin trail of hair above it.

"I'd probably swim right out of this thing," she says, stopping at my knees and reaching behind her to untie her top. It loosens, the cloth barely clinging to her breasts. I reach up and hook my finger between the cups, and drag the material down her chest until it falls to the floor.

"Your tits are fucking perfection. I bet they'd sell a lot of tickets if you swam out of this at a race." I walk my fingers from her navel to the center of her chest, then tap my index finger a few times as if I'm deciding what direction to go. My hand glides to her puckered nipple after a second, and I twist it as I gently tug. Saylor's head falls back as her lips part with a gasp.

"Are you wet for me?"

I squeeze her tit again as she moans, "*Mmm hmm.*"

"Let's see," I say, moving my hand between her legs. I slip under the fabric, my fingers gliding along her swollen, soaking wet pussy.

"You are so wet, Saylor. I fucking love your pussy." Her body twitches against my hand, my dirty words making her open to me. She was wasted on Caleb. I guarantee he never worshipped her the way she deserved. I bet she never truly had an orgasm with him. Not like she does with me.

I slide my left palm up the back of her thigh, grabbing her ass and squeezing before moving to the only thing left covering her body. I tug the final string, and her bikini bottoms drop to the floor.

"Just one taste," I say, glancing up at her. She moves her hands to my neck, then runs her fingers through my hair as she nods.

I'm not sure if she even realizes the way she's pulling my head toward her, bringing my mouth to her pussy, but she is, and I fucking love it. My hands cup her ass as I lean forward and lap my tongue against her pink skin, flicking the very center, then sucking it in.

"Oh, fuck, Rowan!" She grips my hair harder and holds my mouth to her pussy, her legs shifting a few inches wider.

I hum as I taste her, my tongue lathering her until my saliva has completely coated her, along with her own arousal. My cock is pressing against the laced front of my board shorts, and it's aching to feel all of her, every single inch, so when her hands relax in my hair, I let go of her body and unravel the front of my shorts and push them down just enough for my cock to stand free. I don't even have to ask before Saylor's straddling me and guiding my cock into her with her hand. She sinks down slowly, her pussy stretching to accommodate my length. She loops her hands behind my neck and rolls her hips as her gaze meets mine.

My eyes haze, and I feel the sinister tug of my grin at the corners of my mouth as Saylor rides my cock as if I'm the prized mechanical bull at the stockyard's restaurant. Her nipples scrape against my T-shirt until I pull it over my head so my bare chest sticks to hers. I want to buck into her, but I'm having too much fun watching her please herself on me. I like being used by her. She makes me patient.

The slow grind lasts for minutes, my hands memorizing the curve of her ass, the lines of her shoulder blades, the length of her hair as I tether it in my grip and pull her head back just enough that I can sink my teeth into her hard nipple. I could fill her up right here, like this, but I haven't stopped thinking about fucking her on the hood of my car since the first time I tasted her. I want to be greedy with her, just this once.

"Hold on, baby," I say, lifting her with me as I stand. Her legs wrap around my waist, my cock flexing inside of her as I march us out the door and into the garage where my car is parked. Only one of the bays is open, and I move my palm along the wall to shut it, but Saylor stops me.

"Leave it open."

I shift my head to look her in the eyes, and her sex-drunk grin thrills me.

"You're a bad little thing, aren't you?"

She nods and whimpers as her legs squeeze hungrily around my waist.

"Okay, we can put on a show," I say. The sun set half an hour ago, and the sign by the road is turned off, so I doubt we'll get any surprise customers. And anyone who dares to check whether we're open, well, they can fucking watch for all I care.

I move to the hood of my car and lay Saylor back, pulling out of her long enough to kick my shorts down my legs so I'm completely naked, too. I grip my cock in my hand as she parts her legs and scoots down the hood enough to give me easy access. Her pussy glistens from our sex, and I want to paint it with my cum, then fuck her ass in this same spot later tonight.

I need to be careful, though, and not mix the beast up too much with the man who suddenly wants this girl to stay here after. To come here again tomorrow. To bring her things over and get comfortable.

To be mine.

"Can I be rough?" I move toward her and lift one of her legs, hooking it over my arm as I stare into her eyes.

She nods, and it's not a timid yes. She's sure of it. Of this. *Of me.*

I guide myself into her and push my cock in slowly, teasing her with a few inches for several minutes until her cries grow needy and loud. I pull out completely before plunging back inside, pulling her leg to me and driving in until my tip hits her sensitive insides and she gasps.

"Oh, my God, Rowan . . . yes!"

I do it again, this time pumping into her harder and faster. She cries out the same words, her hands gripping against the metal hood, unable to hold on to anything to steady herself.

"I've got you, baby. Come for me," I command, driving into her again. And again. I rock my hips fast, and her body slides with my weight as I lean into her and flex her leg up as high as it will go. I want to touch her in new places, to uncover what pleases her most.

Her hands finally fly up and grip my shoulders, and her eyes open on mine, her stare pleading with me to push her over the edge. When she finally goes, her lids flutter shut as her eyes roll back, and she bites her bottom lip as she hums through her orgasm and smiles. I come seconds later, filling her, then stepping back to watch my cum drip from her pussy.

"My two favorite things are this car and your pussy," I say, running my thumb against her swollen center and coating her with me as she moans. I lean over her and bring my mouth to her ear.

"And later tonight, I'm going to take my third favorite thing," I say, sliding my hand down her pussy and to her ass. I sink a finger inside of her to test how tight she is. I won't be able to go deep, not at first. But the way she moans at this small tease tells me she's willing to put in the work.

"You said you wanted me to ruin you, baby. Are you sure?" I pull back just enough to meet her gaze. Her bottom lip tucked between her teeth, the devil's smirk dusts her lips as she nods and reaches down to circle my wrist in her hands to invite me in deeper.

My father always said Saylor Kelly was a good student.

Chapter 16

IT'S STRANGELY QUIET HERE. Rowan's apartment isn't far from a busy road, and it's barely off the highway. But it's a business district, and it's night. We're basically off the grid.

Our night has been a blissful oscillation from sleep to sex. My body aches from his rough touch, yet I want more. Every single touch from him carries so much energy. It's sensual, and I feel as though anything I ask for he'll deliver without expecting anything in return.

I've been lying naked on his bed for the last thirty minutes, my cheek resting on my folded arms as I stare at his face. His fingertips paint long strokes up and down my back, tracing my spine and shoulder blades, then following the curve of my ass. He wants me that way, and I want him to take me there, but he told me it's not something to rush. I trust him, and I don't even find that scary.

"What are you thinking about?" His gaze has shifted up to mine.

I suck in my lips.

"You. How happy I am here. How free I feel."

His mouth curls up on one side, and his eyes blink slowly.

"Good. I want you to like it here, with me." His eyes linger on mine for a beat, and his teeth grab the tip of his tongue, almost as if they're stopping him from saying too much. I don't care that Rowan has been with other women. It would be foolish to think he hasn't lived, hasn't loved or lusted. I have, and I'm six years behind him. But what I thought was intimacy with Caleb was fake, and I see that now. I don't think his brother ever looked at me after getting what he needed from my body. At least not like this.

"You know, I saw you have sex once. When I was sixteen," I confess. I bite my knuckle as my face warms.

Rowan arches a brow.

"You watched me?" His palm flattens along my back, but he continues to massage my skin.

"*Mmm hmm,*" I say, nodding while still resting my cheek on my arms. "It was at your dad's house, in that garden just off the library, the one in the—"

"The atrium," Rowan finishes with a soft laugh. His gaze drifts above me for a moment as he seems to be picturing the memory. "Everly Segal. She's one of my father's clients' daughters. She hated her dad, and, well . . . you know how I feel about mine. We were . . . *bonding.*"

His eyes drop back to mine.

"*Mmm,* yeah. You really *bonded,*" I tease. I'm not jealous. If anything, I'm curious. That was the first time I saw anything like that, and it woke something up inside of me.

"She seemed so strong," I say, trying to find words to articulate exactly what it was that held me captive for so long.

"She was. She is," he corrects. "She took over her dad's company after that. It was an ugly family break-up. Hostile takeover and all that."

"Does she still work with your dad?" I ask, maybe a tinge of jealousy twisting my insides.

Rowan shakes his head.

"Her first executive decision was to start fresh and break ties with anyone her father worked with. I think she saw my dad for what he is." His mouth falls into a flat line, and the longer I stare at his suddenly guarded expression, the more I think there are things about his father he's not fully telling me. I'm sure for good reason, too.

"What else did you like about it? Watching me?" His shift back to the sexual part of the subject isn't so subtle, and I shift my face into my arms to hide my blush as I giggle.

"I mean, it was hot," I admit.

"Oh, yeah?" His hand traces the curve of my back and rolls over my ass, his fingers sliding between my legs to feel how wet I am. It doesn't take much with him. A thought. One visual.

A wish.

"Yeah," I hum, turning my head just enough to look at him with one eye. My legs part slightly, giving him more access, which he takes, coating his hand with my arousal, then slipping a finger in my ass.

"You like it, don't you?"

I nod. I know he said I need to go slow, but he also promised he'd take me there tonight. It's close to sunrise, and I want him to have me everywhere, today, before I leave this room.

He dips another finger inside, sliding both in and out slowly, stretching me. I arch my back to lift my ass higher, eventually crawling up to my knees while my forehead rests on the mattress. Rowan shifts in the bed, getting on his knees and moving to the space behind me, guiding my hips back until his hard cock presses against my ass. He pushes his fingers in again, deeper this time, and I crave feeling him in my pussy too.

"You sure you want this?" he asks, working me with his hand, coating his fingers with my wetness, and priming me for more.

I nod my head against the bed and moan out, "Yes."

"I'll be slow, easy," he says, drawing his fingers out of me, then replacing the fullness with the tip of his cock, slick with lube. The pressure is soft but wider . . . different, and I gasp in anticipation.

"Tell me if I need to stop," he says, pushing into me slowly.

"Oh, fuck," I moan, my mouth wide open against the bed, my breath gone. At first, the feel of him hurts, the stretch more than I expected. But he rocks in and out, slowly, entering me only a few inches at a time as he gets my body used to his girth.

"Is this good?" His caution and care are sweet, but I'm craving the other side of him, and I want to rush to the place where he's no longer being so careful with me. I back into him to force him in deeper, and it hurts, but only for a moment.

"Oh, you want this," he says, his voice lower and gruff. The sound boils inside of me and makes my belly tighten with anticipation.

"Uh huh," I cry, my teeth biting the sheet as I rock back into him again, taking all of him.

Rowan's hands fly to my hips, and he holds me in place, forcing me to take the stretch before he moves again.

"Breathe through it, baby. Be patient," he says, flattening one hand on the small of my back as he leans into me and reaches his other hand around to my front.

He glides his fingers between my legs, teasing my pussy while filling me from behind.

"You are so wet, Saylor," he hums behind me. His cool lips press against my back as he coats his fingers with me, then sinks two of them inside.

"Gah!" I groan into the bed, the fullness so satisfying. He doesn't thrust behind me for several seconds, instead fucking me with his hand and bringing me near orgasm. Eventually, he pulls out of me slowly, and my ass aches from the stretch and loss of him inside of me. I hear the slickness of his hand wrapped around himself as he coats himself with my arousal and his saliva, then he glides his cock back inside, this time rocking in and out at a slow pace that doesn't hurt but rather, teases.

His hands grip my hips again, and he pulls me back into him as his thrusts grow harder.

"Touch yourself," he commands.

I do, my body flat on the bed except for my ass that is arched up into him, his cock pounding into it while my fingers run up and down the swollen folds between my legs. I circle my pussy and moan as I chase the sensation building in my core. The scream that leaves my mouth surprises me. It's animalistic; nothing reserved about it. It's proud, like an announcement that I am a sexual being ready to be satisfied. I am taking what I want. I come hard, and Rowan fills me from behind, the warmth an unfamiliar sensation in a new place. When he finally pulls out of me, he tucks himself beside me and pulls my body into him, holding me close while he tickles my body with gentle strokes as I catch my breath.

"I liked that," I say after a few quiet minutes.

His low chuckle is followed by his mouth on my shoulder. He bites me softly, then kisses my skin.

"I know you did," he says. "Now, come with me. I'm going to bathe you."

He sits up and drops his feet to the floor before lifting me in his arms and carrying me to the shower. The hot water soothes my aching muscles, and Rowan takes his time lathering my body with burnt amber body wash that smells like him. He leaves me to get dressed while I finish washing my hair.

"What's on your agenda today?" I ask once I turn the shower stream off. I pull the towel from the hook right outside the shower door and wrap my wet hair in it just as Rowan steps back into the bathroom carrying a pair of cotton gym shorts and one of his old T-shirts.

"Thanks," I say, my voice gravelly from the lack of sleep.

Rowan shuts the bathroom door and leans his back on it as he drops his hands in the pockets of his jeans. His head falls slightly to one side, a wet tendril of hair falling over his brow as he smirks.

"You're really beautiful, you know that?" His gaze roams down my body but comes back to mine after a few seconds, and the longer he stares into my eyes, the more my body wants to squirm from the attention.

"I don't know about that, but I'm glad you think so," I say through a nervous laugh.

"*Uh uh,*" he says, stepping away from the wall and taking my hand as I finish pulling his shirt down my body. He turns my wrist over to press his mouth against the inside as his gaze flits up to me.

"You're simply, easily, and naturally beautiful." His eyes hold mine hostage for a long breath, and my chest shakes with my intake of air.

Biting my lip, I finally let the smile slip through as I bat my lashes. He makes me feel so nervous. I'm not used to this kind of attention. I'm more often the strong girl, the good student, or the quiet leader willing to do what's best for the team. I'm the confidant my friends share their secrets with, or the girl-friend who understands when dates are canceled because of family obligations. I'm not so daft that I don't know my best attributes. I'm athletic, and my body has good curves. It's lucky, a little genetic, but mostly these attributes come from years of avoiding my anxieties by taking to the water.

Rowan makes me feel special, like a princess at the ball. When he looks at me, I feel his affection in the heat of his stare. His attraction to me is intoxicating. His attention is a reward. And I know he likes me. So, why is it so hard to ask him to come with me to see my dad's band?

"I have a few clients coming in today," he finally says, and it takes me a moment to remember even asking him about his plans.

"Oh, sure. I should . . ." I glance around the sparse bathroom, my pulse kicking up with a dose of adrenaline. He needs me to leave because he has a job—a business to run. And I'm loitering in here like some doe-eyed teenager.

"Saylor." Rowan takes my hand in his, then circles the back of it with his thumb. I'm feeling flustered, and maybe a bit nervous.

I shake my head.

"Sorry," slips out in a nervous laugh.

Rowan leans in and kisses my forehead, then grazes my bottom lip with his thumb.

"It's not that I want you to leave. But you don't have a car, and I'm the only one on shift this morning, so if I'm going to take you home . . ." He waggles his head, and I crinkle my nose as I squint, feeling silly.

"So . . . you like me here?" I want to hear it one more time.

"I do. A lot." His voice is soft, and there's a quiver in his lips that I'm going to pretend means he's nervous, too.

"Give me two minutes to comb my hair with this thing." I snag his black comb from the sink counter, and we both laugh.

"Okay, and don't worry if you break it. They come in packs of twenty." My fingers slip from his as he backs up to the door, then slips outside to leave me with his ragtag barber tools.

The garage bay door behind his car is open when I make my way out of the bathroom, and Rowan is waiting for me with my bag slung over his shoulder as he leans against his car. I'm never going to look at this car quite the same after what we did on it.

"I got your things, and *not* because I'm rushing you. I wanted to help. But also . . ." He winces, and I glance at the clock on the wall to the right. It's almost seven.

"You're rushing me," I laugh.

He scrunches his shoulder and moves to the passenger door, opening it for me.

"But only because Mig will kick my ass if I'm not back in time to check in our first customer." He hands me my bag as I sink into the passenger seat.

"It's fine," I say. "But I'm keeping this shirt." I pull the collar to my nose and breathe in his scent as he rolls his eyes.

"I may as well give you my whole damn closet, at this rate," he jokes. I'm only up to two shirts and a pair of shorts that I don't think he's worn since high school PE. But if he's offering his closet, there are a few shirts I saw hanging in there I wouldn't mind commandeering.

It's a Saturday morning, so the traffic is light as we cruise on the highway and up into the hills toward my house. The miles are passing quickly, and my window of opportunity to ask is shrinking. When we manage to breeze through the last intersection off the freeway and into my neighborhood, I shoot my shot.

"Would you maybe want to come with me to see my dad's gig? If you get home from the car show in time, I mean. It's okay if you can't, but Miguel said my car probably won't be ready, and I don't really want to go with Cami. She'll get bored."

I hold on to his face, studying every little tic for clues as his lashes flit, but nothing abnormal, and his mouth tightens, but not in a way that looks like he's irritated or put out. When I asked Caleb to go to things with me, like dances or the under twenty-one club where one of my friends DJs on weekends, he always got quiet and seem overcome by dread.

I don't think that's what's happening in Rowan's head right now, but I'm also gun shy. Maybe this is an ask too far. It's not like my father is a stranger to him. Sure, it's been a few years, but my dad still knows the Anderson boys, and he knows I dated Caleb. I get that this will be an uncomfortable coming out as a couple. If that's what we are.

"Let me see if I can scoot out of the auction early. But . . . yeah. I think I can make it work." He swivels his head and hits me with a soft grin that sets my boiling insides at ease.

"Thanks, Rowan. I wouldn't ask if—"

He reaches across the console and takes my hand in his, giving my palm a squeeze.

"I like that you asked," he says, cutting me off before I layer in all the logical reasons I need him to come with me. Truth is, I could find a way to see my father on my own, but I *want* Rowan there.

Rowan pulls to a stop at the edge of my driveway just as the garage door raises and my mom's taillights glow.

"Working on a Saturday. Work, work, work," I mumble. My mom would be thrilled to see me end up the same. She missed half of my swim meets in high school because she was putting in hours at the office or hosting some dinner for David and his clients.

"I bet I could quit the swim team and she'd never know," I whisper.

"She might notice when there's a tuition bill, since that's your scholarship," he points out.

I nod because bills are something she notices. My life has been one long string of trying to level up and fit in. We have always lived paycheck to paycheck, so she can drive the best cars and put me in the top private schools. I know David helped pay for a lot of those things, so maybe the tuition bill should go to him.

My mom's SUV screeches to a halt right in front of us, and her eyes narrow on mine as her head tilts with that special touch of judgement only she can express. I think she's just realizing that my car isn't here, and that I'm in *this* one. With a different Anderson brother. The rebellious one.

"She looks pissed." Rowan shifts in the driver's seat, seeming uncomfortable in his own skin. It's the only time I can recall seeing him this way, and it makes me angry that my mom is doing this with one look.

"She probably is." I turn to face him and lean over the console, pulling his chin to me until our lips meet. I cling to his lower lip, sucking him in for a few seconds, reveling in the feel of his tongue along my lip. When I pull away, my mom has given up and finished backing out of the driveway. I wait until her taillights disappear around the corner before getting out of Rowan's car and scurrying inside to finally get some sleep.

I slide across my yellow velvet comforter, almost missing the envelope waiting for me on the center of the bed. The paper scrapes my knee, though, so I grab it as I roll to my back. I recognize Caleb's handwriting instantly, the way he scratches the letters of my name, something that I always found to be aggressive. I sigh, but open the envelope to see what's so important that he took the time to put pen to paper. Other than birthday cards or notes with flowers, Caleb never wrote me letters. That kind of expression wasn't his thing, so it's not terribly shocking when the first line of his apology note reads:

I'm sorry about the things I said to you, but . . .

I speed through the rest of his words, his reasoning to justify calling me a prude, which isn't even an insult, to be honest. It's a laundry list of his motives for cautioning me away from Rowan, and though he never directly comes out to say it, I can tell he thinks his brother is dangerous. It's Rowan's dangerous side that I like, though, and that's what Caleb doesn't get. If I wanted safe and boring, I'd still be pining for him.

Chapter 17

I HAVEN'T SEEN Saylor's dad since I helped him pack up his truck for the last time. I always wished I knew him better. He seemed like a good soul. So different from the woman who worked for my dad. How Saylor's mom and he ever married baffles me. They were exact opposites. I always admired her dad's character. He held all the cards that day. He could have burnt the world down and made a lot of people pay or pay up, at the very least. But he knew what was best for Saylor, and that's how he drew his lines. He couldn't take her on the road with him, and as much as he resented her mom, he knew Saylor's life would be easier here.

Even dirty money is money, and it can buy opportunity.

I don't know that I could have been such a bigger person. I'm flawed that way. Too bent on revenge. Though, I have managed to keep a lot of secrets over the years. The pain that speaking them out loud could cause innocent people outweighs the temptation to hurt my enemies. I suppose I have some sort of moral compass.

I think I can keep my poker face in check when we watch her father's gig. I just hope he can. He's been the bigger man for a while now. Eight years is a long time to keep painful things in a box. And sometimes, all it takes is a little reminder to set off chaos.

I have a week to ready myself for that test, though. Right now, I need to collect my emotions for my first visit to my dad's office while wired up like a CIA agent. I spent the morning testing sound and capturing clips on the app Mike-Steve had me download to my phone. Everything I record gets sent to him instantly, so this morning his inbox was inundated with my coffee order and a brief conversation with myself about how I need to suck it up and quit being a pussy. I know he listened because the version of him that sold me a car messaged to tell me that he forgot to mention the sound quality of the Vette's speakers. They're sensitive, he wrote.

It's a hundred and four degrees outside, which limits what I can wear to cover the straps wrapped around my chest. I'd feel a lot better if I could throw on a hoodie, or at least toss on a flannel over my T-shirt, but that would raise suspicions. And I can't exactly flip a switch and suddenly show up as the guy who wears a long-sleeve button-down to my dad's office. Jeans and a black T-shirt will have to do.

I'm probably being paranoid. It's not like the wires are bulky, or I'm going to run into anyone insisting on a pat down. It's mostly that I can *feel* them, and that's a constant reminder that I'm about to sell my dad down the river.

I turn the air on full blast in my car and roll down my window as Jersey waves from across the garage. He's holding up what looks like Saylor's part.

"Is that everything?" I holler so he can hear me over my engine's rumble.

"Almost. I got a good deal on this, but she's gonna need some wires, too. That engine fried real fast."

I nod and mentally calculate the amount I'm going to need to cover. No way am I letting Saylor pay for any of this, but I'd also prefer to keep what's going on between the two of us private; at least, private from Jersey. Mig knows the bare minimum, and that's way too fucking much.

"Okay, do what we need to get her running. She can cover it." AKA *I* can cover it.

"Right on, man. I'll need your help when the wire kit comes in. Maybe Tuesday," Jersey says. I build in an extra day because he's terrible at scheduling shit. He'll probably call in sick or something that day.

"I'll be here all week. Oh, but hey . . . I'll have to dip from the auction early Saturday. You think you and Mig can handle the afternoon dockets? I've got . . ." I struggle with the right lie, but thankfully, Jersey bails me out.

"No problem. Deal with your family shit. I know you're still digging out of that hole." He snorts a laugh and nods at me before dropping his headphones back to his ears and returning his focus under Saylor's hood.

Family shit. Yeah, that basically covers anything going on in my life, except for Saylor. I need to start using that as my blanket statement anytime I don't want to delve into details.

I'm going to have to pull from my very pathetic savings to cover the wire harness for Saylor's car. I don't want to write too many IOUs to the shop. That's a bad habit that might land me in the exact hot seat my father's in—though at a much, *much* smaller scale.

I've done my homework on my dad's case—at least the small pieces that Mike-Steve shared with me—and it's the same scam he's been running for years. The same shit he tried to pin on my mom when he thought the feds were sniffing around his brokerage. This time, he's going to pin it on me or Caleb. Maybe both of us. Of course, good ole dad won't pull the safety brake unless he needs to. I suppose that should make me feel better. Less expendable.

My temper is making its way to my lead foot, and I'm suddenly barreling down the freeway at ninety while muttering to myself. Thankfully, I notice as I whip past a pair of motorcycles and let up on the gas pedal before I get myself a felony speeding ticket and a new set of shackles to my dad.

Caleb's car parked in the visitor spot next to my father's provides some relief. Hating my brother will make for a good distraction, and I just might be able to use him to get closer to my dad. I park on the second level of the garage and stuff the parking ticket in my back pocket, mentally noting to have Allison validate it before I leave. I'm bleeding money today, so I'm going to need to save that twenty bucks for better things.

I stop beside a massive pitch-black SUV to scope out my reflection and check my shirt for wrinkles. I also make sure there are no signs that I've got anything going on underneath my white undershirt—like a shit ton of audio wires. Satisfied that the only thing left to smooth out is the stress wrinkle on my forehead, I head to the elevator and start my box breathing to keep my pulse down. Slow counts of four time every breath in and out, as well as the holds in between, until I'm in the elevator and on my way to my father's floor.

The *ding* when the doors open into my father's office lobby acts as a hard reset for me, and I'm instantly focused on getting what I need. The man loves to talk, and he loves the idea of me finally wanting to give in and fit his mold. All I'll need to do is show a genuine interest in his work, and he'll spill something. I'm sure of it.

I've got this.

My gaze hits my brother's first, then shifts to Allison. The two of them are talking at Allison's desk right outside my father's office, and given the way their spines instantly straighten and their mouths shut, I'd guess they were talking about me.

"Oh, look, you're working today instead of floating down the river with a keg of beer." I figure I may as well beat Caleb to the insults.

He chuckles and stretches his back as if he's yawning and bored of me.

"It's easier taking days off when you're on track to make a shitload of money. But I guess money isn't important to you, huh? I mean, you took the day off, too. Saw you at the lake, with Saylor." He drops that bit just to hook Allison's attention. He doesn't know that she's already tuned in and staring at me with lasers.

"Well, money isn't everything," I say, punctuating it with a smug grin that makes his eyes narrow. I'd love to walk away and let him stew on that, but I also need to do what I can not to completely piss Allison off. I shift my focus to her and fish out the parking ticket.

"Despite what my brother may have you think, I'm here to get my father's expertise on a few things. Money might not be everything, but I wouldn't mind having more of it, and I thought maybe I could get a little savvier on investments."

Allison studies me for a whole second that seems to drag on for an hour. Her deep red lipstick puckers as she chews at the end of her gold pen. She finally slides my parking ticket along her desk and stamps it with the company's logo.

"Here's your get-out-of-jail-free card," she says, sliding it back with her own smug smirk in place. Okay, so maybe she's a little pissed off. I might not be able to charm her the way I did when I was younger, but I'm not going to let her pull a power trip on me, either. I know what this is about. I'm not good enough for her daughter. Well, she's not, either. And if she pushes me too far, I might just let everyone know my reasons for feeling that way.

"Believe me. If there's one thing I've learned, it's that jail isn't free," I say, meeting her gaze. I hold it hostage while I slip the parking validation into my wallet for safekeeping. "Is the big guy in?"

Allison breathes in slowly and glances at Caleb.

"Get in line," she says, nodding toward my brother.

My brother rolls his eyes, which only makes me chuckle. I follow him to the pair of leather chairs outside my father's office. His eyes keep shifting from me to anything else, and after sitting next to him in pure silence for five minutes, I finally start to laugh.

"It bugs you that much that Saylor's into me."

His eyes dim, and his head tilts as he shakes with a single silent laugh.

"She's not into you. You're a rebound. A distraction before college." He almost sounds convinced.

"Maybe," I say, leaving it at that.

Who knows, maybe I am simply filler before Saylor takes off to begin the rest of her life. But also, there's something bigger going on between us. I can feel it. When I'm with her, I like the man reflected in her eyes. I forget the failures that led to this point in my life. I'm suddenly a guy who's making smart choices, who's venturing out and being his own man. It's how I'd like to think of myself, but for some reason, it's always been hard to believe those characteristics until now.

Perhaps I'm inspiring Saylor to go her own way, too. And sure, there's a chance that whatever direction she chooses won't have me in it. But I'm in it now, and it feels damn good to be wanted in whatever way this is. Comfort, I guess?

Our dad's office door swings open, saving my brother and I from having to fill more time with grunts and awkward glares. I get to my feet before Caleb, and it amuses me that my brother scrambles to make sure he reaches our father before I do.

"I don't think you two have been this excited to see me since Christmas morning when I bought you that new gaming console." My dad slings an arm around Caleb and guides him into his office while nodding for me to follow. It's a good reminder of my place in this world.

"We were the only kids at school who had the Firefly 2000," Caleb proclaims.

I open my mouth to point out that the console caught on fire after two weeks and the machine was quickly discontinued for massive patent fraud. But saying so would be antithetical to my spy mission and I snap it shut.

"So, what's the occasion?" My dad sits behind his desk, propping his feet up and folding his hands behind his neck as Caleb and I plunk down on another set of leather chairs. These are much firmer than the ones in the lobby. Nobody is allowed to be too comfortable in here.

My brother glances my way, so I clear my throat and lean forward. Asshole wants to put me on the hotspot. Fine. I'll own it.

My hands clasped, elbows on my knees as I sit forward, I force myself to ignore the squeeze from the band around my chest. This mic has been hot since I got in my car; time to make it capture something worthwhile.

"Well, you've always told me that if I was going to get something out of my business, I needed to look beyond the cars and focus on long-term investments, right?"

My father's mouth ticks up on one side, and his eyes haze, probably with skepticism.

I clear my throat.

"Well, we've had a good couple of months. And I was hoping you could show me the ropes a little, maybe help me invest in some of the things you've got going on?"

My eyes lock onto my father's, and I swear there's a computer in that man's head constantly scanning for danger. Several seconds pass before he speaks, and during that time, he simply stares at me and contorts his face into various expressions of suspicion and doubt.

"If you've had such a good couple months, why don't you pay me back those legal fees and rid yourself of your family obligations?" He pulls open a side drawer and takes out a cigar box, opening the lid to offer one to me and my brother. I shake my head, but Caleb practically dives in for a Partagas stogie.

"Do you even know how to smoke that thing?" I mutter.

Caleb shrugs.

"Sure, I do."

He doesn't. But hearing him cough and choke will be amusing, so more power to him.

My father clips the end of his, then hands the guillotine to my brother. He flails with it for a few seconds but eventually gets his cigar clipped.

"I could pay you back, and yeah, it would save me from your frequent lectures on everything I'm doing wrong. But . . ." I draw in a deep breath for effect.

My dad lights his cigar and takes a few puffs. I don't mind the smell of cigar smoke. It reminds me of my father's home office when we were kids, in our first house, before he had an entire building downtown to go to.

"Those lectures are sinking in a bit, aren't they?"

My father takes the bait, and it requires all my inner strength not to audibly exhale in relief. I waggle my head and glance up, playing the part of the slacker he thinks I am.

"Not all of them, but the money ones . . . maybe a little. Or a lot."

My father laughs out hard and flattens a palm on his desk, and my brother flinches in response. He's been trying to light his cigar for a few seconds. I'm surprised that little stunt didn't make him swallow it.

"Here," I say, taking the cigar from my brother and lighting it for him. It's performative, mainly to show off for my father. A man who can smoke a cigar is a real man, at least in David Anderson's world. I hand the lit cigar to Caleb, and as predicted, he coughs his way through his first puff.

"Lightweight," my dad mutters.

I smirk, but cover my mouth with my palm before laughter slips out.

"So, you finally want to make some real money, huh?" My dad leans to his left and pulls open a file drawer. He snags a dark brown folder and slaps it on the center of his desk, flipping it open and revealing documents that look a whole lot like the ones Mike-Steve showed me in the diner.

"I'd like to, yeah. And of course, I would pay you back the money for the lawyer once I've started earning. If that's how any of this works."

I'm playing dumb. I may not have the fancy college degree he wanted for me, but I have a pretty good handle on finances and investments. It's impossible to grow up in our house and not pick up a thing or two simply from osmosis.

"I appreciate that. But I like seeing you make that money work for you. I'd rather you keep it." He holds my gaze just long enough for his words to not quite sit right. I think he likes having leverage.

I nod, though, and force a faint smile on my lips, playing the part of the eager little boy who is happy to get a gift from dad.

"Okay. Well, can you maybe walk me through this?" I scoot my chair in closer and pull one of the documents toward me.

"Hey, whoa, whoa. Why does he get to invest?" Caleb steps right into the *little brother with a chip on his shoulder* role.

"I'm sorry, did you suddenly have your own money, son?" My father gazes at my brother over the rims of his glasses, the way a fourth-grade teacher does a kid talking in class.

It's hard not to chuckle under my breath when my dad smacks Caleb down. I'm not sure which bad guy I dislike more in this room. But I need to get something going with my dad sooner rather than later, and if my brother insists on whining every time I'm in here, it's going to drag this sting operation out for years. Besides, his name is on those contracts too. I may as well use all the tools in the box.

"I wouldn't be totally against having his input on things. I mean, this is what he wants to do after college. And I know you'd like us to get along better, at least on paper." I shift a heavy gaze from my brother to my dad, playing up the appearance that I'm only trying to please my dad.

Our father chews at his lips and nods slowly.

"It would be nice to see both of my boys' names together on a few things around here, flexing our family prowess, so to speak."

I want to vomit, but this is the kind of sucking up that really gets my dad off. He loves power. Always has.

"This investment, is it the one you recommend?" I flip a few more pages around, and Caleb scoots in, immediately sliding them closer to him.

"This one, or one like it. We have a few hot things in the pipeline. I have a few meetings lined up this week. Maybe you'd like to join me." My father's offer has me nearly kicking my feet.

"I'd like that." I meet his gaze and do my best to reflect something close to admiration. It was naïve to think I'd get him to spill his insider secrets to me today, but this is a good start for sure.

"I can make anything this week," Caleb pipes in.

My molars gnash together, but I show nothing except gratitude on the outside. I have to keep this looking legit.

"Don't fuck this up for me," I say to my brother.

And for once, rather than chastising me, my father simply laughs before getting to his feet and pointing to Caleb as he echoes my sentiment.

"You'd better get used to that kind of demand, son. You're dealing with other people's money. You must make more for them, otherwise you're nothing more than a thief." My father's analogy is a bit ironic, yet it resonates with Caleb as much as every piece of advice our dad shells out to him.

"I know. I'll make him money. Then he can owe me for the rest of his life, too." Caleb's glare lingers on my face for a hot second before my dad moves to his door and opens it, signaling it's time for his prodigies—aka stooges—to go.

"You know, it's brave of you to put your life savings in my control. What if I decide to make it disappear?" Caleb stops at the edge of Allison's desk, probably so they can gossip about me when I leave. I pull my wallet out and ready my parking ticket before heading to the elevator.

"You could, Caleb. That's right. But then, you'd be as big of a fuck-up as I am, and I'm willing to bet you'd rather come out looking like the hero than tanking my pathetic bank account." I shrug, and Caleb huffs out an irritated laugh before flipping me off.

I don't breathe until I exit the elevator, too paranoid about the security cameras in there. There are cameras in the garage too, but I'm not on the executive floor. I'm parked up here with the commoners, so nobody is zooming in on me to see whether my face is panicked, or if my brow is covered in sweat. If they do zoom in, though, well . . . fuck, that's exactly what they'll find.

I climb into my car and wind my way down the garage to the exit, handing over my validated ticket to the guardsman before zipping through the gate and south through a handful of lights before pulling into the parking lot for Min's Hot Buns. I'm one of five cars parked here, and I think the other four are all employees working in the bakery. I unclasp my seat belt and tug my shirt up enough to reach the straps hugging my chest. I exhale loudly as the bands fall away from my body, and I pile the wire and mic into my lap.

I pull the small switch box from inside my waistband and turn it off before falling back into my seat with a deep breath. I close my eyes in relief, but crack a lid when my phone buzzes in my pocket. I wind up the wire in my lap and tuck the device under my seat before checking the alert on my phone.

I expect to see something from Mike-Steve, but I guess that's not the way covert operations go down. Instead, it's a short text from Saylor.

SAYLOR: Is it weird that I missed you today?

She isn't asking me for a thing, yet somehow her words overwhelm me in the moment. What starts as a soft laugh suddenly leads to my eyes tearing up, and my chest growing tight. I wipe them dry with my forearm before clearing my throat and rolling my shoulders to pretend *whatever the fuck that was* never happened. I cradle my phone to text her back.

ME: Not weird at all. I missed you, too.

Of everything I've done today, sending that text scares me most.

Chapter 18

THERE WAS a time in my life when I was excited at the sight of my mom in the bleachers, watching me stand on the starting blocks with her knuckles pressed to her mouth. She used to get nervous in the beginning, but then I started to win a lot. After a few years, she quit standing for my starts. And soon after, she stopped showing up at all.

I'm not sure how to classify the expression she's wearing now. It's somewhere between resentful and disappointed, I think. Wait until I break the news about applying to the social work program instead of the business school.

"I think it's great that you swim with the girls. It really motivates them. You know, they look up to you."

I'm not sure whether my boss, Christen, is being honest or simply buttering me up so I don't quit this summer. It's not as if I have another job waiting in the wings. Plus, I kind of like working with younger swimmers. I like teaching them things, and rooting for their wins, however big or small. We have a meet coming up next week, and I'm a little nervous for them. Like, giddy nervous. Not the anxious type that usually sits heavy in my stomach.

I lift myself from the pool, then slide my goggles up my

head, my tight swim cap muting the background noise. Christen hands me my towel as I turn my back to my mother, who has moved toward the entrance. She's leaning against one of the ticket booths, typing things on her phone. It's her way of subtly rushing me. I don't need to see it.

"I was thinking of getting the girls pizza or something after Friday's practice, for team bonding. They've been working hard."

I hold my breath, waiting for Christen to approve it, and hopefully offer to pay for it.

"That's a great idea, Saylor. They'll love it!" She pats my shoulder as she moves toward the office. At least I got half of what I wanted—permission.

I pull my cap from my head and run my fingers through my wet hair as I turn to face my mom. I hold up a finger, and she winds hers in the air, another sign to hurry up. She didn't love hearing that my car was at Rowan's garage. It's all she talked about—my car. Not a word about me being in his car or kissing him. Her silence on the topic speaks volumes.

I'm tempted to stay in this locker room until they lock up for the night, but the hot water from the shower is already turning me into a prune, so after running the comb through my hair and slipping into my linen shorts and tank top, I make my way out to the parking lot, where my mom is now waiting in her idling SUV.

"I know we planned to get dinner, but if we go to the dealership now, we can pick up your rental." She shifts into drive before I can answer, but eventually the dinging of the passenger seat belt alert gets her attention. She stops at the swim club's exit with her blinker on.

"Saylor, put on your seat belt."

"Uh, I will when we discuss this rental car that I'm suddenly getting? Who's paying for that?" I know she's not, and she knows I can't.

"David takes care of his employees. It's nothing," she says, waving a hand at me. "Now, stop being a child."

"Mom, I haven't been a child for a long time. We don't need David to get me a car!"

"It's only a rental."

I shake my head, glaring at her as she looks away.

"Yeah? Where's that rental from? Mercedes? Lexus?" I know it's something luxury. David wouldn't want to be connected to anything distasteful.

"It's a BMW. Like Caleb's," she finally admits.

I laugh hard and shake my head.

"Absolutely not. I don't want a BMW, Mom. I don't need it. My car is going to be ready in a few days, and I can get by—"

"You expect me to just drive you around?" Her wide eyes are glued open, locked on mine, and I'm left nearly speechless.

"It was one shift. I'll walk tomorrow, or hell, just let me out here and I'll find some cardboard and sleep behind the dumpster so I'm ready for tomorrow's shift. Jesus!" I move to turn my head away, but before I can, my mom's palm lands across my cheek. I cover the hot spot with my own hand and blink my vision back in focus.

"I'm so sorry. Saylor, I—"

I exit the car and slam the door behind me as I march down the sidewalk with no destination in mind. All I know is I can't be here, and I won't get in that car. My mom crawls alongside me, though, with the window down.

"Saylor, I'm so sorry. I've been so stressed. And your car not working has me on edge about sending you up north in a few months. I want to get you a new one, but it's not in the budget right now."

I laugh out without shifting my gaze to her luxury vehicle keeping pace with me. The matte finish of the dark green, the charcoal rims and lift kit for all that off-roading my mom will never do. I know how much those payments are. All so she can fit in with that boy's club. I hope it's worth it.

I halt my steps, and my mom punches her brakes to stop with me, flinging herself forward, along with her purse and phone. Her eyes tic as she glances to her feet where I'm sure her purse has spilled out lipsticks, pens, and business cards by the pedals. I walk toward the open window and my mom reaches toward the handle on the inside, but I press my body against the door before she can push it open.

"I'm not getting in that car with you. Not until you tell me the real reason you're so angry with me."

Her expression morphs into a fake apology, but before she can enact her next performance, she exhales, "Fine." Her gaze drops to her lap as she blinks before popping her attention back to me.

"You're ruining your life. With Rowan. He's bad for you, and it doesn't look good for you that you're doing . . . whatever you're doing with him." Her mouth rests in a stern, straight line.

I laugh almost immediately. If only she knew the things I was doing with Rowan. She'd try to have me committed, I'm sure. But Rowan isn't the one she should be worrying about.

"Did Caleb tell you something about Rowan? Did he say he was worried about me?" I scrunch my nose with distaste. I have a feeling Caleb's in my mom's head with this. Not fully, but at least he's a sous chef to her assumptions.

"He has not, other than expressing his regret for how you two broke up."

I laugh again.

"How he broke up with me, you mean. So he could fuck other girls."

"Saylor!" My mom doesn't like swear words. I wonder what she was like when she was my age, if she was proper even then.

I glance to my right, to the roadway ahead, and the few

stragglers from my class still walking home. It's not *so* far. I could take the bus to the main intersection and walk the rest of the way.

"I think we need to get your car tonight from Rowan's garage. I wasn't going to bring that up until after—"

"Until after you overspent on a BMW rental, then took my car to some place that's going to end up charging us double?" My brow is raised so high, it might meet my hairline.

"Saylor, you're blinded by that kid's good looks. He and his friends aren't really experts, and we need to make sure your car is safe for when—"

"When I go up north and start the social work school?"

Now's as good a time as any. We're in it, so why not push through to the other side of this massive disagreement.

My mom's teeth are pushing together. I can tell by the way her jaw flexes. She finally mutters something, the word "ungrateful" one of the few I can understand as she sweeps her hand around her feet to gather the contents of her purse. She tosses it in the back seat when she's done, then turns her attention back to me.

"Saylor, this is exactly what I'm talking about. You're making terrible decisions, and I'm afraid the longer you hang out with those guys, stealing cars and burning down houses—"

"Ha. You think that's what I'm out doing with Rowan, Miguel, and Jersey? Casing joints, hotwiring cars and lighting matches? Do you know how crazy you sound right now? Besides, Rowan didn't steal that car. The guy who brought it to them left them holding the bag. It was hot before they started to work on it, and then the guy skipped town."

My mom shakes her head, her eyes heavy, and her mouth turned down at the sides.

"Mom, you don't really think Rowan's some criminal, do you?"

She looks down again, knotting her hands together. She's honestly worried about this stuff, about me. But it's not so much me as it is her reputation. I'm too tired to throw that back at her now, though. We'll call this round one.

"I'm not getting a rental. And my car will be ready soon. Just . . . drop me off at Cami's." I open the door and slide inside, buckling up and fixing my gaze to the sidewalk outside. After a few quiet seconds, my mom shifts into drive and makes a U-turn toward Cami's house. She doesn't try to sell me on her opinions for the rest of the drive, and I don't pummel her with all the reasons she's wrong.

I let myself into Cami's back yard through the gate, and I kick off my shoes and dip my feet into her pool, kicking around the top step to keep cool. Cami won't be home for two more hours, and my mom knew nobody was here when she dropped me off. We're both done with each other for now.

Cami's answer to all of life's problems is girls' night. Maybe she's right this time.

My face stings a little less under the dim lights of the Velvet Room. I like clubs like this, where it's less about the dancing and more about the vibe. Plus, they take our fake IDs.

I hit Cami with a dose of word vomit the moment she rolled into her driveway. I figured it would be hard to hide the bruise on my cheekbone. Cami says it doesn't look as bad as it feels, but I don't know. Every time I check it in my phone camera or in the Velvet Room bathroom, it looks like I striped my cheeks with blush the way they did in the eighties in those posters my mom still has in the garage.

"Ladies, two Appletinis," the server says, sliding two bright green drinks onto our tabletop. Cami and I meet eyes then both jet our gazes to the server. She points to a table across the bar, where a familiar guy raises a hand.

"Brady fucking Campbell," I mutter.

"Brady who?" Cami slides her drink closer, then leans forward to take a sip before picking it up. They really topped these off for us.

I sigh and shift in my seat as Brady and his friend, who looks like he could be his older, beefier brother, walk toward us.

"He shoots hoops with Rowan. He loses a lot," I say, leaving out the part where Brady then owes Rowan a bunch of cash. My mom's words are still rattling around my head, and I don't want to put things out in the open that make Rowan sound like the degenerate she thinks he is.

"Where's big brother?" I'm fairly certain Brady's talking about Rowan.

I shrug and glance up at the ceiling, then to the left toward my friend.

"He's around," I say, taking stock of Rowan's words of caution when it comes to this guy. He didn't say he was unsafe, but he didn't exactly brand him with a ringing endorsement.

"And who are you?" His friend looks less like him now that they're both close. He's definitely older, though. My guess is thirty. The guy's wearing all black, from his jeans to the long-sleeved fitted shirt tucked into his too-tight pants. The gold chain with a skull pendant dangling from it is the real kicker to his look, and I wince in anticipation of my friend's incoming evisceration of his fashion sense.

"You get this out of one of those candy machines they keep in the front of Denny's?" Cami taps the metal bauble with her long fingernail, and Brady's friend sneers.

"*Pfft*, fuck this. I'm out, man. I'll get us a table." He wanders toward the back room where a few guys are shooting pool, and Cami waves with her fingers before cradling her drink and smiling through her sip.

"Wow, are all your friends teases like this one?" Brady thinks he's clever. I think he's lucky Cami's not that drunk tonight, otherwise she'd spear his shin with the sharp toe of her Louboutin.

"*Hmm*, Cami's special. I'm pretty sure your friend is just a loser. No offense." My gaze drifts to the side and Brady follows my sightline to his friend, trying to impress another table of girls with his Halloween biker costume look.

"Fair enough," Brady admits. I laugh at his humility, but when he joins in on the laughter, it suddenly feels wrong, like I'm giving secrets to the opposing team.

"Hey, Brady?" I set my drink down and push it toward the center of the table. I'm not drinking more of that tonight. It feels like a bribe. I'm sure Cami will make it disappear for me.

"Yes, Saylor?" I hate that he remembers my name.

"You know Rowan isn't really my brother, right?" I fold my arms over one another and lean back in my seat, my glossed lips pulled into a tight smile.

Brady's low chuckle fades as the seconds pass, and my eyes remain steadfast on his. Finally, he chugs the last of his beer and plops his mug down next to my drink.

"Yeah, I know that. He's a lucky guy, though. Fuckin' . . . luckiest guy I've ever met." He shakes his head and smiles softly, tapping the table twice before taking a step back. "You two enjoy your night. And hey, those drinks are my way of telling Row he's lucky, so enjoy them."

"Will do, buddy," Cami says, tipping the rest of hers back and moving on to mine.

Brady snickers as he turns and heads to the back room where he has a far better chance of looking like the prize while standing next to his friend. I roll my neck and give my friend a warning look. She guzzled that sucker pretty fast. It's a weeknight, and I'm not in the mood to hold her hair back tonight while she tosses her cookies.

"I'll nurse this one," she says, still taking a much bigger sip than I'd like.

I slip my phone out of my crossbody bag to check my messages. There's nothing there, though. My mom usually sends some form of apology after we have blowouts like the one we had. We haven't gone at it like that in a while, though. Not since I mentioned potentially transferring from the private school to the nearby public one my sophomore year. I wanted to see what life was like with a bigger class size, with football games that happened under the lights rather than Saturday afternoons. I wanted to ditch the uniform and maybe try my hand at a shop class. But elite swimmers go to Seton Prep, and David made sure I got in. There is always a reason for me to stay, to stick to her plan.

Nothing's changed.

"You're popular tonight," our server says, sliding another pair of drinks on our table. These are pink, and from the smell, I'd say there's tequila in them.

I quirk a brow.

"What is it?" Cami asks.

"Prickly pear margarita shot," our server says. And just then, I notice the writing on the corner of the cocktail napkin.

Good girl. 007

I glance over my shoulder in time to spot Rowan's broad shoulders pass through the exit. His neck tattoos make him unmistakable, and the hint of his profile just before the door completely shuts kicks my heart into action.

Part of me wants to run to him, to ditch my friend and beg him to take me back to his place. But it's enough knowing he saw me tonight, and he liked what he saw. I take the napkin in my hand and wad it up before Cami sees it, and when our server leaves, I scan the bar as if I'm looking for our mystery drink buyer, just like my friend is.

I take a long sip of my pink drink and remind myself that Rowan and I are probably only a season. We're summer. But damn if there isn't a part of me that wonders if we could be fall and winter too.

Chapter 19

THE NORTH PRECINCT is always quiet. Not a lot of crime happening around golf courses, resorts, and gated communities. At least, not the kinds of crimes beat cops handle. Nope. These crimes are for officers like Mike-Steve, who has the conference room set up for our weekly meeting as if it's just another average Thursday.

"Donut holes. How predictable." I snag one of the powdered ones from the plate at the center of the table.

"People act like cops are the only ones who eat donuts, but maybe it's just a conference table thing. I mean, how many of your dad's board rooms have you been in that had snacks?" He grabs a powdered hole and pops it in his mouth, the sugar dusting the mustache hairs that hang over his top lip.

I snag a cinnamon one and shrug.

"Meh, I don't know," I say while chewing. "Those meetings are more of the charcuterie and brie variety."

We both chuckle and nod.

"Fair," Mike-Steve says.

I clap my hands together a few times to brush off the sugar remnants, then lean back in the wheeled leather chair.

"What are we doing here? I mean, do you still want to

hear about my work week, how I'm looking for places to volunteer, my handle on my supposed anger issues? Or . . ."

His grimace cuts to the point.

"We're on a team. We can talk about your father. I think you made some good progress; seems like he's letting you in. Bad news, though."

My gut twists and my mouth straightens as my shoulders drop.

"Not sure how this pickle I'm in gets worse, but please, tell me." I hold my breath, expecting him to tell me I need to go into hiding or some shit.

"That investment he pulled out for you . . . it's legit. We scoped it out based on the few clues you got for us, and it's not the one we're interested in."

"Fuck," I sigh out.

I look out the glass window that separates this room from the front lobby. The officer working the intake desk is playing one of those games on her phone where she has to stack jewels for points. As stupid and banal as that game seems, I wish I could trade places with her.

"It's still an in with your father, so don't get dejected. You'll just need to get him to talk about other options. See if you spot any clues the next time you're in the office. Maybe linger around a cluttered desk near his office. I'm sure your dad isn't putting together these schemes on his own. A lot of the members of his team are profiting more than they should. Anyone come to mind?"

I breathe in slowly through my nose. Allison is the only person my dad would trust. I still think he's using her, though, giving her just enough praise and autonomy to do his dirty work and get to claim she didn't know any better when the cards fall. Unless, of course, he's putting her name on things the way he is mine.

"You watching Allison Kelly?" I ask him point blank,

because I need to know how fucked up my situation is. His long, silent stare tells me enough.

I shake my head and hold his gaze.

"She's a pawn, if anything."

"Maybe. Maybe not. But I bet her desk or computer has the key to what investment you need to try to horn in on. So, my advice?"

I lift my chin, not really wanting advice but bracing for it.

"Get in good with Allison Kelly."

I nod slowly and manage to keep my mouth shut despite the words flashing behind my eyes on a mental billboard. *So, don't sleep with her daughter?*

"Anything else I should know before being redeployed?" I snicker at my light joke, but Mike-Steve is unamused. I clear my throat and utter, "Sorry."

"He's going to burn you. Your dad. At some point, things are going to get too big for him to contain, and he's going to set up you or your brother, or both of you, to take the fall. Focus on getting in on his next inside trade, and make sure that mic is on anytime you're close to him."

His serious expression is punctuated by the straight line of his mouth. I can't even make fun of his sugar 'stache anymore because he's right. I'm fucked. Even if my dad sells me out, I can't count on the feds to bail me out and blow what's probably been years of investigative work. They'll cut me loose, too.

"Understood." I get to my feet, and Mike-Steve does the same. We shake hands, our firm grip on one another holding for an extra second, a little non-verbal acknowledgement that we are both on board.

I cleared most of my morning for this, not expecting our meeting to be so short. Normally, I'd head right back to the garage to drown my worries in motor oil and filters, but I'm not real hip on hanging out with Mig and Jersey on my own today. Jersey's having relationship trouble, and he's the kind of guy who likes advice, and then to kick that same advice around like a soccer ball for hours on end while I'm trapped underneath a vehicle.

What's one more bad idea?

ME: Need a ride anywhere?

I sit in my car while I wait to find out whether I'll be turning left or right out of this place. When my phone buzzes with Saylor's response, my arms and legs are instantly fueled by nerve zaps and eager energy.

SAYLOR: I'm at Cami's and would love not to be.

ME: On my way.

I grin through the short drive, and I'm excited to see Saylor waiting for me by the curb and still wearing that white tank top and flowy shorts she had on at the bar last night when I went out with Jersey. I didn't get enough time to fully study her, and the way that shirt hugs her body.

"Where to, princess?"

Her brow bunches at my pet name, and I feel a little embarrassed. Fucking *princess?* What is going on with me?

"Just trying it out," I say, clearing my throat and shifting into drive.

"I like it. Just . . . didn't expect it."

Yeah. Me neither.

"Do you need to go home for anything? Swim club for work? Shopping? Please don't say shopping."

Saylor giggles as she buckles up, instantly kicking her sandals off and folding her legs up in her seat. I love how comfortable she is in my space.

"I don't need to be at the pool for a few hours. You need a hand at the garage?" She hikes up a shoulder, and there's a sparkle in her eyes that makes it seem as though she's truly interested in crawling under a car with me.

My eyes crinkle and I grimace, but she's so damn cute that I exhale and give in a second later.

"Yeah, I could use a hand. But one rule—no asking Jersey about his girlfriend." I slice through the air with my flat palm.

"Got it. Jersey and the word *girlfriend* are a hard no."

"*Hard* no," I echo.

I rest my turned-up palm on the console, and Saylor folds her hand into mine. Everything about being with her feels easy. At least, the physical things. It's the part where her mom tangles with my father and the fucking pack of wires and microphone under my seat that's a challenge. But for now, I choose to ignore that part. No red flags to see here. Just a guy who really enjoys spending time with a girl. It's something I didn't think was for me, given the shitty example my parents set. But so far, being with Saylor does nothing but feel right.

The latest Deftones album blasts through the shop's open bay doors as Saylor and I roll up. I park just close enough to the workspace for Mig to notice my car pull in. He's bad at masking his expression, though, first flinching when he spots Saylor stepping out of the car, then covering his mouth to barely hide his laughter. He's acting like an eighth grader who walked in on his best friend's first kiss.

"Hey, man." I nod to my best friend, then tap the toe of my shoe into Jersey's as he lies under a sixty-four Chevy pickup.

"Oh, hey. Company." He rolls out on his board, then pushes up to a sitting position, his gaze bobbing from Saylor to me, then to Mig.

"Relax, she's not here expecting her car to be ready. She's here because—" Mig stops his words the second I hold up a hand.

"She's here to learn her way around an engine since she'll be heading up north in a few months." My eyes lock onto

Mig's for a few seconds, and I do my best with my flexed jaw and tight lips to express how much I'd prefer he keep his mouth shut about Saylor and me.

"Hey, yeah. That's a really good idea, actually. You wanna slide under here and take a look? I'm about to change the oil." Jersey isn't being creepy by trying to hit on Saylor. That's not his style. Just mine, apparently.

She glances at me and nods.

"You should learn how to do this," I encourage.

She grins, then immediately kicks the spare roller board toward Jersey. I grab a clean towel from the bin and toss it to him, and he covers the board before Saylor lies back on it. Wearing all white is a bad idea in a place like this, but my creepy side is rooting for her to get just gritty enough to need a shower. After close. When these dickheads go home.

I drop my phone and keys on the counter and slide up next to Mig while I look on at Saylor's long, golden legs stretched out next to Jersey's oil-stained cargo pants. The only thing more jarring to her mom would be if she came home with a guy like him.

He's shaggy, with a full bear beard and a head of hair that looks like the straw of a scarecrow. His mustache is spotty, and his cheeks always seem to be red. He's one of the kindest dudes I've ever met, but he's a bit chaotic at life. He's been on-again, off-again with his girlfriend for two years, and there's a reason we keep him far away from handling the finances and bills. The guts of a car, though? He's like a walking encyclopedia. And he's a decent teacher, so I don't mind so much that Saylor's knees are mere inches from his. Well, I mind a bit.

"How long you give it before he asks her for advice?" Mig whispers.

I chuckle.

"He's asking right now."

We're both quiet, doing our best to eavesdrop on their conversation several feet away. There's a lot of talk about turning things in certain directions and making sure valves are closed, and then we hear the magic words.

"I don't know why Tess won't talk to me about it."

It's impossible to hold our laughter in. The harder we try, the louder our cackling grows, until finally Jersey pushes out from under the truck and sits up to glare at us.

"You guys are assholes. You know that?" He gets up off his board and moves to the front of the truck. "Saylor, join me up here, and I'll show you the rest."

"Sorry, Jers," I say as he scowls my direction.

"Ignore them. You're right to ask a woman for advice," Saylor says, breaking my gaze with Jersey. Suddenly, all I see is her as she steps up next to him and leans over the engine bay.

A woman for advice.

She is a woman. I think that's what's got me so tangled inside, trying to sort out how this girl who was always just that —a girl—is suddenly the most beautiful woman I've ever seen. Did I just wake up one day and see her differently? Or was my mind opened to having something real with Saylor thanks to a massive grudge against my brother? I suppose, in a way, I have him to thank for all of this. Whatever happens.

Saylor's lips slip into a faint smile as her gaze moves between me and the space where Jersey is tipping the oil canister into the opening. Our friend rattles on the same story he's told us, about how he bought airline tickets for Cabo for Thanksgiving without consulting his girlfriend, not realizing she maybe wanted to spend the holiday with her family. Rather than make fun of him the way Mig and I did, though, Saylor listens and digests his frustration.

"You were trying to be spontaneous," she says.

He stands up straight and lets his head fall back.

"Yes! Exactly!" He waves his free hand at her, then toward me. "She gets it, see?"

I nod, and Mig rolls his eyes and flips open the laptop to pour his attention into the books.

"But is it possible that she was maybe planning on introducing you to her family during the holiday? Did she drop any hints?" Saylor's eyes soften as Jersey sucks in his lips and tightens his jaw.

"Fuck," he finally mutters. "She totally wanted to do that, and I completely missed it."

He slaps his palm on his forehead, and Saylor pulls his wrist away with her hand. I shift my feet, wriggling out the spikes of jealousy that prod my insides.

"Don't beat yourself up. Just be honest. You'd be surprised how sexy that is to a woman." Saylor blinks slowly, and her eyes open on me before shifting back to Jersey.

"You really think so?"

Saylor nods.

"You want to go call her right now?" she asks.

"Kinda. Hey, Row, you got this?" He tilts his head toward the open engine bay.

"Yeah, buddy. I got this. Go on," I say, ignoring Mig's low groan from behind the computer screen.

"Thanks, man. I owe you one!" Jersey says, surprising Saylor with a sudden hug that leaves her to look at me over my friend's shoulder.

"What is this?" she mouths, and all I can do is shrug.

"You know you're totally enabling him. He's never going to get anything done if you keep giving him hall passes," Mig says the second Jersey jets out of the garage toward his truck.

"Yeah, I know. But that's what we do, isn't it? The three of us? We have each other's backs despite all our fucking faults." My gaze lingers on the front of Jersey's truck as his daytime running lights flicker on, and it takes a bump from Mig's elbow into my bicep to snap me out of my daze.

"Hey, you know that I don't hold any of your shit against you, right?" Mig shifts his posture enough to insert himself between me and Saylor, who is still hovering around the truck. I blink a few times and drop my gaze with a nod, not so sure about what he says. I'm a lot to handle. My baggage. My decisions.

"Don't do that," he says, snapping to draw my eyes back up. "You and Jersey, you guys aren't the same. He's a lazy hippie, who is, unfortunately, an electrical genius that we need to have around. You're a genius who was born into a fucked-up family dynamic. Two different circumstances. Not your choice."

"Thanks. But maybe some of the chaos is my choice."

I glance toward the truck, and the girl lifting her body up on her arms so she gets a better look inside a sixty-four Chevy.

Mig leans his elbow on my shoulder.

"Nah, that's not such a bad move. I mean, is she your brother's ex? Yeah. And is she younger than you? Yes. But that girl right there has her shit together a whole lot more than most. Age is a number. And your brother's a dick, no offense."

"No, he's a dick."

We both shake with a quiet laugh.

"Right. Well, then? That decision? It's growing on me. My sister loves her, and Cami's got good taste in people. And you seem happy. That's refreshing."

He tilts his head the other way and steps back from the counter, creating a path for me to head to the truck and join my best mistake.

"I might be a little happy," I mutter as I pass through.

I stop along the opposite side of the engine bay, leaning on my forearms. Saylor lifts her head and falls back to her feet before gathering her hair at the nape of her neck and twisting it into this mysterious knot that somehow stays in place. Her cheeks are pink from spending more time in the pool during the hot afternoons. The outline of her swimsuit shows on her shoulders too.

"You learn anything from Jersey?" I squint one eye as our eyes meet.

"Uh, make sure you put the drain plug back in before you

add the new oil. That's my big takeaway." She twists her lips, and I chuckle.

"Well, that's a key component, so yeah. That's good to know. Wanna help me change the filter?"

She nods, so I wave for her to follow me to the supply racks in the back of the shop. I walk her through every little step, from picking the right filter type to removing the old one and replacing it. I let her put the filter cap back in place when we're done, and she gets a bit of oil on the side of her hand, which she proceeds to wipe across the middle of her shirt as well as her forearm and chin.

"You were so close to making it," I tease, gesturing to the fresh oil stain that's likely ruined my favorite shirt of hers.

"Aww, damn." She pulls the center of her shirt out from her stomach and heads toward the towel bin. I stop her before she makes things worse, though, grabbing my sweatshirt from the hook by the counter.

"I'm convinced you did that on purpose just to get one more article of clothing out of me," I laugh out.

"I was missing a piece of winter wear."

She dangles my sweatshirt on a finger and heads toward the hallway, probably for the bathroom. I slide up to sit on the counter just as Mig finishes reconciling our books. His gaze passes me, and I catch the tight smirk on his lips as he stows the laptop in the safe below the counter.

"What's that for?" I have a hunch, and I'm sure my hot cheeks give my inkling away.

"It's sweet, is all, seeing you goofy and shit. You really like that girl." He taps the center of my chest with his fist and moves toward the open bay doors to wait for our next client.

I follow him and lean against the outside wall, bending a knee and flattening my foot against the tan stucco exterior.

"What's coming in next?" I didn't bother to look too closely at the day's docket. I figured I'd still be at the precinct right now.

"Get this. You know that band they're playing a lot lately on the alt channel, Killer Mongoose?"

I shake my head because I don't listen to anything Mig doesn't introduce me to. I'm too busy treading water just to breathe. I don't have spare minutes to spend on music apps, and if it's not on my phone playlist, it's not getting heard.

"Right, well, they're about to blow up. Anyhow, they're in town for a gig, and . . ."

I shift my posture, straightening my spine and drying my suddenly sweaty palms in my pockets.

"I guess a few of the guys are from the area, so it's like a homecoming show and shit. And the lead guitarist has this seventies Ford pickup, with original olive-green paint. And—"

"Fuuuuuuck," I breathe out, closing my eyes and tilting my head back.

"I mean, yeah. Olive green isn't everyone's taste, but—"

"No, that's not it. I know the truck. I know the guy." I peek back inside the garage, to the back rooms where Saylor is still stripping out of her shirt and putting on one of mine. Just in time for her dad to pull up in the same fucking truck I helped him pack when he ended his marriage and left her mom.

"Yeah? His name's Jason something . . . I can look." Mig starts to walk back to the desk, but I touch his shoulder, stopping him.

"It's Jason Kelly. Saylor's dad."

I study my friend's movement; his slow pivot as he mentally puts together the little pieces I shared with him years ago. Mig's always been the one person I could talk to. I've had to hold so many things inside, alone, that when something had to give, I shared the details of Saylor's dad finding out about her mom's affair with my dad . . . at the same time I found out.

"Oh . . . shit." His wide eyes probably mirror mine. My stomach churns, and my mouth feels bone dry.

I couldn't tell Caleb back then, because the less he knew

the better. That fact still stands. And I didn't want to blow up Saylor's life. I still don't. I figured I'd be able to handle a short meet and greet, maybe even a dinner with her dad during his gig. I've been mentally preparing for it. But I'm not ready now. Especially knowing that he must realize I'm one of the owners here. His visit feels suddenly intentional. And it's beginning . . . right . . . now.

"Is that—" Saylor steps through the back doorway and points out toward the lot where a familiar classic F-250 crawls to a stop.

"Daddy!" She rushes toward the truck just as the driver's door opens. My feet, however, are set in cement. Jason Kelly still looks like a biker, though his dark hair and well-trimmed beard are a lot more stylish than when he left. His broad chest maxes out his T-shirt, and I'm not so sure which of us I'd pick in a fight.

"Like I said, it was nice seeing you happy . . . while it last- ed." Mig slaps my back and heads toward our next client. While I dislodge my tongue from my throat.

Chapter 20

I'M INSTANTLY TRANSPORTED to my eighth birthday, my dad swinging me around while I hang on to his neck, a giddy girl happy to see her dad and ready for her birthday cake. My birthday may be a few months from now, but this gift is better than any cake I'll have.

"Why are you here?" It's hard to speak through my wide grin, but I manage as he sets my feet back on the ground. He looks good. Healthy, maybe dressed a little nicer than normal. His band is doing well.

"We had an extra day built in, and since we're still rag-tagging across the country in our own cars, I thought maybe I'd get Nancy checked out by a hot new classics shop I've been hearing about." His gaze drifts over my shoulder. I twist my head and find Rowan a few feet behind me, hands shoved in his pockets and his modest smile pushing dimples into his cheeks.

"Nancy's the truck, by the way," I explain to Rowan. He nods.

"I remember." Stepping forward, Rowan pulls his hands from his pockets, then runs his palm across the front of his shirt before reaching out to shake my father's hand.

"Good to see you, Rowan. This is quite the enterprise you've started." My dad nods toward the sign perched above the open bay doors that reads Old 66 Restoration. It's an homage to the classic route, which runs through the northern part of the state.

"Things are going well. Just gotta keep feeding it, ya know?" Rowan holds his palm at his brow to shade his eyes from the sun as my father nods.

"Yeah, that's the secret. I know a thing or two about feeding the passion, little by little," my father responds.

The two of them exhale with easy laughter, and my chest swells with a comforting warmth. My two favorite men seem so good together. I suck in my top lip when I realize I've put Rowan on par with my father. It feels right, though.

"Mr. Kelly. It's good to see you." Miguel steps up, shaking my dad's hand. The three of them spend the next few minutes sharing mutual praise—my dad for their entrepreneurial spirit, and them for my dad's growing music success. I step back to watch and listen, feeling as though the people I'm surrounding myself with are the right ones.

"Let's pull her in and take a look," Miguel says, holding out his hand to take my father's keys.

"You can sit in here with me," I say, waving my hand over my shoulder to encourage my dad to follow me into the garage.

I round the counter and snag two cold water bottles from the fridge, handing my father one as he nestles into one end of the deep-cushioned sofa while I sink into the other, folding my legs up so I can face him.

"You work here now or something?" He glances down at my sweatshirt—well, Rowan's sweatshirt. I tuck my chin and note the garage's logo on the upper right side of the front.

"Oh, I had to borrow a shirt. I had an oil incident." I don't know why I didn't think through the optics of me being here, but I can't imagine wearing an oversized sweatshirt that's clearly not mine hasn't raised my dad's suspicions.

"And what was the incident?" My father turns his head as Rowan walks up. I swallow hard, suddenly lost for words.

"We did a little oil change lesson. Saylor wants to learn the basics before she heads off for college." Rowan's answer is perfect, and I exhale and smile back at my dad, playing the part of a good daughter simply trying to do the right thing. He seems to buy it, too, because he raises his water bottle for a toast.

"Hey, cheers to that!" My dad leans to his side and points to the other side of the classic Chevy, where my car's hood remains propped open, waiting for new parts. "So that *is* your Toyota, then."

"Yep! Needs an alternator," I proclaim, as if I know exactly what that is.

"Ah. You guys giving her a fair price?" my father asks before taking another sip from his bottle. His gaze settles on Rowan, and my lungs burn with sudden stress. He's still suspicious.

"Friends and family discount," Rowan says, waggling his head. "So . . . free. Yeah. Doing it for free."

Rowan glances behind him, and I think he's making sure Miguel is still behind my dad's wheel. I wouldn't mind paying at least some of the cost. I don't want Rowan to hide things from Miguel.

"That's a mighty kind gesture. I always knew you were a stand-up guy." My dad's gaze lingers on Rowan for a hint too long, and my legs feel restless amid the growing tension.

I get to my feet and move to the other side of the counter. It might be good to have shelter if this questioning gets any more serious. Thankfully, Miguel calls Rowan over to check out something on the engine, and my dad pulls his phone out and begins firing off a few texts. Everyone is busy with their own things, so I take the opportunity to slip back into the bathroom where my phone and ruined shirt are.

My dad is pacing near the bay doors when I rejoin them, so I tuck myself back into the corner of the sofa and split my attention between my dad and Rowan. My father's conversation lasts a few minutes, but when he ends his call, he lingers by the garage entrance, finally calling out to Rowan to join him.

"Be right there," Rowan hollers over the low hum of my dad's truck engine. He and Miguel exchange glances, and Rowan only briefly looks my way before snagging a clean towel and wiping off his hands on his way out to meet my dad.

I do my best not to look obvious, propping my phone on my knees as I watch a video. My eyes are really focused on the conversation several yards away, though. All I can do from here is read body language, and the fact my dad isn't grabbing Rowan's collar or punching him in the teeth is a good sign. There's a lot of nodding on Rowan's part, his gaze lifting periodically to meet my dad's before lowering his head again for more nodding. Eventually, my dad places a hand on Rowan's shoulder, where he pats a few times before squeezing and pulling Rowan in for a short hug.

I scan both of their expressions for more clues when they step back into the garage, but they're both impossible to read. The fact that Rowan seems eager to remain by my dad's truck, though, with his back to me, is a pretty good signal that he's trying to maintain a certain level of decorum between us.

I'll simply have to work the clues out from my dad.

"Are you ready for the fall semester?" My dad's moved back to the sofa and crosses his legs, propping a foot up on his knee, exposing the skull socks I mailed him last Christmas. I smile at the sight, and he follows my gaze. "Oh, yeah. I wear them all the time. They fit my personal brand."

I laugh softly, loving that he recalled my note to him in the package. That's precisely why I bought them for him. While their band isn't necessarily rock, my dad's heart has always leaned toward the grittier side of the industry. I thought the skulls were a nice little rebellion for a folk-rock band.

"You're avoiding the school question. Saylor?" he prods.

I grimace. I might be avoiding it a little.

"I guess I'm ready. I'm not exactly doing backflips for it, though." Other than Rowan, my dad is the only person I've mentioned my lackluster emotions about swimming in college to. I've also texted him about my frustrations with Mom, to which he always redirects me to sit down with her and have an open and honest conversation. I'm not sure if he remembers exactly how difficult doing that with mom is.

"You can always try it for a year. Maybe you owe it to yourself to see how it feels when you're in it, you know?" He pounds his fists together for emphasis.

"I told Mom I want to study social work."

My dad's brow jets up to his hairline, and he chuckles.

"Oh? And how did that go?"

My head falls to the side.

"I think you know exactly how that went."

"She'll come around," he replies, but all I can do is puff out a short laugh.

"We'll see."

A strained silence settles between us, but it's not long before my father feels it.

"So, it's over for good between you and Caleb, huh?" My dad's gaze drifts toward Rowan, at least I think it does. Maybe I'm reading too much into things.

"Oh, that's definitely done. He and I are in different places. And I'm so fine with that." Even if Rowan weren't in the picture, I'd feel relief at not being tied to Caleb anymore.

"It's good you know who you are. And things with Rowan and you aren't weird? What with the breakup, I mean."

My insides spike with adrenaline, but I fight to maintain a

calm exterior, blinking slowly before bringing my gaze back up to meet his. I shake my head and twist my lips, uttering, "Nah. We're fine."

His eyes narrow a hint, his brow lowering the way it does when he's putting me through the famous Jason Kelly litmus test. I might need to sell this harder.

Scrunching up my nose, I glance in Rowan's direction, then back to my dad.

"I don't think Rowan likes his brother very much. So in a way, he's on my side."

My dad chews at the inside of his mouth, nodding after a torturously long second.

"Uh huh." His mouth curves the tiniest hint, but I hold my ground, mentally yelling at my facial muscles to stay locked and steady. "Well, that's good then, I guess. You two seem like you've become . . . friends."

Fuck.

I nod my way through to the end.

"We have."

If I keep this up the entire time the boys are checking out my dad's truck, I'm going to end up running back to the bathroom in stomach distress. Rather than torturing myself, I shift the topic to the one thing I know my father will get lost in for as long as I need him to—music. More pointedly, *his* music.

After twenty minutes of explaining the second leg of his band's tour schedule to me, my dad pulls out his phone to play me a few of their recent live recordings. I've heard most of them from the live streams they post on social media, but I pretend they're brand new to me anyway. I think my dad gets as much joy showing off for me as I always have for him.

Sometimes, I wish I had spent my high school years taking classes online and living on the road with my dad. He always said I'd get bored, but I don't know. I picture myself existing in the stories he tells, and I always see a place for me. I know the reality isn't very practical, but I'm so tired of reality. So tired of rules. Plans. Expectations.

An hour in the garage with him flies by, and I'm disappointed when the slam of his truck hood breaks up our good time.

When my dad gets to his feet, I scramble to mine, overcome with panic that he's leaving. I'm fully aware that he's here for two more days, and that I'm seeing him again on Saturday, but that suddenly doesn't feel like enough. I snuggle in at his side and he loops his arm around my shoulders, hugging me as we stroll toward his idling truck. When he kisses the top of my head, I'm instantly transported to years ago, when I was Daddy's little girl.

"Well? What's the verdict?" My dad bends an ear closer to the hood, then chuckles.

"Yeah, these things are tanks. They sound the same even when they're not running like a river of honey," Rowan says. It's a strange analogy, and my dad and I snort laugh in sync.

"Does that mean I'm not driving a river of honey?" my dad asks, shaking his head.

"No, no. I'd say your honey is just right. The river is full," Rowan says, sticking with this comparison. *Way to commit.*

"Well, that's good. Now, tell me, what do I owe ya?" My father pulls his wallet from the back pocket of his deep gray jeans, but Rowan waves the offer off. Miguel doesn't protest, either.

"Oh, come on. You can't keep giving away friends and family discounts to everyone. I'm doing pretty well now. I insist." My dad holds out a gold credit card, but Rowan rests his hand over my dad's, pushing it down as he shakes his head.

"Your money's no good here," Miguel adds.

My dad's gaze bobs between the two, his tongue held at the edge of his teeth. He finally leans his head to the side and utters, "All right." He slips the card back into his wallet and shakes Miguel's hand before stepping toward Rowan.

"I meant what I said. You're a good man for that. I'm proud of you, what you've got going here." My dad's eyes lock on Rowan's for a beat before he brings him in for a short hug. Rowan's hands struggle with where to rest, his fingers barely grazing my father's back as he embraces him. I don't think Rowan's father has ever hugged anyone, and that makes me sad.

"Thank you, sir."

Rowan's gaze flits from my father's face the second after they break apart, and he immediately begins cleaning around the shop while I hug my dad once more and remind him to save me the best seat in the house for Saturday night.

"Two of them," I add as he gets into his truck. I glance over my shoulder, where Rowan is nervously buzzing around the space. My dad follows my gaze and chuckles, but his laugh is short, and his expression instantly morphs into one of caution, his mouth tight and nostrils flared.

"Just don't lose yourself, Saylor. Okay?" He studies my face for a moment as I nod slowly, promising him I won't. I hang in the spot I'm in as he reverses slowly, rolling up his window by hand, then holding up an open palm as a silent goodbye.

Miguel's already buried himself behind the counter again, slipping the laptop back out from the safe while Rowan runs a broom over the slick garage floor. The place is spotless, so unless he has some strange superpower that lets him see invisible dirt and grime, I'd say this is classic avoidance. We haven't defined what we are, and it's only been weeks, but I believe our connection is something more than two young people passing time. I want to believe that because the thought of not having Rowan in my life this way —with the closeness we've built—hurts. I don't want to go back to our roles from before—childhood friends, the little sister with a crush on her babysitter. I like being a woman in his eyes.

I reach for the broom handle as he moves past me, and he stops his strange, manic behavior when our eyes meet.

"Hey," I hum.

A guilty smile tugs at the corners of his mouth.

"Yeah, I know. That was harder than I thought it'd be, is all." He glances at the open doors, where my father's truck just pulled away.

I touch his chin, nudging him to drop his gaze to me.

"I think he's fine with it, with us. He didn't come out and say it, but it's clear he knows. And he wasn't angry." My right shoulder scrunches up as Rowan's head falls back with his faint laughter.

"Saylor, he's your dad. He's not okay with anyone. And I'm not so sure he's okay with me. But he didn't threaten to kill me or anything, so I guess—"

"What did he say?" I ask, still burning with curiosity over their conversation by the garage doors.

There's a distinct pause in Rowan's breath, and a stutter in our connection as his gaze darts around me for a tick before finally settling back on my eyes. His smile is clearly forced, his lips tight and stretched wide the way a child would draw a smiley face.

"He said he was proud of me for going out on my own, for not taking the easy route and working for my dad." His mouth snaps right back to the curated smile, and I can't help but feel my father said more. But I can tell by the way Rowan's eyes dim that whatever else my father said to him isn't ready for my ears yet, at least not through him. Maybe whatever my dad said is still being processed.

"I know you've got work soon, but after work . . . would you like to come with me to see my mom?" Rowan's mouth pinches, and I feel like there's a glossiness in his eyes.

His sudden, drastic pivot jars me, and I have to shake my head to refocus mentally.

"Wow, I . . . yeah. I'd love that," I say, placing a hand on the center of his chest and standing on the tips of my toes to press a soft kiss to his lips while Miguel isn't looking. "Thank you for asking me."

Rowan holds my gaze as I fall back to my heels, his hand moving to the side of my face as his thumb runs along my bottom lip. His gaze follows his touch, moving back to my eyes again once his hand falls away.

"I want to share things with you. Honesty is sexy, right?" A guilty wince crinkles his eyes, and the fact he locked that little nugget from me away hits my chest with a heavy thud.

"The sexiest," I add, tugging twice on the center of his shirt.

He holds my stare, sucking in his top lip. I let my hand trickle down his chest before moving back to the comfort of the sofa.

"I really hope so."

The whisper is faint, and I'm not entirely sure Rowan actually spoke. By the time I descend into the sofa cushion, he's already returned to sweeping invisible lines along the glossy floor. He slows when he reaches the spot where he spoke privately to my dad, and though the truth has never scared me before, the threat of it now makes me a little uneasy.

Rowan

Chapter 21

"I WANT *you to know I appreciate you, Rowan. You were just a kid when I left. And I always thought it was shit that you walked in on the same thing I did. A kid shouldn't see the guy he idolizes, his father, being so disrespectful to his mom.*"

I've been replaying my conversation with Saylor's dad since the moment we spoke at the shop. I don't know that a day has passed that I haven't thought about the moment he mentioned. All the shitty things that have happened in my life seem to have been born that very second.

It was my fork in the road, all because I decided to go to the office with my mom to take my dad his favorite takeout while he worked late one night. Caleb was busy with video games and didn't want to go. My basketball practice had been cancelled, and I could have stayed home with him, but there was something about my mom's expression, a sadness that dimmed the light in her eyes and kept her mouth from forming anything other than a frown. Looking back, I realize she already knew. It would be easy to blame her for letting me tag along, but I think on many levels her mind was broken as much as her heart.

I've never blamed her for any of it. Not for the choices I

made after, nor the lawsuits she filed against our dad to get her fair share, though his lawyers managed to work those deals in his favor. Not even for leaving us in that house with him. He wasn't physically abusive, and he rarely parented, passing duties off to Gitte, our housekeeper. Mom was starting over. She wanted us to stay in our school, to get the private education she felt our dad owed us. She wanted me to have that basketball team around me, and the chance to play in college if I wanted.

No. I didn't blame her then, and I don't now. But I sure blame my dad. It's his fault I hold people at arm's distance. When people look at me, I fear they see how similar he and I are. When Saylor stares into my eyes, I'm afraid she sees my father's colors, his nose, the shape of his chin. And if she finds out the truth about how he ruined her life, drove away the parent she leaned on when she needed him most, I would understand if she saw the devil when she looked at me, too. Because that's what my father is—the devil. And I'm his son.

I kept the truth about her parents' rift a secret for her sake at first, and my brother's. I did it because her dad asked me to. But now that we've grown closer, now that I've started to fall for her, that secret has been burning a hole through my chest. It's haunted my dreams, like a threat waiting in the shadows to steal my happiness. I've kept my mouth shut these past few weeks for me. Because I'm selfish, and I don't want Saylor to know the kind of man who made me. He's rotten in so many ways. And if she looks at me and sees him, it will break me.

But now, I may not have a choice.

"I was angry back then when I left. Disappointed in my wife, for sure. Angry at your dad, because of his abuse of power. Mad at myself for being so blind to it all. I didn't want to drag things out, make a spectacle. I didn't want Saylor going through that shit, or you and Caleb. Your family has had enough constant scrutiny as it is. But you've all grown up. And the band is doing well. We just need that extra push. We want to

stay indie, but it requires investments. And I think we both know your dad owes me."

Jason Kelly added a stop to his band's tour, not to see his daughter, but to cash in. And hearing him say those words tore me up from the inside out, because the moment my spiral began is the very same one that started his. And if Saylor finds out the truth from long ago over some post-concert dinner she thinks is meant to be a special reunion, it's going to leave a mark—the kind that sends a life spinning and changes dreams, breaks trust, and closes off hearts.

So I'm going to tell her the truth first. All of it. Even the things her dad doesn't know. I'm going to give her complete power over me. And I can't rip the Band-Aid off fast enough.

It's a testing day for her swimmers, and it's hard not to draw comparisons of the ones who leave the water with the best times to their coach. Saylor always finished first, not just when a medal was on the line, but when it came down to a stopwatch at practice. She could have made the team coasting, coming in as a top three time. But that was never good enough for her. She says she's over the competition, but I think she's shifted her focus to backing others on their way to success.

The last swimmer to finish today's freestyle rounds rests at the edge of the pool, disappointment weighing down her bottom lip and red eyes. These kids are twelve, a hard age to handle pressure and expectations. It's the eager parents on the sidelines who make it hard. Their words aren't always supportive. Frankly, they're often not nice. This girl's mom just finished shouting, "I told you to put in more practice. That's what you get."

Reminds me of my father.

Saylor squats at the side of the pool, tilting her clipboard to the side and tracing her finger along a series of numbers. I'm not sure what she's saying, but her sad swimmer seems to be finding her grit. It's not a big smile, but it's a present one. And by the time the girl lifts herself out of the water, she's nodding and pounding knuckles with her coach.

"You're so close," Saylor says as the girl heads toward the locker room with energy in her step. Saylor glances toward the loud parent next, and stares at the woman long enough to make her feel the heat. The woman busies herself with her phone after a few seconds, and if anyone recognizes this avoidance move, it's me. I do it. My dad does it. Caleb, too. Yet one more thing we all have in common.

"You're really good with them," I say to Saylor as she slides her sunglasses to the top of her head on her way toward me.

She sits on the bench beside me and takes the half-filled water bottle from my hand, guzzling the rest down as she squints with one eye open on me.

"I hate the armchair coaching from parents. Not every kid is good at tuning out the extra noise. That girl's gonna be just fine. So, she won't be a freestyle swimmer. Her butterfly is strong. Her mom should hop in and let me time her."

I chuckle at Saylor's rant. She's lit, for sure.

"Sorry," she says, wincing. "I just care about these kids, I guess."

"I know you do."

Her eyes shift to mine, and we lock gazes for a few quiet seconds. It feels nice, and an instant understanding accompanies our silence. She likes helping people. I love that about her.

"Give me five minutes to get dressed, then we can head to your mom's," she says, getting up and tossing the now-empty water bottle toward a blue recycle container. She sinks the shot, and I raise my hands and let out a hushed, mock crowd noise.

"Probably the first shot I've ever made. We aren't all hoops stars." She shakes her head at me as she walks backward, and I hold my tongue because I'm no star either, but I kind of like that she sees me as one.

I head to the car to get the air on . . . and to find my courage. The next several minutes are going to be heavy, and the selfish beast inside is tearing away at my resolve, begging me not to blow the best thing that's ever happened to me. That's what Saylor is. She's a future. A confidant. Someone to love and feel loved with. And for once, I think I may deserve it. But not unless she knows about our families' histories, and the ugly places they intersect.

Her hips sway with her joyful steps as she waves goodbye to her coworkers and skips toward my car. I take a deep breath and push my smile into my cheeks. She smells like chlorine and that vanilla shampoo she uses after she swims. Her hair is down, the wet waves sticking to the bare skin of her arms. She's wearing a green halter dress that screams summer, the top hugging her breasts and the short skirt high above her knees as she sinks into the passenger seat. I hunger to run my hand over her thigh and travel to heaven between her legs, but I don't deserve that yet. It's time to share my darkness with someone, fully and completely. And Saylor is that person. *My* person. I hope.

"You look really nice," I say, sucking in my top lip.

She gives me a coy smile as she buckles up.

"Why, thank you. I thought you might like this dress. I know green is your favorite color." She shrugs off my compliment, but I hold my gaze on her for a beat, wondering how the hell she knows that.

"What? I mean, it's only the color of every birthday cake my mom ordered for you, and despite all the gray and black shirts in your closet, there are a few colors that pop out, like the green hoodie I've been eying."

I shake my head and laugh.

"Don't you dare steal my Notre Dame hoodie. I found that thing in a bar two years ago and it's my favorite sweatshirt." I shift into drive and roll out of the lot, baffled at the details she notices.

"What other things about me do you keep locked away?"

I glance at her before turning onto the main road. I'll be stopping at the burger shop up ahead to grab a late lunch-early dinner for us before we head to my mom's. It's where I plan to bare my secrets, and I hope she'll still be in the car after I'm done speaking. I deserve the rush of new love and infatuation for a few more minutes.

"*Hmm*, well . . . you grind your teeth when you sleep. You should probably get one of those mouthguards," she says, narrowing her gaze when our eyes meet.

"Right, well, I did know that, and a guard is not happening. I've tried. Chewed right through six of them."

My jaw constantly aches from the work my mouth apparently does at night. I know it's stress. It started happening the day I walked in on my dad and her mom. But maybe I'll finally stop hurting myself at night after today. Time will tell.

"Fair enough," she says, a softness touching her eyes. She knows a thing or two about stress.

"So, I'm ruining my teeth. What else?" I need more. My courage is wavering, but she's the heart of what makes me brave. The way she sees me. Everything big and small.

"Okay, how about this? You save all your old IDs and licenses. I've checked out your wallet, and I think it's cute that you hang on to your worst photos from your past."

I wince as I mentally riffle through the images she's seen. My hair has not always been agreeable, and there have been a few photos that look much like the mugshots I've also had taken.

"Relax, I thought they were all pretty cute. Especially the one from eighth grade."

"Oh, God," I laugh out, pinching the bridge of my nose as my face warms. I definitely had a mullet in that one. And not the cool kind.

I suck in a quick breath at the cool touch of her hand on my bicep, and it fills my lungs. I meet her gaze as we pull to the stoplight.

"I mean it. You were cute then. Cute now. Always cute." Her cheeks blush with her sweet compliment, and I think she's a little embarrassed admitting her crush to me.

"Okay, anything else? Did you round up any embarrassing rejection letters from crushes I had in junior high?" I chuckle, but she shakes her head and presses on.

"Nope, none of that. I was too busy locking away the sound of your voice when you hum while you work, and I think I've figured out your favorite Stones song. You like Wild Horses, don't you."

My mouth hangs open in a surprised smile.

"I do. And I didn't know I hummed that loud."

"It's not loud; I just listen to you. I like how you breathe, how you laugh. I love it when you're excited and talking trash on the court when you play ball. I love it when you talk dirty to me. I also love the way your eyes close when you turn over an engine you've been working on. You smile when it sounds right. And you nod when you eat something you like. You have a thing for dark chocolate. You nibble on the candy in the bowl by Mig's computer all the time. And you have a loyalty streak that you wear boldly, and clear-cut integrity. You love your brother despite his massive flaws."

"*Massssssive*," I echo, soaking in every overwhelming thing she's said.

"You're an easy guy to fall for." She sucks in her lips, her smile fighting to burst.

She stopped short of saying she's in fact fallen, but I think she has. I have. And I can't wait to tell her all the things about her that made it easy just the same. But first, I must tell her why she should run from me, and all the pain I'm going to remind her of from this moment on.

I pull into the burger joint's lot, and Saylor shifts in her seat. I park rather than drive to the window, because I'm not sure if I should level her with the hard truth now or wait until her stomach is full. I'm not sure what the polite order of events is in this case.

Saylor unfastens her seat belt and grabs her door handle, eager to head inside, but I can't seem to peel my hands from the steering wheel. She has the door open a few inches when she notices, gazing back at me over her shoulder. Her eyes are pained with sudden worry, the little dents that form above her brow evident. God, my expression must look like I'm about to be ill.

"Are you okay, Rowan?"

I shake my head. Here goes my life.

"Saylor, we need to talk." My lips are quivering with nerves, and my face feels numb. "Oh, God. I'm going to be sick."

I pop open my door and lean out, vomiting acid and coffee onto the pavement. The sour taste matches the ache in my chest, and when Saylor's palm runs up my spine to comfort me, I shiver.

"Rowan, Oh, my God! Hold on, I'll get you some water. We don't have to go anywhere today. You need to rest."

I cover her hand on my shoulder and groan out, "No. Stay. I'll be fine."

I hope I'll be fine. I hope *we're* fine.

"Okay," she croaks, her hand falling away from my body as she shifts back.

The click of her door tells me she's settled back inside, so I breathe in deeply and straighten myself behind the wheel so I can close mine. My head swivels toward her as if my neck is a rusty hinge. The corners of my mouth pull downward toward my chest, and the heaviness of my eyelids makes me want to close them. To sleep. *To avoid.*

"I saw your dad the day he left your mom."

I simply have to start. Saylor flinches slightly at my words, but she steadies herself, breathing in deeply through her nose and rolling her lips together before nodding.

"I helped him load his truck. It was midnight, and you were asleep. Your mom was gone, even though she tucked you in. She left so your dad could go quietly."

Saylor's lips part, and her eyes begin to water.

"Did my dad do something?" she whispers.

"Oh, no. I'm not telling this well, because I'm scared. But no, Saylor. Your dad didn't do anything. Your mom did. She did the worst thing." My brow draws in so tightly my face feels folded. "With my dad. The two of them were having an affair. And I found out when your dad did because I was there. He had suspicions, I guess. So, one night, when my mom and I decided to surprise my dad at the office with dinner, we walked in and found the two of them together."

"Together?" She shakes her head erratically, as if she's trying to comprehend the word.

"They were having sex on his desk. And I could give you the details if you want, because believe me, they are burned in my mind forever. But I don't think you want them."

She shakes her head and croaks, "I don't."

I nod and inhale slowly, bracing myself for all that's still to come.

"Your dad was about two minutes behind us, so thankfully, he didn't see the act, but he witnessed the ugly fight between my parents, and he found your mom in tears and still in a state of . . . undress."

Saylor waves her hand between us, stopping me from painting more of a picture.

"I went to your house while my mom packed up her jewelry

and clothes. I wanted to . . . fuck, Saylor, I wanted to see you. I wanted to somehow protect you from it, I guess. I thought maybe I could come up with some story to tell you that would make life okay when you woke up in the morning and your dad was gone. But your dad already had things handled. He thought of you first. He and your mom agreed on the story they'd tell. They didn't want to dress it up, but they wanted the appearance of any other divorce for you. Two people who simply weren't the right fit."

"Ha, yeah. Well, that's what they were. To the extreme, it seems." Bitterness comes out in her tone.

"I'm sorry, Saylor," I stutter out.

Her eyes lift to meet mine, a strange look of surprise in them. She shakes her head.

"Why would you be sorry?"

My shoulders lift to my ears.

"I don't know. Because I didn't tell you the truth then, or any time over the eight years since. Because I kept it from you, and it was such a big part of your life. Maybe you would have pushed to move in with your dad if you knew. You deserved to have the facts, even if you were a kid."

Saylor leans across the console, bracing on her elbows with her hands circling my forearm. She drags my arm toward her and splays my fingers to grasp my palm. My gaze fights to meet hers, and when it does, I find so much forgiveness in her eyes.

"Saylor, I'm so sorry," I say, swallowing down the weight of everything still to come, the hard part still waiting to be shared.

"You wanted to protect me, Rowan. And you still do. You weren't the one who made the choice to betray our family. And you aren't your father, so stop going there in your head, because I know you are. You aren't him. He's part of your genetic code, sure, but that man . . . he isn't your heart. Not even close." She lifts a hand to my cheek, running her thumb along the two days of beard growth I haven't had the energy to shave. I close my eyes and press into her touch, turning enough to kiss her wrist.

I'm still shaking, my lips trembling, because the hardest words are sitting on my tongue. I blink my eyes open and take her hand back in mine, meeting her gaze and breathing through the death-grip my nerves have on my chest.

"That's not all," I utter.

Her lips part slightly with a short gasp.

"I went to the beach house that night, with my mom. Caleb was at home asleep, just like you. And I was so confused and angry. I wanted to be with my mom, so when she got in the car to drive away, I pounded on the passenger window until she relented and let me in. We drove all night through the desert, and we were exhausted when we finally got to the house. I fell asleep on the couch. My mom busted into the wine and went upstairs. I don't know how many hours we slept, but I woke up to my mom shaking my arm and pulling me to my feet because the room was filling with smoke."

Saylor shakes her head slowly, and I drop my gaze for one final gut check. I have to say the words out loud . . . to *someone*. My eyes flit back to hers.

"My mom set the fire. She burned that place to the ground. But I couldn't let her go to jail for it. That wouldn't have been right. So, when the investigators started asking questions, I confessed. I didn't tell her I was going to do it. I didn't have much of a plan. I just knew that I could handle the punishment, and my mom . . . she'd been punished enough. So I confessed, and when she tried to make me change my mind, I refused. I fought her on it so hard. I begged her to let me. And she was so scared, so fucked up from everything that happened, she gave in and let me make the call. I know she beats herself up for it still, so every time I see her I remind her that it was my choice. I was a kid, yeah. Maybe. But I was also pretty mature. And being a juvenile meant I'd do less time. I'd do it again in a heartbeat."

Saylor's eyes haven't blinked once since I began sharing this part. But they've comforted. The soft shape of them, coupled with the faint smile on her lips, the first look of empathy—true empathy—that I think I've ever seen looks back at me now. I open my mouth and draw in the mix of cold and hot air from the doors having been opened, and my lungs soak it all in. My body fills, my fingers stop tingling, my muscles pump with instant energy. My exhale is joined by an uncontrollable laugh, one that makes Saylor's smile inch a little higher.

"God, that felt good," I say, my open hand clutching to my chest. My heart hammers with relief, and I laugh harder as I run my palm up my jaw and hold my gaze on Saylor in disbelief. "Thank you for letting me tell you. For not looking at me like I'm a monster. For listening."

"And that's why I love you, Rowan." Her words break through the weight of everything, and her eyes finally blink, lashes slowly kissing her cheeks. She doesn't seem afraid. Her words were clear. Easy. Soft. Genuine.

"You love me?" I don't believe her despite all the evidence, and I know it's because I still don't think I'm worthy. I'm still David Anderson's son. There's still bad in there somewhere. She can't love me. She shouldn't.

"I do. I love you. And you don't have to say it back. But I love you, and I want you to know that. I'm glad you told me, all of it. And it's okay that it hurts. It's supposed to."

She dips her chin and peers up at me, waiting for my response. My mind is wild with thoughts, arguments against my happiness battling with reasons I should let myself feel joy.

"Okay," I croak finally, my mouth dry and throat swollen with the lump lodged inside.

"Now, let's go eat. And you're buying. It's the least you can do."

She smirks, and I shake with quiet laughter. She's making this so easy. Too easy. I don't deserve it. But I take it. I take the soft landing. Because that's what I wanted my mom to do when I claimed the consequences for my own. I wanted her to accept my love.

I accept Saylor's. And when my heart heals and I can find the right words, I plan on telling her just how much I love her in return.

Chapter 22

MAYBE I ALWAYS KNEW. I certainly suspected. My mom spent so many hours in that place, surely it couldn't *always* be about moving up the corporate ladder. I think the reason I never tried to know for certain was the other side of the coin — what if it *was* all about getting ahead, even the affair part? Lust has more integrity than prostitution in this case; at least, it does to me.

Rowan's lead foot sat heavy on the gas as we drove here. I can see how much lighter he is after his confession. He's carried that truth around by himself for years. Selflessly. He didn't even burden his brother with it, instead letting Caleb resent him and think less of him, rather than know the truth about what his mom did in a spiral of hurt and rage, and what his father did to cause it. I wonder, though . . . would knowing even make a difference to Caleb? There's a clear line between the person he is, and the one Rowan is, and I think Caleb has more in common with his father.

"You ready?" Rowan's eyes settle on mine as we sit parked outside the quaint apartment complex in the heart of downtown Tucson.

"Yeah, I'm ready."

He leans across the console and pulls my face toward his, kissing my cheek with sweet reverence. I feel like I belong here, with him. To him. Not in a possessive way. In a cherished way.

I meet Rowan at the front of his car, and our hands fold together easily. He kisses my knuckles at the top of the steps to his mom's apartment, and doesn't let go, even as he knocks and we hear her call from inside.

"We're doing this, huh?" He nods and grins like a kid about to get a sticker for good behavior. For such a sexy man, he can be downright adorable.

My hair dried in the car during our drive, so I run my fingers through some of the clumpy waves, very aware of how casual I look. I should have dressed nicer. Maybe been more formal or conservative? I didn't know this was our official hard launch as a couple, and that was before I fully understood how important Cora Anderson's approval was to me.

The door opens as my hand is midway through a knotted lock of hair, and I panic when my eyes meet Cora's, tangling my nails in the matted curl.

"Saylor! Oh, wow. Look at you!" She steps forward to hug me, but all I can do is jut out my elbow.

"I got stuck," I admit in a sheepish voice.

Cora simply laughs, gently taking my elbow and guiding me inside her home while her oldest son follows with a gentle hand at the small of my back.

"Same girl you always were, I see. You were always like a tornado. Even in the water." She closes the door behind me, then turns her attention to my hair situation.

"Let's see," she mumbles, uncoiling my nail from the thick strands that somehow ensnared it.

"I don't even have nice nails. How did this happen?" My shoulders slump, but I'm mostly acting. Cora is so sweet—as she's always been—that my embarrassment is quickly fading.

She has my hand free and is easily working her own comb

through my hair within minutes. Rowan, in the meantime, has moved to the kitchen, where he's scouring his mom's fridge while making comments about how she eats like a bachelor.

"Well, if my sons came to visit more often . . ." she suggests.

He closes the fridge and stands up straight, holding his hand over his heart.

"That's fair. I should come more. And so should Caleb, even if I need to drag his ass here." Rowan moves toward his mom, kissing her cheek as she tilts her head and gives him a hug.

"Come sit, get comfortable. I can order in if you're hungry?" Cora leads us into her warm sitting area, where two leather sofas face a small table made of stone in front of a Spanish-style fireplace. Her home is the perfect complement to her artsy style, the white walls almost like galleries featuring distinctive, Southwestern art. Saltillo tiles flow throughout, every space defined by bright, colorful throw rugs that look like they were woven by hand. The space has a light hint of cinnamon, and the warm oranges and golds make it feel sunlit and bright despite the few windows.

"It's nice here," I say, the only words I can seem to utter now that my chest is hammering with my erratic pulse.

Rowan sits next to me, our thighs touching, and he takes my hand in his, putting everything out in the open. My heartbeat grows louder.

"You can relax, Saylor. Rowan told me you two were seeing each other."

I flash my gaze at him, and he shrugs.

"I had to tell someone besides Mig. Besides, she gives great advice."

My shoulders drop to their normal position, and I relax my back into the leather pillow behind me as I exhale. Then his words fully hit me, and I pivot my attention to him again.

"Advice?"

He chuckles, and his mom utters, "Busted."

"Yeah, I may have . . . Well, I . . . So, when I was here last time—" It's a fit of starts and stops from Rowan, and his mom waves her hand to let him off the hook.

She leans in, her hands cupping a mug of what looks like tea as she rests her elbows on her knees.

"He likes you a lot, and I think he wasn't sure if he was allowed to. So . . . I gave him permission. But . . ." She holds up a finger. "I told him to be careful with your heart, and with his."

Careful. Yeah, we haven't been very careful. It's too late for that. At least, it is for me. Our hearts are involved, regardless.

"I told her the truth, Mom. About . . . about the fire." Rowan sucks in a quick breath, and his hand tightens around mine.

His mom blinks a few times, not seeming to be truly focused on his face until her head tilts slightly to the right. Her eyes flit to mine and hold there, as if she's waiting for me to give her permission, retroactively.

"You have an incredible son," I say, because when it comes down to it, that's the only truth I can give. I don't know that it was right for her to let him take the fall. And I don't know if I would have made a different decision, if I were in her position. But I do know that if the roles were flipped, and it was me able to keep my father out of jail, I think I would. And I'd beg him to let me.

"He is incredible. They both are, even if Caleb is . . ." Her head bobs from right to left.

"Lost," I finish for her. It's a kind word, and he may not deserve that. But she doesn't deserve to hear my honest thoughts about her other son. Especially not since I love this one so much.

"You had graduation. Do you have photos?" She leans forward and sets her mug on the stone table.

"I do," I say through a smile, shifting to loop my cross-body bag over my head. I pull my phone out and slide through my photos to the ones from graduation night. I move over to her sofa to nestle next to her.

"This is me with Cami." She pulls the phone into her own hands and zooms in, inspecting both of our faces.

"That's Miguel's sister, right?" She looks up at Rowan, and he nods.

"You two are all grown up. You're women now. Simply incredible." She slides through more photos, noting the nice waves I curled into my hair for the ceremony. She stops on a group shot that includes me and Caleb, though we aren't standing next to each other. She runs her fingertip over her other son's face, and my chest tightens with guilt.

"He was very handsome," I say, and her smile inches up.

"They're both handsome men. They got the best of us, I think." Her gaze lifts to Rowan, and I try to take my phone back from her before she notices the next photo. Unfortunately, her gaze drops just as my hand meets hers, and there, my mom's face is staring back at her.

"Oh," she breathes out, her mouth locked in a frozen O shape.

"Sorry, I didn't mean to—"

"No, no." She shakes her head and hands my phone back to me. "She's your mom, and that's separate. She's a good mom. You were always a priority."

I bunch my mouth, but hold my tongue, not voicing my doubts.

Over the next hour, I catch Rowan's mom up on the stages of my life that she missed, including the little mailbox incident when I was learning to drive stick shift. I find a few more photos to share, and I even ask her advice on how to handle letting my family know I want to work in social work, or for a non-profit. We both know, I think, that it's my mom who is the tough sell on my plans, but we use the plural *them* as if my father needs to be convinced, as well. It's easier to speak in vague terms, avoiding a path that would villainize my mom. It would be too easy for both of us.

Finally, when the sun about to set, Rowan suggests we should hit the road, and his mom holds up her hand, begging us to wait for just one second while she finds something in her back room.

"She's always loved you," Rowan says, and my heart kicks at the L word coming from his lips. I know he feels it, and I know he'll get there when he can.

"She's always been so nice to me. Nobody braids my hair anymore, not since she left. I don't think anybody else knows how."

His mom rushes back to us after a few seconds, her hands grasping what looks to be various hair product samples. She slips into her kitchen for a plastic bag, dumps them inside, then hands the small sack to me.

"It's not much, but happy graduation. Your hair is going to need some love in college, especially with all the swimming. And I have all these things and figured—"

"Thank you," I say, hugging her, then kissing her cheek. She exhales at my ear, like she's been holding her breath and awaiting my approval as much as I have hers.

"Maybe you can teach me how to braid my hair next time," I say as Rowan opens the door.

"Next time." She smiles. "I like that."

"I'll call you tomorrow. I love you, Mom." Rowan leans back into the door just enough to kiss his mom's cheek, then holds my free hand all the way to his car.

I sort through the samples and products his mom gave me, some of them expensive salon brands I would never be able to buy for myself. Rowan turns his car on, then studies me while I sink both hands into my goodie bag like a hungry kid on Christmas, and I glance at him with a grin.

"I'm going to like some of these, and I'll never be able to

get more." I rub my finger and thumb together to show my lack of dollars, and Rowan covers my hand, urging my eyes to his.

"I'll get you more. I'll get you anything you need. I'll give you the world."

And I know right this moment, despite the language he chose, that Rowan Anderson loves me back.

Chapter 23

THERE'S a lightness to my chest that I haven't felt since I was a kid. I didn't realize how deeply the poison of that secret had seeped into my body until I let it out. It's still uncoiling from my bones, having wound through my ribs, choked my lungs, and eaten away at my arteries for years.

The stress of being me isn't completely gone, but it's gotten easier to exist. I should deal with the biggest secret stowed away under my seat right now, but that one is trickier. There's less emotion involved. I don't have love for my father. I don't even think the blood matters anymore.

Rather than sorting through how the hell I'm going to handle that, though, my mind keeps going back to what Saylor said. She loves me. Exactly as I am. The monster and the mama's boy. The man and the tortured past. All my rough edges and soft insides. An Anderson. The son about to betray his father. She loves me.

And she's going to leave in a few weeks. Sure, not forever, and she won't be far. A day trip away, really. And I intend to push her to take what the universe is giving her to get her closer to her dreams. To find her *own* dreams, too, and own them like fucking mad. But she's still going to leave. And while our six years isn't the end of the world, it still feels like a lot when she has so much life left to experience.

"I see your wheels turning," she says, pulling me from my thoughts.

I roll my head to the side and reach my hand over the console for her to take. She lays hers in mine, and I thread our fingers together.

"You can't see my wheels. You're in the car," I joke.

She rolls her eyes, but a faint laugh still slips out.

"Did my dad tell you that joke too? When you spoke the other day?"

I shrug.

"Maybe."

Of course he didn't tell me that joke. Instead, he told me he's going to ask for what he's owed, and threaten to sue her mom. I need to break that news to her before dinner and his show tomorrow. I'm sure she's wondering what prompted me to share everything when I did.

"Stay with me again. Tonight?"

Her mouth inches up as she nods, her sexy smirk such a fucking distraction from the task at hand. There's little chance of me getting her inside to talk instead of ripping her clothes off. I'm going to have to get her father's plan out now, before we reach the garage.

"Hey, I should also tell you . . ." I rub my chin, and she falls back in her seat, her invisible guard moving into place again. I've really hit her with a lot today. Too late now. I already opened my fucking mouth.

"The stuff I told you today, about my dad and your mom. That's what your dad and I talked about at the garage. That's why he's here, Saylor. He feels like he's owed . . . I don't know . . . something, I guess."

Hearing it out loud, even in my own voice, makes it sound so ugly. I agree that he's due damages, but this isn't a car crash. It was a wrecked marriage. And it's been almost a decade. At this point, it feels like—

"Extortion," Saylor mutters, somehow pulling the word right out of my head.

I grimace, glancing back to the empty road, then to her again. This stretch of desert at dusk is lonely. It can be beautiful, too. But right now, it feels extra bleak. Flat sand, thirsty brush, wilted wildflowers, and a dusty haze from the faraway farm fields that shouldn't thrive in this arid land. It feels thick out here. Quiet.

"I don't get the impression he thinks of it that way. He's still holding on to a lot of anger, maybe, and that emotion can make people do stupid things."

"Like confess to arson."

I suck in my lips and hold my breath, aware enough to know that my knee-jerk reaction to her words won't be kind or deserved. Besides, maybe she's right. I was angry most of my adolescent life, and I'm still angry. It's why I revel in hurting my brother the way I do. All that feeds into my lack of self-worth.

"I'm sorry. I didn't mean—"

"It's fine. And you're probably right." My clipped words leave a coldness in the air, and the silence in the vehicle is palpable. The somberness matches the desert outside.

We ride along in quiet for several miles, the rumble of my tires on the beaten-up road the only thing keeping us company and reminding me that this isn't a dream.

"I'm angry, too." Saylor finally cuts through the quiet. "Just so you know. We're both allowed to be angry. And we're allowed to make strange choices. And I guess . . ."

She lets out a heavy breath. I glance her way in time for her to do the same, and our gazes connect for a short—important—moment.

"I guess my dad has that right, too. The right thing to do would be for me to forgive him. Forgive all of them." She blinks, her body seeming tired, as if she climbed a mountain to get here.

"Doing the right thing is overrated," I say, only partly kidding.

The dark joke makes her laugh all the same, and soon, she moves her hand to my leg. The weight on my thigh is a welcome anchor, and suddenly the night seems hopeful.

I want to tell her to not conflate his greed and need for retribution as a slight. He loves seeing her. She's his light, even if he's blinded a little right now. I could tell when they spoke. I sensed it in the way he clung to her as they hugged, like she could be ripped from him at a moment's notice. Saylor will come to it all on her own, though. Her own way. With, or without me.

Without me.

"Does it embarrass you? Being with me, I mean?"

Her swift laugh at my question eases my worries a bit, but I still wonder if there isn't a piece of her that's getting ready for college and questioning being held back by some drop-out mechanic.

"Rowan, you're pretty much the hottest guy most women with eyes have ever seen. No, I'm never embarrassed to be seen with you. In fact, I wish we were seen more. In public. Together."

My smile doesn't quite reach my eyes, and she calls me on it.

"What are you worried about? Do you need to hear it in Spanish? *Te amo.* How about French? *Je t'aime.* I don't know it any other way, but I'll say it in English again. I love you, Rowan."

I roll my neck and laugh off the embarrassing burn taking over my face as I groan.

"It's not . . . that. I mean, I believe you. And I know that right now, this is very real. But what about this fall, when you're walking in the quad and you drop your books and some smooth football jock swoops in to carry them for you."

"Uh, I hate to break this to you, but first . . . there aren't books anymore. Everything's an e-book. And football players aren't my thing. I'm more of a basketball player kind of girl." She's working hard to convince me, and it's so fucking sweet, but I want her to be sure. I don't want to be some drag on her life. I won't hold her back from anything.

"Okay, fine. But what if there's some baller at your college, and he's nice? I want that for you, if that's what *you* want." I glance her way, and she silently laughs.

"Rowan, I have a baller. And he's nice. And he didn't need college. He started his own business, and it's killing it. And frankly, I don't like to party. Hell, I don't even like to swim, but I'm going to keep doing that until school is paid for. And as for my free time? I'd rather spend it meeting sweet old ladies at the bus stop and helping them carry their groceries. I want to volunteer for things. I want to give myself to something bigger than me and make a difference. I don't need to meet the hot jock in the quad. I'll wait for him to drive up north and spend the night with me in the lodge."

It's pointless to try to remove my stupid grin. I couldn't tell my mouth to behave if I wanted to. And I can't say I didn't give her an out.

"You're a strange woman, Saylor Kelly. Fucking strange."

Her eyes linger on me for several quiet seconds, even after I finally give in and let her win. If she wants to be with me, to try this for real, then that's what I'm going to do. And if she wants to go out in public, and show off what we are and what we have to the world? Well then, fuck it. We'll go right now.

I shift my eyes her way for a beat.

"How do you feel about driving fast?"

Her mouth curves higher.

"I love it."

She probably thinks I mean right now, but I have bigger plans. I haven't hit the drag strip in months. I've been too busy being on parole and trying to keep the garage open. I veer from the main highway about ten miles before we hit the city limits, and I think Saylor knows where I'm headed within seconds of our turn.

The lights glow from the dust kicked up along the track. Professionals haven't raced here in years, but the county kept the track open and started letting amateurs turn out for fun. On the weekends, this place is basically an enormous flea market. But on Friday nights? It's alive with cars that sound just like mine. The minute I pull in and eyes take in the girl sitting next to me, my chest puffs up with the beast.

I find an open spot about halfway along the road, backing in, then rushing around the car to open Saylor's door for her. I take her hand the minute her feet hit the gravel, and I don't let go. I won't. Not until it comes time to race. It may have been a few months since I've been here, but once a few familiar faces shine through the crowd, it's as if I was here only days ago.

I introduce Saylor to Rodrigo and Gus, the guys who run the Friday night races and have for years. They're brothers from Maricopa, and they taught me and Mig all their secret recipes for making cars fast. Not everything they do under the hood is above board, and a lot of it is unsafe, but out here, they're legit. They're here to build community. To turn young guys into them. And given the way the sound of the cars roaring by jolts the blood in my veins, I'd say they've done their jobs.

"You racing tonight, Row?" Gus asks me, the white tufts of hair sticking out of the sides of his Phoenix Suns hat.

"No, not me. But she is."

My gaze zips to Saylor, and she stiffens like a board. Her eyes flash wide and her mouth hangs open as she forces her head to shake.

"Don't be scared. Nobody cares if you lose. It's just for the rush. And besides . . ." I lean in, close to her ear. "You'll have the best car out here."

Her head swivels slowly until our eyes meet again, our noses almost touching. She's positively panicked, but behind all that fear, I see the rush. That girl who likes to win will always be in there.

"Saylor Jayne Kelly. And here's her license," I say, holding out my hand for Saylor to hand it over.

A nervous laugh spills out of her quaking lips, but her fingers fumble with the zipper of her crossbody, and she manages to pull her license out for me. I hand it over, and Rodrigo pulls his reading glasses from his shirt pocket and jots down her number.

"Okay, sweetheart. Here's the waiver," he coughs out.

"Give him a pass," I mutter to Saylor, noticing her hairs spike up at the sweetheart bit. "Rodrigo means well, and he's called me sweetheart, too, once or twice."

"*Hmm*," she groans, keeping her eyes on the sixty-year-old man who once launched a car in the air out on this very track simply because his brother bet him he couldn't.

"You're up in two. Good luck!" He hands Saylor her license, and I swing my arm around her shoulder, urging her stunned body to walk away.

"What are you doing?" She's having a hard time zipping up her purse, so I halt us and do it for her.

"I'm showing you off. And I'm giving you something I think you need. Do you trust me?"

She shakes her head, but her mouth says, "Yes."

"You're so goddamn cute. Now, come on. You've got time for a two-minute lesson."

Once we get back to the car, I walk her through the ins and outs of the race. It's a straight track, a little more than a quarter mile, and there's plenty of room to slow down at the finish line. The tricky part for her will be working the paddle shifters. She's used to automatic, and my car works both ways by design—*my* design.

"It's going to sound strange, and you won't think it's ready, but once you punch the gas, count to three. Every time you hit three, shift."

"How do you know it will be on time?" Her gaze is darting all around the dashboard. I tap on the tachometer to focus her.

"This is all you need to worry about. Don't let it get too high. Stay out of the red."

"Sure. Yeah, no problem. Don't let that clock-looking thing get too high. Drive straight. Go fast. No problem." She's kidding, but I won't let her psyche herself out.

"Basically, yeah. You got this. Now buckle up and go get in line behind that yellow Dodge." I point to the cars getting ready at the spot where we drove in, then nudge her knee inside so I can close the door. She holds it open with a stiff arm, though, and glares up at me with deer-in-headlight eyes.

"You're not coming with me?"

I lean down and lift her chin, pressing my lips to hers.

"I'll come with you later. Right now, I want to watch."

I leave her stunned with the faint smile and the ball of nerves in her belly. Swimming has become so easy for her, it's lost its thrill. If she's going to have to endure it for four more years, she needs to find the joy in competing for herself again. Out here is as good a place as any.

I step away, leaving her with her own thoughts, forcing her to focus as she pulls onto the strip and coasts to the starting line, where she flips a U and gets in line.

"That's quite a woman you've got there," a guy who looks about my age says as he pulls two beers out of a cooler in his trunk. He hands me one, and we pop the caps off, then toast in the air.

"She sure is."

I kick back with my new friend, Doug, our feet crossed as

we lean against the hood of his Chevy SS. We pass time talking about his goals for his engine, and before Saylor's race starts, I give him one of my cards. The second the lights on 007 flash down the straightaway, I'm done pitching my business. Now, I'm simply a fan.

The light goes from red, to yellow, then green, and Saylor squeals the tires at the start, smoke billowing from my Camaro's back end as she cuts down the pavement, neck and neck with the Toyota Supra racing her. The crowd is roaring as they would for any driver, but it feels especially loud for her. Maybe I'm projecting, or maybe it's that she's come halfway and is still right in the guy's sightline. I hear the slight change in my engine as she shifts, and she reaches the final gear right on time. Nothing left but to hold her steady. And when she ends up losing by half a car length, I toss the rest of my beer and leap into the roadway like a fucking lunatic before sprinting to her and helping her stand on her shaking legs.

"I almost fucking won!" Her smile beams, and her eyes are full of honey and light.

Nothing left for me to do but tip her back in my arms and kiss her in front of hundreds of people. And that's exactly what I do.

Chapter 24

OUR HOUSE IS EERILY QUIET. My mom is downtown at a dinner with investors, along with David and a few team members. Of course, knowing what I *now* know, I question whether there's an investment group at all. Or team members. Or fuck . . . *dinner*.

I'm not shocked by the affair. I've had my suspicions over the years. In a way, it makes my mom feel more human. I've always resented the way she puts her career before everything and everyone—else. To know that there was more to the late nights beyond a good performance review? It doesn't feel great, but I can understand it.

Desire.

Infatuation.

Hell, maybe she loved David. Or *loves* him still. Love can make a person stupid.

But David's married again. His wife, Lindsey, is young. And honestly? She's hot as hell. My mom is a beautiful woman, a classy and mature woman in her mid-forties. I've seen Lindsey prance around the Anderson home in a thong bikini, and I just don't know that David is deep enough to desire a woman's mind over a body like that. I have no real

279

reason to believe he's not enjoying the best of both worlds, however.

My phone buzzes on my bathroom counter with a message from Rowan letting me know he's parked outside. He brought me home early this morning, and I spent most of the day sleeping since I get so little when I stay with him. I'm a bit giddy, even though I saw him only hours ago. There's something about the anticipation of him picking me up for a date.

I give my hair one last check. The curls are piled high in a ponytail near the crown of my head. I wanted to feel older, perhaps. More mature, and not at all like the little girl my dad left behind. Something about an up-do has always made me feel empowered. I'm not ignorant of the fact it makes me look a lot like my mom, either. Our relationship may be a complicated mess, but I will never discount the strength my mom can project.

I bought this black dress to wear for my graduation. It's a short swing dress that grazes my upper thighs, and the satiny bodice hugs me so tightly it's hard to take a full breath without feeling like the zipper in the back is going to bust. I like that it's sleeveless, though, and paired with my black heels, it gives the illusion that I'm six feet tall. I want to look down on people tonight—on my father. Fair or not, I'm hurt. And I want him to know that.

I lock the door behind me, then skip down the stone pathway to where Rowan's Camaro is rumbling in the street. He rushes out of the driver's seat and around the front of the car to open my door for me, and his gaze starts somewhere around my ankles and glides up my legs and torso. Rowan looks drunk by the time our eyes meet.

"Well, fuck me."

My lip inches higher on one side as he takes my hand and helps me lower myself into his car. His gaze lingers on my legs for a few extra seconds, his teeth clinging to his lower lip as if he's fighting not to. take a bite out of me right here and now.

"Later," I promise.

He holds his hand to his chest, over the deep gray button down he's paired with black jeans, and I must admit I'm just as hungry for him.

"Gah!" He bites his knuckles before gently shutting my door and skipping back to the passenger side.

"It smells nice in here. I like whatever cologne it is you're wearing," I say, the scent bringing me back to the night of my graduation party, to his body behind mine as he touched me so intimately while everyone's eyes were elsewhere.

"I wanted to make this special. The track wasn't really a date. This . . . is a date. And I know it's important to you." He moves his hand to my leg, rolling it over slowly so his knuckles graze against the inside of my thigh before his fingers flex and await my touch.

I slip my fingers between his, and his gentle squeeze lets me know that however this evening goes, I'm not alone.

It takes us thirty minutes to drive into the northern part of the city, to the Coal Mine Music Hall. It's a big deal that my father's playing here. Cami and I saw one of my favorite bands here only last month. My dad has wanted to break into trendy places like the Coal Mine for years. He and his band have something special brewing now, and I understand that he sees an opportunity to double down. It's the fact he's putting a price tag on those years I missed with him that I can't get past.

"How are you doing?" Rowan lets the car idle as we sit outside the venue. The marquee is lit up with Killer Mongoose's name, and there's a line of people waiting to get in. Nothing that will stop traffic, but it's at least fifty people deep, wrapping around the side of the building.

"Is it possible to feel a lot of things all at once?" A short, pained laugh slips from my mouth.

Rowan leans into me, brushing the back of his hand along my cheek before lifting my chin slightly. His eyes dive deep into mine, his expression serious yet soft.

"It's possible to feel however the fuck you need to. If you want to go right now, we can leave. If you want to walk in there and walk right back out, we can do that too. We can stay for drinks or dinner after the show, or slip out with the crowd and never let him know we were here."

My head tilts to the side, and a wry smile tugs at my mouth.

"He saved us seats, right up front. I'm pretty sure he'll notice whether we're in them or not."

Rowan's head bobs side to side.

"Meh, maybe. He's a musician, though, so he might be all self-absorbed and into his craft so deep that he can't see beyond the lights." Rowan squints, and I laugh.

"He's really good. And I miss him."

Rowan closes the few inches between our lips and dusts mine with a soft kiss before falling back into his seat.

"I know you do."

I lean forward, gazing up at the marquee one last time before taking a deep breath and readying myself for the next . . . however long I can stand it.

"I'm ready," I announce, and Rowan dashes from the driver's side to my door, taking my hand to help me step up on the curb. I notice the way he strategically shields my body from the crowd gathered outside, too, making sure nobody gets a view of what's under my dress as I exit the car.

We make our way to the VIP entrance, and I hand over my ID as I give the worker my name. She sighs as she hovers the tip of her pen down a printed list on a clipboard. I'm not sure whether she's annoyed by her job or bothered by me. I feel my age in places like this, especially when she pulls a blue wristband from the back of the clipboard and proceeds to snap it around my wrist to alert everyone in here that I'm not yet twenty-one.

"I'll take one too," Rowan says, holding his wrist up beside mine.

"You won't be able to drink," the woman explains.

"Don't want to," Rowan responds.

The woman's gaze shifts from Rowan to me, then back again before she shrugs and rolls her eyes, mumbling, "Whatever."

Rowan reaches for my hand as soon as we step inside, and I hug his arm close to my side.

"Thank you," I say, lifting on my toes to reach his ear.

He merely drops his gaze to me with a faint smile as if what he did is no big deal. Perhaps it isn't to him. But it means the world to me. He made a tiny gesture to make sure I feel like I belong, or at least as though we are outsiders together.

I would have been nervous seeing my dad tonight regardless. It's been a long time since we've seen one another face to face. And while we call and text often, it's different than being involved in one another's daily lives. There's a guard that gets put in place, almost automatically.

Now that I know the reason he's here, however, that guard has grown thick. I feel slighted. Even if it's not his intention, it's the byproduct. He has a song that's got a million streams. He could have booked a show in the Valley anytime. But he chose now.

"You okay?" Rowan keeps checking on me. It's sweet. But I must be showing my nerves because he's asked a few times in the last five minutes.

"I'm just anxious. I want it to be over, and that sort of sucks." My mouth falls into a relaxed line.

We step into the roped-off area to the right front of the stage, and Rowan positions himself directly behind me, his arms wrapped around my shoulders and chest as his chin skims the side of my face.

"Remember, we can leave whenever you want. Just say go, and we're gone." His voice is soft at my ear, and the tickle from his day-old stubble brushes the crook of my neck, sending welcome shivers down my spine. I prefer feeling like this, so I wrap my hands around his in front of my body and focus on how incredible it feels to be in a place like this with him.

The venue fills up fast, even in our roped-off section, and I'm suddenly twice as grateful to have Rowan's body acting as a buffer from the sharp elbows and tall bodies squeezing in. I feel a tinge of pride overhearing pieces of conversations around us, actual fans of my father's band, excited to see them live. One woman to our left is gushing about how she's followed them on the road through six tour stops.

"My dad has a groupie," I whisper, looking up at Rowan. He chuckles and teases me about my potential new stepmom, which makes me study the woman with more discerning eyes. She might be a little crazy, upon a second look. But aren't we all?

By the time the lights dim and the crowd engulfing us begins to scream in anticipation, I've nearly buried the resentment I've been harboring since finding out my father's visit is more about cashing in than seeing me. And when the lights go up, coloring his squared jaw and neat beard in deep red and purple hues, I fall into a state of awe.

My father's hands move along his guitar as if he's reading his favorite story, the one he knows by heart. When he strikes the power chords for their opening song, "Honey Thunder," the throngs of fans roar, and his groupie nearly faints. His stoic face remains focused, his jaw rigid and eyes often closed, except for when he looks right at their lead singer, Lyle. They're well into their third song before he scans the crowd, moving around the stage as he plays. When his eyes land on me, I lift a hand and mouth, "Hi." His lip ticks up, and he winks, and the women around me scream, assuming that little bit is for them. I know better, though. He may be in this town to extort money from my mom, but he'll always see me in a special light. I'll always be his star, his one good thing. I need to hold on to that as I work through this pending bump in our road.

Killer Mongoose owns the stage for ninety minutes, blessing their fans with two encore songs, one of them the lullaby my father used to sing to me when I was little. I tear up when he joins the lead singer, their smooth voices blending for "Hush, Little Baby." I'm basically a pile of emotional mush by the time the venue clears out, and Rowan and I hole up at a cocktail table at the back of the attached bar.

The lead singer comes out first; a small group of fans having been invited to chat with the band after their show. It's hard not to notice how many of the fans are beautiful women, and I grimace as the realization hits me that my dad has probably slept with a fair share of women in situations just like this. It's probably unfair to hold him to a certain standard simply because he's my dad, but I guess it's a good lesson to learn—the people we love are still just people. They aren't perfect. And he is single and allowed to be whatever kind of man he wants.

When my dad steps out of the dressing room, a few women giggle and gather. They've been waiting for him, and as he passes by, they hold out their hands and flex their fingers just to get one hand squeeze. It's kind of weird to see. My dad pauses between two of his fans to take a selfie, and he holds up a finger to me and Rowan.

"Sorry about that," he says when he finally peels himself away from his groupies to visit with us. "Ever since "Honey Thunder" took off, things have gotten a little crazy after shows."

My dad runs his hand through his hair, the slicked-back look giving way to his natural waves as a few strands fall over his eyes. I get my hair's texture from him. Same as my height.

"I'm proud of you," I say, catching the gleam in his eyes. His skin has weathered over the years, so the crinkles around his eyes when he smiles seem deeper than I remember them.

"I'm pretty sure it's the other way around. I'm proud of you," he says, lifting his arm up and inviting me in for a side hug. I soak in his warmth and make a mental snapshot of how this moment feels, just in case it's fleeting.

"You all want to slip out the back? I know it's late, but there's a pub on the next block that serves dinner until one. My treat."

My dad's eager gaze makes my gut feel heavy with guilt. I glance at Rowan, hoping to silently signal my desire to stay put. I'd rather not get locked into a meal once our real conversation begins.

"Uh oh," my dad says, likely noticing my hesitation.

He pulls a stool out at our pub table and slides on with his hands clasped together atop the table.

"I'm guessing Rowan finally filled in some gaps for you." I expect a guilty slant to touch my father's eyes, but instead his expression is soft and conciliatory.

"I think I'm up to speed now, yeah."

Rowan's hand moves to my knee under the table, and I layer mine on top.

"I'm sorry I didn't tell you the ugly truth myself." My dad's gaze shifts to Rowan, but only for a moment. "I wanted to."

"I understand. You were trying to not paint Mom as the enemy." I lift a shoulder and bunch my lips into a tight, crooked smile. I hadn't doubted my dad's intentions until now.

His shoulders relax as he exhales and slides his hands toward me along the table. My gaze drops to his reach, but my own hands remain as they are, one on my left thigh and the other on Rowan's hand on my leg. My father gradually straightens his spine and his palms retreat.

"I wanted to let you know before I talk to your mom tomorrow; I plan on reopening our divorce settlement. I'm not trying to be cruel or vindictive, it's only that . . . well . . . when we split, I gave away everything to make it easy on you. But now—"

I shake my head and utter, "No."

My dad's head tilts and his mouth hangs open, as if lost for words. His gaze narrows on me as his brow furrows.

I shake my head and draw in a slow breath for courage. Rowan's hand squeezes my leg, his silent nudge to say, "You can do this."

"You left without the legal battle to make things easy on you."

"Saylor . . ."

"Just let me finish." I finally move my hands up to the table, but I don't reach toward my dad. Instead, I keep them clasped, ready for business. "I know you didn't want me to get hurt any more than having my parents split up already would. But you still left, without plans for how often you'd see me, or insisting on input, or parenting rights—which, I get it. You're a musician, and maybe you felt Mom was the steady one. She had a normal job. She was organized and methodical. She was always thinking about my future. But Dad? I could have used your voice in the room. Sure, there are things Mom is good at, but listening isn't one of them, and you know that. And there were times I could have used the weight of having one parent on my side in an argument."

"Honey, I'm sorry, and I understand." My dad has always been good at listening, or at least he pretends to be. I'm beginning to see that he doesn't necessarily deserve absolute credit, and there are perhaps cracks in my perspective.

"I guess what I need you to know is that I'm glad you're finally dealing with unresolved pain. I hope that your meeting with Mom is civil, though I'm sure it won't be because we both know she will never accept her role in this. She likes playing the victim too much. But beyond all of that, I hope you get what you feel it is you need to finally have closure. I hope you get what you feel you deserve. What you're worth."

The invisible grip around my throat sneaks up on me, and my body begins to tremble as my eyes well up. Despite my breath going scarce, I carry on. I'm almost done. I've come all this way.

"I just wish *I* was the thing you felt you were missing. I wish you had found the motivation to fight a few years ago, when I needed you. I wish I was worth more than a lump of cash to help the band make a new album. Because I gotta tell you, Dad. I think you've been missing out. I'm fucking awesome."

I get to my feet and take in the pained expression on my dad's face. Rowan's warm hand on my back fills me with strength, though. I step toward my dad and kiss his cheek, knowing it's likely going to be a while before I see or talk to him again.

"I love you, and I'm enough."

Rowan nods as he steps into my side, moving his hand to my hip as he guides me to the exit. My dad doesn't follow us out. Deep down I hoped he would, but I also knew he wouldn't. He has fans now. People to impress. I don't fit into his puzzle in a place like this. I never did, and that's why it was easier to leave me behind.

"I'm proud of you," Rowan says as I fight to stave off my tears. It's the same thing I said to my dad, and I know he chose those words thoughtfully, a reminder of how powerful they can be. And my dad will feel them just as I do. He'll feel all my words. Then, hopefully, when he's ready, he'll want to see me to apologize. And he'll mean it.

Everything falls apart the second Rowan closes the passenger door. I cry hard, the inside of the car a pendulum of silent sobs and heavy wails as I let the poison out. I'm not only crying for my dad but for my adolescence, for the missing gaps I will forever have without having a parent around to cheer for me while I race across the water simply because they're proud, not because they see dollar signs and future scholarships.

By the time Rowan pulls up to my house, I've run out of tears and have packed the wounds with a certain amount of false healing.

It's after midnight, and my mom's SUV isn't in the drive-way. It wouldn't be unusual for dinner meetings to roll into late drinks and rowdy locker room behavior. My mom is used to playing the game, and she can hold her liquor better than David. That is, if there was ever a dinner at all. Either way, I'm walking into a home that will be empty for a long while.

"Stay," I hum as Rowan's chest becomes flush with my back, his hand covering mine as I press the last few numbers on the security panel. The door clicks open, and Rowan follows close as we push inside, spinning me the moment we cross the threshold and pressing my back against the door.

I let my small clutch containing my phone fall to the floor and instantly glide my palms to Rowan's face. His rough skin is a welcome distraction from my recent past, and it becomes easier to forget when his mouth covers mine, his lips trapping my bottom one and sucking me in.

There's both a sense of urgency and a pause in time as Rowan's hands move tenderly over my body, his fingers greedily gathering up my dress.

I wrap my arms around him as his fingers walk along my spine until he reaches the tab of the zipper. He drags it down with ease, the tight grip the fabric has around my chest giving me room to breathe. Eventually, the fabric falls to my hips, leaving me bare and cold under the blast of AC filling our home.

Rowan's gaze locks into mine, his hands pushing my dress over my hips until the black silk pools at my feet. I kick it away, then bend my knee to reach my shoe.

"Leave them," Rowan says, pulling my hand away as my

heel falls back to the floor. He steps back, holding both of my hands in his as his eyes take me in. My breasts bare, nipples hard and begging for his kiss, my breath gains speed the longer he admires me. I'm in nothing but my black lace hipsters and heels, but rather than feel self-conscious for being on such display, I feel admired and beautiful. Each time I'm with Rowan, I grow more confident with my sensual nature. I like the way he teases me, and how he silently coaxes me to tease him.

Letting go of one hand, Rowan turns toward the stairs, leading me behind him as he begins to climb. We leave my clothes piled at the door, and I hope my mother comes home to find them after seeing Rowan's car. It will give her a new criticism to stew about, her next lecture to prepare. The gall, too, after the choices she has made.

Rowan walks me to my bedroom, a space that's been stripped of most things from my childhood except for the pink comforter and pillows on my bed. I haven't felt at home here for a long time, and I haven't had a new identity to decorate with for years. I wasn't sure who I was, or where I wanted to go. But now I see it. I see the woman I have become, and she knows her worth and has found her voice.

Rowan leads me to my bed, and I crawl to the center, lying back and bending one knee. He hooks his hand underneath, and he crawls between my legs to peer down at me.

"I want you to enjoy every second, for hours." He lifts my leg and presses his lips to the inside of my knee as his gaze drifts to mine.

"I like that," I whisper. His guilty smirk peaks before he moves his second kiss a few inches higher. He lifts a brow, and I nod while moaning a soft, "I like that, too."

Setting my heel back on the bed, Rowan moves his hands to the front of his shirt, working his buttons open, then slipping the dress shirt from his arms before tossing it behind him.

He unbuttons his jeans next, pulling his zipper down letting his hard-on spring free. He leaves his pants on, though, instead turning his attention back to me. He scoots back enough for his feet to meet the ground, and as he stands, he drags my legs toward him by grasping my ankles. I slide along my comforter, the tufts of cotton gathering under the weight of my body.

Rowan's palms cover my knees, then begin their slow, sensual climb along my thighs. I lift my pelvis, arching my back as his hands move over my hips until his fingers grip the sides of my panties and pull them down my legs. He tosses the tiny piece of lace to the floor, then moves his focus back to my legs, lifting them both and hooking them over his shoulders as he shifts my body until I'm nearly at the mattress's edge.

"Oh," I call out, giggling with surprise as he manhandles me.

Kissing the inside of my thigh, Rowan pulls his cock out and lets his pants slide down his hips as he strokes himself a few times before guiding himself into me. He teases my pussy at first, barely entering me as he pulls out and caresses my swollen clit with the tip of his dick. I move my hands to my breasts and pinch my own nipples, needing relief somewhere as Rowan barely enters me again.

"Fuck, I love watching you touch yourself." His voice is rough, and his eyes are hazed with intense desire as he practices restraint, pulling out of me yet again.

"Rowan, I need—"

Before I get my plea out fully, he thrusts into me until I'm completely full. My head falls back as my arms fold over my eyes, and I moan.

"That's my girl. Let it go. Come undone for me," he commands. "Touch yourself while I fuck you. Be greedy. Be selfish." His fingers dig into my hips as I move my hands back to my breasts.

"Not there," he demands, and my gaze moves to meet his.

He's completely fallen into his dark side, the lover I've grown to need. I tuck my chin a hint and bite my lower lip as my right hand trails down the center of my belly until I flirt with my own hair that leads between my legs.

"Go on, baby. Please yourself."

My fingers slide lower, moving into my wet folds, my index finger circling the plump center that aches for release.

"Fuck, that's hot." Rowan pushes in deeper, gripping my hips as he pulls me into him with every pump. My fingers slide along my wet skin as my other hand works my nipple. I fight against closing my eyes, instead rapt with the intense focus in Rowan's eyes as he pushes into me, his gaze raking over my body. He bites his tongue as my fingers circle my wet pussy, and I cry out with the hint that my orgasm is near.

Before I fall over the edge, though, Rowan pulls out of me and lets my hips fall back to the bed. Gripping his cock in one hand, he points up the bed with the other.

"My turn. Scoot back."

I do as he commands as he kicks his pants from his legs and frees himself of his shoes. Rowan crawls up the length of my body, caging me between his arms as his dick slides along my wet, swollen skin. I nearly come just from the teasing touch before his mouth drops to mine, and he guides his cock into my pussy, tearing into me as his hips rock into mine.

Holding himself up enough to reach his hand between our bodies, he circles the aching nerves between my legs until he brings me to the very cusp. His hands shift to either side of me when the first wave rocks my core, and he holds his torso up with his arms as he drives his cock into me until I'm overcome by the rush of convulsions taking over my body. Rowan growls as his cock releases inside of me, coating me with his warmth as he continues to grind into me until my body feels numb.

Rowan's weight collapses onto me, and I hold him in place so he can't roll to my side and leave me ungrounded. I need him to keep me here, to anchor me to earth, just for the night.

His skin on mine, his pulse counting the minutes so mine can follow. His breath guiding mine. I need to stay here, just like this, for as long as I can. Because when the weight of him leaves, the weight of everything else is bound to move in. And I'm not ready.

Chapter 25

I'M BEGINNING to wonder if Saylor and I are the only people left on earth. It's been too quiet for hours now. She fell asleep with her body tucked into mine, and I don't want to wake her by moving. The faint smile on her lips makes it seem as if she's having happy dreams.

My phone has buzzed in the pocket of my jeans several times, though. Either someone close to me has died or our garage caught on fire. Whatever the impending bad news, it can't be my fault. I've been here, practicing my speech and sorting through the best way to tell Saylor I love her too. I've never said those words, not to a woman, and not like this.

I manage to slip my arm from under her head and pillow, and it takes me a few seconds to wiggle the feeling back into my fingers before sneaking out of bed and snagging my phone from the floor. The notification preview reads Parole Update, so I step into my boxers, then make my way out of Saylor's room and halfway down the stairs so I can call Mike-Steve and see what's so important that it requires multiple calls in the middle of the night.

I press his number as I sit on the steps, looking over my shoulder while covering my mouth to keep my voice low.

"Rowan, where are you?" Mike-Steve's voice is loud, and my instinct is to cover my phone and shush him.

"I'm not at home," I whisper, abandoning the steps and heading into the den so I can close the glass doors.

"I don't need the details on all that. But I need you to get to your dad's office, or his home, wherever he is, and fast."

My heart hammers in my chest, my eyes fixed on the dark living room on the other side of this glass door I keep fogging with my breath. I knew there was a certain urgency to get evidence on my father's securities fraud for the district attorney's office, I just didn't anticipate I'd be deployed in the middle of the night like those blockbuster actors in spy movies. Especially while the woman I've fallen for is asleep a few dozen feet away, oblivious to my final massive secret—the only one I simply couldn't tell.

"Okay, he won't be in the office now. He'll be at home, but I'll get over there. Do I need to wear the wire? What's the play? I feel a little bit like I'm flying blind." I pace the tufted rug that cushions my steps along the hardwood floors, and my hand grips my hair as a physical ease to my stress. None of it is working, though.

"Yes, you'll need to wear the wire. And the key is to get your dad to say something about the news release going out about AirTek's latest AI breakthrough about to blow the company's stock up."

I shake my head, my mind not alert enough at this hour to lock in on every word he's saying. I scan the wooden desk near the window for any paper and pen and find a golden one perched in a crystal stand with Saylor's mom's name engraved on it. It was probably some dumb reward my father gave her for serving him so well, and *servicing* him. Such an asshole.

I pull the pen out and slide open the top drawer in search of a notepad. Instead, though, I find what looks like a press release from AirTek about AI.

"Did you get that, Rowan? They're putting that news out

today. We have a solid source at AirTek, and that tech isn't ready yet. Not even close. So if that news gets out and the stock goes up . . ."

"Yeah, I got it. I'll get to my dad's. I'll get what you need." My chest is burning as my eyes scan the very news release he's talking about. I'm not sure what to think, but I know what I'd like to. I think my father is removing himself from his crimes, the same way he did with our mom. Just as he plans to use Caleb and me.

"Great. I'll monitor when you get there. This could be over fast, Rowan. If you can get him to talk, keep him talking. The more we get on record, the stronger the case."

His ability to remove emotion from the facts is impressive. I suppose mine is too. This is my dad we're talking about. Yet I'm about to wrap him up in a bow and hand him over to the feds. And the only tinge of guilt I have is that somehow Saylor's mom might be involved.

"Okay," I mutter, and Mike-Steve ends our call.

I'm frozen in the leather office chair, my feet flat on the floor as I sit on the very edge of the seat and flatten the paper I found in Allison's desk. I didn't hear her come in last night, and I haven't slept at all. I would have noticed, which means separate from how this press release got here, it's been here for longer than a day.

I flatten my palms on either side of the page and pore over the words without the pressure of holding a phone to my ear. Everything reads legit, not that I know a damn thing about how a tech company rolls out a press release. But there's something funny about the number on the PR company listed as the contact. It's familiar, a six-oh-two area code, just like ours. And the first three numbers are ones I've seen often, pretty much on every business card ever issued from Brogan-Tackerly. But it's more than that. I feel like I *know* this number. I type it into my phone, following my gut, and as I close in on the final number, my contact list pulls up my worst fear. *Allison Kelly.*

"What are you doing in here?" Saylor's voice breaks through the thick silence I've cultivated, and I jump back into the chair and gasp.

"Are you . . . working?" She slides closer to the desk in her socks, her long T-shirt barely grazing the tops of her thighs. I wish I was simply in here making a call to Mig or writing Saylor a love letter. Anything but what I'm actually doing.

"Is that my mom's?" Her brow dents as her gaze moves from the press release to my face. I should probably be a better liar. I've spent years doing it, keeping the fire a secret, and the affair. But there's something about Saylor's eyes, the way they feel as if they're looking right through me, reading my story for what it is rather than the rewrites I wish people would see.

I swallow hard.

"Rowan?" The way her voice cracks and her head tilts breaks my heart.

"I can explain." And I guess I can, but fuck is it going to get messy. And it's only going to hurt her more.

"I'm listening." Her hands are balled at her side, her arms straight as arrows as she sways on her feet.

My long, deep breath does little to settle my nerves, and while I want to look Saylor in the eyes, I'm finding it hard for my tongue to work when I do. I drop my gaze to the press release and my phone, Allison's contact pulled up on the screen, and I shake my head.

"It's such a fucking mess," I mumble.

"What's a mess, Rowan. I'm starting to worry." She steps a little closer, her fingertips now clinging to the edge of the desk as her eyes hold on to mine. I wish I could hold on, too.

My gaze drops again, along with my shoulders, my body sagging in defeat.

"Turns out my dad is guilty of insider trading, and probably a host of other federal fraud charges." My mouth sours, and I know that taste isn't due to my dad. It's for Saylor. It's all for Saylor. Everything I feel is for her.

"Okay, well . . . that probably tracks." Her voice conveys lightness, and I admire her effort to make this into a joke. But it's too serious. And again, it's only heavy because now it touches her. Saylor's world.

I lift my gaze, and I must not be stalling very well, because Saylor backs up a step when our eyes make contact, and she utters, "Oh."

She moves to the chair a few feet behind her, her hands gripping the arms as she slowly sits.

I chew at my lower lip as I mentally organize my words. There are so many working parts to this, and I'm not sure where to begin.

"The day I ran into you up north? When I picked up the car?" I begin.

Saylor nods.

"The guy who sold it to me was my parole officer. Except, it turns out, he's not really my parole officer. He's a federal investigator. And my entire parole was a decoy to get me under the fed's thumb."

Her brow puzzles with confusion, and I shake my head in frustration.

"I know. I'm not explaining this well. But hear me out. When I met him up north, the car sale was a cover. I didn't know until then, and he unloaded all this evidence they have on my dad while we pretended to be talking about a classic Corvette in a Flagstaff diner. Saylor, they want to put him away for years. And they gave me this wire to wear—"

"You're wearing a wire?" she blurts out.

My crooked smile and short laugh are automatic as I pat my bare chest.

"Oh, fair point," she says in a hushed tone, easing back into her seat.

"It's in my car. It's always in my fucking car. It feels like I'm driving around explosives, and it's always on my mind. And I keep trying to figure out how to say the right thing to my dad when we're alone to get him to spill the truth on tape. And it sucks because he tricked Caleb and me into signing a deal that makes us part owners."

"You . . . and Caleb. He tricked you?" I feel foolish as she puts it so plain.

"The truth is, I was so busy sparring with my brother and chipping away at his ego that I didn't pay attention like I should have. I thought we were signing documents for his will. And I knew something felt weird, but then Caleb signed and taunted me, and my father was pushing, and I just . . ." I hold out my open palms to show my regrets. I gave in. I reverted to being that little boy my father used to yell at. The one who wanted him to approve of me, to keep my brother out of trouble. And even now that Caleb resents me, I'm still trying to save his ass.

"Then why are you at my mom's desk? Is she part of this?" Her eyes glance at the press release, and I follow her gaze to the number at the top, the one that matches Allison's.

"Saylor, I think she's helping my dad. And I don't know what to do about it. But some of the clues are just . . . Saylor, they're bad."

Her eyes blink slowly as her lips tighten into a hard line. Several seconds pass before her gaze lifts to mine, and when her eyes hit me, they don't exactly look pained. Instead, there's a distinct shade of anger across them.

"Is that why you're here? Was this all about getting evidence? Snooping in our home?"

I stand up immediately, my defensive instincts kicking in and blending with sheer panic that I'm about to lose her over this.

"Saylor, hold on," I begin, but she's on her feet, too. She snags the press release from the desk and glances at it, her eyes tracking the words. Her scowl etches in deeper before she shakes the paper in front of me.

"It's a fucking press release, Rowan. They get these all the time. It's probably one of their companies, and maybe it's something that came across my mom's desk. There's nothing to this."

"Saylor—" I move around the desk to close the gap between us, but she takes a large step back. I stop in my tracks and press my palms into my eyes as I groan.

When I drop my hands back to my sides, my eyes sting with frustration and despair. I can feel tears glazing them, my vision a little blurry. There's no way to lead her through this without it hurting. And she's been hurt so much.

"Look at the number on the press release. Look at the PR firm's number." I nod to the paper in her hand.

She's hesitant but eventually lifts it to the light. Her gaze moves around the page, then holds steady on the upper right corner. Her lips part with a quick breath, and her hands seem to be trembling. The paper is shaking in her grasp. I move closer, moving my hand to hers, but she takes another sharp step back, the paper ripping in the process, and her sharp gaze cuts right through me.

"Get out."

I lose my breath. My mouth opens to say her name, but I can't breathe. I can't speak.

She shoves my chest, and I fall back a few steps.

"I said leave, Rowan! Get out." The tears are pooling in her eyes, and I want to wrap my arms around her until they stop.

"Now!" Her shrill scream is my sign to be patient, to change course, and do as she wishes. As she needs.

"Okay," I croak. "Just let me get my things."

I leave her alone in the den while I pad up the stairs and slip on my jeans and shirt, stuffing my bare feet into my shoes and picking my socks and wallet up off the floor. Saylor is still standing in the same spot I left her when I reach the bottom of the stairs, and I hover there for a few quiet seconds, hoping . . . waiting. She doesn't lift her head, though. Her gaze is fixed on the center of the floor, half of the press release clutched in her hand, and the only reason I know she's breathing at all is because I can see her shoulders rise with every draw of air.

"I'll be in my car. I'm not leaving here until you make me. Until we talk. Because I fucking love you, and if you think I could ever do something like this knowing it would hurt you, then I haven't done a very good job of showing you how important you are to me."

I slip out the front door, letting it click shut behind me as I drag my tired soul to the curb. I get into my car and pull the recording equipment from under my seat, and simply stare at it. Maybe I should suck it up and let my dad pin everything on me. Take one for the team, even if the team can't fucking stand me. That's what I do.

I flirt with the idea of breaking the promise I just made and driving away, but the thought of leaving Saylor behind hurts too much. She's the only person in my life who is worth it besides my mom. She's all that's good, and her compass is set to all the right choices. I won't give up on us. I won't give up on her.

I drop the keys into the cupholder and move the wires and mic to the passenger seat. I push my seat back so I can force my eyes shut for as long as it takes for either Saylor to accept my version of the story or for the cops to arrest me for stalking or loitering or some shit. The second they close, though, a loud knock at my window makes my entire body jolt back to life.

Saylor's hand flattens on the glass, and her red eyes and full bottom lip are so heavy with sadness. I press the button to roll my window down, and her hand falls away as the glass drops.

"I'm so fucking sorry," I croak, moving my hand to the window's edge, but not so close that I startle her. She made the move out here. It's her choice how this conversation goes.

She lifts her hand and places it on mine a second later, and my chest shudders in relief. Her fingernails scratch along the back of my palm and she holds the tip of her tongue between her teeth, her brow furrowed as her gaze rests on our touch.

"Let me wear the wire. I can get you what you need. I can get my mom to say the right things. Let me——"

I instantly shake my head.

"No."

Her gaze pops up, and there's determination in her eyes. A renewed strength. And no matter what I say, what I think, she's in charge now.

"I'm doing this," she says, moving her attention to the pile of tech in my passenger seat. "Show me how it works."

I draw in a slow breath and look to my right for a beat before giving in.

"Get in," I say.

And so she does.

Chapter 26

THE MAN WAITING for us at the coffee shop near Central doesn't radiate *federal investigator*, at least not in the movie-TV sense. I suppose that's my first mistake.

His unkempt mustache twists in two different directions on the sides, and his belly fully fills the ill-fitting green polo shirt with some generic emblem on the right-side pocket. He kind of reminds me of the grounds crew guys who work the PGA tour that passes through town, but maybe that's the green shirt and khaki pants talking.

"Good to see you," he says, standing and shaking Rowan's hand first, then mine.

He glances around the empty shop, the morning rush well over and the lunch break yet to begin. It's ten in the morning. It took Rowan and me a good two hours to come up with the perfect outfit to hide the wires and wrap my body in the straps.

"You understand what you're doing here? This is aiding in a federal investigation. And you are offering to participate willingly and without expectation for reward or exchange of immunity." He pulls a single page out of a beat-up leather bag sitting beside him in his side of the booth. I drag the paper and pen toward me and scribble my name on the line.

"I'm fully aware. I believe in doing the right thing. I don't have any skeletons in my closet. I'm not my mother's parent, so whatever's in hers she can take care of on her own."

He holds my gaze for a beat, probably trying to read whether I'm truly in for the long haul or simply a jaded young adult. I'm probably both, but I nod and reciprocate with my own serious expression.

"All right then. Let's get this going."

The man Rowan refers to as Mike-Steve pushes generic-looking AirPods in his ears, and I chuckle lightly at the rudimentary tech being deployed. I suppose they've dealt with much worse crimes. White collar exploitations of the market seem petty compared to trafficking humans or drugs.

The investigator heads out a few minutes before us, and I watch over Rowan's shoulder as he drives away, heading somewhere to park and listen to my mom spill all the secrets I can pull from her.

"Are you sure about this?"

Rowan's eyes squint slightly, his mouth turned down on the corners with worry. I slide my hand to the right on the tabletop, and he lifts it in his, pulling it to his lips to kiss my knuckles.

"I'm positive. If she has nothing to hide, then she'll be fine. If she did something wrong, then she won't."

Rowan sighs at my flippant summary, and I get his concern that I'm not seeing the full weight of what we're about to do. But I am. I'm just tired of people disappointing me. I let my head fall to his shoulder and wrap my hand around his bicep, squeezing him tightly as I shift my gaze to blink up into his.

"I promise, I know the potential consequences of this. And if my mother loves me more than her fraudulent career, she'll do right by me. By everyone." I wait for Rowan's slow nod, then I push against his side to urge him out of the booth so we can get to business.

I press the small button tucked against the waistband of my jeans, and Rowan checks the app on his phone to make sure it's reading sound. He nods, then gives me a chaste kiss at the door before holding it open for me.

I head down the sidewalk toward my mom's office with two cold brews in my hands. I know she's there. I texted her thirty minutes ago and asked if I could stop by to talk about my major in more detail. It's one of her triggers, and I'm sure she's spent those thirty minutes preparing her best argument for why I'm making a mistake with my life. The shock on her face when she sees I've spent that half hour getting fit to wear a wire should be one for my memory book.

The lobby is quiet when I step inside the towering glass and concrete building that's been the home to David's firm for as long as I can remember. I manage to snag an empty elevator, which gives me several floors to check my breath and calm my pulse. I wasn't nervous until this very moment. As the numbers climb to my mom's office's floor, I begin to sweat rather profusely. I don't want to mess up the wire I'm wearing, but I need to get some air moving in this space before I feel faint. I pull the taped-together press release from my back pocket, keeping it folded and sturdy so I can fan myself through the final two floors. I tuck the paper back into my pocket and run my palms along my jeans to erase any evidence of the flop sweats. This is as good as I'm going to get.

I worried Caleb might be here when I arrive, so I'm a smidge prepared when he basically pounces on me as soon as he spots me from across the office space. His cubicle is in the very center of the room, one that he's merely squatting in for the summer before he heads off to college.

"What are you doing here? Trouble in lovers' paradise?"

He folds his arms on top of the short divider wall that separates his space from the path toward the actual offices.

"Caleb, let's not do this today, okay?" I keep walking, but his steps quickly join mine. I make a hard stop. Ironically, I'm right next to the water cooler.

"Look, Saylor. I know I didn't handle things between us well at the end. I was a real asshole."

"Ha, ya think?" I can't help my response. I hate that every word of this is being heard by others. Maybe I'll luck out, and Caleb will incriminate himself.

Caleb leans into the wall, crossing his ankles and tilting his head as he smiles. It's a practiced pose, and I recognize it now. He has a handful of them that he pulls out when he knows he needs to turn on the charm. I'm impervious, though.

"I'm trying to apologize." His gaslighting is on point today.

"Good. Keep trying," I say, turning my back to him. His hand brushes my shoulder, though, before I get too far. I spin around and hold up a finger, but remember that Rowan might be hearing some of this. I don't want him rushing in here to defend me, so I leave my protest at the nonverbal gesture.

"Just . . . please think about what you're doing, the optics of who you're with. Rowan is my brother, and I wish we were closer, but he's a liability, Saylor. And I know now that if I want to have a solid future, I need to protect my peace. Rowan really fucks up my peace. Do you understand?"

I stare long and hard at his exaggerated expression, the false care pushing dents above his brows. What a load of bullshit. I thought his confidence was so adorable when we were juniors in high school, but now I see it for what it is—a spoiled kid who refuses to grow up.

All I can do is laugh, then walk away. Before I make it to the conference room, though, where I interrupt my mom reading through a binder of who knows what, Caleb makes one final attempt to sway me away from his brother.

"He ruined our family, you know? When he burnt down that house? Nothing was the same after that. None of *us* were the same."

I have to bite my tongue now, because I know things Caleb doesn't, and as much as I want to throw just how wrong he is in his face, it's not my place. But he needs to begin to think critically. If there's any hope for him at all, hope for he and Rowan to ever have some sort of relationship again, Caleb needs to question things.

"Nothing was the same for him either, you know? You should probably ask him about that sometime. I bet the perspective would do you wonders." I cap off my tip with a tight smile and exhale through my nose, closing the chapter on our conversation for now, and hopefully for a long time.

I shake my head to reset my focus as I pull open the glass door to the conference room. My mom lifts her head from what looks like heavy reading as soon as I walk in, and I can't help but question internally how quickly she shuts the binder.

"I feel like I haven't seen you in ages," she says, her typical smile in place. I think she's genuinely glad to see me. I question whether it's because she loves seeing her daughter or she's anxious to show off me and my accomplishments.

She stands and we hug like acquaintances, her embrace likely because that's how she is with affection, mine as an attempt to avoid her feeling any of the cables strapped under my shirt.

"Looks like you have a lot of work right now." I nod to the binder in front of her as I sit across the table from her.

"Oh, just some light reading on security and exchange rules for marketing. Nothing that can't wait." She pushes the binder to the side while I bunch my lips to morph the wry smile begging to break free. The ironies simply keep lining up.

"Right. Well, I'll try to keep this short so you can get back to it." My comment is both on brand for how we talk to one another, as well as a little relief for how badly I'd love to call her out right now.

"Truly. It can wait. I want to talk about this change in majors you seem hell bent on executing. Have you really researched the outcomes, Saylor? I don't know if you're aware of the drastic lifestyle changes in store for you in shifting a business career to one of social services. And the work, Saylor. You'll probably be spending hours on the streets or outdoors, in heartbreaking situations, at least until you move up into management. And even those jobs aren't valued as highly as—"

"Oh wow, you need to stop," I say, leaning back in my seat and spinning side to side in the swivel chair. I exhale loudly, ignoring the warning Mike-Steve gave me about how loud sounds on my end are amplified on theirs. He'll have to deal with this one.

"I can't stop, Saylor, because you're my daughter. And as your mother, my job is to want more for you than I've had. I want better for you. I've worked hard so you can have any dreams you want. Don't limit them!" Her face is red, and I know she's flustered by me. I've never been like her, and she can't understand that. I'm not suddenly going to change personalities, either.

"Mom, social work *is* my dream. Making an impact on a human being's existence, even if it's one at a time, on a molecular level, is what I want to spend my time on earth doing. It's not a waste to me in the least. If anything, it's the most valuable thing I can give and get in return. I've never felt more certain of my path in my life." I hold her stare, stomaching the shades of disappointment that weigh down her face. I need to pivot now. I've gotten her worked up, so it's the perfect time to draw her into new conversations.

"You sound just like your dad," she mutters, and I breathe out a soft laugh. She made the pivot for me.

"I saw him this weekend. Did you know he was in town?"

She's aware. I know she is because he plans to meet with her later today or tomorrow.

"I heard." Her expression is blank, her words careful and matter-of-fact.

"I went to his show. The band is good. Even you might like their music," I joke.

She lets out a genuine laugh and shakes her head.

"I doubt that."

"Yeah, you're probably right." I lean into the table and tap my fingers along the slick surface, as if I'm playing a piano. I lift my gaze in time to catch the suspicion in her eyes.

"Did you sleep with David because you loved him or because you wanted to get ahead?" I can tell by the slight flinch in her features that she wasn't prepared for me to be so blunt. I'm sure she wonders how long I've known.

"Saylor, this is an adult conversation, and it's very nuanced. There are things you don't know, don't understand."

I suck in my lower lip and lean back a hair, breathing in.

"Well, first, I *am* an adult. So, we can take that barricade off the table. And second, I genuinely want to know. Did you blow up our family over love or for your career? Because I can see one more than the other for you, and it's not the emotional connection one would normally expect." I level her with a hard glare that doesn't let up, even when she shakes her head and mutters something about *nonsense*.

"That's why Dad left, right? Because you cheated. And I am adult enough to understand that perhaps the two of you would have split eventually without the affair. I'm sure you had your reasons to stray, and I'm sure part of him was already out the door. You're different people—*wildly* different people. And I'm not real proud of either of you, to be honest. But you have always, at the very least, portrayed an air of decorum. Professionalism above all else, isn't that right?"

"Saylor." She keeps saying my name as if I'm a toddler about to get a timeout.

"So, it was a professional move then, is that the case? And is it still happening? Are you fucking your boss still? Your *married* boss?"

I'm crass on purpose. I use those words because I know they'll push her buttons. She doesn't speak that way, at least not for anyone of consequence to hear. Her cheeks are getting redder by the second, too.

"Saylor—"

"Allison." I mock her, and maybe that's childish, but it's the right move.

"Gah! No, okay? It's not still going on. It wasn't a long affair. It was . . . a lapse in judgement. I was lonely, perhaps. Maybe sorting out some anxiety. I made a mistake, and it was dealt with."

"Dealt with." I chuckle.

"You have advice on the topic? *Hmm?* By all means, do share." She waves her hand across the expanse of the table, an invitation for me to attack her. Normally, I'd back down. But I'm not intimidated anymore. I'm no longer afraid of disappointing her or losing her support or money. By the time today's done, she may be broke anyhow.

"You lost your marriage. You made a choice. And rather than examining what it all truly meant—and it's clear by your own words you never did the work to unpack why you strayed —you instead dove headfirst into managing everything. Including me. And I've got news for you, Mom. That meeting Dad is trying to set up with you? He plans to dig up those skeletons and deal with them—*financially.*"

Her eyes dim the second money comes into the picture. The way her shoulders tick up, too, is a clear sign that I've hit a nerve. Her financial worth and her status are important to her. Now's the time.

I lean to one side to access my back pocket, and as I unfold the paper above the table, my mother's gaze shifts from curious to terrified in the matter of a second.

"Where did you get that?" she asks, reaching for it. I pull it away and waggle a finger.

"Ah ah, I'll keep this. And there are copies." I meet her frozen expression, her features still and her jaw flexed. I think she may crack most of her teeth if she clenches that hard for much longer.

"I didn't realize you changed jobs, that you are now doing PR for . . . AirTek? Is that the company?" I glance at the paper then back up again, and I find her expression unchanged.

"Saylor, you're out of your element. Honey, I need that back." It's clear she's panicked.

"Yeah, I'm sure you do. I mean, you probably need to send this out after making all those trades this morning. How much did you buy in AirTek? How much did David?"

She licks her lips and opens her mouth to find zero words ready to come out. I don't know that I've ever seen this side of my mom, and I almost feel bad. But I know this glimpse of her is only happening because she's scared of getting caught.

"Did you do this to get ahead? Or was this because you love David? Was it simply a moment of anxiety, a lapse in judgement? How many of these have you done for him?"

"Saylor—" She blurts my name, lunging forward and managing to snag a corner of the paper. She rips it where I'd taped it from already tearing it myself last night.

"Why?" I shake my head and stare at her down-turned gaze, waiting for her to face the truth, to face me. Her eyes flit up eventually, and she's morphed from the frightened accomplice back into the woman who is always—*always*—right.

"How do you think we paid for your private schooling? Huh? Do you think that was simply on my single salary? Do you think David gave away a fifty-thousand-dollar tuition year after year for free? No! Of course not! I had to earn that bonus. By any means necessary!"

"By putting out fake reports to bolster stock prices?" I practically laugh out the words.

"Yes! If that's what it took!" And she falls right into the trap.

"Mom, that's illegal. I didn't need a private school experience. I didn't need the best swim club, or the expensive prom dress."

She rocks back in her chair with a hard laugh at my protests, so I shut my mouth and wait for her to reveal the rest.

"Are you telling me you would have been fine with me pulling you out of your junior high and putting you in public school, away from your friends? And what about those Anderson boys, who you are so intent on being friends with? I guess you've moved on from friends, though, huh?"

I glower.

"That's a bit like the pot calling the kettle black, don't you think?"

"*Hmm*," she grumbles.

Our brief stare-off breaks when she gets to her feet and tears her piece of the press release into tiny bits.

"I don't need that copy anymore anyhow. That one's already been sent, and David's already made his moves. I'll be sure to remember that you don't want the new car that bonus could buy, though. And I hope you're good enough at butterfly to keep your scholarship because I sure won't be shelling out tuition anymore. Since you're so incensed that I did what I had to do to pay for your schooling."

She's breathing hard, and her color is beginning to retreat, her face growing paler, and her arms almost blue. I rush to her side, grabbing her chair and swiveling it around to catch her as she collapses. She's ripping her shirt open around her neck, and her wide eyes look terrified.

Fuck. I've given my mom a heart attack!

"Hey! I need help in here! Someone call nine-one-one! Help!" My voice curdles with my screams. I urge my mom to the floor, but she shakes her head and pushes my hand away.

Caleb rushes in, his cell on speaker as an emergency worker responds. He spits out the address, and they begin asking questions about my mother's state.

"Is she conscious?" the woman asks.

"I'm fine. It's just . . . I can't get a breath." My mom's voice is hoarse, and I doubt they can hear her through the phone line.

"She's awake and speaking, but she's having a hard time breathing. She nearly fainted, too. And her skin feels . . ." I lay my hand on her forehead, and she swiftly swats it away. "Moist. She's sweaty."

Damn it, she's having a panic attack.

I grab Caleb's phone from the table as he rushes to get her a glass of water. I wander out of the conference room door while two of her assistants tend to her.

"I'm sorry. I think she's likely having a panic attack. She's in a stressful job. But can you send someone? Just in case?" I don't want her dying out of spite.

"We're two minutes away, ma'am. Can you stay on the line with us, please? Keep me up to date on her condition, and answer some basic questions?"

I glance over my shoulder to where my mom is now sitting with her head between her knees, and my focus drifts to her hand, which is now gripping the other half of the press release, the part I left on the table when I thought she was ill. She stuffs it into her pants pocket.

"Yes. I can stay on the line."

My pursed lips grow rigid the longer I stare at my mom through the pane of glass that separates the conference room from the hallway. Caleb rushes by with water, and my mom cradles the mug in her hands as she thanks him. She tips her head back as she sips, then asks for help holding the mug when she's done. Caleb is quick to help, and as her gaze drifts from her preferred Anderson brother to me, her signature disappointed smirk slides into place.

"I think she's getting better, if you want to tell them to turn around." My wry tone probably doesn't convey my sardonic mood right now, especially in this situation, but damn, is my mom good. I'm also less sad about throwing her under the proverbial bus.

"It's better that we make sure. The emergency team is entering the building. You should see them soon." I turn when the elevator dings, and then move to the side as the paramedics begin taking my mother's vitals.

"They're here. Thank you so much." I end the call and slip back into the room so I can put Caleb's phone back on the table. I linger as they evaluate my mom for an ambulance ride, and when she refuses, I slip out and take the stairs all the way down to the lobby. Down is always easier than up. That's what makes it so tempting to fall from grace.

Chapter 27

THE RAID IS HAPPENING RIGHT NOW. Mike-Steve said nine o'clock sharp. In the forty-eight hours since I've known it was coming, it's occupied every single waking thought. And I hate that, because in the last forty-eight hours, I've also moved Saylor's things into my tiny home. I want to be thinking about that. Celebrating *that*.

Maybe in an hour I will. Or perhaps I'll begin obsessing over the impending trial, preparing for the hate from my brother and my father's staff, the guilt for ripping away Saylor's mother and leaving Saylor without anyone. And then I can drive myself mad worrying that she'll blame me one day. And then I'll lose her.

"You're doing it again," she says, her fingers pushing into the crease between my brows.

"I haven't stopped," I admit. Her breathy laugh hums against my ear as she lies at my side. Saylor's the only thing that calms the waves in my chest.

She asked to move in with me before leaving for school because of how she left things with her mom the day she pried a confession from her lips. Her moving in here did more for me than for her, though. I firmly believe that. I don't think I would have slept if I didn't have her rhythm to match.

It took a few days for the warrants to come through, and the grand jury indictments are close behind. The plan is for my father to be in custody long enough for the AG's office to formally bring charges, and then fight any bonds being set. His assets will be frozen soon, if they aren't already. In his world, the rats he has for friends tend to scurry at any sign of trouble, so I doubt he'll be able to pay to spend his time waiting for trial in the comfort of his posh home. My only wish is that Caleb is allowed to stay there until he leaves for school. I didn't get it in writing, but Mike-Steve promised. It was literally my only ask out of this mess besides having my record expunged. Caleb may be an asshole, but he deserves the chance to make his own bed of trouble and not have to lie in my father's.

"You aren't the criminal," Saylor reminds me. I take her hand as it massages my head and bring it to my mouth, kissing the back.

"Why do I feel like the bad guy, then?" I roll so we're facing one another, our naked bodies mingling everywhere, legs entwined, chests pressed close, foreheads touching. Her body has been my heroine.

"Because you care a lot more than you put on. You love your family as much as you hate them."

Her truth cuts to the bone.

"*Hmm*, you may be right." My hands move to cradle her face as my mouth covers hers. I want this kiss to last forever, to slow time, and to put off the inevitable for just a little while. But fate happens when it's meant to, and my newest reminder comes with a heavy pounding against the garage bay doors.

I squeeze my eyes shut as Saylor moves to sit up, wrapping herself in my sheets.

"Maybe it's a customer who can't read the closed sign," Saylor offers.

I crack one eye open and smirk.

"Doubtful," I say, as another round of pounding rings against the metal siding.

"A persistent customer," she adds, and I laugh as I get up and slip on a pair of jeans and the black T-shirt I've worn two days in a row.

I kiss her softly before she scurries into the bathroom to shower and change, while I check out the insistent visitor. I had to let Jersey and Mig in on the legal storm going on because I want to keep the business safe. I also want to be closed the day the raid goes down, an act of caution as well as a buffer to avoid the news cycle for the day. I'm sure my mom will call the moment she gets word, and that will be news enough for me. I won't let her know my part in any of it. She's so happy with her life, and if I'm judged by anything at the end of my life, I hope it's how much I loved her and made sure she found peace.

The third round of pounding thunders through the garage as I push the key into the padlock.

"Hold your ass, I'm opening up!" I punch in the code once the backup lock is undone, and the door rolls up with ease as I give it a push from the inside. My eyes are barely able to make out Caleb's face before his fist sails into my nose, and I stumble back several feet and land on my hip and palm.

"Fucking fuck!" The blood runs into my lip, the acrid taste of metal making me want to throw up while I stumble to the towel bin and grab a handful of them to stop the bleeding.

"What did you do? I know this is you, Rowan. It's always you, so tell me . . . what the fuck did you do?" Caleb comes at me, lunging with his fist, but I'm able to block his punch, catching his fist in my open hand.

I push him back, bending his wrist and nearly breaking it as I growl out, "Calm your ass down!"

He shirks me off and runs his forearm along his nose.

"You're not the one bleeding, you shit. What are you sniffling for?" I pull the towel back to test the bleed, and it's already soaking with crimson red. "Fuck," I mutter, tossing the soiled towels into the corner and grabbing a new handful.

"The feds came in today. Did you know that? I bet you knew that already. They tossed every drawer in the office, made Allison and me and the rest of the staff wait in the break room while they took us out one at a time to interview us. I was grilled like I committed some sort of murder, Rowan! The guy warned me that any lie I told meant years in prison. What the fuck did you get us into?"

He thrusts two palms into my chest, sending me back a few steps into the counter. I catch myself against the sharp edge and lunge back at him, pushing him several times until he falls on his ass and scurries to scoot away from me. I squat down, tossing my bloodied towels to the side again as I grab a fistful of his expensive shirt and tie.

"I didn't do shit, Caleb. Dad did. And it's his fault that any of this is happening," I growl.

"You fucking lie!" he screams, his face red, our roles suddenly clear-cut. I'm the older brother. He's my little brother. He's scared, and I'm supposed to keep the bad guys away. Only this time, the bad guy happened to be one of ours.

"He's not lying, Caleb." Saylor's calm voice cuts through the toxic air between my brother and me, and I stand up and take a few steps back to give him space as we both look at her.

"Jesus, Rowan. Your face." She's wearing my clothes, and I'm sure that's all Caleb is focusing on as she pads in bare feet to the towel bin, grabbing twice as many as I've been using before delivering them to me.

"I got it," I say, taking a few from her. She gives me a hard look, though, so I let my shoulders sag before pulling a stool close, then sit and let her tend to my busted nose.

"He got a good shot in," I say, figuring giving my brother credit for the cheap shot might calm him a little.

"I got a few in," he adds. Fucker still can't just take what he gets. He always needs to embellish. I glance at Saylor for a beat, but she's focused on the rage display that walked into her refuge.

For a few long seconds, the only sound filling the garage is Caleb's and my panting breaths, and the occasional *tsk* from Saylor as she pinches the bridge of my nose and presses a second towel into my nasal passages. I can barely breathe. I'm going to need to get this thing looked at. It's broken.

"I don't know why you're defending him," Caleb finally gripes. "They took your mom in. Put her in cuffs. Your mom, Saylor."

She draws in a long, steady breath as she studies my brother.

"Good. She probably deserved it." Her resolved tone only sets Caleb off again, and he gets to his feet to pace around us in circles.

"Oh, he's got you so poisoned. You guys are unbelievable. You're so into this *eat the rich* mantra that you can't even see how crazy you are. Just because our dad makes a shit ton of money doesn't make him a bad person, Rowan. How have you never seen that?"

My heart nearly aches for my brother's naivety. Nearly. But not quite.

"Caleb, I don't think our dad is an asshole for being rich. I think he's an asshole . . . period. He's a bad guy, and he's done some awful things. If you only knew."

"So, tell me," Caleb challenges.

I exhale, because as much as I'd love to rattle off the list, I swore I wouldn't make him more involved than he needs to be.

"Your dad slept with my mom. It's why my parents divorced. And it's why your mom left. And why she set the beach house on fire." *Well fuck.* I guess Saylor didn't make any promises.

Caleb's head shakes with sudden laughter.

"That's absurd."

He knows it's not. I can tell by the nervous tinge in his voice, the high pitch of his laugh, the way his smile isn't reaching his eyes. And when his gaze slides to mine, I can't lie anymore.

"I didn't burn down the beach house," I say, and the way my insides buzz as if with a thousand volts of electricity makes me wonder whether I'm about to die or lift off and fly.

The relief of saying it out loud, for a second time, is intense. Perhaps even more so because it's Caleb I'm telling.

My brother shakes his head and furrows his brow.

"You did, though. You told the police you did it. You went to juvie. It's in your record." All facts. Caleb is right about that.

"Yep." I confirm that part for him.

"So you, what . . . you lied?" His expression is tight; his face pinched with disbelief.

I shrug.

"I lied. For Mom."

My brother's short laugh breaks with a cry, and his eyes well with tears. He tilts his head and glances at Saylor.

"He wanted to protect her. She was angry because my mom's a cheating bitch, and your dad's a real disappointment." Saylor's blunt honesty pushes his tears onto his cheeks, so I snag one of the clean towels from her other hand and toss it to him.

"I don't fucking need this," he says. He blots his eyes anyhow.

"Why don't you sit down and let me tell you everything. From the beginning." It's an offer I didn't want to make, but plans aren't ever set in stone. I must take in the wreckage left behind, and my brother needs the truth more than he needs me to shield him from it.

It takes him nearly a minute to respond, and his acceptance feels halfhearted for a long while as I start from the moment I found out about the affair and slowly walk him through everything that's happened under his nose since then. After an hour, and one trip to the bathroom, where I'm pretty sure he threw up, my brother's body is a lot like a spent balloon, one that is no longer full of air and holds a beautiful shape. He's deflated, and his body sags with grief.

"You quit basketball." It's strange that after all of that, after sitting with it and thinking to himself for several quiet minutes, that's his first takeaway. It's also rather perceptive.

"I did. It didn't feel the same after juvie. The joy was gone." I shrug.

My brother shakes his head, his heavy eyes lifting to mine.

"No, you love the game. I've played you as recently as two weeks ago, remember? You were good. Better than me."

"I know," I laugh out. My brother's mouth quirks up. It's nice to see.

"Arrogant butthole," he chides.

Saylor snort-laughs, which sends the three of us into a short but needed bout of laughter. When we finally calm down, Caleb gets to his feet and walks toward me. The crusty towels, ruined with my blood, are now strewn all over the garage floor. My shirt is done for, too, and I'm sure my face isn't pretty. I don't flinch as he walks toward me because there's not much damage left to do. Plus, I feel his shift in my bones. He's still angry, but he's no longer angry at me. At least, not the way he was.

He holds out his hand and I take his palm and grip him hard, getting to my feet and pulling him to me for a real, honest to God hug. It feels strange, but it also feels right. Maybe the day will come when the strange completely disappears and Caleb and I can be brothers again.

"I think I'm going to see if I can head to campus early, or at least spend the rest of the summer exploring the East Coast or something. Just . . . I don't think I can be here. And it's not because of you—"

"I get it," I say, meeting his eyes with an assured look. I put my hand on his shoulder and maintain our gaze, about a million unspoken thoughts passing behind my eyes as well as his. Neither of us says the hard stuff. I don't tell him I love him, and he doesn't say he's sorry.

But I do.

And he is.

And we will get there.

Eventually.

We all will.

Chapter 28

THE SUMMER WENT by in a blur, even when we were going through hell. It was all too fast, the good *and* the bad. And now I'm looking at surviving what promises to be the slowest eight months of my life. I refuse to count my winter break because I won't get to stay with Rowan for more than a few weeks.

"What if I don't go?" It's the fiftieth time I've said those words to Rowan, and his answer is always the same.

"You have to go. And we'll find a way to make this work." That's the fiftieth time he's answered that way.

I stuff the last of my hoodies into the extra-large duffel bag Cami's family bought me as a going-away gift. I don't think my best friend would mind either if I stayed. She kicked Rowan out of his own bed two nights ago so she and I could have a sleepover like we used to when we were kids. We spent the day in bed watching our favorite movies and eating garbage popcorn, an invention her mom made once when she tossed every random sweet thing she had in her pantry into a bowl of popcorn. It quickly became the official treat for Cami and Saylor.

When Cami tried to turn our one night into a weekend,

Rowan literally carried her out of his home and to her car. He had other plans, though he and I also spent the entire last day together in bed. There were zero snacks involved, however.

The rumpled sheets beneath my bag practically beg me to crawl back under them, but Rowan's right. I deserve this opportunity. I may not love swimming the way I once did, but it's a tool I can use. And maybe now that the clouds have lifted to some degree, I'll find the joy again. I've already started to hear music in my head when I swim, rather than the blank nothing that I forced in before.

"It's time." Rowan's arms wrap around my body, and I grab his wrists to hold him tight, like a safety harness that will keep me safe.

"Remind me again, when will I see you?" I tilt my head to gaze up at him, and he drops a kiss to my lips.

"In one week. And then I'll make it every other weekend. And if you call, I'll only be a two-hour drive away. I promise." He nuzzles the tip of his nose against mine, then squeezes me one last time before letting go.

"And why do you promise?" I love fishing for it, and he always obliges.

Glancing over his shoulder before hoisting my bag, he meets my gaze and winks. "Because I love you, Saylor Kelly. Because I'm *in* love with you."

"Oh, yeah," I hum, my forever smile like a tattoo when I'm around him.

I follow him out his door, waiting while he locks up, then we hold hands as we make it into the garage. Cami leaps from the couch and rushes at me like one of those tree frogs that fly from branch to branch. I catch her as she wraps her legs around me, and I spin her a few times until we're both dizzy.

"I'll see you in two weeks, right? I'll be there for rush week, in case you decide you want to be a Delta, too." She draws a triangle over my chest, and I laugh as I shake my head.

"I won't change my mind, but I'm excited for your visit. Good luck on your bid, though." My friend has decided she's going to fill her social calendar with sorority parties in my absence. I don't know that she'll gel the way she hopes to, but if it keeps her from crawling back to her ex and motivates her to study, I support it.

"Your keys, ma'am," Mig says, holding out my trusty Toyota keychain. He gave my car a tune-up on the house before I head up north. I don't know how much longer I'll be able to make these wheels last, and the prospect of a new one is *definitely* not in the cards now that most of my mom's assets have been frozen. My father offered to get me a decent used car, but I'd rather find a way to do this on my own. I may change my tune when my car conks out on an icy hill, however.

I hug Mig and Jersey before turning back to face Rowan as he holds my driver's door open. He's following me up to my dorm with Mig's truck, which is loaded with the rest of my things. I'm not used to cold weather, so I may have gone overboard in the sweatpants department. And my blanket game is on point as well. Between winterwear and the mini fridge, my dorm essentials have taken over most of the spare space in the cab and the bed.

I slip into my car, and Rowan closes the door halfway, leaning over the opening and meeting my gaze to make sure I'm ready for the hardest part yet to come.

"Are you sure you want to do this?" I hold his stare for a breath and consider backing out, but I know it will only fester in my heart if I don't make a stop to see my mom before I leave for college.

I nod.

"I need to do this."

"Okay. You're the boss," he says with a smile. "I'll follow you."

He pushes my door shut, then kisses his fingers and taps

them on the window. I touch the same spot and watch him walk behind me toward Mig's truck.

How did I get so lucky? How am I the girl who made him fall? His tall, lean body is cast straight out of a Hollywood romance, and the way his hair has grown out over the last three months makes him even more appealing, especially when he runs his hand through the waves like he is right now. I bite my lip and catch the last possible glimpse of him before he steps into the truck and cranks the engine.

I back up along with him, and he waits as I pull out so I can set the pace. I'm not sure whether I would rather speed there to get this over with or take my time to put it off. It's going to happen either way so I stick to the limit on the highway, and on every road, until I'm parked in front of the house I grew up in.

Rowan sits in his truck parked behind me, its engine idling as I get out and step onto the sidewalk to meet his waiting gaze. He gives me a thumbs up, and I flash one back in return, though that gesture feels minuscule for the task at hand.

"You got this, Saylor," I say to myself, blowing out a heavy breath and relaxing my shoulders as I straighten my spine.

I march up the pathway to my old front door, and rather than ringing the bell, I simply push it open. I figured it would be unlocked. My mom said she would be waiting for me when I texted her. She's sitting on the center of the tan sofa with a magazine open on her lap when I step inside. Her face lights up, but my focus zips right to the ankle bracelet locked above her right foot.

"Well, this is it," I say, walking across the empty room toward her. She gets to her feet and tosses the magazine to the side, but kneads her hands together nervously rather than reaching for a hug. We've never been physically affectionate, so it's for the best. It would feel forced if we hugged right now. We need to work on getting better with words first.

"I like the couch," I say, gesturing to the very basic sofa.

They repossessed most of our furnishings as part of the deal my mom made. She gets to keep the house, which is mostly paid for, but it's a shell of what it was. I think there's a bed in her room, my old furniture in mine, and then this sofa. I can see beyond her to the dining room, and it looks like there's a folding table set up with a tablecloth over it to dress things up.

"It's all only temporary. I'll bounce back. You know me." She seems so sure of her plans, which, why wouldn't she be? That's where my mom excels. Goal setting and action steps, that's the Allison Kelly way.

"I know you will. Maybe it's your chance to change up the place. Try a little color and less leather," I suggest. My mom scrunches her nose, sticking with her expensive and very boring taste. Maybe my next olive branch to her will be a pink flamingo statue or a bright blue throw pillow.

"You said they'll stream your swim meets when they start, right? And I can find them on the website?"

I nod.

"I'll make sure to text you the link each time," I say, almost forgetting the promise the minute I utter the words. She hasn't watched me swim in years.

"I hope you do," she says, though, which gives me a sudden pause.

Our eyes meet for a quiet breath, and for the first time since our world imploded, I feel an emotional lump threaten to choke me. I clear my throat and glance around the bare walls. All her art is gone, too.

"I should hit the road. I'll let you know when I make it there. Rowan's following me, so I'll be safe."

My mom leans to her side to peer out the window at Rowan in Mig's truck. Her eyes slant with what I think is envy.

"Good. I'm glad you won't be alone." Her gaze comes back to me, and my body itches from the awkward vibes that always seem to creep in between us now. It was one thing when we were always arguing. Now, the power shift has only made things feel sad.

"I'll let you know about Thanksgiving. I'm sure Cami's family will be hosting something, and maybe—"

I let the thought linger there, and my mom only nods. We both know the silent rules. Maybe we'll be in a better place, and we can both sit at the dining table together.

"I'll see you soon," I say, moving my hand at waist level for a tiny farewell before heading back to the front door.

"Hey . . . Saylor?" Her voice quavers, and the sound sends a shock through my chest. I stop, my hand on the door knob, freedom only a few steps away. But there's something so desperate in her voice that I must see it through. I turn to her as I say, "*Hmm?*"

Her eyes are glassy, and her mouth is a tight line as she mashes her lips together. She's trying to find her courage. It's one of the few ticks she has that I do, as well. When we struggle for words, our expressions are so similar.

"You know, right?" She bobs her head side to side, and for a moment, I consider answering *no*. But that would be the old me, and I'm trying to be healthier with my relationships with my parents. No more passive-aggressive baiting. Only honesty.

I nod.

"I do, Mom. And me, too."

She nods back, her tight mouth forming a pained smile.

I shut the door behind me and breathe in through my nose, one last reminder of the dry desert air and my mom's sage bushes that have fizzled into tumbleweeds now that the water hasn't been running to them for weeks.

I march straight to Rowan, and he rolls his window down as I approach. I lean into the truck, lifting myself up on my elbows so he can caress my head and tell me everything's okay.

"I'm proud of you, baby. That was hard. I know it." He

kisses the top of my head and releases me so my heels fall back to the ground.

"It was the hardest thing I've ever done. Worse than sending her to the wolves." My eyes sting, but I don't want to give in to the pressing need to cry. Not today. I won't give up my excitement for this. If I'm going to be sad about anything, it's going to be about Rowan driving away when he's done moving me in.

With nothing else to tackle before our drive up north, I head back to my car and dial Rowan so we can talk on our speakers all the way to my school. The one time there's hardly a lick of traffic—and it's today—is the day I wish would slow down.

We park side-by-side in the main student lot, and Rowan proceeds to haul my things into my dorm room while I sort my clothes and make my bed. My roommate is sweet. Her name is Megan, and she has curly short hair that she pulls into ponies on either side of her head. I can tell we're opposites in a lot of ways, but she seems to have good energy. I choose to see opportunity in her, and the way she eyes Rowan's ass as he stands on my bed and pins lights to the ceiling above us means she has good taste in men, too.

The afternoon cheats me more than this morning did, and it's near sunset before I have time to accept that this is it. My next phase. The biggest of all steps. And Rowan's and my first real test. If we can make it through this semester, I'll feel solid about our future. But I don't pretend it won't be hard. If anything, Rowan is surer than I am of everything. Sometimes I wonder if he even owns a mirror, or simply doesn't know what he looks like.

I walk him down to the front desk, where yet another student worker checks him out, and I plant a terribly inappropriate kiss on him to claim my territory.

"Hey, I have an idea," I say as he brushes the thousands of

stray hairs that are tickling my cheeks away from my face. I'm sure I look like a wild animal. Moving is hard work.

"And what is that idea?" he asks, sliding his hands around my back and dropping them into the back pockets of my shorts so I feel his massive hands on my ass. I blush, but I also grin.

"Now that we've moved everything into my dorm room, let's move it back to the truck, and you can take me home with you."

I blink expectantly as he laughs. Of course I'm joking, but also . . . not.

"I'll be back up here in a week. In fact"—he steps back to look at his watch as if it tells days and not just time—"I'll be back in five days, four hours, and fourteen minutes."

Oh, wow. Maybe his watch does.

"Okay," I grumble, sinking into his chest as he wraps his arms around me. I breathe in his scent, wanting to have a reminder of him when he's gone.

Rowan lifts my chin and takes my top lip between his, sucking gently and holding me still for long seconds.

"I love you," he says against my mouth.

"I love you, too," I echo.

And I let him go, because I have to.

Our first night apart wasn't easy. I didn't really sleep, and I was only half listening to my roommate share stories about herself. I wanted to be present, but it was hard when half of my heart was two hours away.

Last night was easier, though. Mostly because I had classes to locate before my first day, which is today. And the sheer expanse of campus doesn't give me much wiggle room between my courses. My mom would be impressed if she saw the online planner I built to keep me on task—and on time—for the next three and a half months. Plus, now that I'm overwhelmed with the reading list from two of my courses, on top of the swim schedule coach just locked us into for the season, I think I've accumulated enough distractions to survive a week without seeing Rowan's live face. Video chat will do.

I just finished my first afternoon swim session, and while I didn't feel the drive I once did, I didn't hate the water. Putting in the work was fun rather than an escape, and even being out of breath feels like a gold coin moment. I'm finding myself again, little by little, and I'm excited to see what parts of the old me come along to join the new.

"Nice work today, Saylor. I can tell you worked hard this summer. I'm excited to see your times," Coach Cruz says as I fish my suit out of the spinner to take home and finish drying.

"Actually, I owe the credit to a bunch of twelve-year-old girls."

My coach quirks a brow, and I laugh.

"I coached a youth team this summer, and it was just easier to get my laps in with them. Some of the girls were fast."

Her mouth curves, and she leans against her office door as she folds her arms.

"Coaching, huh?"

I nod, and excited butterflies flutter in my belly.

"I really loved it. I might want to investigate doing it more after I graduate." I shrug, expecting her to placate my whims with some positive coaching phrase. But instead, she straddles the bench and tilts her head to the side as she peers up at me.

"I know you're only a freshman, but how do you feel about being a captain?"

The weight of that responsibility stops my heart at first, but when my pulse kicks in again, the butterflies are back.

"Would it make some of the uppers upset? I don't want to step on toes. I respect the pecking order," I say, though really, I think that's all bullshit. The best should be in the pool. I have a feeling Coach Cruz feels the same way.

"Maybe, at first. But the ones who have a problem are the ones who don't put in the work anyhow, so maybe it's the nudge they need to get their shit together. What do you say?"

I shut my locker and spin my key ring in my thumb, trying to imagine myself in the role. It's easier than I expected. I look back at my coach and nod.

"I say hell yeah." She holds out a fist and I pound my knuckles against hers, riding the flutter of competition in my belly all the way to my car just outside the facility.

I can't wait to share my news with someone, but I'm not quite ready to move my mom into my go-to call list. It's almost closing time for the garage, though I'm sure Rowan is buried underneath some car while Radiohead blasts in his ears. It's always been the water for me, but for him, it's the underbelly of a vehicle.

I swipe his contact to call him, then let my phone ring on speaker as it rests on my thigh. He picks up after a half ring.

"Wow, were you just sitting there waiting for me to call?" I picture him like one of those contestants waiting to ring a buzzer.

"Uh, no. You're in my ears," he admits.

"Oh," I deflate a little, and he must be able to hear it in my tone.

"I wore AirPods in case you called," he quickly interjects. My smile returns, and I swipe over his name to pull up the photos of us together that I saved along with his info.

"I had my first swim day," I say.

"And?"

"And . . . I liked it," I say, moving the phone to my cupholder before I clip my wet hair into a knot on top of my head. "Coach wants me to be captain."

"Babe, that's incredible!" I hear the clatter of his board

rolling along the garage floor, and picture him sitting up with his legs outstretched and his face smudged with oil.

"You might piss a few people off," he says, his mind going right where mine did.

"Yeah, but what's new, right?"

He chuckles and adds, "True."

I push my key into the ignition and turn my car on, but rather than the welcoming sound of the whir and rumble, I get nothing but a quick ticking sound. Like a bomb.

"What's that?" Rowan's ears are too good.

"Nothing. It was me. I'm sure I just . . ." I crank the engine again, and this time, the ticking stops and turns into nothing.

"Damn it," I mutter.

"Where are you?" His tone is urgent, and I picture him pacing and searching for his keys. In fact, I'm sure that's what he's doing right now.

"I'm at the swim facility. It's fine. I'm like a quarter mile from my dorm, and there are a ton of people around. I can leave it here and walk. It might be good for me to get the exercise this week anyhow. I was a bit gassed after my laps."

I grab my bag and sling it over my shoulder before locking my car and heading toward the main path that cuts through campus.

"*Hmm*, I doubt you were gassed. I'll be up Friday to give it a look," he says, and I smile, noting he moved his visit up by a day. "Okay, so tell me about this captain gig while you walk. I want to stay on the phone with you."

The wheels slide along the garage floor again through the phone, and I picture him resting the phone on his chest as he slides back under his latest project. My voice and his passion build him the perfect bubble to escape to. I love that I'm part of his formula.

"Well, I don't know much yet," I start. Rowan asks me a few questions about the team, none of which I can answer after only a day, but he keeps me talking for the seven-minute walk back to my dorm. He makes me put him on speaker to say hi to Megan, and then makes me take him off it so he can promise to do dirty things to me on his first visit before we say goodbye and end our conversation.

All it takes me to forget that my car is basically DOA and parked on the other end of campus is one night's sleep. I go to my first class then dawdle on my way back, indulging in one of those iced coffees with the swirl of cinnamon and caramel on top. I'm still in a sugar coma bliss when I cross through my dorm's lobby for swim practice and step out into the parking lot.

"Oh, shit!" The lack of my car in the spot where it should be brings it all rushing back. And the thing that gives my panic an extra edge is that Coach texted me thirty minutes ago about sharing my role as captain with the team today. *Before* practice.

Regretting my Birkenstocks and the weight of my backpack, I suck it up and kick off my shoes, holding them as I sprint along the gravel pathway that cuts up the hill and to the swim center. My feet feel the sting of a thousand Legos underfoot thanks to the jagged stones I can't seem to avoid, but I make it into the locker room with minutes to spare.

My nervous energy comes out in my bouncing knees as I sit in front of my locker and wait for the rest of the team to arrive. Thankfully, when everyone files in and Coach announces my new role, it's met with cheers and even a few handshakes from the girls I worried would resent me most. I guess being Allison Kelly's daughter has conditioned me for the worst. It's going to take a lot of deprogramming to kick this.

I take my new role on with vigor when we hit the pool, giving tips when I can to cut times for some of our younger swimmers, and when I suggest we swap the order on one of the relays Coach has mapped out, she agrees. She urges me to challenge for one of the spots, but I'm not quite ready for that big of a takeover just yet. And if I'm being honest with myself, I don't think my times are there yet. Part of leading is making decisions for the team above myself. And maybe that's what attracts me to this job so much.

I'm the last one to finish my laps, and I promise Coach I'll shut off the lights and punch in the alarm code when I leave the locker room. Since I'm alone, I set my phone on the bench and dial Rowan while I change out of my wet suit. Just like yesterday, he answers the moment it rings.

"Yes, Captain?" he teases.

"That's the best you can do?" I drop my suit in the spinner and begin combing out my hair.

"Oh Captain, my captain?"

"That one's solid. Much better," I say, slipping into the long-sleeved gray T-shirt he gave me the first day I hung out at his garage.

"How was the first day on top?" I don't hear the usual echo when he talks, so he must not be in the garage tonight. I wonder if he's done early, in bed, or out lying on his car, staring at the stars. We spent a lot of summer nights together doing just that.

"I think I'm really going to like it. I'm honestly less invested in improving my times than I am in improving the team overall."

The spinner dings with my dry suit, so I snag it and tuck it in the top of my backpack. I'll keep my Birkenstocks on for the walk back, so I flop them on the tiled floor and slip my sore feet inside. I did a little damage on my barefoot trail run.

"Looks like someone found their calling," he says, and I sit with that thought for a beat before opening the door to head outside.

"Maybe. It's the right fit for now."

"Fair enough." I stop when I realize his voice is hitting me from two directions.

"Hey, are you—" I step around the corner to find the familiar trailer bed with my vehicle clamped down for the long ride back to Rowan's garage. I walk along the length and then there he is, leaning against his Camaro, parked where my car spent the night.

I drop my backpack to the ground and say fuck it to my shoes and feet, kicking them off so I can sprint to him. He catches my full-force leap into his arms, and my lips begin kissing his neck upon impact. I don't even care that he's salty.

"We couldn't even make it three full days." He chuckles.

"Hey, I think this counts as four," I contend.

He quirks a brow, and I shake my head and wave him off.

"Whatever. Now, kiss me."

His hands slide up my head and into my wet hair, tangling into the strands as he spins until I'm sitting on the hood of his car. It's my favorite place to be, and I nearly forget where we are when he bends me back just enough to drop kisses down my throat.

"How would Megan feel if you maybe slept somewhere else tonight?" He bites the center of my shirt. Well . . . *his* shirt.

"I don't think Megan is sleeping there tonight. She met a guy. So, she'll feel just fine," I say, pulling his waist snug against mine. I feel him hard between my legs and briefly flirt with the idea of reckless behavior. There are cameras literally everywhere, though, and I really do like this captain gig.

"Then the lodge awaits, my captain," he says, taking my hand and helping me back to the ground. He gathers my tossed shoes and slips them back on my feet, then hands me his keys.

"Oh, I don't drive her. That's *your* baby," I say, promptly giving them back. But before I can, Rowan wraps his hand around mine, forcing the keys into my palm. His gaze holds mine for a few seconds as I mentally work through this gesture, at first tilting my head, then nearly tearing up when he nods.

"Rowan, I can't take your car," I protest, though not very hard. I want to take this car. I fucking love this car.

"It's yours now," he says, stunning me. I thought he was letting me borrow her, not keep her as my own.

"Rowan, I don't know. Isn't this your most favorite thing?" I lean against the driver's side door as he rests his hands on either side of me and leans in close, dusting my lips with his before pulling back just enough to meet my gaze.

"It was. But I have a new favorite thing now. And it isn't even close."

Epilogue

Four Years Later

IT FEELS like I'm always signing important shit in diners. I'm not sure what it is about these places, this one in particular, but it's my business office of choice, I guess.

Dante's Diner in Flagstaff is where I signed on to break free of my father and the lies I'd been carrying for years, so it seems fitting to be the place where I plan to put down roots. *Real* roots.

"What do you think? You ready for this?" Mig signs his portion of the contract, then passes it to me. I sign without hesitation.

"Hell yeah, I'm ready." I push the done deal across the table to the broker and the notary, then fall back against the orange vinyl booth with a massive exhale.

Four years ago, Mig, Jersey and I were treading water to keep our garage open. We were working our asses off, me often twenty-four-seven. It never felt like we were going to make it to that magical plateau where we could close on the weekends and pay ourselves real salaries. But it turns out when the love of your life is two hours away and busy, you find ways to fill the time.

I filled mine with business outreach. My dad might be a criminal, but he had a good nose for business. The legitimate ones he invested in all had something special. Our garage had that, too. I knew it. So, I sucked up my pride and made some amends with my brother. Turns out Caleb is kind of the shit at investing—legitimate investing. He found us some partners who not only loved our brand but wanted to see it flourish. Better yet, being that they were in the high-end auction world and traveling most weeks, they wanted to remain hands-off and simply reap the rewards of our connection.

We own the Phoenix shop outright now. Every brick paid for. Every repair on us, too, but we have contingency funds to pay for things. Contingency funds . . . ha! That's something Caleb got me on board with. And now we're expanding up north, near the university where my girl is planning to coach next season.

Turns out this town is full of rich people with massive garages, and people like that want their toys to run well—and they want to swap them out often.

"Mr. Anderson, here are your keys," our broker says.

I hold them in my palm, letting the weight sink in before curling my fingers around them.

"Thank you," I utter, shaking his palm with my other hand.

Mig and I follow the real-estate guys out of the diner, and I walk Mig to his new truck. He's a solid friend and gave me his old one for a dollar. We wrapped them both in the business branding, so I'm advertising while driving around.

"I'm gonna take off and get back before rush hour." Mig grasps my hand, and we give each other a bro hug. "I'll head up next weekend, and we can start the demo and get with the contractor, yeah?"

"Sounds good, man. And hey, thank you."

My friend's gaze settles on mine for a moment, a hint of surprise in his expression. Being grateful is something I've worked hard on over the last four years, and I think it still shocks him when I show my feelings.

"Of course, dude. I believe in you. I believe in us!" He points between his chest and mine. "I mean, plus we have Jersey. But I don't really believe in that fucking guy."

We both laugh at our wanderlusting friend, who is currently learning how to retool German cars in Munich, and racing on the actual fucking Autobahn.

"Hey, he gives us our niche," I tease, repeating words Jersey used when he sold Mig and me on the idea of sending him to the Munich program.

"He's a niche in my ass," my friend grumbles, and I laugh as he climbs into his truck and holds up a hand for goodbye.

I wait for Mig to pull out before I head to my truck to text Saylor and see if she's done setting up her office. She officially graduated a week ago, and the school offered her the head coaching gig a day later with the blessing of her coach, who just retired. I could tell she wanted to say yes when she called me with the news, and I promised her we'd make it work. I've managed to keep the new shop a secret for ten months, so I sort of already knew it would work. I wanted to keep a secret for a good reason for once, to surprise her and get to see her eyes light up when she steps foot into a space that she and I fucking own.

Both of our names will be on this deed soon, assuming she says yes when I pop the question in about thirty minutes. I'm never fucking nervous, but I now can't seem to stop sweating. The damn ring in my pocket is wedged so deep into the denim from my constant checking that I'm afraid I won't be able to pull it out when the time comes. I suppose that's step one hundred in this whole thing, though, and I'm never gonna get there if I don't fire off this text and take step one.

ME: Made it to town. You ready to get picked up?

My leg bops with nervous energy as I wait for her to text back. She thinks we're loading up her studio apartment and moving her things to the one-bedroom we talked about renting. I canceled that shit as soon as the realtor cashed our check for the shop, though. It comes with Saylor's dream apartment on the second floor. It's a one-hundred-year-old building made of red brick and iron, and the downstairs used to be a bar up until the fancy clubs started moving in near the college. The apartment's been empty for years, so I'm sure we'll have our work cut out for us, but we'll get to make it ours.

SAYLOR: Yep! I'll be outside.

ME: On my way.

I blow out my nerves and toss my phone in the console before shifting into drive. I practice every word I plan to say on my way to the athletic complex, then promptly forget them all when I spot Saylor standing outside the doors with two duffels in her hands and the world's best smile on her face.

Somehow, my pulse settles into a steady rhythm at the sight of her. It's still pattering at a good clip, but more like a train and less like a jackhammer.

"Showtime, Rowan," I mutter to myself, hopping out of the truck at the curb and racing around to help Saylor with her bags.

"I still have packing to do. I'm so sorry I'm not more prepared. It's been . . . *ooof!*" She blows up at her loose hairs, and I tuck them behind her ears as I cradle her head and pull her into me for a kiss.

"No worries at all. We've got time." *More time than she knows.*

I help her into the truck, closing the door and feeling my pocket in one more display of OCD. Ring is there. Way in there.

I hop in and pause for a moment before shifting into drive. I practiced so many versions, but now that I'm in the moment, I can't think of a single one of them.

"Something wrong?" Saylor drops her phone to her lap and turns her attention to me. She's so cute in her cut-off shorts and sockless sneakers. Her T-shirt is tied at her back, probably to keep her cool because she's been busting her ass all day. I bet she'd love a shower right now, but I don't think I can wait for her to take one. I *definitely* can't wait while she packs the rest of her things. I know how much shit she has. It could take days, for all I know.

My head swivels to face her as I chew at the inside of my cheek.

"I want to show you something. It won't take long. Promise." I hold up two fingers like a scout, and she narrows her gaze with suspicion. Her smile curves into one cheek.

"Am I going to like this surprise?"

I threw her a party for her birthday at the pub in town in March, which is how I learned that she's not a big fan of surprise parties, or a lot of people. Lesson learned, and damn are we destined to be together. Two hermits for life.

"It's not a party. We'll make it quick." That part's an exaggeration, though I suppose if she throws the ring in my face and bolts, it won't take very long.

"Okay, *007*. Show me your special something."

My mouth ticks up and I nod.

"All right."

I pull out of the campus lot and take the back route to the building, mostly to deter her from guessing before we get there. Once parked in front of the rounded bay window, Saylor grows incredibly quiet and still. I think she's starting to imagine a bigger surprise when I let her off the hook by handing her the keys.

"Wanna see our new place?" I quirk a brow, and she stares at me with an open mouth.

"No fucking way." Her voice is low, laced with caution.

I pull her face to me and press my mouth to hers, her lips fumbling to form a kiss after being frozen in shock.

"Yes, fucking way," I say, holding her gaze for a beat before hers drifts behind me to the polished concrete steps she has commented on every time we walk by them.

"Come on," I say, hopping out of the truck and zipping to her side to help her onto the curb.

She shuffles her feet at first, her head tilted upward as she looks at the tiny details of the kind of architecture that simply doesn't exist anymore. I'm able to get her to focus when we reach the steps, and she puts the key in that opens the small vestibule that leads to both a door on the right and a set of stairs to our new home.

"It's all ours. Well, this part is Old 66 North, but the upstairs . . . that's just you and me." I push open the down-stairs door, and it creaks as I push it wide. The bell hanging above still rings, most of the dust having fallen off from the various walk-throughs Mig and I have made in the last few weeks.

"You're expanding?" Her wide eyes swing to me, then scan the wide-open space waiting for our rebuild.

"We are. I'll run this location while Mig handles Phoenix, and Jersey will bounce between the two."

"Jersey," Saylor mutters through a raw laugh. "If he shows up at either of them."

I chuckle at her laugh, then guide her through the space, pointing out where we plan to have displays of some of our best work, as well as the office area. There's a small bar that we plan to turn into the main counter, a leftover remnant from the building's earlier days. We've found a guy who can retrofit the ornate wood and turn it into something special.

"And we'll put the bays in here," I say, waving my hand along the whole wall that leads to the alley in the back. "We've already started permits with the city to pave our portion back there, and then it should be easy to get cars in and out."

"Rowan . . . it's amazing." She spins slowly, and I almost drop to one knee. But I want to get her in her dream home first, to make our first memory in the place we'll live. I sweep her into my arms instead and carry her back to the steps, climbing up until we reach our new front door.

"Now, I'd carry you over the thresholds, but fair warning, there's a hole in the floor." I wince, and it takes her a moment to read my face and see that I'm not kidding.

"Oh. Yeah, uhm. I'll walk on my own."

I gesture to the keys in her hand, and she pushes the second one into the lock, swinging our new door open. The mustiness has faded a bit since Mig and I were up here last week, and thankfully, they've kept the curtains open since then as well because otherwise, I'm afraid we'd accidentally find the hole I mentioned.

"Rowan," she gasps, covering her mouth as her eyes flicker like a child waking up to snow on Christmas. "It's . . . it's everything."

The sight of happy tears touching her eyes is more than I hoped for. I stand back as she runs her hand along the built-in wooden nook by the door, then continues into the family room, sliding her feet along the old wood floors.

"I love the dents and dings. I want to keep them. Can we keep them, Rowan?"

She turns to me, and I'm already on one knee. I couldn't handle it. Seeing her sense of wonder, seeing her so happy, literally brought me to my knees.

"Oh," she gasps, covering her mouth again and dropping the keys to the floor.

I push my hand deep into my pocket, snagging the edge of the setting with my fingernail to retrieve my grandmother's ring, and I hold it out for her to inspect while I force feeling back into my smiling numb lips.

"Saylor Kelly, I love you. And it may seem like I'm a grumpy wreck sometimes, but since I met you, I've learned a lot about myself. I've learned what I'm capable of. I've learned how to love someone with all my heart, and to tell the world so. I've learned to forgive, even when I don't want to. And I've learned to share the hard things, not just the happy ones. Most of all, though, I have learned that while I *can* live without seeing you every damn day, I just don't want to. So, what do you say? Will you turn me into a clingy motherfucker? Will you be my wife?"

Saylor's hands clasp around mine, her fingertips sliding up to meet mine where the crown of the antique ring showcases a princess-cut diamond and two sapphires, her favorite color of blue.

When she begins to nod, I exhale, my head a little dizzy from holding my breath.

"Yeah?" I want to make sure.

"Yes, Rowan. Yes, I will marry you." Tears trail down her cheeks as she lets me push the ring onto her finger. The fit is a little big, but nothing we can't fix. We're used to growing into things, she and I.

"You should know, I asked your dad for permission. Like an old-fashioned cuss." She laughs through her happy cry, nodding as she runs her arm over her nose and falling into my chest for my embrace. I hold on as I sway her, never wanting to let go.

"And my mom?" She tilts her head up enough to meet my eyes.

Saylor and her mom have made strides in their relationship for sure, but there's still a lot of trust that needs to be rebuilt. They talk several times a week, and sometimes they cover deeper ground. But mostly it's still casual, the kind of conversations had between coworkers. Maybe this proposal can be the first of many, though. A way to wedge open the door to becoming family again, however that needs to look.

"I thought you might want to handle that," I say, and she nods.

"I do. I will." She snuggles against me, and I reach into my pocket for my phone, pulling up her favorite song while I sway her in the middle of our dusty, perfect apartment.

The chorus always hits me, but something about hearing Mazzy Star's haunting voice preach about fading into you hits extra hard this time, and I hold on a little tighter.

"I can't wait to see it all evolve," she says, shifting her head enough to gaze up at me. I bend down to kiss her softly, then smile and hold on to her amber brown eyes and promise to make everything in this place exactly the way she wants it.

She shakes her head, though, then sets me straight, wearing her own devil's smirk.

"We'll make it ours. Just like we made us."

THE END

If you enjoyed THE OLDER BROTHER, you may like these Ginger Scott books:

The Moon & Back

Johnny Bishop crashed into my life like a hurricane. Not once, but twice.

The first time, we were teenagers. He was the star quarterback destined to save our small town's high school team. I was the music nerd desperate to shine, but always falling short.

Until him.

Johnny was good at football, but he was great at music. And when I realized we shared a love of performing, I fell for his charm. I drank in his words and was hypnotized by the way he sang. I was never fully in the spotlight with him, but the way he held onto me and kept me close felt good enough. His star was bright enough for both of us, and his dreams were worth all the risks, even if they were my dreams first.

But when he left our town--leaving me in it--the damage in his wake was devastating. I spent a decade trying to piece together my broken heart. A decade trying to avoid his music, a nearly impossible feat considering he was selling out arenas and piling up Grammys. While he tore through city after city, I built a quiet life as a music teacher in my hometown.

I'd made peace with the fact that a now famous rockstar once held my hand and told me he loved me. But when he shows up unannounced, begging for help, I'm sucked right back into his gravitational pull.

I want to hate him. I want to punish him for turning his back on me. But I can't when he's so broken. And the more time we spend in our present talking about our past, the more I start to wonder if maybe Johnny left to save us all from the storm.

Maybe that story about me and the famous rockstar has a lot more story to be told.

Southpaw

Sutter Mason is sick and tired of ballplayers. And pitchers? The worst!

She's over their inflated egos. Done with their magnetic charm. And as far as she's concerned, the broken promise the last ace left her with was her final strike in the game of love.

The problem? Her dad is the coach of the hometown minor league team. And the hot new lefty who just joined the squad? He's her brother's new roommate. This time around, instead of falling for the player, she's going to use him to get what she wants—the perfect case study for her psychology thesis.

No dates. No feelings. Zero extra innings. Simply a business relationship that ends when the season is done or Jensen Hawke is pulled up for prime time.

Arizona Monsoon rookie Jensen Hawke is laser focused—on proving he's more than just hype, on breaking the league's strikeout record, and on getting called up to the big leagues.

Jensen doesn't do relationships. He doesn't even really do friends. But his stubborn attitude is getting him in trouble on the mound. His control comes and goes. His curveball is a mess. And every time his roommate's cute sister points out that it's probably all in his head, he wants to scream.

But when a single conversation with her seems to up his game, Jensen decides maybe he's got time for one relationship while he chases his dream. Just a little positive mental coaching. Nothing but two people working toward shared goals.

So what if Sutter Mason gets him more than anyone ever has. Believes in him in a way that makes him believe too. Looks at him like he's actually special. And so what if he's starting to feel things he swore off for good.

In baseball, sometimes all it takes is one spectacular play to change the game. And Jensen Hawke and Sutter Mason didn't see each other coming. With love on the line, everything is riding on this next pitch.

Southpaw is a standalone, new adult, enemies-to-lovers, grumpy-sunshine baseball romance full of angst, steam and swoon.

Hold My Breath

Fractions of seconds can do lots of damage. One decision can ruin lives. A blink can be tragic. And loving a Hollister...can hurt like hell.

I would know.

They say the average person can hold their breath under water for two full minutes when pushed to the extremes. Will Hollister has been holding his for years. The oldest of two elite swimming brothers, Will was always a dominant force in the water. But in life, he preferred to let his younger brother Evan be the one to shine.

Evan got the girl, and Will...he got to bury all of the secrets. A brother's burden, the weight of it all nearly left him to drown.

The daughter of two Olympians, my path was set the day my fingertips first touched water. My future was as crystal clear as the lane I dominated in the pool—swim hard, win big, love a Hollister.

My life with Evan burned bright. He gave me arms to come home to, and a smile that fooled the world into believing everything was perfect. But it was Will who pushed me. Will... who really knew me.

And when all of the pieces fell, it was Will who started to pick them up.

In he end, the only thing that matters are those few precious seconds—and what we decide to do while we still have them in our grasp.

Acknowledgments

Well, this one was fun. ;-)

I love to stretch my writing in new directions, and while I've dabbled with family drama themes plenty, I've never added a touch of taboo and quite this much steam before. I dare say, I liked it. I hope you did too.

The Older Brother has been such a fun journey for me, and I must thank my team for rooting me on the entire way. As always, I am forever thankful to you, Autumn, for standing in my corner and pushing me when I doubt myself. The Older Brother might never have been without your encouragement, and I'm so grateful to you—for ALL the things. Brenda, my editor and unflappable rock, your steady guidance never steers me wrong. You roll with my crazy punches and keep me on track, polishing up my chaos. Thank you for being my own, personal wizard.

I've found quite the writing groove thanks to two of my best author friends, and I would be remiss if I didn't shout out Kacey Shea and Rebecca Shea (no relation, though I do call them my two Sheas lol). My office hours with you at Panera and Wildflower Cafe produce the best words. Thank you from the bottom of my heart for being my word-sisters. Love you both so much.

I'm so lucky to have a family who believes in me and roots for me, always, regardless of what I write. My mom and husband read everything I write, and they're both bad liars so I'm pretty sure they like my books for real lol.

And to my readers, this one is for you. Every bit of it. You've been with me through it all, tagging along for my coming-of-age stories and my twisty psychological YA thriller, for my sports romance and my angsty rock star, through my series and my standalones. I hope you enjoy this sexy little thing I wrote. It's a bit dark for me, and definitely amped up in spice. It was a lot of fun, so I think I'll do it again sometime. What do you say?

About the Author

Ginger Scott is a *USA Today, Wall Street Journal* and Amazon-bestselling author from Peoria, Arizona. She has also been nominated for the Goodreads Choice and RWA Rita Awards. She is the author of several young and new adult romances, including bestsellers Waiting on the Sidelines, The Hard Count, A Boy Like You, This Is Falling and Wild Reckless.

A sucker for a good romance, Ginger's other passion is sports, and she often blends the two in her stories. When she's not writing, the odds are high that she's somewhere near a baseball diamond, either watching her son swing for the fences or cheering on her favorite baseball team, the Arizona Diamondbacks. Ginger lives in Arizona and is married to her college sweetheart whom she met at ASU (fork 'em, Devils).

FIND GINGER ONLINE: www.gingerscottbooks.com

facebook.com/GingerScottAuthor

instagram.com/authorgingerscott

tiktok.com/@authorgingerscott